Scalp Point

Francis J. Smith

ISBN# 9781706022091
First Edition 11/2019
Edited by William Smith and Ann Tanyeri
More books at www.centervillebooks.com/

Cover Photo Courtesy Jeremy Richards at
https://ww.jeremyrichardsphotography.com/gallery/html

Editor's Note: Robert Rogers is best remembered, if he is remembered at all, for his daring escape at the end of what came to be called The Battle on Snowshoes, which took place a few miles southwest of the present village of Ticonderoga, NY. In truth, there were two battles on snowshoes, fought a year apart (January 1757; March '58,) and remarkably, in almost the same place. It was at the conclusion of the second battle when Rogers famously slid down the front of Bald Mountain (or not,) the edifice now locally known as Rogers' Slide.

Dedicated to Francis' uncle, Captain William James Smith (1920-1950.) Bill was born in North Creek, New York and raised in Witherbee (NY.) He was a veteran of World War 2 who remained in the service and was presumed killed in the Korean Conflict, at the Battle of the Chosin Reservoir. Like so many of the American GIs at Chosin, and many a ranger around Ti and the lakes, Bill's remains have never been recovered.

Table of Contents

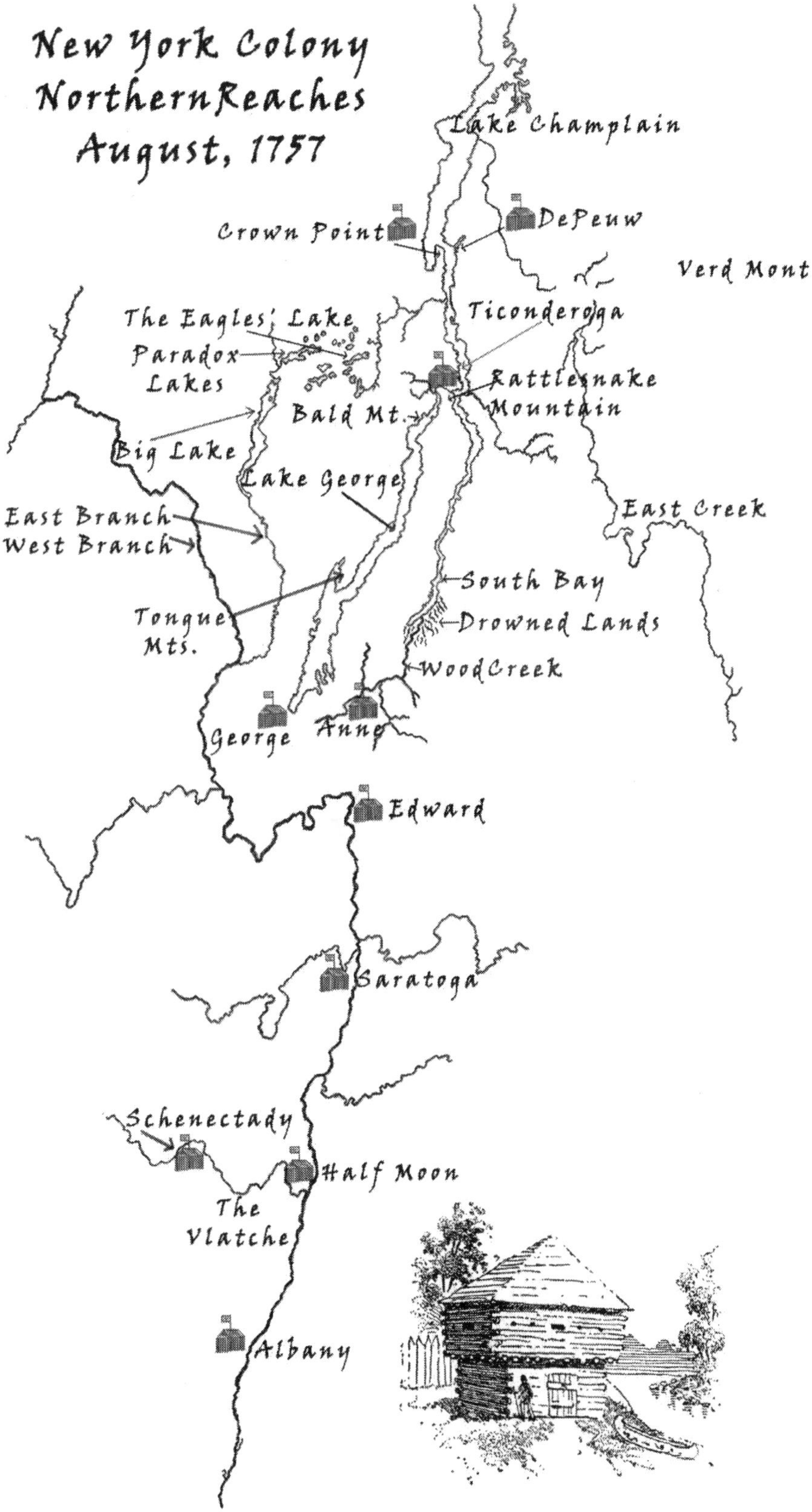
New York Colony
NorthernReaches
August, 1757
Lake Champlain
Crown Point
DePeuw
Verd Mont
The Eagles' Lake
Ticonderoga
Paradox
Lakes
Rattlesnake
Mountain
Bald Mt.
Big Lake
Lake George
East Branch
West Branch
East Creek
South Bay
Tongue
Mts.
Drowned Lands
WoodCreek
George
Anne
Edward
Saratoga
Schenectady
Half Moon
The
Vlatche
Albany

When you be reporting in, don't forget nothin' and always tell the exact truth of evur'thin you seen and done. Youse can tell it however you want later, in the taproom or 'round a fire. T'aint nothing the men appreciate more'n a baldfaced liar what can spin a yarn which don't hurt nobody but goddammit, when you be tellin' it to your superior officers, give 'em naught but the truth.

–Anonymous ranger paraphrasing Robert Rogers.

Chapter I – Carthage Must Die

I was born in 1720 to Dutch immigrants, in the back room of my Father's tavern, the Full Sail, in the frontier town of Albany, New York Colony. As a young man, I fought in what was called, here in America, King George's War. In Europe, they called it the War of the Austrian Succession. For me, a ranger scout, it was simply The War. It lasted in Europe from 1740 to 1748. In our forests, it lasted officially for a shorter time and unofficially much longer, as our wars did. It was our third go at the French and their Indian friends and it ended inconclusively, frustratingly for us.

Toward the end, our rangers were getting to where we felt we could stand up effectively in the woods against our enemies. Our ranger boss, the intrepid Joseph Blanchard out of New Hampshire, had learned us to fight what we called Indian Style, which meant spooking through the forests on foot and in canoes and on snowshoes, even sometimes on skates. We struck from behind rocks and trees and vanished, although we mostly just watched, to gather information for the British, who often failed to act upon what we brought. Us rangers could sometimes make the French and Indians pay for their incursions but we were too few to contend against the larger parties what came up the lakes. Our regular forces, our British cousins, were woefully inept at our sort of warfare and were not inclined toward adapting to it. With all their years in North America, they still insisted on wearing the red coats we called widow-makers and they were incapable of grasping the simplest ideas of wood-craft. They preferred lines of men with flags flyin', drums beatin' and volleys firin', which was how it was done in Europe, a rather foolish way of doing things in the American forests.

Or anywhere.

Before the war, when I was not a man but still a lad, I became a fur smuggler to the north and afterward I carved out for myself a solitary life as a trapper in what I called my Paradise Valley, a lost land west of the lakes, Lac du Saint Sacrement and Champlain, which two lakes were a corridor between the warring empires. My Paradise, at a distance from the lakes sufficient to preclude unwanted visitors, was yet close enough so I might spook the enemy, for even in times of peace they were the enemy. England and France had each long maintained a claim on the lakes and whenever men from the different sides met out there, one side or the other usually came away with woodland trophies; hair. Even in times of peace.

For the lone trapper, the dangers never went away, yet I seldom got into trouble, even on my forays down the lakes. Shepherd a large party and the Indians would come onto the tracks. Not so with the lone spy. He left scant traces for an enemy to follow.

By the end of the war, devastation was near complete, our frontier was abandoned, the farms and settlements above Albany were charred ruins. The forests began taking back the clearings. With the peace treaty signed in Europe, the frontier came slowly back to life, yet over us there hung the certainty another war must come. The country being contested was too rich, too lush. Holding it meant wealth and power and so our northern and western borders would flare again and the brave settlers in this wilderness would be the ones to suffer, which was too often the way of things. Our British masters, for masters was how they saw themselves, did little to prepare for war. No new military structures were erected in the north. Saratoga Fort, thirty miles up the Hudson River from Albany, remained our northernmost post, the loneliest, too. With nothing beyond Saratoga except some few cabins, we could in no way contest French incursions. No system of support or supply did we maintain; our brave settlers were left precariously out there unprotected.

In the years following the war, I spent my winters mostly trapping the north woods. The cold and snow served to keep the French and their Indian allies close to their forts and camps. Summers I was mostly in Albany with occasional sojourns to my Paradise to gather ginseng and wild horseradish, both in demand in town. I ventured north of New York Colony, into the Saint Lawrence River Valley which was the property of the French and east to the Connecticut River. Mostly did I stay in the mountains to the west of the Champlain and Saint Sacrement corridor. These mountains which our fearsome Indian allies, the Mohawks, called Haderondah, which word meant Bark Eaters, an epithet the Mohawks put derisively upon their northern foes who, with the extreme harshness of the land and the depredations of the Mohawks, were often reduced in winter to eating trees. This Haderondah we white men corrupted into something more palatable to us, thus, Adirondacks.

Out to the west, beyond the mountains, was the most incredible land, lakes and ponds, grasslands surrounded by pine forests, watery bogs, a country filled with furbearers and game, an easy country to wander. A canoe afforded passage for mile after mile and with only short portages between waterways which were generally placid. The land had the look and feel of having never been trod upon, at least not by a white man. I got lost often and cared not, being content with seeing what was there.

In those years, as I entered and passed through my twenties, I was in full vigor, as some would say, although I wore my years perhaps more heavily than most men. Certain of the finer folks around Albany Town thought me crude. They often mocked me, though always outside of my hearing for their being afraid of me and for knowing of my prowess with the war hatchet and knife. Some said I was a spy for the French. I never bothered telling 'em different. Those close to me knew the truth, them others didn't much matter. Those who knew something of what I was doing up north, why I seemed to vanish most winters and for shorter intervals in summer, and always returning with profitable furs or herbs, and there were too many of those people for my liking, said I was a fool to venture up there but I never seemed to get into trouble unless I went looking for it, which I did not.

In my scouts around Champlain and Saint Sacrement, I saw much sign of the French and their Indian allies but they seldom took notice of me. The Indians were constantly admonished by the French not to start any trouble but such was the Indians' thirst for scalps, I stayed well hidden, grateful the French and Indians were wary of penetrating the forests to the west of their corridor, less they wander too close to the land of their eternal enemies, our Mohawks, who, greatly to my benefit, claimed the lands where I was ensconced though they rarely trod there.

The French were in greater strength on the lakes as the years wore on. They fortified Scalp Point and rebuilt the palisade on the other side of the lake, and with more Canadian settlers moving into the area, they were obviously intent on permanence. I told this to the Albany authorities. They, for their part, duly noted it and did naught to counter it.

Fervently, futilely, I wished for no more war to interrupt the pattern of my life. I had taken some harsh personal blows in the last war, the loss of persons dear to me, although the worst blow, the death of my beloved wife and baby boy, came not as a result of the war but for some stubborn, nay, rash actions of my wife. I wanted no more of it. I only wanted to stay in my valley to hunt and fish, yet I understood there could be no peace until the French issue was resolved.

****

At the age of fifteen, when I had first decided upon a life in the forest, my mother, who had taught me to read and write, had insisted I put all my adventures down on paper. She thought, for a man choosing to live his life in the wilds, writing might be a way to keep a hand in civilization, keep me from going entirely over to the beasts. I made a promise to her, which I have kept, and truthfully, I did hope my writings might someday generate interest amongst the public.

In the time before and during King George's War, I had a friend by the name of Arnold Baldwin who helped me with my writing. Arnold was an Englishman, come over, an educated man whose book learning availed him naught when the Canadian Indians razed Saratoga. Arnold they tomahawked and scalped, his beloved wife Priscilla they took back with them to Canada, the secret of her fate forever locked in the deep woods.

Arnold had used to talk about what was called the Punic Wars. In ancient times, two mighty empires watched one another over the blue waters of the Mediterranean Sea, same as we and the French watched over trackless green forests. Those ancient powers, Rome and Carthage, were voracious, neither willing to settle for anything less than the complete obliteration of the other. Altogether they fought three wars over the course of a few centuries and with uneasy peace between times. Arnold said how England and France were like Rome and Carthage, each determined to have all the North American continent, which, we seemed to be realizing, was even more vast than what we could have imagined.

"So we'll go on fighting," my younger self would always say, "until one side or the other is destroyed."

Arnold would smile.

"Cartago est mundi," he'd say. Carthage Must Die.

****

In the spring of 1754, when I arrived in Albany to drop off my furs at one of the riverside fur sheds, the town was buzzing. War was surely coming. Soldiers were arriving daily and there was the additional excitement over the expected arrival of important politicians from New York Town and from some of the other colonies, coming as delegates to what was being called the Albany Convention. This conference was by the summons of our British masters, king and council, the purpose of which was two-fold. To determine what measures the colonies might take to better coordinate their war efforts and to preserve the support of our Indian allies, the mighty Iroquois. Those indomitable tribes had long held the balance of power in North America and did they go entirely over to the French, as seemed possible, we were doomed. Convincing them to stay neutral was about the best we could hope for, although neutrality didn't mean many of their warriors would not go over.

One of the delegates to the conference was a Pennsylvanian by the name of Benjamin Franklin, a politician who was also a newspaperman and a tinkerer, an agitator who delighted in stirring the pot, any pot, and who threw down a most audacious proposal to the delegates. The purpose of the conference, Franklin said, besides securing the continued allegiance of the Iroquois, was the coordination of mutual aid amongst the colonies and against the French, the lack of which coordination had plagued us dearly in all our past wars. Franklin advised the conference to look to the Iroquois for inspiration. Those Six Nations, as the Iroquois called themselves, after a sixth tribe, the Tuscarora, joined the original five, had for centuries preyed upon one another, which also made them vulnerable to getting ravaged from the outside. They had finally and of necessity come together in a confederation which made them into what Franklin, same as Arnold, called the Romans of North America. Yet, Franklin said, thirteen colonies of civilized men risked destruction for the reason they could not agree on anything. We, too, must unite, Ben insisted, and he proposed we do it by forming a single American government to be made up of a legislature elected by and representing each of the colonies and a governor appointed by the king, said government to conduct military affairs in the name of all the colonies.

This went somewhat beyond what our British Lords had intended. Even many Americans thought it outlandish. Our very own American king, men joked. Other men called it treason, although I suspect the idea found favor with many who dared not say so. I thought it was sensible as a way to conduct the war but doubted anything would come of it. The colonies, all so different one from another and with so many issues between them, certainly needed to stand as one against the French but uniting, men feared, meant any one colony might raise itself above the others. My own experience told me a New York Dutchman such as myself and a dour New England Yankee were about as different from one another as men could be, and them southern folks who passed sometimes through my folks' tavern might as well have been from the other side of the moon.

Franklin seemed to me to be a dreamer although, and as I got to know him, I found him to be a most practical and clever man. He created a sensation with the woodcut he disseminated in support of his proposal and which seemed for a time to be posted everywhere one looked. Join or Die, it showed a snake chopped into pieces, each piece labeled as one of the colonies. King George the Second, I suspect, was not amused.

Franklin took supper most nights in Pops' tavern and there were always men wanting to sit down and either talk earnestly or josh with him, none more than Pops, and even did most of the men disagree with Franklin's notion of our colonies uniting, he was a politician of the sort our rough frontiersmen could abide. Often did men in the common room rail against Ben for his notion of us learning from the Iroquois. White men were civilized whilst the Indians, the men said, were dirty varmints. Franklin seldom argued, he just smiled.

Ben enjoyed his wine and charmed everyone, my father and mother included, and me too, I suppose. Each night when he came in, he and Mother played out the solemn ritual they had established. He would take a place by the fire, Mother would come over with a glass of wine on a board, Franklin would lift the glass and gaze admiringly at the wine. He'd take a sip and proclaim, "Here is God's constant proof of His love for us. He so loves to see us soused."

Sitting with Franklin before the fire in the Full Sail on the night when the conference approved his proposal, I listened as men congratulated him on his success. Franklin said it was doubtful all thirteen colonies would approve his plan, a necessary step before it could go to the king, who would surely reject it. Franklin said few of the colonies would even bother looking at it. Seeing the serenity on his face, I realized he understood his proposal was doomed for now but was confident our colonies would someday come together in the manner of the Iroquois. It was as if Franklin understood something the rest of us didn't. Ol' Ben, Father said, was planting a seed.

The more urgent talk going around was of war. The previous fall, rumors had the French on the move, engaged once again in erecting forts on land claimed by the English, this time in the Ohio country. Out there was a hornets' nest gettin' jabbed. The French were erecting a barrier up the Saint Lawrence to the Great Lakes and down the Mississippi to New Orleans, this to keep us pinned to the coast. A young colonial officer was dispatched out there to dissuade the French from their encroachments. The fear was the officer, Washington, with too few men and with his inexperience and ambition, would light the spark which would bring on the war.

So although war was not yet officially declared, the troubles were surely coming, my days of happy pursuits in the forests to be interrupted by the folly of nations. Rumors and counter-rumors flew at the conduct of affairs thus far, the certainty the Indians would soon be engulfing the frontiers in flames. Yet our main problem remained, to resolve the infernal bickering between our politicians, which crippled our efforts. With the powdered wigs arguing in their stuffy chambers, our frontiers would shrink and burn, our settlers would remain helpless before the enemy.

Incredibly, the Quakers in our neighboring colony of Pennsylvania insisted the Indians be treated with brotherly love. The Quakers controlled the Philadelphia Assembly and refused to allow even a single keg of desperately needed gunpowder for the defense of their western settlements. The Quakers did not believe in violence; the French and Indians made gleeful mayhem out of the Quakers' intractability.

Worst of all, William Johnson, who, as Commissioner of Indian Affairs had done so much for our cause, had been deposed. Bill it was who had for years maintained our relationship with the Iroquois tribes, especially the Mohawks, who were situated closest to us. Bill's good work was all that stood between us and annihilation and his dismissal, prompted by the jealousy and avarice of the politicians, allowed the French to extend their influence over the Iroquois. A steady stream of tribesmen flowed north to join their many brothers and cousins already amongst the French. An open split with our Indian allies could only be averted by the timely return of Johnson to office, but nothing, it seemed, no matter how dire, could convince Johnson's enemies of the need to reinstate him.

****

I stayed around Albany for the excitement, but when fall came again and with things simmering down and with war still not yet declared, the allure of the north was upon me and I returned to my Paradise, to trap and to keep an eye on the French. Trapping season went deep into the spring of the year 1755, longer than usual, the ice staying late on the ponds. The fur was prime, which prompted me to stay longer than I maybe should have. When the spring breakup came, I was ready to leave, the way was clear, and I canoed down the East Branch and the Hudson.

I came to the Hudson's Falls. Here, the river, heretofore flowing east, turned abruptly to the south for its fifty-mile run to Albany. This river bend I knew well. It had an Indian name too long for any white man other than Bill Johnson to pronounce. Indian words flowed smoothly off Bill's tongue. We called it the Great Carry. It was the starting point for the two carries which led up to the water routes to French Canada. One carry was the fourteen-mile trail to the northwest, to the headwaters of Saint Sacrement, which lake connected by Portage Crick to Champlain. The other was to the north and slightly east, to a junction with Wood Creek and on to the South Bay, the lowest part of Champlain. This latter trail, which went through the infernal swamps we called the Drowned Lands, had the advantage of avoiding Portage Crick which, connecting the lakes at Ticonderoga, was often the setting for ambushes by Indians and pirates. Both Saint Sacrement and Champlain flowed north; the latter, more than a hundred miles long, went almost to the French city of Montreal.

The only habitation of any note at the Carry had been the fortified house of the fur-buyer John Henry Lydius. I had but few dealings with Lydius, except to avoid him. My first mentor in the woods, the crafty smuggler, Hugh McChesney, had always warned me to stay away from Lydius, who had a French wife, spent much time in Canada and was, according to Hugh, a spy for the French. What else Hugh said, Lydius was in collusion with the fur-robbers on the river. Once, smuggling with Hugh, our party had nearly lost a fortune in furs along with our hair, to Indians what was lurking around the Carry and were, according to Hugh, working for Lydius.

Now, here, the British were raising what would be our northernmost fort, and I, coming downriver and hearing sounds ahead, men's voices, bawling oxen, axes against trees, trees crashing to the ground, pulled in to shore and hid my furs and canoe. I made my way down along the riverbank to the fort-builders' clearing. They had made good progress since I had come by in the fall, the fort would be completed soon and would be most welcomed and overdue, the fulfillment of what had long been talked about, a stockade on a bluff along the east side of the river. Stoutly built, the fort would enhance our security and would facilitate any advance we might make toward Canada.

I got into the camp. It was colonials and British and some Mohawks what was lazing 'round a cask of rum whilst the work went on around them. A British artillery company was showing our colonials how to load and fire the big guns, the British calling out orders in their arrogant fashion and sending cannonballs crashing into the trees on the other side of the river. Colonials manning one of the constructed walls, jovial for having drawn guard duty and not the heavy work of fort-building, called out in derisive mockery of the British. The men I spoke with knew war was coming and were eager to get on with it. They said they sometimes took arrows and gunshots from the woods, so our fort-building had raised the ire of the French.

I stopped in at the sutler's for a drink, he maintaining a makeshift watering-hole in the back room of his post, and who was there but my friend from the last war, British sergeant Thomas O'Brien. Me and Tom exchanged hearty greetings and commenced quaffing rum. Tom had heard I was again trapping in the north, thought me crazy and said so, and said he had feared for my life. He told me the war was on, although still not officially declared, and he was eager to hear what news I brung. When I finished telling what I had seen of the French up north, he gave me the military situation.

He confirmed what I considered to be the best news. The British general newly appointed in charge of all military affairs in North America, in one of his first acts, had reinstated Bill Johnson as Commissioner of Indian Affairs. So the general, whose name was Braddock, had some understanding of our New World, unlike others of those who came over, and we now had a chance of preserving our alliance with the Iroquois. What else Tom said, even with war yet undeclared, the British were preparing offensives on three fronts.

An army of redcoats was come ashore in Virginia, commanded by this Braddock, the army intending to push the French out of the Ohio country. Braddock's expedition, if successful, would stop the raiding out west. In the meantime, whilst the army prepared to move, the people suffered.

Tom said Braddock was hacking a road through the wilderness and I sneered. "So's he can march with flags and drums and with his soldiers dressed in their finest. Sometimes it seems to me your generals care more about how their troops look on parade than they do about putting 'em into a situation they can fight from." Tom gave me his hard look, one eye enlarged, the other nearly closed, and I thought he might take a poke at me. Tom was quick with his temper and his fists, but he backed off by agreeing, at least somewhat, and asking plaintively how the hell we could fight the French in the Ohio without first building a road to get there. "The time it will take Braddock to build his road," I said, although I saw Tom's logic, same as he seen mine, "will give them snakes time to prepare a greeting." I said as how with or without a road, the scarlet coats, those widow-makers worn by the British, would be juicy targets for the Indians sure to gather on the flanks. The coats even had long tails on the backs to hang up on the brush, which would hinder, nay, kill, plenty more of those brave men. Although he was a lifelong British soldier, Tom had seen enough of our colonial rangers and militia in the last war to know his British would have to make some adaptations before they could win in the forests.

Which didn't mean Tom held a very high opinion of colonials. He had naught but respect for our ranging corps, he having often gone with us into the woods, and he conceded our militia could fight for as long as they had something to hide behind. Still, he felt as if we Americans, for so we were beginning to call ourselves, were only good for sniping and could not be depended upon in a stand-up fight. He said we were poorly officered and were without discipline, and it astonished and infuriated him, how we got to decide who was to lead us, and often, which orders we would obey and which we would not. "Rights!" Tom always spit the word, and he'd harangue about professional soldiers not concerning themselves with rights nor of the fitness of an order. A soldier need only obey. In Tom's eyes, colonials were an unmanageable rabble prone to fleeing as soon as the first shots were fired.

Tom talked of another prong of our offensive, our part, which would push north from Albany and take Crown Point, which we rangers called Scalp Point and the preachers called the nest of vipers. An army of colonials, two thousand of us and with however many Iroquois as could be cajoled into coming along. Tom, when he told me who was to lead us, sputtered with even more indignation. Bill Johnson.

An army of the king commanded by a bloody colonial, although Johnson hailed from Ireland, and I understood Tom's disgust. Johnson had no military experience. None. "Johnson," Tom said, "has enough to do just keeping his Mohawks quiet. He's not ever been in a fight, knows naught of the soldierin' life." Yet, when I said I didn't expect anything other than disaster for Braddock and his professional European army and said how a lot of good men would die for being unfit for wilderness warfare, I saw the sadness in Tom's eyes. Many of those who had gone with Braddock were Tom's friends and he despaired of ever seeing them again. He said he was fortunate to have drawn duty with supply. The chances he'd get into trouble were less, and unsaid, and understood by both of us, he liked the nearness of what he called the charms of Albany.

Tom maybe didn't have one good word for Johnson as a soldier but the old sergeant clearly understood Johnson's value as a liaison with the Iroquois. Tom said even with Johnson's reinstatement, our politicians hadn't stopped interfering with his work with the tribes. Many of the Iroquois, including just about the entire Seneca tribe, disrespected by our politicians and sweet-talked by the French black-robes, had gone over. The Seneca orators spread discord throughout the entire Iroquois League and only Johnson could keep the tide from becoming a deluge. His harangues in favor of the English cause and his use of lavish gifts, many at his own expense and for which he asked and was often denied reimbursement from the government, was at least keeping some of the tribesmen neutral.

The French argument, how the English armies had feet of clay, was a powerful one against us. "The courage of mice," the French said. Surely the mighty Iroquois, so proud in war, did not wish to align itself with such as us. Many of the sachems heeded strongly to such words and moved their camps north, to the banks of the Saint Lawrence River, or indicated they would simply stay home when war came. And even those who agreed to come forward and fight for us did so with a not unreasonable stipulation. They would not fight if others of their nations were present on the other side. The Iroquois' Sacred Council Fire maybe flickered and sputtered but it was not yet gone entirely out.

Our third prong, also departing from Albany, was an expedition to the west, led by another man with no military experience, Massachusetts governor William Shirley. Shirley was to reinforce our Oswego fort and attack the French posts on the Great Lakes, no easy task with French naval superiority out there.

Sergeant Tom livened his telling with swigs from a tankard. He was a prodigious drinker, and when it was time for him to return to his duties at the supply house, he said he had a convoy of empty wagons heading south to Albany in the morning. He told me to load my furs into one of the wagons and he'd put his official military seal on the canvass what covered them. This would keep any and all from having a look underneath and would give me safe passage, thus saving me risking losing a winter's worth of work to the fur-robbers or the Albany authorities. The former would cut my throat; the latter, suspicious of good furs, might confiscate my cache and arrest me, or, and each time I got stopped, they would levy a bribe, which they called an assessment.

After dark I fetched my furs, brought them in and loaded them, along with my canoe, into a wagon. I covered it with a tarp and slept on top of it. The next morning just before we pulled out, Tom brought along a soldier who'd stay with me until my furs was delivered. Tom then gave us a basket with bottles of French claret. We said our goodbyes, me and Tom fairly certain we'd be seeing more of one another before the war was over.

The road was poor, wagons kept getting stuck, we all had to help pull them out, and whenever wagons came from the other direction, it was us without loads who had to get off to the side. Took us three days to get to Albany. I was impatient with our progress and wasn't sure I had done the right thing in accepting Tom's offer. I could have made the trip in a day, had I stayed on the river but with so many soldiers and officials of one sort or another and with plenty of Indian sign, it was better this way. Besides, me and the teamster and the soldier had some good talk and each time we finished a bottle of the claret, one or another of us would watch for a big rock along the side of the road and when we seen one, we'd stand up and hurl the empty bottle against it, most emphatically smashing the bottle to pieces. When we got to Albany, the teamster took me in to the fur-buyers' shed and him and the soldier helped me unload my cache.

Chapter II – Monica Louise Saint-John

I spent most of a day negotiating with the fur-buyers who tried plying me with whiskey, same as what they did with the Indians. Loosen us up so they could cheat us. Always mindful of how I had sometimes been shorted as a younger man, I refused even so much as a drink, tempting as it be, until I had struck a deal. Did pretty well for myself, my furs were, as usual, superior to most of what else was coming in, and I left the shed a happy man indeed, whistling a merry tune, my rifle over my shoulder, my pockets jingling.

The streets of the town, as well as the taverns and shops, was bustling with troops, in from the south and east, staying a few days and going on to the north or west. Their mood was confident. Our armies, especially Braddock's and according to those who had seen it, were invincible. We would not be thwarted by woods-loping Canadian Frenchmen and their capricious Indian allies. English discipline and firepower would overwhelm the enemy. Our colonials did seem to me to be more fit than in the last war and better equipped, better clothed, better fed, but still I felt the old unease for knowing what so often happened to our armies when they ventured into the woods.

Late in the afternoon, still whistling my merry tune, I stopped at the apothecary to drop off a small amount of ginseng with the proprietor, Eric Studdard, my best friend since we were boys. With the look he gave me as I entered, he was asking, same as always, was there any news of his father, carried off by the Indians in the Saratoga raid, same as Arnold Baldwin's wife. I told Eric I had no word and I knew he wished he was a member of the militia so he might get revenge against those who had taken his father but with his two oldest boys, ages fifteen and sixteen, having gone off and joined Shirley's army, Eric felt his place was in Albany with the rest of his large brood and his shop.

Eric thanked me for the ginseng, said his customers had been askin' about it, and me and him talked over glasses of rum. Our talk was mostly about the coming war. Eric gave me the news from his sons. Shirley's army for Oswego and the Great Lakes was hampered by a lack of transport. Delays were common, the bateaux-men were grumbling and laying aside their oars at the slightest provocation. A large French army was said to be awaiting Shirley out on the lakes. If Shirley got beat, the western frontier of our New York Colony would be laid open. Settlements to the west of Schenectady were reporting sightings of Indians. We had to strike soon else the French would hit us first. We talked on, the afternoon shadows lengthening, and with Eric having gone into the back to fetch something for a patron, the front door opened and a woman came in. I was looking at her whilst trying to seem not to be, she was looking back at me with no attempt at coyness.

She was tall for a woman, nearly as tall as me, although I was only of middling height for a man, neither tall nor short. I thought she was beautiful, which of itself didn't mean much. Having just re-entered town from a winter alone in the woods, even the plainest woman would have looked damn fine in my eyes, although this woman was in no way plain. Not truly beautiful, perhaps, she tended toward stout and with shoulders somewhat broad for a female, which, with the way she carried herself, proud and erect, served to add, not detract, from my estimation of her. She had nice features, a large bosom and shiny black hair tumbling from beneath a wide-brimmed straw hat. Her dress, long and loosely worn, was more for comfort than for fashion, although no dress, no matter how loosely fitting, could conceal the curves underneath. She wore an apron and a hooded cloak, as was the custom.

She walked boldly up to me and in a lilting London accent, spoke my name. "Kenneth? Kenneth Van Kuyler?" I stammered, somewhat taken aback by her boldness. "Are you Kenneth?" she repeated in her strongly accented English and with her face close to mine, for I had not answered her question. Eric, just having come out of the back, laughed.

"Kenneth he was," he said, "before you stole away his tongue."

He introduced us. Her name was Monica Saint-John.

"Yes, I am Ken Van Kuyler," I rather stupidly said, it already having been established who I was, and now both of them were laughing at me, the woman's laughter gentle, mirthful. She was studying my face, bright as a British soldier's coat. I was thankful for having just refreshed myself with a sponge bath, a shave and a haircut, and for having put on new buckskins, as was my own custom whenever I re-entered civilization from a long absence.

"Your mother," she said, "has heard you are back in town and sent me to ask why you have not been to see her." I mumbled about being on my way, and Monica's green eyes sparkled unabashed, for there was nothing coquettish about her. She looked me up and down, appraising me. She smiled, apparently satisfied, and said again as how my mother wished to see me at once. She turned and went toward the door, for she had come to the apothecary for the sole purpose of fetching me.

"Appreciate the ginseng," Eric said. "Now go along with the lady."

I looked at him and looked back at Miss Saint-John. She was at the door now, one hand on the knob, the other on her hip, one foot poised as if to begin tapping out her impatience with a child or a puppy. We went out of the shop and with me walking a few steps behind, for with her long legs and with her purpose accomplished, she was a fast walker, or was I walking more slowly so to afford myself a better view of her? Truth was, I was smitten by her looks and bearing, the sway of her form as she moved.

I felt the need to say something, anything, and I said I was surprised she was working at the tavern. She stopped and the look she gave me made clear she too considered her status as a tavern wench to be beneath her station in life. I apologized and babbled about how what I meant, ever since the time Anneke, a girl Mother had hired, had run off with Bill Johnson, only to be abandoned by him, Mother had been loath to hire young women, preferring older women and free blacks, if she could find them. "I am acquainted with Squire Johnson," Monica said, "and doubt I would run off with him." Walking side by side now, I bumbled yet another apology for having maybe impugned the lady's honor by implying she might be seduced by William Johnson.

I inquired was she just over from England, for so it seemed. She, with a slight, proud lift of her chin, said she had been the wife of a promising young captain in the Forty-Fourth Foot, a part of Braddock's army. Her husband had perished from sickness on the Atlantic crossing and she had come up to New York, which, before the British took it from our Dutch and renamed it, we called New Amsterdam, and thence to Albany to find someone she thought she might know from home. Turned out she was wrong and stranded in Albany and probably, although unsaid, destitute, Mother had given her a job dispensing food and drinks in the tavern.

I was interested in learning more about her and as we passed by a public house, I asked if she would like tea. She assented, we went inside and took a table, and over tea and sugar plums, she opened up to me.

She said she was much taken by the beauty of the countryside, the delights of the northern spring. The breaking up of the ice on the river, the annual awakening of the forests, the swelling of the buds on the trees, the flocks of birds along the Hudson flyway. She said having got through the winter, she was sad to think she would not get to experience our summer before earning money enough for passage back to England. I said I hoped she saw more of it too and glancing at her, I saw how my burst of unintentional ardor had put the little smile back on her face.

She turned the conversation away from herself and toward me, and spoke in an animated way, and with the knowledge she had of me, I wasn't blind to what she was, another trap set by my dear mother, who had never given up her efforts to turn me away from my woods' life. I sensed there was a conspiracy afoot. Monica and Mother both wanted something and were using one another to mutual purpose. Of course. Mother had prepared the way for me with Monica. Mother had disapproved of my first wife, Mary, an Indian, and since Mary's death, Mother had tried settin' me up with different women, wanting, no doubt, to ensure my next wife, should there be one, would be white, preferably Dutch, though she seemed willing now to settle for an Englishwoman. Another wife, Mother reasoned, might break me of my enthrallment of the north and convince, or coerce me, into becoming a civilized man, a prosperous Albany tavern-keeper. The more Monica talked, the more I heard my mother's influence. Monica knew all the good things about me, and if she knew the bad, she didn't say so.

The flattery was pleasing but I wanted to hear about her, not me, and steered back onto herself, she talked about having managed to come to America with her husband, which would have been difficult and which I ascribed to the amazing power of such a woman. She said how grateful she was to my mother but it was stressful for Monica at the tavern, with no strong man to protect her from the ribald jibes and grasping hands, although she quickly assured me, anytime a patron went beyond what was considered permissible, Father Kuyler's Dutch fists boomed loudly in her defense.

After a time, Monica got back to talking about me, about my exploits to the north. She was intrigued by how I was something of a mysterious character around Albany, what with my vanishing in the fall of the years and returning in the spring with a rich cache of furs and always with valuable knowledge concerning the French. As she talked, a bitterness came into her voice, my mother's bitterness against the authorities, as well as the citizens, who were not so grateful as they should have been for the risks I took for their benefit.

With regard to my fur business, she asked, “Are you a smuggler, as some say, or have you happened upon some lost land known only to you, as others maintain?” I might have said how, having heard so much about me from my mother, she could judge for herself. Instead, I asked her to please not speak of my secret in a public place. It was carefully guarded, whatever I be, although with the passage of the years my secret was maybe less well-kept than I imagined.

Gazing at her whilst she talked, I was reminded, by her looks, not her temperament, of Priscilla, wife of my late friend Arnold. Priscilla had been a tall woman too, and with a reputation around Albany, and later up at Saratoga, as a harridan. Here was perhaps another warning but I took no heed; physical similarity in no way meant a similar disposition. And besides, I was probably one of the few persons to have seen the softer side of Priscilla. I remembered the portrait Arnold treasured of his wife as a young woman. Portraits sometimes lied, often lied, else the artist might not get his full commission but I saw how Priscilla had once been, if not beautiful, then at least fetching. The middle-aged Priscilla had been intimidating with her size, a big-boned woman taller than most men, including her husband, and there was no abiding her hawk-like gaze and shrill tongue. Still, I could believe she had been beautiful as a younger woman.

So entranced was I, and what man does not relish such a woman as this Monica recounting his deeds of bravery, I ignored the warnings. In Monica’s eyes, I must have seemed to be a man who, properly steered, could be harnessed into proprietorship of the Full Sail Tavern, as profitable an establishment as there was in Albany, although every last duit was hard-earned. Did she already see herself as the wife of a respectable tavern-keeper? Had she spent enough time in the tavern to have deemed the drudgery worth a share in the profits? If this were how she saw me, she might be a threat to my freedom, to my sojourning to the north, and yet and realizing it, I stayed in my chair, held there by the flattery and admiration she seemed to hold for me and I was smitten with how she lifted her chin with indignation for the way I was treated by the Albany folks. I couldn’t help feel I wasn’t disrespected nearly as much as what Monica had been led to believe, but gazing at her across the table as she talked, I was flattered to think a lady of such breeding and intelligence, even brought low, could set her sights on a mountain man.

I would have had our conversation go on longer but all too soon our teacups had been refilled and emptied again, the plum platter was a smattering of crumbs and she suddenly remembered her errand, to fetch me to the tavern. We were back on the street, hurrying, and now it was I who was smiling. Miss Saint-John feared Mother's wrath whilst I had no such fear.

****

We arrived at the tavern. It was raucous, food and spirits flowing, the din terrific. The crowd was mostly young colonial soldiers, rowdy, hard-drinking, far from home, many for the first time. Monica looked on approvingly as Mother greeted me. Pops was surely glad to see me safe but cut short his welcoming, he had just one man helping him with the dispensing of drinks and with all those thirsty patrons. I retreated to the kitchen for some supper, and from where I sat, I could see Monica and Mother, deep in animated conversation, oblivious to the raucousness. It was obvious they liked each other plenty and equally obvious with their glances in my direction, their talk was about me. I couldn't hear what they were saying but I could imagine the excitement in Mother's thick Dutch accent and the approval in Monica's English lilt. Father yelled to them more than once to get back to work, they finally heeding him.

An army clerk came in and presented me with a note in Johnson's scrawl. Bill had got word I was in town and I was to go up to headquarters immediately. I stuffed the note into my pocket. I was thirsty and would have some beer and hopefully more time with Monica but the demands of the boisterous common room kept her from me and Mother reminded me how "William Johnson does not like to be kept waiting."

I headed back across town and up Yonkers Street, to the fort at the top of the hill, where Johnson's headquarters was located. His orderly told me to wait. I told him, "Either get out of my way or Johnson can go to hell or come and find me instead of me findin' him. I don't give a fat damn. No son-of-a-bitch of an Irishman is going to keep me waiting." I knew my loud declaration would draw Bill out of bed or wherever the hell he was, and I pushed past the orderly and into the back office.

Surprisingly, Johnson was still huddled with a few hard-set officers over lists of supplies and rosters of men. A nearly naked Mohawk was passed out on the floor, a spilled glass of rum alongside him. Johnson shook my hand warmly, slapped me on the shoulder and introduced me to his officers. He passed me a rum. He talked glowingly about his army and about testing the mettle of the French. "Crown Point will soon be ours," he assured me. "And after Crown Point, on to Montreal and Quebec." I recalled the words of Sergeant Tom, how Bill Johnson was drunk on more than just rum. "Tell us what you saw up in the north," Johnson said. "What is the enemy doing? What is his strength?" I stepped to the map on the wall, illuminated by the candle one of the men held up to it, the light flickering our faces in and out of shadow. The map showed the northern reaches of our colony and beyond, the Champlain Valley and Canada. It also contained blank areas which I might have filled in, had I been asked.

My telling of the situation and our talk kept circling back to Scalp Point. For the last twenty-five years, the French had maintained a fort there and even before the fort it had been the place from which the French launched their Indians and the Jesuits proselytized the Iroquois. Also, according to the rumors around Albany, the smuggling of furs had flourished in those parts, the way to riches for those daring enough and savvy enough to survive. About this, I had some personal experience.

Johnson asked plenty of questions about the Scalp Point fort which was a rock castle. Four-stories high, rounded and made of black limestone and with cannons on each of the levels, the castle had for years dominated the straits. It loomed large too, in the thoughts and plans of Englishmen. Whilst I spoke of the presence of so many French regulars and marines up there, the regulars in gray and white, marines in blue, veterans of many a European campaign, I was scornful of the fear which showed in the eyes of Johnson's officers.

On the east side of the strait, the fortifications, less formidable and of wood, not stone, were getting strengthened. The palisade, long rotting and falling away, was stout and strong now and bristled with men and guns. Camped on both shores were French woodsmen in tan and brown, Indians in all sorts of dress and undress.

The Mohawk there with us in the room had awakened. He, nearly naked and with his body heavily tattooed with the strangest designs and shapes, grunted and held his cup out to Johnson for more rum. Bill shook his head, no. The Indian grunted again, which grunt revealed nothing of his mood, nor did the manner in which he walked out of the room give any indication.

Johnson saw I had been staring at the Indian's tattoos, particularly the cluster of identical small marks on his thighs. Bill asked did I know what those indicated. I did, he told the men, "Each represents an enemy scalp taken." More than thirty. Bill got talking about how proud were the Mohawks of the tattooing, a subject of amazement to him but clearly of less importance than what we had been discussing. Bill said more of what I knew, how the larger tattoos signified many things, tribe and clan, fealty and valor; deeds, dreams and visions. He said the tattoos attested to the astonishing degree of pain the braves could endure without flinching or crying out. It was supposed to make a man more courageous than he already was, in preparation for the day when he might get tested at the fire-stake.

This was not the first time I had seen Bill interrupt an important meeting to get onto marveling about the Iroquois. I knew from experience there was no stopping him once he got started, my glance at his officers told me it wasn't their first time either and they shared my frustration. We listened impatiently and yet it was not lost on me how Bill's admiration was genuine, and with how it played into the Iroquois' devotion to him, it was of great advantage to us.

I finally interrupted his discourse by putting my finger on the map a little below Scalp Point, where the lakes, Saint Sacrement and Champlain nearly came together and were connected by Portage Crick. This place, called Ticonderoga by the Mohawks, was of the utmost strategic value and I said if Bill didn't get there soon, the French would have themselves a fort there, out where the promontory narrowed the lake.

Bill asked more questions and with him not offering a refill on the rum, I raised the cup slightly a few times so he'd know it was empty. I thought I might have to walk out, same as the Indian had done, if I did not get my drink. I had been thirsty for a long time. He filled my cup, I said something about our own fort which was going in at the lower end of the falls, at the turn of the Hudson, adding as how it was about time. He agreed. The fort, Bill told me with a mild disgruntlement, was getting called Lyman, for the man charged with building it. Johnson said he was steadily dispatching men up there, enough so the outposts and work parties would be well protected just by the sheer number of men sent.

More practically, Johnson was starting a ranging company and he wanted me to be a part of it. I refused, told him I was no more inclined to take orders from him or his officers than I was from the bumbling redcoats. I said I would scout the French, maybe even hunt them, for I had grown fond of the hunt, but I would do none of it as a part of his army.

I did inquire as to whether or not Joe Blanchard, who had so ably led us rangers in the previous war, would be leading us again. Johnson said Blanchard was too old and infirm and would stay home and recruit New

Englanders for the service. Robert Rogers would command our rangers.

"Rogers!" I said. "He's naught but a pup." Johnson wasn't interested in arguing Rogers' fitness to lead, and truth was, I wasn't either. Rogers was awfully young for such responsibility, no more than mid-twenties, but he had been scouting along the New England frontier since he was a lad. Blanchard had recommended him as a man of uncommon ability and there was nobody's opinion I trusted more than Joe's. Still, Rogers' appointment concerned me. It wasn't his youth nor his loose scruples. Nor his propensity for clandestine dealing with the French in times of peace. I had engaged in my own share of this sort of nefariousness which Rogers called trading. Others, including me, called it what it was. Smuggling. No. My feelings toward Rogers didn't have to do with any of it, nor of having worked for him and his partners, moving goods around New Hampshire, which had not been a bargain for me and which left me with the feeling they had not played me fair. What bothered me was the grandiose opinion Rogers had of himself. He reckoned to be a big man someday, his boasting not unlike how Bill Johnson had talked of hisself when he arrived in the New World so many years ago from Ireland, damn near penniless. Bill had made good his boasting, becoming one of the most influential men in the colonies and one of the richest. Trouble was, deep into the woods with enemies lurking was maybe not the best place to be with a man whose reputation was foremost on his mind.

Johnson told me Blanchard and Rogers had both asked about me. Both had urged him to sign me up. Bill said he presently had just a single company of rangers, sixty men, but Rogers, on his way to us from over east, was bringing more, a mix of former rangers from the last war and recruits handpicked by Blanchard and Rogers. Assisting Rogers was his younger brother, Richard, whom I also knew.

Johnson told me our rangers' base camp would be at Lyman. He then bragged how carefully he had chosen the placement of the fort, never mind this lower landing of the Great Carry was the most obvious place and was far more familiar to me than it could ever be to him.

Johnson said a road had been started over toward Wood Creek, where sat the charred hulk of old Fort Anne, a post of bygone days, now in the last stages of rotting away. He said this road would be his invasion route to the north. "Only a fool," I said, "would go by way of Wood Creek." I had much experience with the creek and the surrounding bogs. Johnson had probably never even been up there. "The ground," I said, "is naught but swamps with water too foul for drinking and with too many places for ambush." I shuddered to think of our inexperienced men strung out for miles along the narrow waterway, open to sniping from the tree-lined banks and not able to help each other in a fight. The entire army might get picked off a few men at a time, those what didn't get sucked down into the bogs or died for drinking the water. "Them Drowned Lands," I said, "always give me the shivers. Once, an entire army got swallowed up in there and it could happen again. It be a damn fool place to meet an enemy who will know more about your intentions than you'll know about his."

"Your way to Scalp Point," I said, "is Saint Sacrement and Ticonderoga. Build your road to the south end of Saint Sacrement and sail to the north, where the enemy is ensconced. You are not going to sneak up on them anyway, so go the way you can keep your army together." Johnson raised his hand for me to stop speaking, he not appreciating my going against him in front of his officers, which I should not have been doing. He dismissed them and we talked deep into the night.

Johnson said his army would be made up entirely of colonials with just a few British along as advisors. "Any lobsterbacks you got," I said, "order 'em out of their bright coats. Give 'em a chance, at least." Johnson grinned and asked did I think a colonial such as himself could order British officers to shed their coats, of which they were so proud, and which admission pointed out the absurdity of a colonial such as him at the head of one of our armies. "You're the damn commander," I said.

He asked about the smuggling trade which, even with the troubles, flourished. I denied knowing anything about it. "I never saw no such thing," I said. Bill had never done any smuggling, only had he bankrolled some few trips. One such trip resulted in the deaths of all the men in my party 'cept me, and when I finally made it back to Albany after stumbling around the north woods for weeks and nearly going stark, raving mad, Bill and his partners demanded I make good their losses!

I hammered out with Johnson the same arrangement I'd had with Blanchard in the last war. I would not join but, and with Rogers' assent and the approval of the higher-ups, I would become what was called an attached. Working along with the rangers, getting paid same as them but not subject to their discipline or to the discipline of the British, and with the right to cease the attachment anytime I felt fit to do so. They also could break the attachment.

"My army leaves for Lyman in a few days," Bill said, after we had talked it all over some more. "The rangers already here will be leaving tomorrow, an hour before sunrise. Can you be ready?"

I said I could.

Bill then decided it was time we did some carousing, which we had used to do often, when we were younger. I demurred, this puzzled him initially, then a thought put a grin on his face.

"You've met Monica," he said, and certain it was my mother had spoken to Johnson of her scheme to unite Monica and me, for Mother often confided in Johnson, and no doubt Bill, unknown to Mother, had made his own unsuccessful play for the dark-haired, green-eyed English beauty. Few women ever failed to succumb to Bill's seductions and with my apparent victory over him in an arena where he seldom lost, he conceded amicably. We had a few more drinks and I stood up to go.

"I'll see you up there at Lyman," he said.

"Keep your hair," I said.

I went out, stiffened into the north wind blowing cool and strong. The moon was down in the west. I walked down the hill, shuddering against the cold, the walk clearing my head some. I arrived back at the tavern, expecting I would have to spend the night in the shed in the back, the doors long since bolted and I not daring to wake Pops but as I got around toward the back, the side door opened slightly. Monica had been waiting for me. Holding a candle in a dish and dressed in mobcap and an opened robe over a nightgown that fetchingly ended above her knees, she led me into the darkened taproom. She lit a few more candles and we sat at one of the long wooden tables. She poured us some ale and we soon regained the rapport we had established earlier. Deep in conversation, she invited me into her quarters, the tiny, low-ceilinged room located behind the stairs to the loft.

She sat on the edge of the bed and with me next to her, my hands on my knees, I told her I must leave in a few short hours. She pressed my shoulders gently backward until my head was against the wall. She went on talking and seeing me struggling against sleep, she snuggled in beside me. "Rest, then," she said, and pulling a blanket over us, she apologized for having talked so much and said what I needed was sleep, not to be listening to a woman's babbling. I murmured how I could stay wrapped in her charms forever and to hell with having it out with every damn Indian what came up the lakes. She laughed ruefully and said she hadn't realized how the allure of her charms might be in competition with the urge to thrash woodland savages, but she said it with playfulness, and added as how she was grateful for at least having got the better of the comparison. Then, and more seriously and with my head in her lap, her fingers twining my hair, “Oh, please do be careful. Please stay safe. All my thoughts go with you and I pledge to wait here faithfully for you.” Wait faithfully for me? Hearing this, I should have lifted my head up out of her lap and got on my feet and away. What more warning did I need to take flight from this woman? Yet I was content to drift into blissful sleep in her arms, convinced hers were the sweetest of words.

****

There came a banging on the front door of the tavern. Someone was calling my name and yelling about getting moving. I was an hour late; the rangers had already left. I looked for the woman who'd been lying with me. She was gone, and had I dreamt her? Dreamt the dark hair and long shapely legs? The alluring eyes and voice? The full womanly form pressed against me as I drifted off to sleep? I was conflicted. I wanted her to have been more than a dream yet I was not unaware of the relief I would feel, had she not really lain with me.

Going into the tap room, I saw her behind the bar. Humming softly to herself whilst she stuffed into a knapsack the provisions she had prepared for me. Meat, bread, sweets.

Ignoring the warning voice in my head and the shouting, which was coming from the alley which ran alongside the tavern, I took her hand and fervently promised to show her my mountain lair, the country she wanted to see. “If you have no other plans, of course.” She said her plans might be put off for a time. We held each other at the door. I was reluctant to leave her, with Bill Johnson prowling. Mother came in her nightclothes and hollered, “Goddammit, go, afore the loudmouth in the alley wakes your father and he gives both of you the thrashings you deserve.” Mother spoke harshly to Monica too, about gettin' her day started and although Monica jumped, Mother's harshness toward her was without bite.

I stepped outside, the orderly sent to fetch me said, “The rangers are scouting on foot up the river to Lyman, looking for signs of trouble.” I was to hurry the hell up. Dawn was lighting up the eastern sky as I made my way toward the fort.

Chapter III – With Rogers to Lead Us

I canoed to Stillwater and got in before the rangers and when they arrived, Rogers was not with them, he not yet having come over from New England. Most of the rangers, what few there were, hailed from south of Albany. They were strangers to me and were not frontiersmen, which made them suspect. I went to see the company commander whose name was Willett. He made it clear he was ill-disposed toward scouts who could not get out of bed in the morning. I agreed and we went up to Lyman, or what there was of the fort, and waited there for Rogers and the rest of the ranger companies.

We waited two weeks. The summer wore on without much getting done except work on the fort and a widening and smoothing of the old carry trail to Wood Creek and the South Bay. Work on the road went slowly, the mosquitoes and flies a constant harassment. Many of the men sickened. We rangers used the time to scout close around the fort, and to look after the road builders and train our men.

A large party of Indians was sighted south and east of the Hudson and I led a party of rangers down to have a look. It was a sparsely-settled area with the homesteads precariously situated. Most of these cabins had been erected since the conclusion of the last war and were easy pickings for the torrid raiders. There wasn't much we could do except survey the damage and when I got back, Willett told me he had heard from Rogers.

The raiding had been heavy over in western Massachusetts and the Hampshires and now it was abating, Rogers figured there'd be plenty of Indians heading north. This assumption was probably correct. There were two main routes down and back for the northern Indians. One way was the Connecticut River trail which started somewhere up in eastern Quebec and more or less followed the Connecticut River. The other was Lake Champlain and the Drowned Lands. The more western Indians came down either the Ottawa or Saint Lawrence rivers to Montreal and from there, they came up Champlain to the South Bay. A trail ran south-east from the Drowned Lands to the Connecticut trail.

We moved farther up, beyond the road-builders and to where we were to rendezvous with Rogers, no more than a day's march from the

South Bay. No fires were lit, sentries were posted, the men hunkered down for some sleep. The sky was clear, the air warm enough so a man hardly needed a blanket.

Willett asked me to go up and have a look, to see were there Indians heading for the South Bay. He asked did I want to take any men with me. I didn't, and I was gone, moving quickly and staying off what few trails there were. I skirted the hills and the worst of the lowland bogs. Toward nightfall, I got in to the connector trail. Tired from the hard walking, I needed sleep and too bad I no longer had my dog with me. A faithful companion through the last war, Old Blackie could always be depended on in situations, to watch whilst I slept. I slept more deeply than I should of, and sometime later, I knew not how much so, I awoke. The woods was silent and dark, the moon in and out from behind the clouds. I listened. The ominous quiet meant there was probably something.

It wasn't long before I seen Indians, in a single file along the trail in the moonlight. They had captives, men, women, children, with tethers 'round their necks and loot on their backs. The captives were staggering with the weights they carried and were trying to stifle whatever noise they was making, for the kicks and blows they took for it. With my eyes adjusted to the darkness, the sleep gone from my eyes, I watched as they passed scant yards from me. I figured there were ten or twelve raiders and as many captives.

Well, this old friend stayed where he was after they were gone and a damn good thing for there were more. Plenty more. Over the next hour, three parties of ten or more came past and with ones and twos between the parties. Some had prisoners, some didn't. They passed close enough to my hiding place so I heard an occasional French or Indian word, so close I could smell 'em. If I so much as moved, I too would be bound and carrying a heavy load north. Or dead. A woman captive looked me straight in the eye and I feared she might betray me without intending to, though she did not.

For two hours I watched 'em go by and I stayed still for another hour after the last of 'em was gone. With silence around me again, I moved out slow and easy. I made my way back, eyes darting 'round at the deep shadows blown by the north wind which was up strong, a steady mournful wail through the trees, a lamenting spirit crying for the fate of those who had fallen to the savages. I had seen it all before, lived it all in the last war, and now the terrible blight was over the land again. The hordes out for mayhem, vicious and cruel. Scalpings, mutilations, burnings the work of these fiendish devils.

I got back to Willett's camp and Rogers was there, not with his entire contingent and instead with just a single company, sixty men, the rest to follow later. Rogers shook my hand, said he was glad to see I was joined up and he asked were there Indians. Plenty, I said. Heading to the South Bay where their boats were stashed, and as I told this, I seen his eyes was gleaming. He asked could we get up there in time to hit them. I said yes. The trail would take 'em wide around some swampy ground and with how we were situated and did we cut to the northeast, we could traverse north of the worst swamps whilst the devils was looping around to the east. This should get us out along the trail ahead of them. I showed Rogers on a map what would be the best place for settin' an ambush. I then said as the noise of a fight would draw in any other Indians what was close by, we should just hit the last of them. Hit 'em fast and get the hell out.

Rogers sent orders back to the militia at the road builders' camp for them to come up on the double-quick. The rangers sent to get 'em were to bring 'em to a rendezvous with us farther along. In the meantime, Rogers, with half his ranger company, a slightly understrength company of militia and twenty Mohawks, seventy-five men, would go up ahead and set his ambush.

There was concern amongst the men for Rogers taking us out from the militia, who would be our backup, did we get into a situation. Somebody said out loud what most was thinking. What did Rogers expect to do with no more than seventy-five men? Rogers wasn't saying, could be he didn't know yet himself, but whatever he decided, it would tell us plenty about him.

I told Rogers this part of our own New York frontier was not entirely uninhabited. There was a small settlement north and slightly west of us. Rogers was surprised to hear this and asked wouldn't the folks have departed. I shook my head. I did not think they were gone. The settlement was recent, the folks had been warned about venturing so far north with a war about to commence but had gone anyway for knowing it was good land and them wanting to get there afore anybody else. Neither me nor Rogers doubted their courage, just their sense. They had built a blockhouse, I'd seen it, it was a good one. Smaller war parties going down into New York had avoided the settlement on account of the blockhouse but it must have rankled the Indians each time they went wide around it and they had probably always intended to hit it and with so many Indians raiding New York Colony, same as in New England, now might be the time. Rogers asked could I get out there and have a look and still get up to the South Bay in time to join him. I said it'd be plenty of hoofing but I figured to do it. In the meantime, he'd go to the northeast and set his ambush.

I left at once and late morning the next day, I approached the settlement. Smoke from burning cabins and barns billowed up as white pillars in the windless air. I came across slain folks at their cabins, in their fields and along the trails and especially at the blockhouse, which was aflame, as were the few cabins around it. Folks scalped and mutilated; livestock piteously hamstrung. Bawling, unable to stand, crazed by their circumstances. Often did the Indians not kill the cows and oxen and only cut the hocks so the white men who came behind would have to put the beasts out of their misery.

The raiders were only just gone, they having struck at first light, as is usual with them. There were survivors. They told me the Indians had got into the blockhouse before anybody was aware of them. The Indians clanged the bell to bring the folks hurrying in to what they thought was safety. One woman told me she and her eight children were almost in when a boy come running the other way saying it was Indians doin' the ringing. The woman and her brood hid in the woods.

From what I seen, the destruction, bad as it was, could a been worse. The savages had done their work quickly, probably fearful for the closeness of the fort and road-builders. This, if true, proved the importance of all the work our side was doing.

The folks said there were many hundreds of Indians. This was surely an exaggeration, still, there were plenty, by the sign, and with Frenchmen, for I had seen boot and shoe prints.

There was naught I could do for the folks and with the likelihood these Indians would come in behind Rogers, I had to get up to warn him. I promised the folks to get help to them as soon as I could and I loped off into the woods.

Spooking behind the Indians, I came to where their main party had split into two, their usual tactic when they were in enemy country. The lesser of them, twenty or so and without captives, had gone to the northwest whilst the others, fifty of 'em and with the captives, stayed north and east.

I followed the bigger of the parties, which seemed more directly headed for the South Bay, their sign plain enough in the daylight. I saw the bodies of those who for one reason or another it had pleased the red men to dispatch. I seen a headless body and a little farther along was the scalped head, on a pole, an old granny who could not keep up.

The Indians turned more directly to the north than northeast and it seemed they might be headed along the route I had intended taking and which would have got me looped around in front of them. A trail which followed what scant dry ground there was through the swamps which was up ahead. Maybe this war party, having raided deeper down into New York Colony before hitting the settlement, had hid their boats up along Wood Creek. If this be true, they'd bypass Rogers' ambush, which would be a good thing as it would mean less Indians for him to fight. I had at least to follow 'em long enough to ascertain their route, and as it was and after they had got in close to the Drowned Lands, they turned to the east to avoid the worst of the swamps and which turning put them square toward Rogers, if he was where I figured him to be. I swung around to the north and got parallel and alongside the raiders. This was more dangerous than following 'em for I was now traversing a narrow corridor between the Drowned Lands and the trail. If the Indians got wind of me, I would have nowhere to run, 'cept deeper into the swamps where they would hunt me down but it was the only way, if I was to get to Rogers in time. I walked hard most of a day. It was hills which were no more than rounded humps and with plenty of watery bogs between 'em.

Just before dark and onto flat, dry ground and beneath primeval oaks which were centuries old, I was again back following alongside the trail to the South Bay. I got to the ambush place. Rogers wasn't there and from the sign, plenty of Indians had passed by without him hitting them. He would have had time enough to get into position so where the hell was he? I had a bad feeling I might be the only Englishman other than the captives within miles of the bay. Me and all those Indians. I hadn't heard any shooting, though, and Rogers wasn't the sort to turn tail and run so I figured him to be around somewhere.

Deciding not to go on in the dark and settling myself in a bed of leaves a short distance from the trail, I heard a turkey call, the ranger signal. The call was repeated a few times. With no rangers around, it might have been Indians trying to trick me so's I'd come in. I listened some more, the woods deathly silent around me. The calls had hushed the birds and squirrels, so they were nervous too. I moved around some and got a look at the sign in the last light of day and decided it was just one man, a ranger, and after some careful spooking by each of us, we joined up. He gave me some news which was a shock to me.

Instead of setting an ambush along the trail to fast hit the last of the Indians and high-tail afterward, Rogers had gone up to the South Bay to pick a fight with as many Indians as was there. I asked had anyone tried talking him out of it. Damn near all of ‘em had reminded Rogers the Indians congregating at the bay sometimes numbered in the hundreds and this looked to be one of those times. Hundreds of them, seventy-five of ours.

I asked the ranger what Rogers intended doing with so few men. The ranger said Rogers, when asked the same question, had just grinned and said he’d figure something out when he got there. How Rogers saw it, for too many years the Indians out of Scalp Point had stashed their boats at the South Bay and raided south without fear of getting cut off. This time, he intended it be different. The man was not short of ambition and as trepidacious as I was for Rogers’ recklessness, he was doing what I had always wanted. Taking the war to the Indians instead of waiting on them to hit us. Just he was maybe doing it at the wrong place and time.

Me and the ranger spent the night and with I knowing the country and him knowing where Rogers was, we was moving at first light. Those few times when we checked the trail, we couldn’t either of us believe how much fresh Indian sign there was. Indians enough and still coming so we had to make our own way through the thickest parts of the forest.

We got in with the company no more than a mile from the South Bay. Rogers, gleeful, said there were more Indians than he could have hoped for and even with my telling him there were more coming from the other direction, he was undaunted. He said he had men out to watch for the militia and guide them in, said they should be arriving soon. I had doubts the militia could get up in time to help us out. The rangers he’d sent to bring ‘em were raw and unfamiliar with the country. They would have to be damn good to do all of what was expected of ‘em. Rogers conceded we might have to fight without them, which again had me wondering what to hell Blanch had been thinking when he recommended Rogers for command.

Rogers got up into a pine tree, the woods were silent around us except for the hammering of a big woodpecker what was knocking about for something to eat. Rogers came down from his swaying perch and said there were two-hundred Indians. Said they were neither hurrying nor readying for a fight so they didn't know we were nearby. He said there were some few men in white uniforms. These were French regulars.

A ranger from our perimeter came in and said the Indians from out of New York Colony was coming. He said there were a lot of them. We were now in a vise between two large enemy forces. Rogers' Rangers, as we had begun to style ourselves, might be about to get wiped out afore having fairly got started. The glorious career Rogers set for himself was about to get snuffed.

Rogers formed us into a half-circle from which we could fight in one direction or the other, or both at once, which seemed more likely. We were on the ground and behind cover with primings checked, hammers cocked. We seen a man ghosting through the trees from a direction other than what we had expected the Indians to be coming. We had our sights on him. Rogers went out and slapped the man on the shoulder. It was his brother, Richard.

Richard had been bringing in more of the newly constituted ranger force, out from New England. Two companies, neither at full strength, eighty men. "Some seasoned, most green, all tired." They'd been on the way to Lyman and hitting the carry trail above where the men were widening it into a road, they'd started south and had met the militia coming up. Apprised of our situation, Richard had turned around and come at the double-quick.

Richard said the Indians were two hours behind him. Rogers said this was time enough for him to hit the Indians already there, then turn and hit those what was coming. I seen the disbelief in the eyes of some of his officers.

Richard was grinning. He was always eager for action, same as his brother, and with our force now up near a hundred and fifty and with how many Indians was on the shore and both sides with more coming, the possibility of a good-sized battle was brewing, the outcome to be decided by who got the most men into it the quickest. Rogers intended it be him. Richard's men were New England frontiersmen, no strangers to the depredations of our adversaries, and were spoiling for a fight.

Rogers got back up in the tree and when he came down, he told us more Indians was arriving on the shore, which we knew anyway by the whoops and the firing of guns in greeting and in celebration of their successful raiding. Rogers sent me with thirty men, including the Mohawks, in a swing north and west through the woods, to the high ground overlooking the shore where the enemy was preparing to evacuate. I was unsure of myself, leading Mohawks, I having never before worked so closely with them. I marveled at how silently they moved. More silent than the best rangers.

Rogers was to circle around on the other side, Richard and his men would advance abreast of the trail. I would remain hidden whilst the brothers hit the Indians a double blow, Robert first, then Richard. The direction of the hits would push the Indians toward my hill and I would strike when they got up to me. We should do well with this arrangement. Already panicked by the rangers, the sudden appearance of Mohawks would take the fight out of the northern Indians.

I got my men behind the ridge and snuck to the top with a couple of Mohawk chiefs. Hidden in the tall grass, we watched the Indians, on the strip of cleared land along the shore. They were greeting one another and boasting of their deeds. The captives were grouped together and was singing a psalm whilst the Indians burnt a man alive. A warning to the others or maybe it was intended as one last slap across our faces, one more black mark we must someday avenge.

There came a change over the Indians, a murmur going through 'em. They was finding out about us, and whilst some prepared to get hit, others began hurrying their captives into the boats and shoving off. We had to get in fast and how agonizing for the captives, taken away even as they sensed relief was at hand. We could hear their laments as they were moved out onto the water.

A band of Indians burst into the clearing, shouting alarms and there came a devastating fusillade from the side of the clearing opposite to us. There were whoops and screams as the Indians, without cover, took the brunt of the firing. Richard's men volleyed, then Rogers again. They knocked down scores of Indians and put the rest into disorder as they got thrown back against the bay. Some ran for the one place seemingly open to them, my hill, where they might a thought they could make a stand. They got partway up the slope and our Mohawks, hidden in the grass, rose up screeching and firing down into 'em. Our war-whooping, warclub-wielding devils charged off the hill. Never had I seen such fear as what was in those northern Indians at the sight of Mohawks rising up from cover and gettin' after 'em.

The Indians' confusion was about total, we had 'em from three sides and were gettin' in on 'em with hatchets and knives. It was a nasty fight, hand to hand, knife to knife, ax to tomahawk. Some of us got down to the shore and peppered those Indians who was in their canoes but not yet beyond the range of our guns. A few of 'em we knocked out of their boats. One, thinking himself safe for being far enough out on the water, gestured with a finger across the throat of a woman captive. I took aim, fired, he tumbled over the side and into the water. Our men cheered but the ill-fated woman went over too and floundered, her clothes made heavy by the water. I figured she drowned. I reloaded quickly and took another Indian at an even greater distance. Too bad for them, my gun was a rifle, not a smoothbore, and in King George's War, a decade before and on account of my gun's accuracy and distance, the men had taken to calling it Old Nitpicker. I was showing this new generation of red men they too would have to learn respect for the distinctive crack she made when she spoke against them, same as their fathers and elder brothers had learnt.

With the surviving Indians having fled into the woods, Rogers put a ring around us so we didn't go chasing after 'em. We'd pursue soon enough but not in disorder. With plenty more Indians out there and surely coming in fast for having heard the commotion, we were now in about the same situation as the Indians had been when we'd hit 'em, which is to say, open to fusillades from the woods and with our backs to the bay.

We had took some casualties, although not nearly so many as the foe. We had some few dead and plenty had gashes, cuts and bruises, clothing ripped and bloodied from the close-up fighting. Some of our men were for getting into canoes and pursuing those Indians which had got away with captives. This, Rogers forbade. He said there was naught we could do for those which had got taken. Others of the captives had got killed in the shooting or had got struck down along the shore. We had rescued plenty. One young lass, nearly naked, unscathed and on her knees, arms lifted, praised us as if we were the Hosts of Angels come down to snatch her from the jaws of Hell.

The Mohawks and some few of our men were scalping and looting, Rogers said for them to stop, not because he was against it, which he was, but because he was anxious to get us out of there. The Mohawks ignored him and he left them alone for knowing they weren't going to pass up scalps on his nor anybody's orders. Only did he make it clear to the chiefs there'd be no scalping of our own dead or the dead captives, neither.

Whilst we was assembling, a scout came in to tell us the Indians which had been raiding New York Colony was arriving. The scout said there were a lot of 'em. Rogers told this to the men as if it were good news and said it meant we could kill 'em all to once instead of hunting around the woods for 'em. The men laughed at this.

Gunfire broke out a ways to the west, a battle, which confounded us. Who the hell was out there, besides Indians? The noise grew in volume and another ranger came in with the news it was the militia. They had got up and hit the Indians from behind whilst the Indians was readying to come at us. We cheered for the militia and for the rangers whose good work had brought 'em. We advanced to the sounds and with more good work by our officers and scouts, we got into the Indians from the side opposite from where they was already engaged. The Indians probably outnumbered us, it didn't matter. With us getting them from two sides, they were whipped. Rogers put out pincers to outflank the Indians, this failed, the fight was hot for a time then it slackened as the Indians melted into the forest to the northwest.

Rogers was for letting them go. Our men were exhausted and Rogers knew how even beaten Indians could be rattlesnakes in the brush. The militia commander, eyes flashing, scoffed. He said he'd been rushed up here to kill Indians and by God, it was what he was going to do. The damn fool seemed to want to chase 'em all the way back to Scalp Point. Or Montreal. Rogers again cautioned against pursuit. He knew how rashness could squander a victory and he damn sure didn't want to be chasing Indians through the woods with militia.

The militia captain declared he outranked Rogers and following a brief council, from which Rogers was excluded, the militia officer said we was going after the Indians. Whilst we were forming up, Rogers and the captain jawed at one another, the captain calling Rogers a coward. This, with the boldness Rogers had shown in getting up with the Indians and hitting 'em, was, to us rangers, beyond belief.

The captain raised his sword and pointed it toward where the Indians had gone and off he went with his men. Rogers had little choice except to go along, which we did, though with less recklessness than the militia. The enemy was made to fight a retreating action which they, after their initial confusion, did well. We was getting scattered and the Indians, with quick sorties, served us some hard blows. They'd strike and get back into the brush afore we could get onto 'em. They'd maybe got whipped but now and with us fighting their kind of battle, they were reviving.

The action moved west. Rogers had his rangers fighting in pairs, two men behind cover, one firing whilst the other loaded. The favorite trick of the Indians had always been to wait for a man to shoot, then jump him with tomahawk or warclub whilst he reloaded. Now, and with a trick of our own, we learned 'em a painful lesson. When an Indian came in against what he thought was an unloaded gun, our second man got him. I got one in this way, up so close, the tip of my gun barrel scorched his breast and I saw the startled look in his eyes as my bullet tumbled him backward over a log.

I spent most of this fight moving from cover to cover and holding back a young ranger not over sixteen years of age. Me and him moved together, loading and firing, and when we caught up with the fight, we were able to deliver our shots with good effect. He got an Indian, his first ever, and how he did carry on! I had to wait whilst he collected the Indian's hair and attached it to his belt. He was full of himself now and was even more anxious to go off in blind pursuit, same as the rest of the fools. "Son," I said. "You'll live longer and do better if you go slow." I tried to get others to do the same but afraid they'd miss the action and get out-bragged later, they kept on. Big hurry to get themselves killed. Tried to tell 'em there'd be plenty enough French and Indians for those of us who went slow but most would not listen, not even with the Indians continuing to set their ambushes, which was costing us.

I picked up a French musket to back myself with in case the boy took off. I kept it loaded and strapped across my back. It was reassuring, an extra gun bouncing along my backside, and with our rangers out front now, we came to a considerable stream. Plenty of Indians had got there ahead of us and had gone across. I was sure some, at least, were hidden on the far bank, to blast us when we came over. Rogers thought so, too, but the militia officers would not consider the possibility and with the way the captain was waving his sword and exhorting his men to keep going and with Rogers raging against it and the men hesitating, I had a remembrance of a most ugly occurrence from the last war. At a crick same as this and with us chasing Indians, Joe Blanchard had said better it was to outflank 'em. An argument ensued and got so fierce, a British officer raised his sword and got his redcoats around Blanch with their pig-stickers. Our militia and regulars formed up and marched into the shallow crick and got met with a devastating fire from the other side.

Now, and with the militia officers ganged up against our ranger boss and him a young man without experience or reputation to back up his words, I saw in my mind the slaughter from ten years ago. Men crossin' a crick without flankers or cover fire and getting hit with a devastating fusillade. Caught in the open, knee-deep in the water, easy targets for the enemy, many brave men died for such rashness. Now and did we go, it would a been a simple matter for the Ottawas and Hurons, hidden on the other side, to knock us down. We might drive the Indians from their cover but far too many of us would perish in the doing.

I became enraged enough at the thought of it to throw down my hat and stomp on it and demand we do it Rogers' way, else we too would get slaughtered. So startling was my outburst, it convinced the men they would be marching into certain death. Few of the men knew me but most knew who I was, or what I was, a scout more experienced with Indian wiles than their officers, and if the men didn't figure to listen to Rogers, a young fellow only just setting out to prove himself, they surely listened to me. My tirade had no such effect on the officers who insisted we go over. The men made the officers to understand, they, the officers, were welcome to go but the men were entirely disinclined to follow.

So we did it Rogers' way by sending men in both directions along our side of the crick, thus outflanking the Indians. They withdrew and since we never actually saw them, our militia officers said afterward the Indians hadn't been there. Said the Indians had fled across the brook and kept going and the time it took for us to do the flanking was time enough for 'em to get away. The sign over there told a much different story.

With the Indians vamoosed, one way or the other, our running battle was over and with our men scattered over a wide area, we worked to bring 'em together as quickly as possible. Small parties and even lone Indians would be prowling for any of our men out by their lonesome. We made camp in a clearing and rangers leading militia began gathering the men and bringing 'em in, along with our dead and wounded. Gather 'em up and get the hell out. We put the wounded in the center, our dead we buried in a pit quick-dug by the militia. Our orders were to bring in the enemy wounded too but few got brought. Easier and more satisfying was it for our men to mostly finish 'em off.

It was now late in the day and with us exhausted, we would not leave until morning. Try to move through the dark and we would lose our way, the men would get scattered and us rangers would have to gather them all over again. Better to rest. Fires were lit, supper cooked, there was a sip of rum for the thirsty men, not much was said. Our canteens were low or empty and I advised Rogers about the waters in and around the Drowned Lands. Fetid waters to kill an already weakened man.

"Drink tomorrow," Rogers told the men. "When we are away from here."

Missing men came in all night, an uneasy time with the pitiful cries of the wounded. Rogers sent rangers back to the fort for help and in the morning, some others of us, myself included, scouted the best way back to the portage trail. Rogers warned our militia before we got going about Indian vultures what might still be around. Our column, when we finally got underway and with plenty of wounded men and the difficulty of getting them through the woods, moved slowly.

We saw sign of Indian stragglers. There was some contact, shots in the woods. Rogers had sent his brother to follow the enemy, to ensure they was gone. Another detachment was sent to the South Bay to stove in any canoes still there. When this second detachment got back to us and reported having chopped the bottoms out of more than thirty boats, Rogers got us together and told us of it. We cheered, and when Rogers feigned sympathy for the poor Indians who'd be walking home, we laughed.

It was after dark when we arrived at the road builders' camp where we would spend the night. A relief force out from Lyman arrived during the night, and the next morning and with our pace hastened for the help and for having got onto the part of the trail which was now a road, we arrived back at the fort by early afternoon. Along the way, some of our wounded, including some rescued folks, succumbed.

Chapter IV – Reckoning the New Ranger Way

Joe Blanchard's leadership in King George's War had much to do with our success, scant as it was. Joe had used us rangers as scouts, bringing information the regular army could use in making its plans. Joe had mostly avoided battle, he had too few men, so it was exhilarating for me, to have gone up to the South Bay with Rogers and whipped the enemy. Still, I had misgivings for how eagerly he took his entire command into a fight and thereby risked more casualties than maybe what we could afford. Rogers had been good enough to succeed and had shown an understanding of Indians and their ways, a necessary talent for any man who would engage them. He was audacious and lucky. The first trait, without the second, might someday be his demise, ours, too.

And yet and despite this difference between Rogers and Blanchard, it was Blanchard who had insisted loudly enough to Johnson for Bill to have put Rogers in command of us. Maybe Blanch realized, same as some others, including me, how the rangers' role in this war had to be different from what it was in the last one. With our ranks bolstered, we had at all times to be going for Frenchie's throat. To keep them and their Indian friends from moving freely through the forests and having safe places for refuging. Knowing this, Johnson had looked for someone different from Blanch and had found him. Whether or not this was the right way to go, we'd find out.

I, even with my apprehensions, was pleased with all I had seen. Many of our folks considered the last war to have been an English victory. It was not, and Blanchard and Rogers were right. We could not achieve victory until we were able to meet the Indians as equals in the woods. If this new war was to be the final deciding contest, the French would have to be without the old advantages they had always held over us.

The South Bay had long been a safe disembarkation point for the Indians. Too remote for us to get to in a hurry and close enough for them to hit us in numbers and get away. Secure the length of Champlain, the Indians had always come with impunity from Canada to Scalp Point and then to the South Bay where they left their boats unattended and with confidence the boats would be there when they got back. This was evidenced by the large number of boats and by how little effort the Indians had made to hide them. Now, and with a fort at the Great Carry and a road to the Drowned Lands and with a more aggressive ranger force, it was hard not to think everything was going in our favor.

What I mostly questioned was whether or not it was wise to hit the Indians whilst they had captives and if there was little or no chance of rescue. The Indians had learned the value of hostages, they could be exchanged for all the things the Indians depended on getting from the white man; muskets, powder, bullets, the iron cooking pots and shiny beads so coveted by the Indian women. Was it not perhaps better sometimes to let the Indians get away and barter later through the Montreal authorities? Maybe, but such was not to be Rogers' way, for what man could stand by as folks was dragged into captivity?

****

The colonel in command of the fort, British regular John Montresor, held a conference with all the officers who had been in the fight, to ascertain what could be learned from it. I had breakfast with Rogers and his brother before the meeting. The battle had been Richard's first time seeing the Iroquois and he marveled at the ferocity they showed against their enemies of antiquity. He shook his head to think how the sight of a mere handful of Mohawks roaring up out of the tall grass had spread such panic through their northern foe. As a New Englander, Richard's previous dealings with Indians was with those out of Canada, fierce, for sure, but not so fierce as Mohawks. He said he was glad the Mohawks was on our side. I said I was too but I cautioned him, "Expect 'em to be not so unrestrained when fellow Iroquois be on the other side."

Rogers told us about an officer of French regulars who was amongst the prisoners we took. He and his brother officers had come along to get their first taste of forest warfare. The officer said they had come down expecting they'd stay together and hit the road builders, then the fort. The Indians had insisted they'd fight in their usual fashion, which was to break up into small bands and disburse into New England and New York. They could not be induced to go against this inclination, which frustrated the French. Warfare for the French was about strategy and tactics, the loss of many men sometimes the price paid to gain an objective but for the Indians it was scalps and spoils and keeping their men alive. The lesson for the French was how this was North American warfare, not European. The red men were as no allies the French had ever worked with before.

Frenchie would have to adjust.

Rogers told us the captured Frenchman had been saved from the Mohawks by one of our patrols which had come across them just as they was readying to torture and burn him. The Mohawks knew Montresor would take any white captives brought in and they intended having their fun whilst still in the woods. The Frenchman had already witnessed the suffering put upon some few Canadian Indians, the disfigurements, the collecting of body parts, including, sometimes, heads. Otherwise it was hair, hands, fingers, ears and whatever else and all whilst the tortured man was kept alive. Imagine Frenchie's relief when our rangers showed up and his dismay when the Mohawks, their hands on their belted tomahawks, refused to give him up. Only what convinced the Mohawks was the rangers saying Rogers would pay most generously for any Frenchmen brought in. So they did and Rogers ransomed him with a goodly portion of the loot taken by our men, he promising to repay the men for what they gave. Afterward, Rogers put in a chit to the colony for reimbursement, the chit was denied and Rogers had to make good on it. This would happen often throughout Rogers' time in command and would contribute to his ultimate undoing.

Whilst we was finishing our breakfast, a militia man came up and thanked Rogers and me for speaking up as forcefully as we had back at the crick when the officers insisted we charge across. "Your officers," Rogers said to the man, "ain't accustomed to taking orders from me," to which the man said they'd learn quick enough. "Those," I said, "which can keep their hair for the time it takes to learn it."

Rogers invited me along to the officers' meeting. I listened as Montresor praised the conduct of the rangers. He said the militia had fought well too and he lauded the effective trick of two men fighting together from behind a single cover. He said this enabled us to kill many more Indians than we might have otherwise and it kept more of us alive. An officer remarked how even after the Indians caught on, the threat of it would serve to dampen their brazenness. Montresor's officers urged him to incorporate it into the training of all our forces.

Montresor told us he and Johnson were intending a lightning-strike force. Led by rangers and rotated through the army, the force to be ready to move out at any time, day or night, overland or by boat, whenever an enemy was reported. The force would be quick to the aid of the settlers, the wood-cutting parties and supply convoys, thus freeing the rangers to scout, which would always be our most important duty.

After the Montresor meeting, Rogers and his brother called their own meeting with the ranger force. Our men sat on rocks and logs or lay in the grass whilst Rogers spoke. Most of our men, without any first-hand experience with Rogers and knowing of his rigorous standards, maybe expected him to chew them out for their mistakes, small as those mistakes may have been. Instead, and without ignoring any of what we had done wrong, he praised us. This was the first fight for many and he said he was pleased with how we had bloodied the enemy. We had suffered losses we were ill able to afford, we had not enough ranger material, but I think Rogers had seen enough to feel he had us going in the proper direction.

Rogers reinforced the importance of our not having rushed ahead as the militia had done when we seen the Indians fleeing, A hurrying man was out of breath when he got up to a fight and didn't shoot so well as a man who was more deliberate in advancing. Rogers, too, talked of us fighting in pairs. "Unless your partner is shot dead, do not leave him. A wounded man can sometimes reload for you. If your partner is killed, find another pair of men or a single man, but do not charge into the enemy alone." He said many of our men, whilst hidden, had stayed in one place too long. "Keep moving else your smoke will give you away and you'll get filled with lead. Move around. Keep to cover, but move. They will think there are more of us."

He talked on all of what he envisioned we would become. An army of woodland fighters who would be at their best when things got hot. He sprinkled in some humor which was mostly at the expense of the French and Indians and he ended more somberly by saying our biggest problem in the past had always been our thinking the enemy to be more formidable than maybe they were. He said he would never feel as if his men were any less capable in the woods than were the enemy. This was a promise as well as a challenge.

Afterward, I sought out the young ranger who had shared cover with me in the fight. His name was Ephraim Woolman and here was a chance, I thought, to do some good. Told him the kind of fight we had engaged in was what could win us the war. I pointed out, and he concurred most eagerly, how between us, we had shot a good number of the enemy.

****

More soldiers and supplies kept coming in to Lyman and with the increase in traffic came a corresponding increase in trouble. Sniping along the Hudson and along the wagon roads. Sudden, small ambushes, shots from shore, swift canoes in the current. Any party on the river or in the woods, no matter its size, was at risk. Orders were issued for boats to travel together and keep to the middle of the river. Those which didn't were liable to get hit from the tree-lined banks. Orders were to not go ashore. So often our least-experienced militia and boatmen, hearing a single gunshot, dashed into the woods thinking there was but one savage and finding plenty more.

****

I was in the straw bales of the stable, asleep, and was awakened by gunfire and loud huzzas. I stumbled outside to word of a great victory for us on our western frontier. Braddock's army, his long, proud column of marching men, had met the enemy in the woods and delivered them a devastating blow. Our cannons fired in joyous celebration; rum was dispensed but the details were murky and Rogers said, "If Braddock got his cannons up to the walls of Duquesne, why then, I believe a victory has been achieved. But if the fight was in the forest, the news is wrong." The next we heard, two days later, was the fight had been in a brushy ravine a few miles from the French fort. I knew what the next message would say. Sure enough, an express rider came in with the news. Braddock was dead, his army defeated and turned back in a panicked rout. This was from James DeLancey, the governor of New York and could be taken as reliable. The western country would be in flames as never before, all the remaining settlers would be thrown back; those who did not move fast enough would be caught up. The folks down along the Virginia and Pennsylvania borders and the Carolina backwoods would be in for bad times. I pitied those folks for what was coming for them.

With news of Braddock's defeat confirmed, the morale of our army fell like a duck shot on the wing. Most of our Mohawks vanished. The news was followed by Indian raids along the border of New England. Tales of tragedy and woe. Many of the troops with us were from over there. They had joined up with the expectation they'd be going against Scalp Point, the root of their troubles, and the inactivity, Johnson's army was still in Albany, did not sit well with them.

****

Finally, in August, Johnson came up to Lyman with his army, two-thousand men, which raised our total now upwards of three thousand. Only now did Johnson realize the truth of what Rogers and me had been saying, how the road should be built to the head of Lake Saint Sacrament. The road to the Drowned Lands had proven advantageous to us in getting up there and hitting the enemy but Johnson's objective, as laid out by the late General Braddock, was the Scalp Point hornets' nest and for this, Lake Saint Sacrement was the way to go.

Johnson recalled the men who were working on the road and no sooner was work begun on widening the old carry trail to Saint Sacrament than Johnson inexplicably decided to resume work on the earlier road. He had to be convinced all over again, more time lost. Finally, a large party of ax-men was sent, well-guarded by rangers and colonial levies. The sound of axes and of falling trees rang through the forest. In short order, the road to Saint Sacrement was completed through fourteen miles of wilderness.

Our move up to the lake was painfully slow. A drunken three-legged turtle could have raced Johnson to the lake and got there sooner. The first day, Johnson moved his army no more than four or five miles afore stopping for tea. He and his staff sipped leisurely whilst the army lay scattered along the road in terrific heat, waiting for goddamn tea time to be over. The next day we moved even more slowly, if it were possible, so Johnson and his officers could dine along Halfway Brook beneath an awning spread as protection from the sun. They ate a cooked meal and drank rum punch whilst the army ate stale biscuits.

I wasn't with the army when it finally arrived at Saint Sacrement and when I came in, the men told me Johnson had renamed the lake for the king, henceforth, Lake George. Our soldiers relentlessly mocked Johnson for the pompousness with which he had done the renaming. This mockery I saw for myself a few evenings after I got there. A crowd of men was gathered around a drunken soldier who was attired in a purple robe and had a long pink feather in a hat nearly as big as him. With his sword uplifted like some great discoverer of olden times, the jokester proclaimed the lake in honor of the English king. The men, all mostly drunk, thought this hilarious. I felt embarrassed for Bill. Regular British officers would have had the man flogged for his insolence; Bill was probably too drunk to have noticed.

****

A week later, Rogers and me were leading a small patrol out along Otter Creek, thirty miles southeast of Scalp Point. The day was nearly gone, we were about to turn for home. One of our men was up in a tree having a look around when he spotted smokes, a lot of them, off to the east. We decided we better have a look. If it were Indians, we'd have to send a warning over to New England. Our patrol of twelve men moved cautiously along and getting in close to what was a large camp, we seen it was colonial militia. We snuck past their sentries, who were not posted very well, nor alert enough, and got into the camp without them seein' us. Rogers was furious. He told them to douse their fires. "What in the name of the Almighty are you men doin' wandering around the woods?" A hundred men on their way to join Johnson, who they assumed was by now besieging Scalp Point. They'd got lost for not knowing the woods and afraid they'd miss the action, they decided on a more direct route so's to get to Scalp Point before the fight was over. Their officers were mightily embarrassed to learn Johnson had only just got up to the lake. So they did not want to be late. Ha! They'd have got some welcome, this band of fools, honored guests had they marched into the Scalp Point stronghold. Blood sport for the Ottawa. Rogers had them abandon their camp at once, even with dusk falling. "We're all of us getting the hell out of here. No telling who might have seen your smokes." We moved them out until dark, then rested a few hours whilst our rangers scouted around. We tried to keep going through the night but with how the colonials thrashed about and fearing we'd lose 'em in the dark, we hunkered down and soon as the sun came up, we were moving again. We brought them safely in to Lyman. Rogers said as how we had only made it in for there not being any Indians around to attack us, nor even small bands which might have harassed us.

****

Johnson's army, grown to four thousand men, was spread between Lyman and the camp at the south end of Lake George. We had some Indians; Mohawks and Mohicans, sometimes up to the number of a few hundred, though this many was never available for very long.

Everyone, even the Indians, were disgusted with Johnson's camp which weren't nothing more than a clearing in the woods. No palisade nor bastions, nor barracks or cookhouses had been erected. The forest came right up to the clearing on every side and there was foul-smelling swamps close by. A stench born of the wastes of men improperly disposed. This I could not abide and I just about refused to enter the camp. Soon came diseases. Men sickened. A few, but in increasing numbers, died from the filth. The men began to feel justified in going home.

The supply wagons coming up the carry trail from Lyman got hit often, small attacks costing us men. Meanwhile, Johnson, nearly naked and with his face painted, danced away the nights with his Mohawks, just about the worst foolery for the troops to witness, their commander engaged in absurd frolic. Religious sermons were preached constantly. Half the New Englanders in the camp, it seemed, were reverends of one sort or another. Men who should have been seeing to the rendering of the camp into a proper fort were instead seated for hours on the ground, listening to these praying fools.

The horrifying details of Braddock's defeat became known to us once the survivors got out. Four-hundred dead, as many wounded, and this out of a total of two thousand. All the baggage was lost, guns and ammunition, wagons and horses, food and rum. Enemy losses, killed and wounded, weren't much more than fifty, and what was maybe the worst of it, the Indians had watched as our men, who still outnumbered the enemy and might have regrouped and held 'em back, instead ran off in abject panic and didn't stop running until they got to Philadelphia. The French, in the eyes of the Indians, must have seemed to have some very powerful medicine.

Braddock's defeat was not really an ambush, more a clash of fighting styles, with the British standing in lines and delivering volley after futile volley at a cleverly concealed enemy. A little common sense on the side of the British and the fight would have been winnable. But not for as long as the goddamn fools ordered their men to stand in the open. I heard the stories and doubted them not, how when the Virginia troops and even some of the British regulars tried to hunker down and fight Indian-style, the pompous commander and his equally pompous officers called them cowards and ordered them to stand straight, not hide behind cover. Not a fight so much as a deadly game of nine-pins is what I would say.

The flight of the British meant the frontiers would burn. And burn they did, the Indians now having a nice new road to trod for raiding into Virginia and Pennsylvania. Thank God for young Mister George Washington, who was making a reputation for himself, tirelessly leading the Virginia militia in bloody skirmishes. Outnumbered and with too much territory to cover, Washington and his men valiantly struggled to hold back the tide. They showed how effective a force could be if properly led and allowed to fight in a way more fitting for the deep woods.

Johnson, despite boasting of his intention to march to Scalp Point and beyond, showed little inclination toward advancing. He seemed always to be hung over from too many drinking bouts with his Indian brothers. His Mohawks saw more of him than did his own officers. The number of rum kegs and oxen consumed, the latter of which should have been hauling freight, had our men grumbling. It was profane what went on. The Mohawk scouts rarely left the camp except to get more of their tribesmen to come up and carouse with Johnson. They were surly to the colonials. It seemed more dangerous to meet one of these Mohawks in the woods than it was to meet a Huron.

Johnson, men grumbled, was afraid to go against Scalp Point. Maybe he was right not to go, his army could not even camp properly, how in the hell could it move through a wilderness? And surely the French were not waiting idly for us, as we seemed to be doing for them.

Bill was no part of a military man, his appointment as commander was political, his knowledge of military matters, as even he admitted, was minimal. His strength was the council fire and spirited harangues, not making war. More of our men died on account of his poor facilities in the camp. Our rangers patrolled just to get away from there. Johnson, whilst interfering in Rogers' decisions regarding the disposition of our scouts, showed little interest in the information we brought back.

Johnson did manage two things, neither of which seemed important at the time but would prove crucial later on. Firstly, and with the road from Lyman coming through thick forest all the way up to Johnson's camp, he cleared out a field of fire the last hundred yards along the road. With the woods on three sides and the lake behind us, he should have pushed back the woods on the three sides instead of just cuttin' a strip. With his clearing facing south, men joked Johnson had got himself so badly turned around in the woods, he was expecting the enemy to come at us from Lyman and not from Scalp Point.

The other thing he did was to have his teamsters haul a large number of bateaux up from Lyman. The men howled at this. Transports for an army which wasn't going anywhere.

Chapter V – Key to a Continent

Johnson held a meeting with his officers and afterward, Rogers told us some of what had got talked about. When asked why he had not built any defensive works, Johnson said he was of a mind to advance down the lakes and so was not too interested in defense. This enraged some of the men and caused others to shake their heads. They well knew Johnson wasn't going to Scalp Point. One officer, much too politely, in Rogers' estimation, told Johnson if he wasn't going to attack, he best get ready to get hit. It was too late for a stockade but something needed to get done. The way we were presently set up, the trees and brush which came up almost to the edge of the camp offered an advantage to an attacker and scant cover for us. Rogers, well aware of how Johnson never acted upon sound information and instead procrastinated, which was the situation now, remarked to me as how the opportunity for an offensive had clearly passed over to the French.

"They're coming, sure as hell," Rogers said to Johnson in his somber New England accent. "What are you gonna do then?"

****

Rogers said he was taking two companies of rangers up to Scalp Point and asked did I want to go along. "Hard to keep a hundred men hid in the woods," I said, but as foolhardy as it maybe was, I was excited to be going up there with so many men. To prove to both us and the French we could do it. We would be led by Rogers and his brother and John Phillips, a long-time crony of the boss, and with me advising since I was about the only man amongst us who was familiar with the lakes' country.

We left at sundown in canoes down Lake George and next morning and looming ahead over the lake though not yet visible to us for being around a couple of bends and with the morning fog, was the towering edifice of Bald Mountain. Montagne Pelée to the French, Old Baldie to us. I told Rogers this was a most advantageous lookout position with a long view up the lake to the south. I said the French surely had a watch-post at the top and we would have to get deep into the woods to get past them.

Rogers said he wanted to have a closer look at Baldie. I reminded him the French were up there. He grinned and after getting our boats and men hidden in a secluded cove on the west shore, me, Rogers and Richard snuck through the woods and got into cover along the south side of Baldie, from where we could somewhat see the front. They were impressed. An eight-hundred-foot rockface sloping out and down into the lake and naturally denuded of trees and brush except at the top and some few other scattered places.

I hoped this obscured look would satisfy Rogers. It didn't, he insisted we go to the top. I said the trails, one from the north, the other from the southeast, would be watched. He asked if I couldn't sneak him up along the landward side which was heavily forested.

I took him and Richard up, and closer to the top than I cared to get, we spooked from hiding back in the trees. The French had a prospective-glass mounted on a swivel and positioned for looking south up the lake. They most likely kept a man at the glass at all times and they'd have fleet Indian runners prepared to take word back to their fort at the first sign of us.

We got back down with our men and after dark, we crossed the lake to the east side and walked to the north end and to the top of Rattlesnake Mountain. This was an eight-hundred-foot hill which rose up over the Ticonderoga Valley. Rattlesnake and the adjacent South Mountain were the northernmost of the backbone of highlands which ran the entire east side of Lake George and separated it from the valley of Champlain to the east, that lake stretching as a blue ribbon all the way into Canada.

We could see down onto where Lake George emptied into the Portage Crick. Here was a most worrisome aspect of French encroachment. Two blockhouses, newly built and hitherto unknown to us. One on each of the flats along either side of the narrow debouchment. The blockhouses were proof the French were taking the next strategic leap, control of Lake George. I could only shake my head. Bill Johnson's officers had long been telling him to get moving and now it was too late. Did he come now, the blockhouse cannons would smash him.

The trail along the west side of the lake from Scalp Point to Ti was getting widened into a road so Frenchie was intending plenty of traffic. Discernable through gaps in the trees as a brown ribbon through dense forest, the trail stayed close to the shore, only did it curve away to avoid the worst swamps and gullies. It ended at the wide pool at the bottom of the lower falls from whence the crick became navigable down to the promontory.

West, out across Portage Crick and rimming the western edge of the Trout Brook Valley were the Three Brothers mountains, in a line, each rising higher than its eastern sibling. Beyond the Brothers and off into the receding distances to the northwest were the tallest of the Adirondack peaks.

Closer in to where we were, just northeast of the Brothers began the escarpment which ran along the west shore of Champlain, all the way to Scalp Point. Just over the top of the escarpment and down the other side was my cabin, my lakes and ponds and beavers, my secluded glade. My Paradise. I could see it in my mind's eye and I banished all thoughts of it. Such thoughts could get a man killed.

We next moved around the mountain to the east, to where we could see down on the Ticonderoga promontory, a peninsula which intruded into Champlain. The promontory was slightly higher ground than what was around it and with how it skinnied Champlain, it was a natural place for a fort which, here, would deny passage out of Portage Crick and through the Ticonderoga Narrows. Rogers asked why the French had not yet built anything here. I said they would, soon enough, if Johnson did not get off his ass and get here first. Rogers laughed.

I told him any fort situated down there on the promontory would have a glaring weakness and asked did he see what it was. He looked at me as if I were an idiot. He, though never having been here before, had at once seen the deficiency of which I spoke. Artillery positioned exactly where we were standing on Rattlesnake could bombard and smash anything built down there, no matter how stout.

The greater significance of this, which Rogers also got immediately, was how the advantages of location and height of Rattlesnake Mountain, which, although it weren't no more than a hill and with how it loomed over the promontory, was the single most strategic piece of ground in all North America. This would not seem possible for our continent stretching thousands of miles, an uncharted denseness from the shores of the Atlantic Ocean to whatever lay along the western edge but it was nevertheless true.

The distance between New York and Montreal was four-hundred miles and the waterways, the mighty Hudson and the two lakes, constituted the only route of passage for an army between the two. I had once heard an Albany politician who would never have dared to stand where me and Rogers was now standing declare the lakes to be the key to the continent. If such were true, then control of this hill meant control of the portage and thus of the water route between us and the French. It was an astounding notion, the fate of an entire continent controlled by a single mountain that wasn't even a mountain, just a hill, and yet both the English and the French, so far at least, had ignored it.

We went north along the lake. Traversing the highlands along the western side and with plenty to show Rogers, it took us a day and a half to get to where we could look down upon the entirety of the Scalp Point peninsula. From as high up and as far back as we were, the men down there, their forts and boats, was toy-like, and gazing down on 'em, me and Rogers silently contemplated yet another truth. Here was the place we must vanquish if we were to someday live without fear.

The fort was perched almost on the water, where the lake was at its most narrow. It was built of black stone, a square with a bastion in each of the four corners. The bastion closest to the lake, indeed, it had the appearance of sitting in the lake, was a massive four-story black castle, a rounded turret said to contain forty cannons. Rogers asked had I ever been inside the castle. I said yes, once, as a guest of the French during an interlude between wars. I said in there was a Papist chapel, barracks, a bakery, an armory and much else.

At a distance well out from the fort was a wooden palisade. Scattered around between the palisade and the castle were soldiers' encampments. With not enough room in the fort for all the men billeted there and with the French understanding the danger of disease from too many men in close quarters, they often posted their men around in small camps. Scattered but close enough to support each other and to watch the various points of concern. This made them more vulnerable to an attack but to the French, an attack by the English was laughable. Did Johnson even begin preparing an advance, the French would know from their spies and did the English come down either lake, the French, from their outposts, would see 'em in time to draw in all their men.

Outside of the palisade were Indian encampments. Crude wigwams, huts made of bark and animal skins. Plenty of Indians, by the size of the encampments. "Praying Indians," I said. "Under the thumb of the black-frocked Papists who are always eager to unleash their fiends."

Just south of the fort, on a rocky point jutting into the lake stood a windmill and north along both shores were fields, orchards and clusters of peasant dwellings. Boats plied the waters and were pulled up along the shore. Bateaux and whaleboats, birch and dugout canoes. At anchor in the deeper water of the bay, north of the fort and with cannons protruding from their gunports were two twin-masted schooners. The crews on the ships wore blue, which represented another escalation in the war, for these were sailors. With their cannons, the bigger of the ships looked to have ten, the smaller, six or eight, the ships could sail unchallenged anywhere on the lake, thus making it impossible for Johnson to attack successfully. Did he try, the ships could get in behind him and give him trouble. On the east shore across from the castle was the original stockade fort, Depeuw, built back in '31.

We headed back to Johnson's camp. Along the way, I showed the men things which might save lives and those which might take 'em. At Snake Rock, where a stream debouched into Champlain, I told them to watch where they stepped for this was a place overrun with snakes of every kind. Adders, water moccasins, six-foot black snakes, even the occasional rattler. Watch where they stepped and watch for the Indians who often hunted the slitherers.

This patrol, as audacious as it was, was satisfying for having taken a large number of men into and out of enemy country without being discovered. Small patrols bringing back information and prisoners would always be our primary mission but Rogers wasn't going to be satisfied just with sneaking a few men. He intended taking the war to the enemy, even did Johnson choose not to. I also think Rogers was getting swayed by the newspapers publicizing his exploits. This was bringing him fame as well as recruits. With so many men eager to become rangers, Rogers and his officers maintained the highest standards. They rejected most of the aspirants, kept only those judged to be the best and put them through a most rigorous training during which many more of them dropped out or were let go. The caliber of men making it into the ranks thus was high and the recruits were given time to assimilate into their units. Drill was long and hard. Not the way the British did it with tedious dress-parade and all the men shooting to once and not hitting anything and bayonet charges in long straight lines as if the trees and boulders would move out of the way when they seen us coming. Our drill was sharpshooting, silent tramping, finding one's way to a rendezvous. Things to save lives in the woods. Much needed to be learned before Rogers would let a man go out on patrol.

****

Late August and for the second time in a few short months, I was on my way to scout the Connecticut River trail for hostiles. I would be fifty miles north of where I had scouted it back in the spring. My mission was two-fold. Our Iroquois were telling Johnson there was a horde of Indians coming from the west. The Indians which had wiped out Braddock in the Ohio country coming now to do the same to Johnson. This western horde, as our men called it, and according to those northern cousins of our Iroquois, would soon be arriving. Neither me nor Rogers believed it. With all the scalps and rum Braddock had gifted the Indians, they'd be a long time celebrating and once they sobered up and did they come east, they'd come in dribs and drabs. More likely, by their nature and having whupped Braddock, they'd go home to brag.

Secondly, I was to locate the base camp of the parties which were still raiding down in New England. Our victory at the South Bay hadn't entirely stopped the raiding, just it made the Indians skittish about using the bay as a place from which to launch their raids. We were fairly sure they had a camp somewhere to the east and maybe a little south of Scalp Point. Close enough to keep the camp supplied and south enough down from Canada so the Indians, in perfect security, would be well along toward the places they raided. I was to find the camp so's Rogers could come up and wipe it out.

My intention was to go first to Scalp Point to see had all those Indians arrived. If they had, I would abandon the second piece of my plan and get back immediately to Johnson. If the enemy was not present, I would go in search of the base camp then check Scalp Point again before going home.

I had three men along with me. I was accustomed to working alone. This had not been a problem in the last war with Joe Blanchard but Rogers always insisted I take men, to show them how to properly spook the enemy and to be used as runners, sent back at intervals with what news there was. Rogers and me would always argue over this. I preferred working alone, but truthfully, runners was useful. And taking less experienced men along, whilst risky, was probably necessary. Rogers didn't have a lot of veteran scouts and those he had he might lose at any time and he wanted as much of our knowledge as possible passed on to the others of the men. I couldn't blame him for any of this, I just didn't care for it. To his credit, Rogers always made sure his new men were rigorously trained before he allowed them out for this kind of close-up work.

One of my men was Ephraim Woolman, who had been with me when we battled the Indians at the South Bay. I trusted Ephraim though he was but a youngster. Already a skilled woodsman when he'd joined up, Ephraim had proven himself to be brave, resourceful and eager to listen and to learn. He had the makings of a pretty good ranger.

We got to Scalp Point and observed from a place along the east shore. The western Indians had not come, which information I sent back with one of my men. The others of us watched for another day, then, leaving at night, we proceeded into the vast flatlands on the east side of Champlain, which was Verd Mont on French maps. We followed the trail out of Scalp Point and toward its joining with the Connecticut River trail, which led down from the wilds of eastern Quebec, the homeland of the fierce Abenaki.

Verd Mont was a rich and fertile country. Numerous cricks and rivers flowed down to Champlain, there were groves of lofty pines and beech trees of astonishing girth and with tangles of thick roots twisting up out of the ground. My men, always with an eye for settling after the war, said anyone good enough to survive here must prosper.

With plenty of Indian sign along the trail, we stayed off it, just did we keep an eye on it, and after two days' hard going, we came to the ridgeline which marked the eastern edge of the Champlain Valley. We got into the mountains and to the Birdseye, a mountain shaped like the head of a snipe, a long ridge running to the southwest to form the beak and with naked ledges perfectly forming the eye of the bird.

Using the Birdseye as a landmark, another day of trekking whilst still alongside the trail from Scalp Point and deeper into the mountains, and about where we figured we was getting close to the intersection with the Connecticut trail, we got a whiff of smoke. We scrambled up onto a low hill behind a ravine which was a dry moat across the front and which would be difficult to cross for how deep it was. Indians coming past, without any reason to scout the hill, would be disinclined to cross the ravine. We had got onto the hill from behind so not to leave sign across the front. A good place to sit and watch.

We lit no fire and had a supper of dried corn and jerked meat. At dark a woodland mist sprang up, a summer fog which hung low to the ground. The scent of wood smoke getting stronger, a flume of sparks rose up from a big fire not too far from us. I told my men I was going in for a look. Having already told them to keep their pipes in their pockets, I now reminded 'em about Indian noses, which, even immersed in the scent of their own fires and pipes, might catch a whiff of our tobacco, did we burn any. In my most stern voice, I warned 'em to stay quiet.

The slightest noise, the scrape of a rock, the bump of a canteen,`might alert the Indians.

I snuck up to where stood the camp and peered through a natural opening in the trees. In the clearing around the fire were twenty Indians and a few Frenchmen. With all else what was there, I was quickly satisfied this was the base camp, not simply an overnight stop for a raiding party heading in one direction or the other.

There were stick and bark wigwams and a more solid structure, a cabin which was probably a storehouse of supplies and gifts for distributing to the Indians and it was why the French were here. So the Indians didn't take everything all to once instead of just accepting what was doled out to 'em. Gutted deer hung from the trees; I smelled roasting venison.

There were captives bound with thick ropes, a man and a woman, four children. Probably a family whose cabin got burned out. The bucks were showing the captives the knife and tomahawk blades which was getting heated and the bark cups getting filled with glowing coals. The woman was entreating the Frenchmen to intervene. They, smoking their pipes by the fire, ignored her.

It was just the man who would suffer this night at the torture stake. The woman and her brood had value and would be spared, so long as they could keep up on the trek to the north. The torturing would get done here for the Indians, same as our Mohawks, knowing any white folks brung in would get taken from them, thus robbing them of their sport.

The Indians were talking soothingly to the man, even did they stroke him gently on the cheeks and shoulders. It was the custom of the Indians to speak in generous tones to those they were about to torture. Indeed, part of the ritual involved tending to the victims to keep them alive for as long as possible, the savages priding themselves on how close they could bring a man to death without extinguishing the last spark of life. Often, when their victim seemed about to expire, the fiends would bring 'em back with the most generous coaxing, only so they could perpetrate more foul deeds upon them. Caressing, they called it.

I thought how the Indians would've got a good laugh had they found three rangers lurking around their place of villainy. How effusively they would have thanked us for coming in on our own, thus sparing them the trouble of fetching us.

The Indians were from a few different tribes and with some probably headed home whilst others was goin' off south to raid. To one side and sitting cross-legged in a circle and passing a pipe were the older bucks. These were the chiefs, hashing out the division of whatever spoils they had taken or sealing the arrangement they would abide for the time they were joined up for raiding.

I backed away and rejoining my men, I told them we'd found the camp and said we would not be leaving until the moon came up. Not fully, just enough to give us sufficient light to get away without making any noise. In the short time we waited, the drumbeats started along with bursts of sparks and the perverse howls of the savages, the despairing screams of the man and of the woman and children, a long night to be endured.

I kept an eye on my men, to keep 'em from doing anything stupid. Fighting Indians in the daylight was one thing, spookin' their camps at night was another. My men were surely capable in the woods but neither of 'em had ever been in a situation as fraught on the nerves as this and did the captives' laments get to be too much for 'em and did they get mad enough for us not doing anything for the captives, there was no telling what they might do. I kept giving 'em my most severe look.

Finally did we get out of there and even as we got beyond the sounds of the torturing, it weren't possible for me to cease hearing it in my mind and when we stopped for a few hours' sleep, my thin blanket was useless against the shivers which ran through me. I thought how even this very night we too might have got tied to trees.

We went south and slightly east and crossed Otter Creek high up in the mountains, plenty of extra walking but better to get far enough away from the trails to avoid trouble. We turned west again and with two days hard walking, we got back to Champlain for another look at Scalp Point. The expected army had still not arrived. I sent a man back to report to Rogers and me and Ephraim continued south, still along the east side of Champlain. With so much Indian sign around the lake, we stayed buried in the woods. We came again to the lake, at Ticonderoga, where we had intended to cross over and get onto Rattlesnake for another look at the Ti valley but when we got there it was dark and we seen pinpoints of light on the promontory.

I told Ephraim there was another place where we could cross and we once again proceeded south and came to a narrows. Here the lake was less than a thousand feet across. We took off our clothes and secured them, along with our guns and accouterments, on top of a log, one we hoped might stay afloat and remain stable long enough to get us across in the calm water. Before we started, I told Ephraim not to worry with the time it would take us and did the northward drift of the lake seem to be moving us toward Ti faster than we was making the other shore. A sandbar extended out from over there and we'd touch bottom with our feet whilst yet a distance out. We pushed off, immersed to our necks. We each kept an arm draped over the log and kicked without splashing, Ephraim in front, me behind. The water was warm; the biters swarming our heads and faces, we didn't slap 'em for the noise it might make.

Turned out our log was more difficult to control than what we had anticipated and with the northward flow of the lake and a strong south wind rising, the waves got bigger with whitecaps and we was getting pushed hard north. Soon we could see the campfires at Ticonderoga and we was hearing voices. Ephraim was nervous and straining with his legs and feet for the sandbar. I dared not speak, to remind him how firelight and voices always seemed closer in the dark than they were, just each time he glanced back, I gave him a cold look. The lights got bigger, we could see the shadowy movements of men. I didn't know did the sandbar extend this far north and I felt as much relief as did Ephraim when his feet touched bottom and I heard him exhale. We were not long in gettin' ashore. We checked our powder, put our clothes back on and some fast walking got us to the bottom of Rattlesnake Mountain.

I told Ephraim we would have to move fast to get to the top and into hiding afore first light. Otherwise and whilst goin' up, we might get seen from below. I also told him there might be French and Indians up there. We got started, up along the edge of a ravine. Uprooted trees and loose boulders impeded us. We were forced to each seek our own way, the climb difficult in the extreme. It took an hour just to get to the top of the ravine. Here we rested just long enough to catch our breath and resumed climbing this ever so steep hill.

We got to the top whilst it was still dark and were now eight-hundred feet straight up from the floor of the Champlain Valley. We ate from our parched corn and strips of meat. The Portage Crick was low this time of year, yet we could hear the water spewing down over the rock ledges.

At first light, with the smokes of the cookfires rising up around the valley, we looked down on the promontory. There was a French presence, half a dozen soldiers, regulars, by the cut and color of their coats. A few woods-lopers and Indians; tents pitched, mules staked. Whilst we watched, one of the regulars unraveled a measuring chain and laid it on the ground, another got out what appeared to be an astrolabe, what sailors such as Pops used at sea. Frenchie hoisted the wood and metal device up onto a tripod and focused it on another man who, at a distance, was holding an upright pole at the top of which was a red ball. The man with the astrolabe, whilst turning his knobs, spoke to another man who began scratching with paper and ink. There was no mistaking what they were doing. Surveying, and for what reason was plain. The commencement of erecting a fort.

I sent Ephraim over to South Mountain to see did the French have a presence on Lake George and I moved back around to the northeast. Two flatboats, each with three smaller boats on 'em, were moored in the pool at the bottom of the lower falls. The boatmen had been having their breakfast and finished now, they lifted the smaller boats onto the shore and began carrying them up the portage trail. With how slender the boats were and with how they tapered at bow and stern, these were whaleboats, not the more ponderous bateaux. Bateaux were for transporting men; whaleboats, more agile, was for getting around swiftly.

The men arrived at where they usually put their boats into the water, a short way down from where the lake entered the crick. Here was an Indian encampment. It wasn't raiders, it was men, women and children, netting and smoking fish to trade with the soldiers for gunpowder and whatever else.

The men with their boats continued along past the encampment and were soon out of my sight for the steepness of the mountain and for them passing directly below me. I got back onto South Mountain and worked around to the southwest, to where I might get a better look. An odor wafted up from below. The farther I went, the stronger was the scent. Sweet, not unpleasant nor unfamiliar, though I could not have said what it was. I got down as close in as I dared and still not able to discern the source of the smell nor see what the men were doing, I climbed up into a tall pine tree for a better look. This was dangerous for the possibility I might get seen by the men or by the Indians, yet I felt it was necessary. Just I didn't go all the way to the top of the tree.

The men had arrived at the last shelf of flat ground along the east side of the crick, just below the blockhouses. Here the flats were cleared of trees and brush, the ground bare except for the stumps of trees, and I seen more than thirty whaleboats, upright and arranged in curved rows.

I couldn't figure why the French would need so many boats for an army which, when it arrived, would already have transports enough for having come up Champlain. Unless, and with the French always moving with alacrity, they wanted enough boats waitin' to save themselves the time it would take to portage. They could simply quick-march their men from one landing to the other, get into their new boats and come up Lake George and hit us before we knowed they was arrived. But that didn't make sense. Even with as many boats as was there, it weren't enough to carry an army the size of what was said to be coming, whether it be red men or white. And besides, the portage trail from the lower falls to the Lake George landing, as short as it be, could be covered quickly by men carrying boats regardless how big or heavy.

Whaleboats or bateaux, this many boats suggested to me the truth of another rumor which had been going around. That the army coming would not be red men from the west. It'd be regulars out of Montreal and Quebec. Indians didn't have the skills nor the discipline for handling whaleboats for the reason they didn't ever have a need for 'em. Canoes was all Indians ever needed and when they got to Ti or to any portage, they'd simply pick up their boats and carry them, same as they had been doing for thousands of years.

And what else the presence of so many newly built whaleboats told me, with their men arriving at Ticonderoga in heavy bateaux, the French wanted the swifter, more agile whaleboats not to facilitate an attack but to ensure their immediate supremacy on Lake George afterward. What was coming wasn't a raid, it was an invasion, the French intending to move deeper down into English territory and stay there.

There was a lean-to shed and after the men had arrayed their boats with the others, they brought brushes and pails out of the shed and began slathering the boats. The sweet smell, stronger now, was caulk, oakum dipped in pine tar. No boat made of fresh boards could be launched without first caulking the seams and creases. The caulk was brushed on in layers and clumps and needed time to dry. Hence the curved rows and the boats propped upright, leaned into one another instead of laid on the ground or stacked. The wind off the lake, funneled between the blockhouses, would speed the drying.

The French also probably wanted to keep the boats at a distance from the Indian encampment. With summer waning, the night air cooling, the Indians would have a big fire going and the French wanted their boats shunted out of the way of any sparks or embers.

Whilst I was up in the tree, along came a black bear, big and shaggy and with a face like a pig. He, too, had been drawn in by the sweet smell. The excitement in his movements and his snorting showed his arousal for the scent which seemed now to be wafting along this entire side of the mountain. The bear got up on his hind legs and scratched at my tree with his front claws. He seemed to know I was up there and I hoped he did not think me the source of the smell, else he might join me in my perch. He snorted, shook his shaggy head in bafflement and ambled off down the hill.

The boatmen finished their work and departed back along the portage trail. They left their boats entirely unguarded. This was a slap across our faces. A mockery, the assurance on their part we dare not come against them. Or, and with how near up the boats were to the blockhouses, the French might simply have assumed no British force of any size could get in there, which was true, but what about one man, alone? I had a wild notion to go down there and burn the boats. Make the French pay for their insolence.

With how the boats was arranged it wouldn't take much to get some fires going. The boats would shield me from the blockhouses and would shield my fires whilst they grew. I reckoned two or three fires properly located and hidden long enough might merge into a single conflagration, something to delay the French advance up the lake. And even if it didn't, it would at least show them we had some fight in us.

Riskiest part for me would be getting to hell out of there afterward. I could grab a canoe from the Indians and go between the blockhouses and onto the lake. Paddle through as if I belonged. Go hunched and the sentries might figure me for an Indian getting onto the lake to fish. If they challenged me, an Indian grunt might be enough to get me past 'em in the dark.

With how advantageously it all looked to be laid out, it might have been a trap. Leave the boats unguarded for having seen me up in the tree and hide in the bushes and wait for me to come down. No. They'd not expect me to try to burn their boats and anyway and did they know I was spooking along the mountain, they'd already have put them Indians on me. Beatin' their drums and whooping as they surrounded and shrank a circle around me, same as if they was hunting deer or a panther.

The more I studied the situation, the more I tried to convince myself it wouldn't be possible. I should just forget it and get to hell out of there. Yet, I hesitated. I am not a religious man, the only precept with meaning for me was the one about the Lord helping those who helped themselves and surely Providence was speaking to me now. Daring me to help my-self.

I decided I must try it.

I clumb down out of the tree and moved farther down South Mountain, stopping in those places offering a vantage from which to scout it all more thoroughly. I worked around to the band of cliffs along the front of the mountain, about halfway to the top, and got in with Ephraim just south of the cliffs. He was anxious to get going. I asked was there French or Indians around the lake. He said no, the blockhouses marked their southernmost presence. I gave him the last bits of information to take to Johnson and told him of the plan I was working up in my mind. He could only stare wide-eyed at me whilst I spoke, and when I finished, "Nuts!" was what he said. I did not disagree but I said torching the boats would buy time for Johnson. "Time to do nothing," Ephraim said, and again he was right. Still, and as crazy as my scheme was and as much as Ephraim insisted I abandon it, I felt I must make the French pay for disrespecting us. I told Ephraim I could find no fault with his objections but being a stubborn Dutchman meant I didn't have to listen to reason. I ordered him to go. I wanted him well on his way afore I got my fires started. It was more critical one of us get through to Johnson than it was to burn Frenchie's boats. I told Ephraim to move fast and stay the hell off the trails and the lake. With luck, he could be at Johnson's camp by tomorrow night.

With him gone, I was alone with no one else to watch out for or to draw attention. I figured the game was best played this way. I moved back north and got in close, awaiting full dark. I still had doubts and I might not have been disappointed had a detachment of soldiers arrived to watch the boats through the night. However, none came, and by now I was maybe too excited by the thought to give it up.

I got back around to where I was looking down on the boats and I laid out the sequence of actions in my mind whilst checking constantly to ensure no one was about. In the last light, I moved down closer and by full dark, I was along the crick and sneaking toward the Indian camp where a fire was gettin' going a little way back from the shore. Flurries of sparks shot up into the night sky but no drums beat, there were no whoops or musket shots to indicate a long night ahead for a captive. The Indians around their fire were subdued. It's how they were on nights with no one for the torture stake and same as when we had been scouting the trails along Otter Creek, I thought how joyously the savages would have welcomed me into their midst. I thought too how much worse the torture would be here, if such be possible. Indian women and children were often more vicious in their deviousness than were the men.

I got a canoe onto the crick, a few quick, powerful strokes got me up to where the whaleboats awaited. I got started before the moon came up, going first into the shed where I sniffed the kegs and buckets. Caulk. I took two buckets, they were heavy but not so much I couldn't quickly carry them down to the boats. I made two more trips with two buckets each time and got between the rows and beneath the boats, like entering caves or wigwams. I placed the buckets in those places which seemed best suited for getting something started. The boats had plenty of wet caulk already on 'em, the planks were fresh pine and thin, no more than an inch thick, good for burning. With my buckets positioned, I grabbed up a handful of long-handled straw brushes and working like a white-washer, I smeared the undersides of the boats overhead of the buckets.

I jammed the handles of the brushes into the buckets so the brushes were upright and the bristles nearly touched the bottoms of the boats. I got a small torch going and used it to ignite the bristles. The flames licked the caulk-smeared hulls. This created ovens, the boats catching, beautiful sights I could have gazed at for a long time but did not, for it behooved me to get the hell out of there.

Back in the canoe, the next thing for me was to get past the block-houses and onto the lake afore anyone got a glimpse of fire behind the wall of boats. Even a dancing reflection might give me away but I must not appear to be in a hurry. I stayed along the east side; the blockhouse closer to me, to my left, was no more than twenty feet away. Defiantly, probably foolishly, I hurled my hatchet so it struck the side of the block-house and stayed there. "Que vive?" came a voice from inside. I grunted in imitation of an Indian, something all rangers were learned to do, and expecting I might get a musket ball in my back, I yet paddled without hurry. No bullets came and onto the lake and once past the one small island just beyond the first bay, I commenced paddling hard.

With the wall of boats concealing my fires and knowing the soldiers in the blockhouses would be looking south onto the lake and not north along the crick, I was hopeful some of the boats would catch before my scheme was discovered. The damage didn't have to be total. Even a partially burned boat might have to be scrapped or might require extensive repairs and a few boats burned or charred would give me what I most wanted, a strike against our arrogant Gallic foes.

The canoe I had taken was a good one and I went swiftly up the lake. The wind, still from the south, obstructed me somewhat but I understood it was my friend, working to my purpose back at the crick, swirlin' inside the boats, fanning the flames. The wind gusted, I exulted. Blow like a smith's bellows, my friend! I kept a fast pace, my arms were strong, both from years of this work and the thought of the Indians what might be in pursuit. I could feel their hot breath behind me. I knew there would be plenty of them.

Time was now critical, time for my fires to grow unobserved and time especially for me to put some distance between me and the hornets soon to be swarming. I stayed along the east side of the lake and just before I rounded the point which would put the debouchment out of my sight, I allowed myself a look back. I had hoped for a glow as if the northern lights were up in the sky but naught was there but blackness. Had the boats not had time to catch? Had my fires burned out? Had they been found and extinguished? Were the Indians even now coming up the lake to punish me for my rashness? My euphoria crashed, I cursed my failure. Time now only to flee.

****

The dawn coming in, I approached the Lake George Narrows and knowing the Indians often lurked around the islands in their war canoes, I put ax holes and a couple of big stones in the canoe and sank it in sixty feet of water. I made my way through the woods along the west shore. I stayed slightly up along the higher ground, the lake somewhere off to my left. I had not seen nor heard any pursuit but surely it was out there and coming fast.

I worried about Ephraim. Did he get safely in or did his scalp dangle now from an Indian's belt? One of us had to get through. The enemy force hadn't arrived but whether it be Indians or French regulars or more likely a combination of both, and even did I burn all their boats, they'd be down on us almost as soon as they got to Scalp Point.

****

Nightfall, disheveled and exhausted, I got to the camp and cleared my way in with the sentries. Hurrying toward Johnson's tent and even in the dark, I seen he had still done naught to prepare for an attack. He was courting disaster with his laxness and it angered me and not for the first time, risking my life for such a negligent commander. I considered not telling him about the boats. If he thought even some of them had got destroyed, he would procrastinate even more. Yet I must not withhold anything. It was the ranger way, to tell everything without exaggeratin' nor lyin' nor decidin' what was best to tell and what weren't.

Inside Johnson's tent, I waited whilst his orderlies roused him. They told me they had seen nothing of Ephraim. With Rogers and his officers gathered, I told 'em over mugs of rum all of what me and Ephraim had learned and they began debating what course of action to take. Rogers, supported by some few others, demanded an immediate, two-pronged advance. A main party to go to Ticonderoga and drive the French to hell out and a ranger detachment into Verd Mont to destroy the Indian camp. Johnson vacillated and I knew the arguments would go on a long time, which was Johnson's way, to chew on things without swallowing.

Before I could tell them of my burning the boats, Ephraim burst into the tent, flush with excitement and with two blood-dripping Indian top-knots hanging from his belt. With the officers looking on in astonishment, Ephraim eagerly pumped my hand. Congratulating me, which I at first supposed was for my having got in safely but as we listened, he said he had been slowed up by a couple of Hurons and before he got so he could move south and from atop a high ridge, he witnessed a glow of flames to the north. Like some hellish inferno and with the fire so high in the air, he swore it must a got into the trees and burned its way up the mountain. He went on about it, which further confounded the officers, since I had not yet told them what I had done. Ephraim said he could a watched it all night but didn't, and said he was glad to have been well on his way when the fires got going. Johnson finally asked Ephraim what the hell he was talking about and now it was Ephraim who was astonished. He turned to me. "You've not told them?" I shrugged and in a few words, I told what I'd done. When I finished and in the presence of the officers, Rogers rebuked me, although not harshly. He said it was a foolish risk to have taken and he was thankful for not having lost a valuable scout in such a misadventure. When he finished, he winked at me.

One of the officers speculated it was possible, even likely, the French wouldn't have had at hand the means with which to immediately put water on the fires. The officers laughed at this. Boats burning so near to the lake and Frenchie without buckets. Another said he'd give a month's pay to hear the fulminating which must have been going on. Said it must have been a long night for poor Frenchie, trying to save his boats or just standing by helplessly whilst they burned. Someone said it was too bad the French would assume it was all the result of their own carelessness, a tossed match or emptied pipe. I said they'd think no such thing; there be no mistaking a ranger hatchet like the one I'd stuck to the side of the blockhouse.

Rogers turned to Johnson and again demanded we advance at once. Johnson wouldn't commit and Rogers, scathing, said Bill must either go on the offensive or prepare a stout defense, and whichever he chose, he must do so at once. Rogers then scowled and answered his own demand, saying Johnson would do what he always did. Nothing.

Chapter VI – Eastern Branch, Western Door

I took an early morning bath in the lake and went for breakfast with some of the rangers. Word of my exploit had got around the camp and I became a man of standing with the troops, garnering handshakes, slaps on the back, guffaws and disbelieving shakes of the head. Burning those boats had done something I hadn't anticipated. It lifted the spirits of our men. I only hoped it hadn't further convinced Johnson no immediate steps need be taken.

****

A few days after I got back, a staff officer came to me with orders to report to Johnson. When I arrived, the fancy tent was crowded with officers, Rogers included. There was tension. Something big was brewing. I figured the enemy army must be on the way down to attack. I was asked to step to the map and fill in a few of the blanks, all of which concerned what the officers kept referring to as the Western Route of Invasion. I had no notion what they were talking about, or why, and no one bothered explaining anything to me but I soon put it all together.

Johnson's western route was the East Branch of the Hudson, more or less. The invasion route started at Scalp Point and went west, overland, up into the mountains and perilously close to my Paradise Valley, then turned down what I called Big Lake and to the East Branch of the Hudson and to its joining with the main branch thirty miles west of Lyman. Johnson's Mohawks were charged with watching this route and now our red men were saying the enemy's vast reinforcements were coming this way, to hit us from a wholly unexpected direction. I had a fleeting image of thousands of French and Indians tramping through my Paradise, an image I quickly dismissed as preposterous.

The officers were looking at me. I was the only man, even among the rangers, with any familiarity with this western route, I having used it often to get back and forth to Paradise, and knowing it as well as I did, I damn near laughed in Johnson's face. To think an army of any size might come this way. Not even the stupidest goddamn British officer who had never been north of New York Town should have believed such a move was possible.

"There be no navigable waters," I said, "running from Scalp Point to the west. There can't be, for it is a steep hill up which it would not be possible to portage war canoes nor supplies needed for campaigning."

"You've done it, haven't you?" Johnson said.

"Walked west from Scalp Point? Aye," I said. "But not with a boat over my shoulder. And supposing they did get themselves out to the East Branch. This time of year, it ain't much more than a lazy crick without water sufficient to accommodate an army of the size you're saying."

"And with them two big lakes laid out flat as tables for 'em," Rogers said, impatient with what he considered to be a waste of our time, "they got no reason to go the long way."

Bill asked would it be possible for the enemy to bypass the lakes by plunging south from somewhere along the Saint Lawrence River, something else the Mohawks had maybe suggested. I was dumbstruck.

"I suppose," I finally said, "getting down to Big Lake from the Saint Lawrence wouldn't be impossible for men what was fools enough to try it. Trouble is, with how little water there is this time of year, they'd be portaging through some of the most god-awful wilderness known to man. Besides, the northern Indians are unfamiliar with it on account of it be Mohawk country and them northerners is scairt of trespassing."

"The Lower East Branch, below Big Lake," I continued, "did they reach it, is a most frustrating stretch of river. It turns constantly on itself in lazy bends, so much so, I sometimes expected to see myself going the other way." A few of the men snickered, Rogers gave me a warning look. I heeded the look and calmed down some. "That army, if it exists," I said, "and if it's somewhere up along the Saint. Lawrence, will come at us through Scalp Point. They will not come the way of the most difficulty." Johnson, in his haughty way, said as how he was well aware of the wrongness of what his Mohawks had reported but as commander, he'd had a duty to ask. Trying to save hisself the embarrassment and not fooling a single officer there in the tent with us.

Rogers said it should have been rangers watching this back door, not Mohawks. Johnson replied by saying the rangers didn't need the extra burden, truthful flattery which gained him nothing with Rogers.

Johnson called in King Hendrick, a Mohawk chief of great repute. Hendrick agreed with my assessment, and Johnson asked him why, if he knew it to be impossible, had he not said so, and why hadn't Hendrick sent more men to verify what his scouts were saying. Hendrick shrugged his shoulders. The fatalism of these otherwise strong people was tough to understand. It served to make them unreliable allies at all times. No matter how capable the Indians were in the woods, they could never be trusted, a truth Johnson never conceded. Capricious Mohawks sent on some crucial mission might decide instead to go hunting or fishing or might wander off on a frivolous errand they thought necessary. Often, one of Rogers' parties might wait days at a rendezvous for the Indians to show up. Or they might never show. Such was how Indians conducted themselves, by their own customs and methods, and nothing the white man said or did could ever change them.

Rogers then spoke what every man present was probably thinking but dared not say, on account of Johnson's affinity for the Mohawks. The routes spoken about, from Scalp Point to the East Branch or down from the Saint Lawrence, were so outlandish, there was no way the Mohawks, who knew the country better than any, could a believed it. Yet they had suggested it and might they be complicit in an attempt to trick Johnson into sending a part of his army off to the west whilst an attack came from the north?

For me, it was a confirmation of the need for rangers to become the eyes, not only of this army, but of all British North America. If Johnson wanted to know what was transpiring to the west of us, he'd better send rangers for a look-see. I didn't say this, it wasn't my place, and I didn't care to be chasing Mohawk rumors with an attack up the lakes imminent. What else I might a said but didn't, if the French could coordinate a diversion and a major attack so many miles apart in the woods and do it with the timing necessary to carry it off, we might save ourselves a lot of trouble and just all bow our heads to the French King Louis.

Rogers conceded there were probably Indians to the west, the Mohawks seldom made something out of nothing, but surely not so many as the Mohawks were saying. Probably a raiding party not connected to what might be coming along the lakes. Rogers said finding out the truth of the rumor was a ranger mission and with his men exhausted with all the work they were doing, he could spare no more than a few to go.

With Johnson unable to decide on how big a force to send, Rogers, not wanting to waste men, bluffed, saying if a large force was to go, he would lead them. Johnson inquired as to whether or not Rogers had been pushing himself too hard and should maybe send someone else. Rogers growled, "I'm no more tired than my men." The meeting broke up, all were dismissed except Rogers. He stayed another hour and when he came out, he said to me, "You coming?"

We were gone within the hour, just ten rangers and with no militia and without Rogers. With Johnson having called Rogers' bluff, Rogers had been made to back off. The lakes were still the obvious route and Johnson wasn't going to allow Rogers to go west in search of a phantom army. Leading us in his stead would be his brother Richard, a capable ranger. We were to go overland, southwest, ten miles, to a rendezvous on the Hudson with a company of militia which Johnson had ordered up by canoe from Lyman. Rogers said something about Johnson being more willing to draw men away from Lyman than from his own camp. He said for those of us who were going, it'd be time off from the war. "Find a comfortable place along the river, hunker down, have yourself a few quiet days and come back in." Then and more seriously, he told us Johnson was mostly sending us to keep faith with his Mohawks but there might be something to what them Mohawks were saying. "Get out there and get back," Rogers said, "so's not to miss what's coming here. And expect trouble whilst you're out there."

Late afternoon we met up with the militia out of Lyman. Not a full company and instead just thirty men, so the commander at Lyman was no more anxious to disburse his men than was Johnson. We paddled up the river for a few hours more, our progress swift, our intention to get out and back as quickly as we could. A hot summer's day it was, a man's strength was quickly sapped if he be not careful. The militia talked as if they were disgusted with the foolishness of it all. Some no doubt were sincere, others were just as glad to be away from Lyman with an attack coming.

I was in the lead boat with Richard. He joked about going all the way to Scalp Point and hitting it from the west. Leastways I hoped he was joking. Early evening, with still another hour or two of daylight and with Richard satisfied we'd gone far enough for one day, I told him there was a place ahead where we could camp. "On the north shore, high ground along the bank and with a swamp behind it so nobody can sneak in on us and with the best water you ever tasted bubbling up out of the rocks. Spent plenty a night there myself."

We pulled in, the men made sure the canoes were well hidden and they refreshed themselves at the spring and slept or rested quietly in the tall grass along the bank. No cookfires were lit, there was little noise of any kind. I took Ephraim and two others up along the side of the river. We went no more than a mile and got into cover across from where a wooded promontory jutting into the river from the south shore created a small backwater bay.

Vigilant but relaxed because we didn't expect trouble and speaking in whispers, I began regaling Ephraim and the others, all youngsters, about a battle fought in the last war just across the river from where we now were. A handful of Indians had shown themselves over there and taunted us to come over. We had two-hundred men, the Indians were no more than twenty, an obvious trap, but our British commander foolishly obliged. Our men got onto the water and got hit with heavy fire from the point whilst crossing and when they did finally get over and were getting out of their boats, hundreds of Indians came swarming out of the woods.

I kept on with describing the battle until I seen my men were giving me astonished looks. I got what they was thinking and I laughed. They weren't much more than boys and same as most youths, they couldn't grasp there had been events playing out before they was born, or before they was old enough to have had a part in it. For them, the world didn't get spinning until they come along.

We stayed the night in the brush, two of us dozing whilst the other two watched. I had given Ephraim command of the dawn watch, this was a sign of my trust in him as this was the time for most Indian attacks, and thus and when he shook me hard at first light, I was alert at once. He said there were Indians and he pointed to the other shore. I seen 'em, a dozen, maybe more, under heavy cover and scarcely moving. Ephraim said he only knew they were there for have seen 'em arriving. They were unaware they were getting watched nor of how close they was to our detachment of forty men. I sent one man back to Richard, then a canoe came suddenly down the river, on our side. It was a ranger canoe which must have been hidden somewhere upriver and which had got found. Indians used our stashed canoes same as we did. Three Indians going past us, so close and with us on a bank which was raised up from the water, I could a damn near taken an Injun by the topknot and lifted him out of the canoe. They, after checking the bank without getting out of their boat nor seeing us, moved across the river to where the others were. We backed off the hill, bellies to the ground, each taking our own route back to Richard, routes which was decided upon beforehand.

I told Richard we seen around ten or so Indians and said it was probably a raiding party and not scouts for the western army coming the back way to hit us. The officer in command of the militia, Beaumont, asked how I could be sure it weren't scouts for a much larger party. I gived him a look, though I could not refute the possibility of what he was saying, for as unlikely as it was, we didn't know for sure.

How Richard saw it, we was well situated to wipe out the Indians, however many they be. With us up on a hill and with the swamp behind us and an old Mohawk trace between us and the river, they'd come down the trace in a single file and would be easy plucking.

Beaumont saw it differently. He said if there were more Indians than we figured, the swamp and the river, rather than working to our advantage, might seal us off from escaping. Richard had got us into a jam and he had better get us out. Richard said it was too late and anyway he did not believe there was too many Indians. Beaumont reminded Richard we were there for scouting, not fighting. He said even if this wasn't the anticipated attack, we might still be outnumbered and by how many we wouldn't know until we got into it. He suggested we just let the Indians go on by. Richard said big or small, he wasn't for lettin' 'em go without a greeting and besides, and if we didn't kill 'em, they'd raise hell down in the settlements. Beaumont said we had a larger mission than looking out for the settlers. I expected Richard to get all over him for this callous remark. Instead, Richard didn't say anything. He was pondering how to prepare his ambush, so I said it. "Protecting the settlers is what rangers are about, and any man who don't know it had ought not to be here." Beaumont gave me a look as if how dare I infer he was a coward.

His umbrage, though, didn't keep him from keeping on, and what he said next filled me with shame for him being an American, same as me. He said he didn't know how good his men might be in a fight. Richard and me both gived him hard looks. An officer denigrating the capabilities of his men so's not to have to lead 'em into a fight. When Beaumont again said we ought to allow the Indians to go on by, I could only hope his men had more fight in them than what he did. If not, we were in for it because Richard wasn't going to pass up an ambush, especially one which was already laid out for him.

Richard would not allow his eagerness to override his usual cautions. He shifted the men around, to ensure they were under cover and in good position for when the Indians came. He told us not to shoot until he gave the word, then blast the hell out of them. "Make every goddamn shot count, boys," he said, his voice tinged with excitement. For many of the men it would be their first firefight. For some, maybe, their last. Me and Ephraim were behind a large beech tree whose thick girth offered cover.

No Indians came and the longer we waited, the more we felt something was wrong. Either us forward scouts had made Indians out of brush and stumps in a dawn mist or the Indians knew we was there and was preparing their own surprise.

A single musket shot roared from behind us, from out of the swamp, and back there erupted in smoke and noise. So the Indians knew about us and if there be enough of them and did they rush us at once, they might have pushed us off the hill and it would have been them on the high ground and us below and with our backs to the river. Fortunately, they didn't charge in and only fired from cover. Probably on account of them not knowing how many we were nor how we was situated.

This gave Richard and me time to get our men repositioned and the battle, such as it was, was sniping on both sides. There did not seem to be a lot of Indians. I said the war party was a small one. Beaumont insisted it was bigger than I thought. Richard said the Indians, from the glimpses of movement and the shots, were working out along the edges, probing the extent of our lines so they could get curled around us. He said they were unlikely to rush in, even did they secure both flanks. This would have meant bunching their men and exposing 'em, which was not something Indians cared to do. More likely their intention was to cut off any avenues we might have for sneaking out.

Richard pulled some men from our line and used them to try to stem the Indians' flanking movements, him on one end of the line, me on the other. Neither of us was successful for the Indians were too well hidden. Fortunately, when Richard had set us up for what he expected would be us ambushing the Indians, he hadn't neglected a defense against what was happening now and our situation, although precarious, was far from desperate. We still had the high ground and thick cover, and boxed as we were, the swamp and the river would keep the Indians from hitting us along a wide front. Any attack in strength would come on one end of our line or the other, where the swamp ended. Both these points we had covered. Our position also included the spring. Cold water bubbling up out of the ground and flowing down the hill to the river.

****

The sniping was sporadic most of the day, Richard was at his best, a leader of men in a fracas, same as his brother. The Rogers boys surely loved fighting up close. Richard's eyes shone bright through the smoke of the burning powder and he peppered the Indians, he being an excellent shot with a smoothbore musket. He kept a wounded man loading for him and constantly had a primed musket in his hands and even as he kept an eye on the flow of battle and directed and encouraged us in the fight, I seen him wing a couple of Indians, both of whom maybe thought they was hidden pretty good.

The fight, hot as it was at times, lacked resoluteness and by late afternoon, any man showing himself on either side got peppered; hats raised up on sticks got blown away but otherwise there were long moments of quiet, enough to convince our men the Indians had vamoosed 'cept for a few who stayed to keep us pinned whilst the others got away. More likely they knew they had us boxed and was content to wait, for what, we wasn't sure, until around sundown when we heard French voices. Canadian bush-rangers arriving, plenty of 'em, and with more Indians, by the whooping, all sure to put the fight back into those already there. The enemy's numbers were now surely more than ours, the firing would pick up considerable come morning for the French were always more bold than the redskins and it was likely they'd try to get in on us. Our men were near to panic. I was hearing talk, how the claims of the Mohawks had proven true and we was confronting every goddamn Indian in North America. I even heard some of the men saying we ought to surrender. I knew what surrender would bring, and what else I knew, the men were not going to believe anything I told 'em were it contrary to what they was thinking. Richard understood too and went up and down the line at great hazard to himself, to steady the men.

After dark, Richard and me held a conference behind our beech tree. Our casualties so far were slight and we didn't expect the foe would try to get in on us in the dark but our dearth of powder made it unlikely we could hold out once daylight came. I suggested a breakout during the night. I said we could take along the less wounded but those badly hurt would have to be left behind. Richard said he would not desert his wounded whilst he still had an intact fighting unit.

"My esteemed friend," he said, after me and him had talked it over some more, "I think it is time you went for help. We shall otherwise not get out of here. You are our best hope. What do you say, do you volunteer?" Not really a question. More an order. I had known it was coming. For myself, might as well get killed out there as in here. As hot as was our situation, how much worse could it be out there? Seemed I was to find out.

Getting through the enemy lines was going to be difficult; the Indians would be alert for such an attempt, and seeing they had us on three sides, I decided I'd try the river. Get into the water and swim quiet until I got far enough down past 'em to where I could make a run for it. First thing, I stashed my rifle partway up a tree where no savage would find it. That favorite gun of mine was too good for some redskin to have. If possible, I would come back for it later. It would do me no good in getting out, and strapped across my back and bouncing, it would only hinder me. Speed was what counted now. If I had to fight, I was lost. When it got dark, I got down to the river. I took off my buckskin shirt. Armed only with the knife and hatchet in my belt, I got knee-deep in the water and an arrow skimmed the surface about where I was standing. I scrambled back up onto shore and into cover and another arrow whizzed out of the darkness. I waited a few minutes and there came a gunshot and a musket ball thwacked into the tree I was behind. I couldn't figure it. It was dark, not much moonlight, and were they seeing me all the way from the other side of the river or were they in closer, in their canoe on the water? I put my shirt on and went back to Richard. We talked about what other possibilities there might be. "There's the middle part of the swamp," he said. "There don't seem to be too many of the buggers in there. You might try it." I worked my way to the center of our line and spoke to the rangers there, to get an idea were there any gaps in the enemy positions. They showed me where there weren't too many Indians and I might have a chance of slipping through. They shook my hand, wished me luck and I moved silently down the hill and into the marsh.

The black water up to my belt in some places, the swamp was the remnant of an old beaver flow; marshes, mudholes interspersed with clumps of solid ground, stumps and vines, but without any sign of fresh cuttings or drag trails, things this old trapper always looked for, even in the thin moonlight and with his life in the balance. Traversing the thickest part of the swamp, I avoided the solid ground, where the Indians would most likely be, and how I was fortunate enough not to meet any of 'em, I do not know, suffice to say I did not. Got pretty damn close to 'em a few times and when my presence brought forth a sudden burst of shots, I realized I had got turned around in the dark and was heading back toward my own lines. Finally, by use of every cover I could find, I was through the swamp, and when I felt I was out from any pickets or outliers, I commenced running. My steady strides ate up the ground. It was twelve miles to Johnson's camp.

****

Going Indian fashion, trotting steadily, I came onto an old Mohawk trail. Even with the trail overgrown for not getting used much, it was risky to be on it but not using it would have cost me too much time. I seen plenty of Indian sign, more than what Indians would leave, likely it was old traps set for unschooled militia. The crick crossings was the most likely places for ambush and each time I came to a ford, I moved downstream afore crossing. Always downstream because Indians sittin' in ambush on the other side of a ford would be watching for anything drifting down. Even a mud rile was sometimes enough to get 'em after a man.

****

Toward morning, I got to the Lake George camp, cleared my way in with the sentries and was soon in Johnson's tent. His orderly awakened him. I expected Johnson would get a relief column up at once. Instead, and to my utter astonishment and disgust, he looked at me in a way which I understood all too well for having seen it before. It was self-pity, and it was why it was just me and him in the tent, why he had not called in any of his officers. Johnson was cracking under the strain of leadership and at just about the worst time and he wouldn't want his officers to see it. Bill and me had known each other for many years and only with me would he allow his indecision to show. He began carping about the unfair burden he carried and when he said as how he envied us scouts, we had only to spook and keep ourselves alive and not carry the responsibility for other men's lives, my astonishment turned to rage. There was much I could a said about his leadership causing so many good men to die but I couldn't get into it. Richard needed help. I thought how Johnson's indecision paled before the leadership shown by the Rogers brothers. They maybe didn't always make the right decisions but they at least made 'em quick, which speed was often as important as being right.

Johnson continued dithering, I got my face up close to his, told him we needed men, "Now!" Johnson asked how many Indians was Richard facing and when I said it was Frenchmen too and I didn't know how many, he seemed to push the whole thing back onto me. I was a scout, it was my duty to bring him the information he needed and I had failed him. Everybody always failed him. He then said he didn't think it would be prudent to send a large force, he might be attacked in the meantime. He used my own words against me, since I had told him this wasn't a force of many hundreds come down the western route and was instead a raiding party, deadly for sure, but not connected with anything bigger. Johnson said Richard would have to handle it with the men he had whilst he, Johnson, awaited the main thrust of the enemy, which might already be coming up the lakes. "What Richard is up against," I said, seething yet with a need to control my anger, "is maybe not connected to what's coming, but there's plenty more of them than him and if we don't get out there quick with men, he's a goner." Johnson repeated what he had said before, "If it is naught but a raiding party, Richard must get himself out." I said Richard couldn't get out. "He's boxed," I said. "It's why I'm here." Johnson began pacing. "Dammit," I said. "Decide!"

Finally, a relief force was authorized, ten rangers and fifty militia. I was to guide them. We would go overland whilst Johnson sent word to Lyman to dispatch another fifty men by water and with medical supplies and provisions.

I got the men going, the rangers leading. I told them I would catch up. I had a quick gobble of stew, some of Johnson's rum and a re-arm, and got started. The rangers and militia were going along the trails I had come in on and when I came to where they had gone off the wrong way, I figured Richard was done for. I set out after them and didn't get too far before I met the militia coming back. They had realized their mistake and had turned around. I asked where the hell were the rangers. The militia said the rangers had decided they could find their way to Richard without using the trails and had gone into the bush. I asked the militia why they hadn't gone too. "Easier it be on the trails," their captain said.

I hurried them along as best I could, even whilst insisting we go with flankers and scouts, which slowed us some, though what slowed us most was the militia themselves. I never seen men move so inexpertly, even on well-marked trails. The harder I pushed 'em, the more frustrated I got and the less anger I felt toward the rangers for having abandoned them. And with all the noise the militia was making, I feared we'd get ambushed before we got there. Late afternoon we got back in with our rangers and a short while after, we came abreast of the river. We were yet a few miles from Richard. We strained to hear the gunshots which would tell us he was hanging on. Silence meant he had got wiped out. We waited, there came a shot, then another, then a brief, steady firing. Our men gave a whoop. Some of ours, at least, was holding out.

I spoke with the ranger boss, a youngster, one of those Warners from over in Connecticut, and we agreed it would be a mistake to go any farther in the dark. He began spotting around the militia against the possibility of an attack during the night. Pickets were put out; our lines were set so's to be contracted to offer protection where necessary.

I had given Warner a stern upbraiding for his having left the militia behind when they were coming out from Johnson's camp. He hadn't argued nor tried to defend his actions and now, watching him placing his men in a way to make it damn near impossible for the Indians to get the jump on his outfit, I was impressed with how his youth belied his abilities.

This was something I would see more of in the years ahead. Robert Rogers was shrewd in selecting and grooming those who he felt would make good leaders. Mostly it was youngsters who, did they live long enough, would form a solid officer corps and who might make names for themselves.

Sometime after midnight, with our men well situated and with me confident Warner would lead every man to his proper duty, I told him I was going to sneak back in to Richard's position. Warner was dubious. I told him I was of no further use where I was and said someone had to let Richard know we were arrived, what we intended and what we would expect from him. Warner assented. "For God's sake, be careful," he said.

As I was preparing to go, one of our pickets reported the militia out of Lyman had arrived. They had stashed their boats and were finding their way to us by torchlight. This would surely give away our presence, which we hoped had so far gone undetected. Me and Warner hurried out to the militia and told them to halt immediately and douse their torches. We then worked out a plan with them for the morning. Warner did most of the talking, he was an astute young man and sure of himself, and when he finished, he turned to me and asked did I have anything to add. I said the Indians would have a plan too and both sides would try to get moving before the other and whichever side struck first would have the advantage in whatever came.

Then I was again sneaking through the swamp. The night was without the moon, I made out a few Indians silhouetted in the darkness and had little trouble slipping past 'em. No doubt some of 'em heard me swishing the water but with the darkness and with the direction I was going, they must a figured I was one of them, maybe going in to see could I grab a scalp. A few wished me luck in my skulking, least I think they did, and I nearly collided with one old pipe-smoking warrior who paid no heed other than to grumble. Now came the most difficult part, getting into the lines without getting shot by my own side. I tried to remember how Richard's men were deployed, easier it would be to slip past the militia than the rangers. When as close as I dared get, this old friend lay still. All was quiet. No night birds or animal sounds, the air filled with the lingering stench of burnt powder. I figured there must be a picket nearby and I waited until there came the scrape of a musket barrel against a rock to my left. Another sound from over there and I knew it was militia, not rangers. I edged away from 'em and gauging about where I figured the next sentry would be, I slid between 'em.

Richard was still behind the big beech tree. His arm was bandaged, he was no longer able to do any shooting. I could see the asking on his face as I approached. I was his last hope and had I brought help? I told him a hundred men would be coming to his assistance at first light. He shook my hand with fervor and whilst I told him what young Warner intended, I could see Richard was conjuring the possibilities. I asked how had it been with him. He said half his men were dead or wounded, his powder was all used up and he couldn't have lasted much longer. He said the Indians had hit damn hard first thing yesterday morning, so hard he figured he'd be overrun but the men, including the militia, had fought superbly. Desperately. He said once they beat off the attack, there was little more than sniping until last evening when there'd been a flurry of shots which had seemed to signal another attack though no advance was made. Could be the Indians knew a relief force had arrived and the shots was the raiders saying goodbye afore they headed down into the settlements for easier pickings.

I gave Richard more details of what Warner was intending. Richard agreed it was a solid plan. He had been hoping the enemy would depart through the night, now he hoped some, at least, had stayed around.

The rangers went down our lines to give the news to the militia. The rangers knew how a roar from us would alert the foe to the change in fortunes and so, and before giving the tidings, the rangers had advised the militia not to raise any huzzas, which some did anyway, so great was their relief.

As the dawn came in, we waited behind trees and in the tall grass. We would charge out as soon as Warner, able to cast a wide net with as many men as he had, came up. Our own line was thin. Sweat ran down into my eyes, my vision blurred. The French and Indians, were any of 'em still there, were deathly silent. We heard the relief forces coming but no gunshots, then we began seeing our men approaching through the swamp. They were beating the bushes cautiously and as they got up to us, we knew the enemy was gone. Must have become aware of Warner and vamoosed for having lost their advantage of numbers. We came out from cover and shook hands with Warner's men. Our men were glad for the fight being over though for some, such as Richard, there was disappointment for not having given the enemy one last kick in the arse.

Fires were lit, food was cooked and eaten. Scouts were sent out to make sure the enemy was gone. Another militia company came in from Lyman. The wounded were tended, loaded into canoes and sent downriver under guard. The scouts got back in. They had found the remains of the Indian camp on the other side of the swamp, the ashes of the fires still warm. Stuck hard into the soil was a pair of crossed spears highly decorated with feathers, paint and colorful quills, a warning.

I was sitting by a fire, Richard came by. "Soon's the men are finished eating," he said, "we'll be starting back. I don't aim to miss out on the fighting down to the lake, which is surely coming. I'm grateful for what you done. If not for you, a lot of good men would have died."

Chapter VII – Devils in the Afternoon

Richard and me reported to Johnson, who looked terrible, eyes puffy, face pale. Campaigning was going hard on him. So much time spent in debauchery with his Mohawks, he was sinking into a morass of booze and wenching. Deeper he sank, and the leadership of our army, so necessary to our survival, was in jeopardy. This was something else Richard and me had talked about, with Richard saying as how Johnson, with no military experience, had maybe convinced himself the commanders on the other side were better than him, thus diminishing whatever confidence Bill might have had in his own abilities. I didn't think so. Having known Bill for many years, I knew how highly he regarded himself.

Nothing much about the camp had changed, which was in its own way infuriating, although most of us were too fatigued to raise any hell about it. With everyone knowing the French were coming, why hadn't Johnson begun preparing? We were now late into August and there was not even a breastwork, and except for our front, where the road came in, the forest still came right up to the edges of the camp and never was a more dismal location chosen. Two low hills, one each on the east and west sides of the camp, dominated the area. In addition, the land was swampy around the hills which created unhealthy conditions which, in the heat of summer, had manifested into increasing numbers of sick and with men dying each day. The lists of those unfit for duty were as long as the muster calls, with most of our men down at one time or another.

Soldiers complained about Johnson frittering away the campaigning season in the Mohawk camp. They said Johnson slept all day and never showed himself until nighttime when he came out to dance with his red friends. So much alcohol got sent over to the Indian camp, they stayed drunk, and after they consumed almost the entire beef herd, they started on the transport animals. The Mohawks, ensconced in the camp, sometimes refused even to venture forth to scout. They were contemptuous of us, as we were of them. Fistfights took place, an open split seemed imminent. In a battle against the French, these allies might turn on one another.

Bill had a pretty squaw, the daughter of a chief, and except for some drunken bouts with her relatives, Bill hardly seemed to leave his tent. He paid scant attention to his army; his orders often made little sense. A rumor had it he'd struck a young lieutenant for a caustic remark, which, true or not, caused resentment. Our troops, in a foul, pestial camp and doing nothing whilst the enemy pillaged the New England frontier, were getting edgy and more hostile toward the leadership. All the trouble was coming out of Scalp Point, yet we made no advance toward this place of the devil.

****

Rogers came to me. Said he knew I wasn't rested enough from our battle out along the Hudson but he needed me to go up and have a look at Scalp Point. Our scouts were reporting more activity up there than usual and a ranger had just come in saying the French army had arrived.

I took two men, Ephraim Woolman, who had got through the recent battle unscathed and another, name of Nathan. This Nate I knew only by sight. Hard not to notice him, with his great height and skinny frame and a most amazing hat, an albino wolf's head with white wolf-skin flaps along the sides and back and with the wolf's snout and eyes always tilted forward and down. Rogers said Nate was a solid man in a fight whether it be with axes, knives, fists, didn't matter. I shook hands with Nate, we meeting for the first time. He was long and lean and with eyes compelling with how they took the measure of a man, same as the wolf's milky-blue eyes seemed to do. I was glad Nate was on my side.

We started up the mountains along the west side of Lake George and on our second day out and seeing too much fresh sign, we holed up. Come dark, and using one of our hidden canoes, we crossed over to the east shore. I left Nate at a place where he could watch Lake George, me and Ephraim carried the canoe up over the mountain and down the other side, to the Champlain shore. We crossed the lake, I posted Ephraim a little south of Ti and around dark and having moved steadily all day, I reached a favorable vantage along the Verd Mont shore opposite to the Scalp Point citadel. I got into hiding and spent the night.

The morning came in cold and raw, the fog lay thick, impossible to see across the lake though it was not a great distance. Terrible for spying but welcomed enough by a man deep into enemy country and needing to stay hidden. I waited whilst the fog cleared and as the weather slowly burned off, the mist lifted and the long-awaited danger showed itself. The French army had arrived. Boats on the water and moored along the bay; bateaux, whaleboats, twenty-five-foot war canoes, supplies piled on the shore; shot boxes, powder barrels, salted meat, all the accoutrements for a campaign.

And men, so many men. Buckskin-clad Canadian bush rangers and nearly naked Indians but mostly it was French regulars in their white and powder-blue uniforms. They were not the eight-thousand reputed by the Mohawks to be coming. More likely no more than a few thousand, enough to rip into Johnson's army and maybe into the Great Carry fort after they finished with Johnson. With neither place strong enough by itself to beat off an attack, both might fall, one after the other.

Then came another nasty shock. Ephraim arrived breathless at my post to tell me a flotilla of boats had gone past his hiding place, another entire army heading south on Champlain. Ephraim said he reckoned he'd seen fifteen-hundred men. I asked was there regulars. "Plenty," he said. So the army was bigger than what I was seeing and had apparently divided with some staying at Scalp Point whilst others moved south to attack.

I sent Ephraim back to report. Told him to go by way of Lake George, stay off the water and pick up Nate along the way. I set out down the east side of Champlain, along the lesser used of the Otter Creek trails. I went at a steady trot and was soon across the lake from Ti. Here was a small encampment with whaleboats and canoes on the shore and some few men, Canadians and Indians; the invading army was not here.

****

I trod the lonely paths along the eastern shore of Champlain, the cataracts and riffles of the cricks splashing around me. The hardwoods dark and gloomy for the trees permitting no sunlight, I passed through ravines and in every dapple of light, every shadow blowing in the wind, I seen what I thought was an Indian.

It began to rain. It came steady then stopped, though the sky stayed cloudy and the wind came up. It was hard to move fast in clothes wet and heavy, yet move I did, all day. I stayed mostly up on the ridges, just slightly back from the lake. It was steeper going but I figured there'd be plenty of Indians prowling the shores. Staying higher up also enabled me to keep watch over Champlain and as it was and from a side ridge and with the mountains rising dark and craggy over the lake below, I saw a whaleboat come 'round a bend. The whaleboat was crowded with French officers, their battle flags snapping in the stout breeze over their heads. Behind them came the flotilla. Bateaux, whaleboats and canoes, a hundred boats headed south for Lyman. Ephraim's estimate of fifteen-hundred men seemed accurate, no cannons did I see.

With the last of the flotilla gone past, I slipped on down to the Champlain shore. It was not yet dark when I got there and I used a log to get across. Did Indians or another part of the army come by whilst I was crossing, I'd be spear fishing for 'em. I got to the other side and passed through a notch to the Lake George shore.

I moved at a steady trot all night. Owls hooted at my passing; wolves mourned from afar. Along an eastern-facing slope and with the rising sun filtering through the treetops and striking the bare ledges and before I knew it, I was in close to a rattlesnake den. Warning rattles all 'round, fat snakes takin' the sun on the rocks and coiled in the patches of ferns and tall grass. Here was an extra load on my overworked mind. The snakes were sluggish for only having just begun to absorb the heat of the sun but would strike quickly out of their torpor. I moved a step at a time and poked at the ferns and grass with a stick to give the snakes time to move away. Once, stopped, I felt the weight of a heavy snake sliding over my foot.

Along the lower east side of Lake George, a marsh abutted the shore. This I knew I must avoid for the time it would take either to get through it or go around. The latter course would have entailed getting well south of Johnson's camp before turning north again. The only way was to find one of Rogers' hidden canoes and make the last part of the trip on the water. This would be faster but more dangerous. This close to the camp, there were islands and bays where Indians often lurked. We had sometimes to come up in force and clean them out. I could only hope our men had been up recently.

****

Early morning, I was pushing hard along the lake, the prow of the canoe busting the high waves; the spray stinging cold. I came into sight of Johnson's camp and it was certain neither of my men had got back yet. Soldiers were at their usual morning tasks, which meant most of 'em was around their cookfires. All calm-like and serene, they was about to get hit a death blow and here they sat like ducks on a pond. Right there on the shore, about where I was headed, a preacher was on a stump, Bible-thumpin' for a hundred fools crammed together. Many of 'em appeared to not even have their guns. Who could believe it, the French were invading New York Colony and our garrison was as serene as a park lunch in New York Town.

I jumped out of the canoe, rolling it and getting myself wet all over again. I at least managed to grab my gun before it went into the water and approaching those men around the preacher, I pointed my gun in the air, pulled the trigger and hoped she'd fire. She did, and now and having drawn the attention of the men, I waved and shouted to get 'em moving. "Big force headin' for the South Bay, more'n a thousand! Maybe two thousand!" The men stared blankly at me and all to once they began to scurry. The preacher eyed me fiercely from behind bushy black brows and he cursed me to Perdition for breaking up his oration.

I ran through the camp shouting, "To arms, to arms! The French are coming!" More men were giving the alarm, drums began to beat, and by the time I burst into Johnson's tent, I had the camp in an uproar.

Johnson was stumbling bare-assed and bleary and muttering what was all the noise about. He had trouble focusing, his eyes seemingly popping out of his face, barely seeing it was me. Some commander! Whilst he splashed water from a basin on his face, I told him about the French and Indians, bolstered by regulars and probably intending to hit Lyman first, then come up the road for us. I told him there was a whole other army still at Scalp Point and I couldn't say would they be coming too. Johnson moved around his tent, getting into his clothes, his nubile squaw trying to keep herself covered whilst balancing him so's he could get his legs into his trousers. Flashes of the girl's copper skin from under the coverlet brought me pangs of memory. I had once been wed to just such a beauty as this. Officers came in and out of the tent. Finally, Johnson finished dressing.

Outside and with all the officers and plenty of men gathered 'round him, Johnson asked for a volunteer to take a warning down to Lyman. A volunteer because the way led through fourteen miles of lonely forest, a road overhung with hills, ledges, trees; dense country surely teeming with Indians, and Johnson would not order anyone to go. A waggoneer by the name of Adams said he would try it. Every man in camp should a thought about Adams' chances of gettin' through. He was a brave man. He was also doomed.

Our bateaux, laying about since they'd got brought up from Lyman, were now put to desperate purpose. Along with wagons, logs, stumps and all else what could get heaped into a barricade, the bateaux were hastily, nay, frantically thrown up around the camp, mostly to the south-east where the carry road from Edward came out of the woods. Men began removing brush from in front of our barrier. Trying to do in minutes what should a been done all through the summer.

Meantime, scouts came in and confirmed the French were heading for Lyman. Johnson ordered five-hundred men to march down there. A second, smaller force would go to the Drowned Lands with the intention of destroying the enemy's boats and ambushing them on their return.

Johnson only had about twenty-five hundred men, including his Mohawks and I didn't think he ought to be sending so many of them away. Lyman had men enough, all of whom were behind walls and with cannons. The wily French might march as if to Lyman then swing around and hit us instead and I thought worrying about Frenchie's boats was gettin' ahead of ourselves. As wrong as Johnson's intentions seemed to me, it must have seemed so to the officers as well, yet nobody said anything. Until, and as the two troops was forming up to march, it was old Hendrick, the ancient Iroquois warrior of renown, famed war chief of the fighting Mohawks, who challenged Johnson. Now a fat old man, Hendrick had once been a most formidable warrior, reputed to have been the greatest of all and much revered by his kinsmen. He had not reached such venerable status by bravery alone. His fame as an orator and sage was as great as the respect he'd earned for valor. The words of the chief were always worth heeding. Now and using the name the Mohawks had given Johnson when they adopted him into their tribe, Old Hendrick spoke to him from a short distance so all could hear.

"Warrigueghey, hear well," Hendrick said. He bent over and we could almost hear his bones creaking. He picked up a stick and held it over his head for all to see. The grounds became silent. Hendrick broke the stick easily into two pieces. He then picked up a number of twigs in a bundle and raising the bundle up over his head, he tried to break it and couldn't, which meaning was impressed on us all, except Johnson. Or maybe Bill grasped the wisdom of the gestures and chose to ignore it, for instead of keeping all his men at the camp, he ordered those who were to go to the Drowned Lands to go instead with the others to Lyman.

Hendrick jumped rather stiffly up onto a wagon box. "Warrigueghy," the chief said. "Hear again my words." He pointed to the relief force. "If they are to fight, they are too few. If they are to die, they are too many." Johnson shrugged and ordered the men to depart, and Hendrick, with the change of heart so common to Indians and so baffling to white men, declared he'd go, too.

This wise old Iroquois, though fluent in both English and French, spoke now in his own language, which few of the whites present could in any way understand. But he spoke so passionately and his voice held such richness and deep resonance, the fluidity of the motions accompanying his speech so spellbinding as to hold every man. He finished by raising the war whoop as he jumped down and only then did the troop start along the portage road toward Lyman.

Johnson provided a horse for the old chief, who was too lame to keep up with the detachment. Hendrick mounted the horse and straight as an arrow, he rode out at the head of his Mohawks, into the woods and down the lonely path so fraught with danger. About an hour after they departed the containment and not having enough flankers out, they blundered into an ambush. A lot of good men got killed. Many more would have fallen if not for the presence of Hendrick. There were Iroquois on the side of the French and seeing the old man, who they too venerated, and not wanting him hurt, they called from concealment to him and the others of the Mohawks to get away and thus the trap was revealed before the entirety of our column was enveloped.

Still and despite the warning, the Mohawks received a blow from which they would be a long time recovering. With most of the hidden Indians belonging to tribes long dominated by the Mohawks, thirty Mohawks were killed or wounded in the first barrage, a substantial loss for a tribe already reduced in fighting men. Among the wounded, though not mortally and left behind same as so many others as our men staggered back toward camp, was Hendrick. Unable to defend himself, he was easy prey for the Huron boys who came upon him. Too young to be allowed to fight, the boys were accompanying their fathers and elder brothers. The boys finished off the old chief and took his scalp. As well-known and as feared as Hendrick was by the Hurons, imagine the start those lads had gained on a warrior's fame. Imagine the boast they could make until death took them, too.

Our colonials suffered severe losses and retreated back toward the camp. Some few rangers and colonials held the rear whilst others helped along such of the wounded as could be recovered. Any left behind would be butchered by the Indian flood sweeping over them.

****

Having done what little I could to clean and dry my gun, I was in the line of men at the barricade when word of the ambush and of our retreat came in. Nothing to do now except wait. I looked to my either side, into the tense faces of our militia and I was uneasy for what they would do when the enemy arrived. Would we hold or would we flee?

Soon, and by the sounds of firing and the shouts and screams and the smoke, the action was fast approaching. On every side except where the road came in, the forest came to the edge of the camp. This would assure our enemy of cover when they got up.

The sounds of the fight gettin' louder, a relief contingent was sent to help our men get in. I went along with the column and as we got out there, the first of our retreating men burst out of the woods and into the clearing. They was hollering and running for holy Hell and bumping us as they went past and saying we ought to have been running too. When most but not all of our men had streamed past, the last of 'em came in a running fight with the French and Indians. I aimed and fired at a French officer who was waving his sword. He took my ball in the throat. Then, and reloading whilst walking backward, I gave a close shave to another Frenchie. A militia man alongside me went down with a ball in his calf. I slung my rifle on my back, picked him up and carried him in. Back behind the barricade, I passed him to a colonial who was eager to take the wounded man, any wounded man, to the hospital in the rear. I looked to shoot more of the enemy but dared not, for those of ours still twined in with them, and with so much firing, it was damn hard to see anything in the smoke. Our men were loading and firing as fast as they could and was as likely hitting our retreating men as not. Those of our men coming in were grapplin' with the foe right in front of the barricade. Some of the Indians, even whilst bullets whizzed around 'em, waved scalps.

The last of our men got in and we beat the enemy back from the barricade. They hunkered down in the woods along either side of our camp and began peppering us. Arrows and musket balls flew thick out of the brush and from behind trees. The shooting from the hill on our right became almost too hot to bear as the Indians and Canadians enfiladed us. Our men wavered but fought well enough for having a barricade and for knowing we'd get slaughtered did we break and run. Besides, and with Indians on three sides and the lake behind us, there wasn't any place to go. It was fight or die and we poured as much lead into them as they did into us. Men fired from close up and grappled with knife and tomahawk; our too-few bayonets jabbed and clashed against lances and spears. I even seen men bashing other men on the head with rocks.

The Indians were jumping around in the brush and trees which made it hard for us to hit 'em. A ranger alongside me, a toothless old codger, cussed. "Dad-blasted varmints! Stand still so's I can plug ya!" Despite the bullets and arrows, I laughed.

We heard drumrolls and from out of the woods came a sight to take a man's breath away. Ranks of French regulars in white and powder blue and at their head, the grenadiers, the tallest soldiers plucked from the different regiments and wearing lofty, brass-fringed fur hats to make 'em look even taller than they were. A fearsome sight with how the sun glinted bayonets, gorgets and brass hats, the French confident the mere sight of themselves would panic our men, our rabble, as they thought of us. The Indians thought so too and raised up bloody scalps on sticks and gave us their peculiar ululation, the scalp halloo, a whoop of different cadences and meanings which said now they would soon be putting our hair on sticks too.

The firing slackened on both sides, the field became eerily quiet for us gaping at the grenadiers and the Indians salivating for all the scalps they'd collect as soon as the regulars dispersed us as they surely would. The only sounds were an occasional Indian yelp and the commands of the French officers, the tramp of the grenadiers' feet, the swishing of their coats and clicking of their guns as they got arrayed for advancing.

Whilst our men gaped in awe, the only Britisher present amongst us, engineering officer Lieutenant-Colonel Billy Eyre had the presence of mind to try and bring up our two small cannons. I seen what he was up to and with him not able to do it by hisself, I went along our line clapping men on the shoulder and pointing 'em toward Eyre. Most was too frozen to move but enough of 'em helped so we got the cannons up and swung 'round and pointed down the road. The French regulars commenced marching toward us whilst we frantically loaded the guns with damn near anything a man could think to put in there.

The grenadiers were almost to the barricade when our cannons fired. The grapeshot we had stuffed down the barrels, musket balls, stones, nails, chains, chunks of metal, tore into their ranks. A hurrah rose up from our side as the smoke cleared and we seen the heaps of crumpled, bloodied Frenchmen. With their front ranks decimated, their back lines came up, the soldiers stepping with magnificent courage over their own dead and wounded. We, meantime, got our cannons reloaded and gave 'em another blast. This time as the smoke cleared, the French, victors on so many European battlefields, were running away.

We gave another huzza and sent a volley of lead into 'em. The French Canadians and Indians on our flanks, outraged, scalded us with a close-up, angry firing but their ululations rang as false in their ears as in ours for the truth which was felt over the battlefield. They would not break us. We would hold, the day would be ours. Every man there, American,

French, Indian, felt it. Everybody but Johnson. In the first of the fighting at the barricade, Bill had got hit lightly and retired to his tent, never more to be seen on the field. Only after it was confirmed the enemy was in retreat would he re-emerge. His absence had the not unfortunate consequence of putting the directing of our men into the very capable hands of his subordinates.

There came huzzas over on our right. I looked and never and for as long as I live will I forget the sight which I now seen. An officer up on an overturned wagon and with bullets flying around him and with his hat at the top of his sword, was waving it and hollering. Our militia, with a mighty roar, scampered up and over our makeshift wall and got after the enemy who, when they seen us coming, high-tailed into the woods.

We had beaten off a most ferocious and sustained attack and now we was after them, our officers did more good work in organizing a pursuit. The enemy would yet have plenty of sting. Whilst chasing 'em along the road to Lyman, we saw evidence of the slaughter of our men from the morning's battle. This spurred us into a rampage over a distance and against a thoroughly-whipped enemy. Our men butchered 'em, even those who, exhausted and scared, tried to surrender. Retribution, though not justifiable, was swift. I make no attempt to judge others, I not taking part in such things myself. I simply say the same was done to us earlier when it was ours who was retreating.

Our pursuit continued down the road and by a small pond known thereafter as Bloody Pond, a relief force up from Lyman fell upon the enemy's front whilst we engaged on their rear. This fight lasted a full hour and ended with the enemy getting driven off. We didn't pursue them any farther and with so many dead French and Indians, we simply tossed the corpses into the pond. Later, I heard we had thrown some of our own in too, our men too fatigued to get up a burial detail.

Among our prisoners was the French commander, Baron Dieskau, a brave man with two or three musket balls in him and who had nearly become one of the butchered. Dieskau congratulated Johnson for what Dieskau said was a masterful performance in Johnson's conduct of the battle. Said he couldn't believe how stoutly our irregulars had stood up to his professionals. Dieskau credited this also to Bill, and what Dieskau said next was to be repeated over and again in our camp. "In the morning you fought like boys, at noon like men, and like devils in the afternoon."

Chapter VIII – To Smoke You in Their Pipes

The Mohawks were much aggrieved by the loss of Hendrick and of so many of their tribesmen and were furious over the rumor which our colonials mostly discounted but which festered among the Mohawks. In with the Huron boys who had slain the great Hendrick were some few Mohawks. These were Caughnawagas which were Mohawks what had pledged to the French and abandoned the tribal homeland to take up residence in Canada. The greatest of all Mohawks slain and scalped by the children of his own blood. A terrible humiliation for the proud Iroquois who, already seeing the dissipation of their once mighty confederacy, were powerless to do anything about it.

The Mohawks directed their frustration and rage toward Bill Johnson, the only true friend they'd ever had among the whites. The Mohawks confronted Bill, an angry mob gathering in front of his tent to demand he give them the captured French commander and any other prisoners he was holding. Johnson refused and a heated exchange took place in the Mohawk tongue and whilst the argument was going on, a young brave slipped inside Johnson's tent, where Dieskau was, and if not for the timely intervention of the doctor, the brave might have got hisself a most illustrious trophy.

The Mohawks persisted in demanding they be given all the prisoners and they howled with fury for Johnson refusing. The Mohawks needed captives to assuage their pride and for adopting, to rebuild tribal power. They had plenty of prisoners already, which no man could safely take from them but they would not be satisfied until they had them all. The Iroquois chiefs, full of bluster, stomped their feet and called Johnson bad Indian names, trying to intimidate him but he held fast and dealt with them. Knowing rebuffing their demands might compel them to depart, he patiently calmed them. There were still plenty of scalps and loot to be had on the battlefield, they had only to collect what was there. I suppose everybody dead in the woods, friend and foe alike, was treated to the hair-snatchers.

Johnson gave the Mohawks bullocks for roasting and some watered-down rum to celebrate our great victory and to drown their sorrow at the losses they had suffered. Bill did the best he could to convince the Iroquois to pursue other sport and they went away disgruntled.

After the Mohawks had been disbursed, Dieskau, heavily bandaged, and already with a notion of the answer to the question he now put to Johnson, asked what might have been his fate, had he been given over to the Indians. Their intention, Johnson said, "Was to burn you, by God. To eat you and to smoke your flesh in their pipes. For revenge of Hendrick." Dieskau feared the Mohawks might try again for him. "Fear not," Johnson said. "Before they can have you, they must kill me." Johnson soon after sent Dieskau down to Albany under heavy guard.

Our Indians claimed the major credit for the victory, and in truth, they were a factor, just not the decisive one. The work of our officers, Titcomb, Folsom, McGinnis, Eyre, and Colonel Williams, beloved of the Massachusetts men, shot dead almost at the onset of the battle when our relief force going down to Edward got ambushed in what would be famously known thereafter as The Bloody Morning Scout.

Perhaps most heroic of all was Phineas Lyman, a veteran of many a woodland fight. Lyman, taking command when Johnson, wounded, retired to his tent, had the major part in organizing our reserves. He put them in at just the right places and times to carry the weight of battle. His loaders from among our wounded kept more men shooting more often, and it was Lyman who, late in the fight, led a Massachusetts company into the woods on our right flank from whence had come so much devastation to our side and which action had precipitated the final rout from this place. If our army had more leaders like those, we could win this war.

Some of our officers tried to get Johnson off his arse and moving against Scalp Point. Resolute action might a taken the snakes' den but Bill demurred, mindful as he was of the other part of Dieskau's army, still at Scalp Point. Johnson feared throwing away all we had gained. His refusal to advance, his dismal, some said cowardly performance in the battle, finished him in the estimation of the colonial levies. Already well disillusioned with his leadership, their confidence he would never regain.

****

With the Braddock disaster of just a few months before, our people had been hungry for something, anything, and our victory in the Battle of Lake George gave us what we craved. Our newspapers sensationalized what they deemed our great victory; Bill Johnson's martial fame would be toasted not just in New York Colony but all up and down the seaboard. Bill at least looked the part.

The British, also smarting from the Braddock disaster, made much of the work of Billy Eyre as the only Britisher present at our victory. Our colonials, the British said, would have been routed if not for Eyre. Such a sniffling insinuation, same as the British claim the battle was more a draw than a victory, was drowned by colonial huzzas. I conceded our newspapers maybe exaggerated our victory but victory it was and not the draw both the British and French were saying, each for reasons of their own. How our newspapers stated it, confronted by European regulars, our farmers, shopkeepers and tradesmen stood their ground unflinchingly. Truth was, we flinched plenty, same as any men would of under such withering circumstances, just we didn't flinch so much as to cause us all to run away. We had gone from near panic to staving off defeat to turning the enemy, to sending him back down the lake. To those who said it was less than a victory, I could only reply by saying we killed more of the enemy than they did of us, we got their general, they didn't get ours, and when the battle was over, it was them running for the hills. As for the greater significance of the battle, this I leave to the theorizers.

Some of us wondered why Dieskau had left half his army at Scalp Point. Someone said those left behind were a blocking force, in the event Johnson came down one lake whilst Dieskau was going up the other.

Hah!

Another man said my burning the boats along Portage Crick had convinced Dieskau to come up Champlain instead of George, which, the man said, set into motion the events which led to our victory. I didn't think so. The boats bringing Dieskau's army out of Canada, even were they heavy bateaux, could have been moved up the Ticonderoga portage to Lake George, did it fit the general's purposes to do so.

Some wondered why Dieskau had attacked Johnson instead of our fort at Lyman. All the men and supplies for Johnson came through the lower fort. Did it fall, Johnson, with Dieskau between him and his base, would have withered on a severed vine.

Dieskau had the last word on all counts. He conceded he had left part of his force at Scalp Point as a defensive measure, and as for the whaleboats, he said he had issued orders for their construction and he verified what I had seen as the reason for 'em, back when I burned 'em. To establish control of Lake George following his expected victories over both Johnson and Lyman.

Dieskau had been informed of the burning of the boats, and advised it was the work of a single man, the vanquished general appreciated the man's courage, and as Johnson's prisoner and before he was sent down to Albany, Dieskau asked to meet the man. I dined with him and Johnson. Candlelight, wine out of fancy goblets and a damn fine supper of veal, potatoes and red cabbage, all served on Johnson's best china.

Dieskau, who was German, not French, I found to be an interesting man. Haughty, stiff-mannered, a professional soldier of the European sort who made their living by hiring themselves out to whichever king or prince paid the most. A true soldier of fortune but a gentleman most gracious in defeat. I think I offended him by eating with my knife instead of with the sparkling silverware provided.

He said his loss of the battle was the most embarrassing reversal he had suffered in all his years as a fighting man. Stunning because so unexpected. Every man among his regulars was certain the sight of them marching down the road would send us fleeing. No colonials could stand against these veterans of many a European battlefield. We were mostly first-timers so maybe his men had reason to be contemptuous.

Dieskau spoke ruefully about having attacked Johnson instead of Lyman. He said he had intended hitting Lyman first but his Indian scouts had insisted Johnson's camp would be the easier plum, due to its negligent defenses, and with the Indians balking at a frontal assault against the walls and cannons of Lyman, Dieskau had been made to alter his plans.

Our newspapers speculated on the possible consequences, had we not stopped Dieskau and had it worked out as he intended. He might then have brought the rest of his men down from Scalp Point and taken Lyman, and with all the Indians who would have flocked to him and with naught between him and New York Town, the campaign might have ended with French grenadiers in a triumphant Wall Street victory parade.

The final pieces of our victory came to me on an evening over the winter when I returned from a scout and walked into one of our larger ranger huts where a dozen men were gathered. Rumors had been going around saying Johnson was to be replaced and my asking, "Is Johnson gone yet?" was corrected by one of the men. "Baronet Sir William Johnson," he said. I turned sharply toward the man, nobody said anything but all the men were looking at one another and at me and they seemed amused about something. They all knew of my contentious relations with Johnson. “Aye,” the man said, trying, same as them others not to laugh and explaining, “It seems we could not have beaten Dieskau without Johnson’s sterling leadership, or so it was reported to the king, who saw fit to reward Bill with a baronetcy and a pot of gold as well.”

This brought out the laughter. I could only shake my head, even as I laughed too. That goddamn Johnson. “All of us,” a ranger said, “knowed he weren’t much for leading soldiers.” Another said, “If the king wanted to reward him, he shudda pinned turkey feathers in his hair and paid him off in wampum beads instead of gold.”

“And Phineas Lyman got his reward too,” a man said, “for saving Johnson’s bacon in the fight.” Here was something, for surely the valiant Lyman was deserving. The fort which Lyman built and which had been named for him, Johnson had renamed Edward in honor of the king’s grandson. The laughter erupted, though this time with an edge, the men there were mostly New Englanders, as was Lyman. It was jealousy of Lyman, no doubt, which had prompted Johnson to erase from the maps the name of the man who had built the fort strong enough so the Indians refused to attack it and who then masterfully directed our forces after Johnson retired to his tent. Johnson had thus managed to disparage his rival whilst at the same time ingratiating himself with the king.

A ranger asked in what direction must a man be facing if he be shot in the ass. This brought out howls of laughter. As originally reported, the wound which had prompted Bill to leave the field was a mere scrape of a musket ball across the back of his hand. Now men were saying the ball, or another ball, had taken him in the arse. I knew the men were not being fair. I had seen Bill after the battle, he was wounded in the hip more seriously than what the men would admit. And in fairness, Bill had done good work before retiring, he steadying our men at the barricade when the French and Indians first came at us. This I had witnessed, as had some of these rangers who were now choosing not to remember. I had known Bill almost since he first arrived in the colony from Ireland. A shyster, a womanizer, a smuggler, a politician, a crook according to many, but never had I any reason to doubt his personal courage.

In a way it saddened me, to hear the men scorning Bill, but in another way, I felt the men were right. It was how Bill got by, a charmed life, and to give Bill his due, even as the men laughed at him for his supposed cowardice, there was no denying the good work he was always doing with the Indians, what he did better than anyone else ever could. If not for Bill, we might a been at war with the entire Iroquois League. Many of the Iroquois who might otherwise have sworn eternal enmity toward us were instead backing off from their support of the French and were at least willing to listen to us.

We then got into the rum and drank a number of toasts, as was our custom, and during a lull and having seemingly run out of men to lift a glass to, I proposed a toast which proposing might have been, in a room full of New England Yankees, more dangerous even than standing up to the French grenadiers. "To the Baron, Bill Johnson," I said, and the men raised their cups. They could grumble at Bill for his reaping more laurels than what he maybe had earned but they understood it was always so in wartime. To the commander went the praise or condemnation, whichever was to be dispensed. The men drank to Bill for an important job well done, just not the job for which he had been rewarded with his title.

For years afterward, whenever those few of us who felt we knew Bill well enough chided him over his perhaps undeserved glory, he was a big enough man to laugh along with us. And once, also much later and when I was alone with Johnson and we were both sober, he admitted he owed a good part of his victory and thus his title and his gift of money, to Phineas Lyman.

****

Two days after the battle, I left the camp and headed up to Paradise Valley for a much-needed rest and to spook the North Country. I dared not go down the lakes for fear of lurking Indians. Instead, I walked the mountains, a circuitous trek along the western shore of Lake George. I hadn't gone more than half a day when I came upon a clearing where a band of Iroquois had stopped on their way home and made sport with four Huron captives, three men and a boy. The Hurons had been tortured at the fire-stake. The meat of legs and arms was stacked alongside what had been a cook-fire and with the stink of burnt flesh and the flies, it was clear the Hurons had been cannibalized, probably ritually. Boiled and eaten, their story plainly written in a lonely clearing in the woods.

The four armless, legless torsos with scalped heads attached, were propped with sticks around a firepit. The lips and the skin around the lips had been removed, all probably whilst they were yet alive, which presented a ghastly spectacle of toothy grins, as if the Hurons, too, saw the humor in the deviltry played upon them. With their pipes clenched in their teeth, they reminded me of my old friend, Arnold Baldwin. He'd been scalped too, although he hadn't been boiled and eaten, but he'd had a toothy grin and with a briar pipe always between his teeth. The boy, no more than ten-years old, I figured for the son of one of the men, brought along to do the camp chores, as was the custom. Youthfulness would in no way have spared him from any of what was done to the men.

I put the palm of my hand over the bowl of one of the pipes, the ashes were still warm, and I got to hell out of there. The Mohawks were our friends but with their blood aroused, I surely did not care to meet them in the woods.

****

I got to my cabin where I craved solitude and peace. The only sign I saw was of a bear and the usual deer. The first night and all the next day, I slept in my old bed, the one made of woven rope strands, my one real luxury in my mountain abode. Sleep sorely needed and most welcomed. It felt some good to be back. Trouble seemed to keep away from this door. Outside my secluded realm, all the world as I knew it was aflame with war, pillage and death. Here, so close to the war yet so far, it was calm and secure, an amazing sanctuary where life went on unaffected by the noise and clamor around it. Here, for a short while at least, was peace.

Mornings this time of year tended to be foggy; the days, after the fog burned off, were bright and clear. It was the best time of year to be up here, early autumn, the land free from the mosquitoes and horseflies whilst the days still held some of the heat of summer, although, and with the heat slipping away, the nights were cool for the sleeping. A few of the hardwoods had begun shedding their leaves, most were still in full verdure. Groves of elms, hillsides of birch shining in the bright sunlight, the colors sharp and focused. Things to embrace. To put aside thoughts of the awful events and dangers, of the incredibly long hours spent under arms in the forest. To instead bask in the wondrous beauty of the land. At least so it felt.

It had been this way for me in the previous war, coming to my Paradise for desperately needed rest despite it being so close to the French. The taut nerves, the straining, the constant threats, all those elements of scouting made it necessary for a man to stand down between forays. Otherwise he was not able to sleep until falling into a deep slumber which might last for days and leave him more weary than before. Along with the fatigue, my back ached fiercely. A man could accustom himself to sleeping on the hard ground but even in summer the ground was damp and my back always suffered for it. I was getting on in years, I was mid-thirties, and wasn't sure how much more woods-romping I could do.

In the mornings, I'd climb up out of the canyon to the ledges overlooking the Eagles' Lake. I'd sit up there with the sun striking warm on me and think how amazing it would be to live here in peace. It was a harsh country, almost too harsh, but the virgin forest abounded in riches of different sorts and did a man persevere, the hardships could be overcome, his reward would be wealth and prosperity.

After a time, the diving osprey took a fish from the lake and as the bird rose up into the air, the timeless ritual was enacted as the bald eagle swooped in and took the fish from the osprey in mid-air. The lake was so bounteous, the osprey simply took another. I tried to convince myself the way they interacted was better than our own. To share in the abundance. But who would be the eagle, who the osprey, who to soar, who to submit? We were prideful men for whom submission was worse than death and who must fight to have it all.

I spent considerable time up on the ledges pondering such things whilst the humanity flowed back into my soul. Unfortunately, this interlude was interrupted early one morning by the sound of loud booms which jolted me out of sleep. Cannon fire! I rushed outside in my linens. Had Johnson come north after all, to surprise the French, and me too? But as I listened, my excitement faded. It wasn't cannon fire. It was the blasting of rock down at Ticonderoga, no more than seven or eight miles from me, and I had an idea of what it meant.

Frenchie was getting started on his Ticonderoga fort.

The blasting went on all day and after a quiet night, it re-commenced the next morning. My respite from the war at an end, I redirected my thoughts to the outside world and proceeded down into the Champlain Valley. The blasting was right there along the base of my mountain, the French blowing out the rock with charges of gunpowder, then sledgehammering the debris. Others of them were busy clearing a road from their quarry down to the lower falls of Portage Crick where the rocks would get loaded onto scows for the short trip down to the Ticonderoga promontory. Also, and right there at the falls, Frenchie was erecting a blockhouse, a large two-story affair with swivel guns, and by its location, up against the falls, the blockhouse was to be a sawmill. Frenchie was, as always, taking advantage of British lassitude to encroach deeper into territory which, by treaty and custom, was ours. He'd soon have a base to extend his dominance farther south along Champlain.

I went up to Scalp Point and spooked for two days. Here, another ritual was getting played out. The habitants, as the peasants were known, were getting started on bringing their crops into the barns and once this was done, they would depart for the winter. Same for the soldiers and Indians. Schooners, sailing boats, barges and scows, all would be taking 'em away. The winter garrison of Canadian militia and French regulars would be small. We could take them simply by hitting in the interval between the departure of their troops and the first deep snows, or even after the snows. Johnson, though, wearing his laurels, was indisposed toward moving and risking, in seeking a bigger prize, the loss of all he had won. The French who stayed to man the fort over the winter would go about their duties unmolested and without fear of us disturbing them.

****

I returned to Johnson's camp to news both good and bad.

When I had departed the camp for Paradise, neither Ephraim nor Nate had yet got in from our last scout, when we'd found Dieskau's army. Now I heard Ephraim had still not got in and was presumed lost whilst Nate had been found, at least what remained of him, a charred carcass tied to a tree no more than a mile from the Lake George camp. The man who told me about it said Nate had been tortured and killed in a manner to leave him so disfigured and bloodied as to be scarce recognizable. His scalp, most of his fingers, his ears, nose and eyes were missing. His stomach was torn out, his guts wrapped around the tree. Usual practice was to wrap a man's innards and put burning coals inside of him, all whilst he yet lived. It bothered me to think Nate had been so close to making it in when they got him. The man said Nate had maybe been captured somewhere along the way and got dragged here. It was an ugly picture in my head, this stoutest of rangers trussed hand and foot, those powerful eyes seething up from the bottom of an Indian canoe. I said as how anybody who knew Nate knew there be not enough Indians in the woods to drag him from one end of the lake to the other. And no Indians foolish enough to try. Nate was a hellcat and would not have surrendered so they must a jumped him as he was getting in to the camp, then brained and trussed him whilst he was knocked out.

The militia man who told me about it wondered how Nate took the torturing. Did he suffer bravely or did he blubber and beg for mercy? I asked had Nate's heart been ripped from his chest. The man gave me a nod, which confirmed Nate had died bravely for no Indian would ingest the heart of a coward. I asked was Nate's albino wolf hat missing when they found him. It was and I vowed to kill any Indian I ever seen wearing such a hat. Even if it be a Mohawk.

After reporting in to Johnson, I came out of his tent with Rogers and he said he had something to show me. We walked toward our ranger huts, on the outskirts of the camp. We came to some tents and to what I figured was a fresh company of rangers, men I did not recognize. There was a fancy marquis tent. Rogers pulled aside the flap and grinning, he ushered me inside. Behind a table sat my commander from the first war, Joe Blanchard. Joe got up and came 'round the table, as happy to see me as I was to see him. We grinned and cussed and pounded one another on the back and shoulders.

Good old Blanchard, the original founder of the rangers. Ill-health and creeping age had limited him to recruitment and training duties back in New Hampshire, at both of which he was performing admirably, and with a fresh company of sixty men to be delivered, he'd decided to bring them along personally. Joe was fifty-years old and even with hard years taking their toll, I was sure how, when he brought his company over, the men, most of whom were less than half his age, would have struggled to keep up with him. It's how he was in the woods, a first-rate leader under the most trying of conditions. He got back behind the table and sagged into his chair and as we talked, a sadness came over me.

Joe had been a tall rangy man, immensely powerful, and seemed now not so big as I remembered. The hard life he had lived had left its mark; he did not look to be in the best of health.

Still, it was good to see the old man again. The words which passed between us now were few but significant. The dangerous times shared in the last war were recalled and spoken of briefly. Blanch said he was taking his men down the lakes. Said their New England frontier was suffering same as ours, more than ours, and they had come on the promise of going against Scalp Point, the root of the troubles. Having arrived too late for the battle and feeling outraged for Johnson not advancing, the men were spoiling for a fight. Blanch said he was eager too. I think he understood it was the last time he would raise a hatchet and a whoop in the direction of the French. He asked me to go along. It weren't no secret I preferred working either alone or with just a few proven men and not with sixty recruits and besides, I had one very compelling reason to decline, but goddammit, if Blanch wanted action and wanted me in on it, I was damn sure going.

"I'll go," I said. "You know I will, but look here. I'm going home to be married."

"Married!" Rogers said. "You?"

"Yes, me." Sometime before we defeated Dieskau, I had sent a letter to Monica, asking her to marry me. I hadn't received a reply back so I couldn't be certain of her answer but I was confident she would assent. "I can't stand before the preacher shot full of arrows," I said to Blanch. "So let's not be too over-anxious, huh?"

Blanchard, back in his chair behind the table and staring at me, burst out laughing. Rogers and me looked at him and he said he'd heard, whilst back in New Hampshire, about the ranger who got into Frenchie's boats and burned 'em, and before the man what was telling it could say the ranger's name, Blanch had blurted, "T'was Kuyler, was it not?" The man said yes, it was, and Blanch belly-laughed, same as he was doin' now. I couldn't help but smile. Then, no longer laughing but with the amusement still in his eyes and looking affectionately at me, "You are one crazy goddamn Dutchman."

****

With most of our men hidden back in the woods, me and Blanch and a few of the men looked out at the French doings along the Ticonderoga promontory. There was an encampment, rows of white tents. Regulars were drilling in a nearby field. Engineers was laying down the outlines of the fort. Rocks was getting sorted, mortar pits dug. Habitants with pickaxes and trowels worked under the direction of master stonemasons. Oxen roped to pullies dragged massive beams which got laid on the ground for raising. Supplies were getting unloaded from the two French ships at a wharf which was still getting constructed. On a flatboat was a water-wheel for the sawmill, soon to be creaking, spinning out a steady supply of lumber.

Earlier, when I showed Blanch where I had burned the French boats, the blackened ground, the swath of charred trees up the mountainside, he'd laughed. Now, he was mad. For him, the rage of French busy work seemed a negation of all he'd done in the last war. He had always pushed the British to get here before the French, for us to take the war to them before they brought it to us. This we hadn't done and now there would be one more obstacle to overcome in our march to Montreal and Quebec.

We went up to Scalp Point. The castle and fort walls were manned, the French were still there in strength. It seemed their winter exodus to the north was slower than in years past and with more men staying than usual. Probably it was to support the work down at Ti and was as well a wariness of Rogers and a fear the Mohawks would come for revenge for their loss of so many men. Little did the French know and fortunate for Johnson and for those of us who were prowling, the Mohawks was more whipped than the French knew. The Mohawks, same as the others of the Iroquois tribes, had suffered for years from all the wars and from the defection of so many of their people to the French, the power of their League diverted by the Jesuits having converted so many of them to the Papist religion. Their stomach for fighting had long been on the wane and now and with their losses in this latest battle, the Mohawks would spend the winter close to home, desperate to re-group and rebuild.

All whilst we spooked Scalp Point, Blanch had Ticonderoga on his mind. He dearly wanted to hit the sawmill. Burn it down, which would wreck or at least delay the French working on their fort through the winter. I talked him out of it. With the French alertness and with the time it would take to get in there and get a fire going, it weren't something our new men could handle without severe loss.

Blanch joked about giving the recruits seats up on Rattlesnake whilst I snuck in and did the burning. Show the new men how a real ranger went about his business. "On second thought," Blanch said, "if they seen what was expected of 'em, we might wake up of a morning to find 'em all gone home."

We stayed around a few more days, alert for any chance which might arise. None did, and finally, regretfully, me and Blanch shook hands and he departed with a small escort for his home in New Hampshire. I led his company uneventfully south and we arrived back just as the officers were going to a meeting called by Johnson, enough men so the gathering was held in the open. Some of the men were excited for thinking we was going against Scalp Point. Most knew better and were not surprised, just resigned, when Johnson announced he was shutting the camp down for the winter. He maintained he wasn't getting supplies enough to keep the camp open. He'd keep a winter garrison at Edward, the rest of the men he was sending home. He said he was leaving too. Having not ever really taken to the soldiering life, he was anxious to get back to his Indian business and his wenching.

Rogers asked would I stay over with the rangers who'd be wintering at Edward but when I had arrived back, Monie's letter awaited me. She had accepted my offer of matrimony. When I read the letter and reread it to be sure I wasn't dreaming, men said I carried on like a wild Indian. Her letters were always wonderful to read but this time all the new and little things she put into words were eclipsed by the most joyous words in the language. "Yes, Kenneth, I consider it an honor to love you and will do so 'til death do we part." She sent me into paroxysms with her assent, my emotions got carried away. My dream for us to settle at Paradise would have to be delayed for the duration of the war but we could embark immediately on a life together; anywhere with her would be a paradise for me.

For now and with the money I had stashed with Eric, we could purchase a place near Albany. We should be able to do pretty well; homesteads were going cheaply. With the Indian troubles, many people were getting out and moving back downriver, or even returning to England or Holland.

I was anxious to get started on our life together. With hard work and could we get through these troubled times, we would prosper in all ways. We would move north when the time was right. In the meantime, it would be enough for me simply to be with her.

Before I departed, the rangers threw me a party with fresh venison, rum, and plenty of ribaldry, and with everybody thoroughly drunk, the subject of pay came up. I spoke to Rogers about it and we went over to see Johnson, who kept saying over a bottle of fine claret how grateful he was for my services. He reminded me of the times we had womanized together when we were young, a subject of no interest to me now. He opened a second bottle and we set to upon it, he talking long on nearly every subject but pay. I went along for a while but when he called to his squaw for yet a third bottle and with me already drunk and anxious to be on my way, I cut him off. "Damn it," I said. "Turn me loose. Pay me so I can get the hell out of here." He answered in a snotty manner and soon we were in a drunken argument. Told him if I didn't get paid right away, I would never work for him again. He demurred and I accused him, rightly or not, of spending the army's money on the parties he'd held all summer with his smelly Iroquois. I said I pretty much reckoned I could take my pay out of his hide if he'd just step outside. He laughed, a cold laugh, and with the look he fixed on me, I supposed he was taking my measure, thinking on whether or not he wanted to try me. He was a bigger man than me but he was living a softer life than I was, and with Rogers cooling us off, Johnson backed down graciously. He went to his private funds and took out more money than what I figured I had comin'. He said, as he handed it to me, "In truth, Ken, you, with your good work and honest opinions were worth more to me than any man. You have my thanks more than I can say." Quietly I took my leave of this strange man, packed my gear and headed out. A company of New Jersey rangers was going on furlough and I walked as far as Edward with them. Then I got a seat in a bateau headed down the river.

Chapter IX – Silly Hans

Monie was overjoyed to see me. Since I had first departed for the north in the spring and until now, I had only managed two short visits home. Short, but sufficient to establish an even firmer bond between us. She had been hearing all summer and fall of the sickness and the battling and about the toll it was all taking on the men, and her joy, when she received my proposal, and her joy now at seeing me, made my heart jump more. Never was there such a feeling as this! For three days and nights we talked of our future and the night before we were to be wed, Mother and Father surprised us with both a trousseau and a dowry. Sarah and Mother had secretly filled the trousseau, a chest containing all the pretty and practical things a new bride might want, and Pops presented me with a cloth sack full of coins, as if he were the father of the bride, not of the groom.

The next morning, dressed in fancy rented suits and tricorn hats with gold trim, Pops and me sipped rum in the otherwise empty common room whilst Monie was in the back with Sarah and Mother and some of Monie's friends. I asked Pops what the hell could be taking Monie so long getting ready and did she want to be late for her own wedding? Pops supposed whatever was going on behind the door had to do with Monie's hair. He said Monie and Mother had near drove him crazy the past few weeks, fretting over what to do with Monie's tresses, as long and dark and straight as an Indian's and impossible to work into the curls and ringlets appropriate for a bride.

Finally, the door opened and Monie came out. She watched me to see did I approve. I thought she was a vision. They had given up on the curls and instead had lifted her hair up off her shoulders and back and piled it beneath a bride's cap. This had the effect of accentuating the white of her neck, the delicate sweetness of her face. The cap had swirls, woven lace and netting. Two ornamental little wax birds clung to the netting, so realistic they might have broken into a chirping melody and there were some bright red wax-cherries as well.

The gown she wore was a sky-blue silk print with a stenciled flower-pattern. It was cinched at the waist, tight against her amazing curves;

her long sleeves opened at her wrists into lace cuffs over white gloves. The front of her gown, squared, and embroidered with imitation gold thread, was low-cut and showed plenty of cleavage. She wore a necklace, pearl earrings, and pinned to her chest, a gold brooch. Her green eyes sparkled with happiness.

We rode in a rented carriage to the old Dutch church, my bride and me, Mother and Pops. We processioned into the nearly-full nave, I leading, followed by Eric and Sarah, our legal witnesses, then Mother, escorted by the gallant Sir William, who, in town on Indian business, surprised us by showing up at the church just moments before the ceremony was to begin. Lastly came Monie, on Pops' arm, him a few inches shorter than her and beaming side to side at our guests as he and Monie came down the aisle. Pops was filled with all the pride of a man giving his own daughter in marriage.

A few of my ranger friends, on furlough, were in attendance, saying they had to see it to believe it, and although they had spiffed themselves, still they filled the church with their not-unpleasant woodsie scent. One of them was the scrawny, toothless old fellow who had stood alongside me at the barricade at the Battle of Lake George. He, with a formidable wife nearly twice his size, emitted a guffaw at the sight of Pops and me in our outfits and got for it his wife's sharp elbow like a knife-thrust into his ribs. This got some of the folks, including me and the scrawny ranger, laughing.

After the ceremony, Monie and me, holding hands, led our guests on the traditional bridal walk through the streets and with the passersby applauding whilst admiring my bride who was, of course, beautiful. We arrived at the Full Sail where Mother's friends had dinner waiting, every good dish known to the frontier and some traditional Dutch delicacies.

****

With the generous gift from Pops and the fur money I had stashed with Eric and with what little Monie had saved, we set out at once to search the countryside for a new home. We soon decided on a place and bought it from the widow of a Swede who'd been killed at the Bloody Morning Scout. She and her young children were moving back south of Albany, to a hamlet along the King's Highway known as Fishkill, to be with relatives. She'd had most of the fall work completed, most of the crops harvested, when she'd received word of her husband's death. We gave her a fair price, the transfer was properly recorded in Albany. We bought a wagon and two mules and when everything was in order, we loaded what goods we had and set out for our new home.

The farm was eight miles or so north of Albany, along the Vlatche, in the crook of the last big bend of the Mohawk River before it emptied into the Hudson. It was an easy day's journey from Albany along the Schenectady Road. Our own road, cut by the previous owner, was a mile long. Rougher than the main road but passable by wagon, our road burst abruptly out of deep-shaded woods at the top of a rise, thus affording a sudden and generous view of the farm, spread below as a clearing in a saucer-like hollow. On the day we arrived to take ownership, we stopped at the top of the rise and Monie squeezed my hand as we gazed down in silence at our farm, bathed in late-afternoon sunshine.

The cabin was situated directly below the ridge where the road came out of the woods. On either side of the cabin were well-tended vegetable gardens. To the left, on a wooded hill back in the trees was a spring, the water flowing in a brook cutting the length of the yard. To the left of the cabin were the outbuildings with some on either side of the brook and with one of our two ornate cedar bridges situated there, although the brook was sufficiently narrow so a man could leap or even step across it. The previous owner had built a dam at the bottom of the downward slope of the gully, to the far-right from where we were looking, thus forming a half-acre pond filled with turtles, bullfrogs and fish.

There was a barn with a stable attached. The stable was of a size sufficient to accommodate my mules and the four young beef cows and the two milkers what had come with the farm. The barn bulged with corn and hay. There was a chicken coop and pigsty, although the chickens and pigs most often ran loose, the chickens to peck insects in the dusty yard, the pigs to fatten on acorns and beechnuts in the nearby woods. There was a corn crib, also bulging, a toolshed and lean-tos for keeping stacked wood out of the rain. A massive chestnut tree overspread the yard, shading the cabin. Cornfields and pastures surrounded the farm on all sides except for where the hill overlooked us, and around the clearing were the fields and pastures and beyond these, the deep woods.

The cabin was an impressive ten-logs high, sufficient to accommodate a loft, which we would use for storage and as a sleeping place for our children when they came along. The door was stout double-boards with two heavy bars for securing from the inside, the floor was puncheon logs set so close together it was as if they were a single smooth floorboard. We had brought along a woven rug to cover most of the surface. The fireplace was brick, not stone or wattle, and our rather too large, too fancy bed, the bed we'd paid a king's ransom for and which Monie had insisted upon by saying we deserved at least this one simple luxury, took up fully a third of our single room. I put up rods and hung curtains for pulling around the bed at night. There was a table and chairs and in front of the fireplace, two rocking chairs.

As I set about organizing my new farm and my new life, it occurred to me there were fewer pigs and chickens than what had been posted on the bill of sale. I presumed it had to do with the pigs roaming the nearby woods and maybe getting into trouble and to a fox getting into the hen-house but when I realized I was short one milking cow and some few other things, including an expensive, brand-new plow, I was angry and disappointed. The woman from whom we had purchased the farm had cheated us. Thinking further on it, she hadn't seemed the sort to deceive and I remembered the warning she had given me. My nearest neighbor was a man named Barnes, his shabby place the only other farm on our road, just a holler away, and she had paid him to look after things in the time between her departure and our arrival. Her warning was to watch him, for he was a shyster.

We set immediately to preparing for winter. I got the remainder of the crops in and worked long days cutting and stacking wood. Monie gathered the last of the vegetables from the gardens, planted the tulip bulbs Mother had gifted us and worked putting the cabin the way she wanted. At night, in each other's arms, we talked long hours of the future and of the dreams seemingly coming true for both of us. This was the best time of my life. I was completely happy and cared not one whit if I ever went north again. Certainly not to fight. Monie seemed as happy as I, which was the wonder of it all.

We spent time in the woods together, sometimes hunting deer, which were more plentiful near the crops and orchards of the farms than they ever were up north. Monie carried the light musket I purchased for her but after downing her first deer, a stub-horn yearling fawn, she cried for what she called the noble creature and vowed never to take another. I tacked the tiny antler-set to the side of the barn with all the many sets already up there and when she insisted I remove it, I teased her, saying as how it was in with the others and I couldn't recollect which was hers. She was adamant, though, and I obliged her.

After this, when she came along, she was mostly content to allow me to do the shooting whilst she followed the tracks of the woodland critters in their search for sustenance and marveled at the silent beauty. Sometimes she carried bits and crumbs in her apron and scattered them for her "Poor dear things." Other times she gathered acorns or pinecones for decorations to make our house cheery.

Ducks and geese were easier for her to kill, although most times when she shot, either with gun or bow, she missed, which didn't seem to bother her. With the fowl heading south, I blasted every morning into the geese alighting on the pond. We had fresh goose for a month. I hurled sticks high up into the chestnut tree and brought down clusters of the nuts for roasting. Monie joined me but she wasn't very good at it and got frustrated. She threw like a girl; I had used to gather the nuts as a boy, for roasting, and had a surer eye for it.

Working with some of our neighbors, we put out nets on the Mohawk River and caught messes of fish to sell and I taught Monie how to fish in our pond. With her woman's patience and feel for the subtle bite, she was a great, if not immediate success. She'd go to the pond in the mornings for fish to eat along with our eggs, or late afternoon, for our supper.

Monie loved this life, and with us close enough to town so she could visit and shop, for she was not a solitary woman and thrived with folks around, we visited Albany often over the winter. We saw a lot of Mother and Pops, Eric and Sarah. Which was certainly different from my previous solitary winters up in Paradise Valley.

The winter I spent cutting down trees, to clear more land for spring planting. The more land was cleared, the greater the value to the farm. I cut and split firewood which I hauled in my wagon to Albany or Schenectady. The money I used to buy things for our household.

Monie always insisted we find time for ourselves, as distracted as we were with work. Love left to itself and not nourished, she said, soon must die like a squash left after the frost. So when the pond froze, I cleared the snow off the ice and taught her how to skate. She quickly picked up on it and it was beautiful to watch her gliding with controlled grace over the frozen surface. Sometimes when I was working in the yard, she would try to sneak up on me, to pelt me with snowballs. She had no chance of getting close to this old scout but I'd feign obliviousness to humor her, or get around on her backtrack and give her a pelting. We'd romp, throw snow on one another and usually finish by rushing to the hayloft or to bed, to re-consummate our deep and abiding love.

I trapped some, not the prime pelts of the north. Skinning pelts, I told Monie, was a squaw's work but I could never get her to work the skins. I had to do it, always in the barn, never in the cabin.

Monie was fascinated with the wolves' howls in the night. She said they sounded sad, as if bereaved, and so I shot one and brought it home to show her the malevolence in the eyes and snout, which only served to increase her fascination, if not her sympathy. The winter was severe, the wolves ranging near and far in search of food. Some of our neighbors lost stock to them. We were also wary of two-legged wolves from the north. Scalp Point and Ticonderoga were only a few days' journey away and at any time, the Indians might come down upon us. From what we heard of the news, Billy Eyre, commanding at Lake George, had gone through with Johnson's plans for disbanding our army, sending most of the men home.

There were some Indian scares over the winter, not all the reports were false, some small farms in outlying places, mostly north of Saratoga, got burned out, people killed or taken away. My rifle was always near to hand and I kept a musket pistol and knife in my belt always. As far south as we were, hostile activity was at a minimum, though we kept a vigilant watch upon the countryside. I never trusted when things were quiet and I helped organize our closest farmers into a local militia. Every day through the winter, in fair weather and foul, a few of us patrolled the area and met to report our findings. At the first sign of danger, all of us were to meet at the river and take boats moored there to Albany. We saw scant sign of hostiles. When trouble doesn't come, there is the tendency to relax. These are the most dangerous times. We did occasionally see sign of a lone Indian or two but as often as not they were Mohawks. I met sometimes with a wider circle of men, at a tavern on the Vlatche, to discuss military affairs and to gain a broader perspective.

One night at Pop's tavern, we learned the British were sending an army over to replace the one Braddock had lost. The army was already on its way and within a month's time would be arriving. Good news, except the soldiers, upon arrival and before the campaigning season began, were to be boarded with and at the expense of, the private citizens of the colonies. We were incensed at this development, the grumbling everywhere was ferocious, it seemed to be the only thing anyone wanted to talk about. The passions raised were easily as strong as those raised by the French troubles. "Feeding them damn lobsterbacks all winter," a man said, "is just fattening the hogs for the butchering." His point was well taken. Most of our colonists had barely enough food for their own families, or claimed so, and now they had to feed strangers who would lay about all day and expect to be given the best and the most at the supper table.

"Their hair will be groomed thick for hangin' on scalp poles to the north, come winter next," a man said. "For surely it will be their end."

"Hide your daughters," another man said.

Everyone agreed, for anything other than garrison duty, the lobsterbacks were useless. In the forests and on the rivers, we had seen their unfitness. "Damn the British!" a man in the common room said, banging his tankard of flip on the table. When the enemy was upon us, we figured the redcoats would be little enough help.

The grumbling about this and all the other vexing problems often kept the taverns open late into the night. In these times, when armies gathered and dangers abounded, the tavern-keepers profited. Men often spoke of their prowess and I recalled an observation of my father, who had fought at sea. Those who bragged the loudest were the first to shirk when the lead started flying. It was the quiet ones who did the work. My own experiences told me there was no bragging to be done. Surviving a battle was the same as winning at cards, the luck of the draw.

Soon, the matter of quartering troops came to pass. First came word of the British having landed in New York. Then the officers arrived in and around Albany. They ignored the pleas and cussing of the locals and assigned lodgings for the troops. Then came the non-commissioned officers with lists in their hands, then the men. They were boarded in New York Town and up the river as far as Albany. We were far enough out to be spared a lodger but from what we saw of these soldiers, they were uncouth even by our frontier standards, not the best of English society. Their fighting skills were lacking as well; they got pummeled in brawls in every saloon and along every dusty street in New York Colony. We understood the soldiers were for the general good, for England and the colonies but folks deeply resented the extra place at the table and it was all worsened by British imperiousness which grated on the nerves of the colonists. All of which benefitted nobody, except the French.

One lobsterback boarder, at least, found out he wouldn't be spending the winter months lazing about, as he had maybe anticipated. This was the private with the misfortune, or good fortune, to get assigned to Pops' tavern. Men told me how the first day the man came in and sat down by the fire and demanded a drink, Pops kicked the chair out from under him, lifted him up off the floor by his collar and held onto him whilst Mother presented him with a mop and a pail. I saw the man on our trips to town, he working hard in the tavern, either out of fear of Pops or maybe because Pops and Mother, whilst demanding much of him, also made sure he was the best fed of any of 'em. Some others, eatin' no better than dogs, were, I think, envious.

****

Mother hoped my marriage would put an end to my forays to the north and I wasn't sure whether she was wrong. At her urging, I suspect, Pops began badgering me again about taking over the tavern. He was making plenty of money but his age was starting to tell. He was weary from having worked hard his entire life, first as a lad on a Dutch farm, then as a bosun in the Dutch navy, and for most of his life as the face of the Full Sail Tavern. He was still man enough to use his fists, or, as often, the threat of his fists, to quell any trouble in the tavern but I think he was tired of having to put out all the fools who, deep in their cups, felt as if they could make a name for themselves by whipping the old Dutch barkeep. I encouraged Pops to sell, just not to me. No way would I get into the rum trade. He and Mother had enough money saved for them to live their old age in all the crude comforts Albany could offer. He said he could not quit with all those thirsty soldiers and with business as good as it was. He only promised to think more seriously about it once the troubles were past and business slowed. I doubted he would. Work was all he knew.

The winter was a cold one, which reminded me of past winters at my cabin, and as devoted as I was to Monie, it was a difficult adjustment for me, to winter so close to Albany. Thoughts of the north began creeping in, those deep, silent forests blanketed with snow, the fresher snow weighing heavily on the evergreens, the only sound the thud of the white stuff falling from the branches, the branches snapping in the cold north wind. It helped me to talk about it with Monie, and although my yearning I tried to disguise, she must have known by the intensity with which I spoke of the beauty of the country, the deep clear mountain lakes, the high peaks, the trackless forests. How a man must read the clouds to anticipate the weather and read as well the signs in the snow and mud, the passage of every living thing. I told her of the richness of the land, the incredible lushness.

Monie had nightmares, about Indians, I was sure, although she would never say so, for sometimes at night she would get up out of our bed and go to the door, to assure herself the thick iron bolts were secured. Still, and despite her fears and usually as we sat in our rockers before the fire drinking hot rum or lay comfortably in bed, she'd ask to hear about the

Indians. I would try to put her off it but she'd insist and I could tell she was conflicted, same as so many of the folks who never saw the hostiles up close, repulsed and yet fascinated, afraid to hear it and wanting very much to hear it. Same as she felt about the wolves, except without the sympathy. She'd get up so incredibly close. Her eyes would shine with the excitement of the telling, it was as if she wanted to experience it, although I knew she didn't, and I was adamant she never would.

She was anxious to see Paradise Valley, to go there to live, but for as long as the situation was such, it was impossible, and not just because of the savages but because of the many difficulties. The forests were entirely foreign to her and before I could take her north, I would have to prepare more comforts than what were there now. Perhaps, when the war was over, we could live at the Eagles' Lake. For now, we could only dream of the future and how it should be when it arrived.

Sometimes she'd tell me about life in London, the place of her youth, the crowded city as foreign to me as the emptiness of the woods was to her. She told of people packed close together in firetrap tenements, people working themselves to death whilst others were destitute from a lack of work. And the rampant lawlessness. Thieves of every sort, pick-pockets and grifters, masked highwaymen, and so many places where it was unsafe to venture, especially at night. I marveled to think it was the British Isles which were civilized and yet a man could walk the streets of Albany at night with little fear of trouble. Surely we had crime and just as surely we were no better than they, same as they were no better than we. Monie said it was more than just the abject poverty of so much of the population. It was the hopelessness making 'em different from us. Despite our nearness to danger, nay, to extinction, we knew we might prosper. Men such as my father came to the New World with nothing and by striving, they built comfortable lives for themselves. The people of the Old World, crammed into cities such as London, had no hope for the future, whilst here in the colonies, the future was us.

That winter I spent a lot of time adding to my journals. Monie helped me with the writing, adding many good corrections. Her father had been a clerk in a big firm and same as Mother had done with me when I was a child, Monie's mother had insisted, over the objections of Monie's father, that her two children, both girls, receive at least some education. Monie had taken to it and was able to read, to do cipher and to write in a beautiful hand.

When we would go over my writings, my wife would sometimes

betray a prior familiarity with some of what I had written. I often chided her for having perused the writings before we had met, when she was setting her snares for me. I always left my journals with Eric and with the understanding no one was to see them. I had enemies amongst the Albany politicians and did they know of my writings, they might send the sheriff to confiscate them. Despite these strictures, Monie seemed to know a lot about me and seemed sometimes to be feigning seeing for the first time things I sensed she already knew. I would tease her, saying she had used her feminine wiles to seduce Eric into showing her my journals. She always insisted Eric would never betray my trust, which I didn't doubt. One night before the fire and with the journals spread on the table, Monie bashfully admitted it was Sarah who had unlocked 'em and I smiled to think of the two of them gigglin' and gaspin' like school-girls over my scribblings whilst Eric was busy with his shop.

Though I missed the woods and the fur-gathering, I was happy. Most of my winters had been spent hard at work in the north, this winter was a farmer's winter for me, busy for sure, but with my load lightened by the snow and the cold and the shortened days. The life of a trapper meant terribly hard work through winter and an easing in the summer. Now I was a farmer, it would be long days from spring through fall, sunup to past sundown, and in winter, when a trapper was at his busiest, I had time to rest and to reflect and even to read some of the few books Monie had lugged all the way from London. Truth was, I rather enjoyed my leisure and felt as if I would be sorry when spring came.

My trapline brought every kind of fur except for beaver, the furs of a lesser quality than what I was accustomed to. Monie sometimes joined me in checking the traps. She enjoyed being afield on snowshoes and I enjoyed having her along. Sometimes we went on skis, long slender pieces of varnished wood with upcurved fronts. Useless in deep woods, the skis, when strapped securely to the feet, enabled us to move rapidly and silently through open fields and over good trails. The skis were a hindrance in thick brush; fairly open ground was necessary for their use. They worked best on the ice. When the snow was too deep on the frozen ponds for skates, the skis served admirably. I thought how useful they would be in the North Country for getting around the lakes and ponds.

We were introduced to skis by a family friend, over on a visit from Holland, a nice old fellow who had grown up in the same village as my mother and father. They had not seen Old Hans for years but had kept in contact by post. Hans brought news of home whilst Pops told him of occurrences in the New World. Monie and me went down to Albany and spent a few weeks with Hans, eating and drinking, swapping stories. I told him how what kept a mountain man alive was understanding and observing the world around him. I regaled him with tales of the North Country, how the osprey fished and the eagle robbed him and of the moose in winter, of deer, snakes, bears and most especially, the beaver.

Hans told me about the beaver craze in Europe. Beaver blankets, coats, and even perfumes, but, he said, it was mostly about the hats. Felt hats were such a sign of wealth and fashion, no man of standing would be seen on the street without his elegant beaver hat perched on his head. Here was the other side of the coin, as it were, from my own experience with the critters. I admitted to never really having thought about what happened to my pelts once I laid 'em on the counter at the fur-buyer's shed. My only concern was for the price, I had not considered what it might be about the pelts which fetched such outlandish profits.

I told Hans of the ferocity of the Indians, he marveling at the idea of Stone Age people standing in the way of advancing civilization, and in what I took to be a condescending way, he said as how their ultimate defeat and eradication was inevitable. I was offended at this as it seemed to belittle the efforts of men such as myself. If we were going to win anyway, what need was there for us to risk our hair in the fight? I told him of my late friend Arnold Baldwin who had used to say the same thing about the inevitability of the outcome until a tomahawk blow to the top of his head sent him 'round the bend. Hans saw I was getting hot and apologized, saying inevitable didn't mean it wouldn't come without a heavy price, and thus an argument was avoided.

I explained to Hans the differences between Canadian-born French and those over from Europe and we agreed it was the material support of the French and Canadians making the Indians so indomitable. "Without French backing," I said, "the Indians could not stand against us." Hans was a worldly man and whilst musing on the relationship between the French and Indians, he hit on something I had long contemplated. In their contact with the English and Dutch, the Indians tended toward civilizing, not always to their betterment. It was not always so with the French. For them, the pull seemed often to be in the other direction, with so many of the French abandoning civilization and embracing life in a wigwam. Also not always to their betterment.

The more I told Hans of the north, the more he longed to see it. He would have loved a trip up to the lakes but he was old and it was dangerous. I did take him hunting a few times and when word came of a panther taking sheep and calves somewhere to the west of Albany, Hans and me went out there and after two days hard tracking, I got him into position and he, using my rifle, downed the big cat. We made it into a rug with the head still attached and packed it for Hans to take home with him. This was, I suspect, the highlight of his sojourn in the New World.

One day, as Hans and me returned from hunting and approached the gates of the city, the late-afternoon sky darkened as if for a storm. Hans began to hurry and was puzzled by my lack of urgency and puzzled as well by the single dark cloud which, low in the sky, seemed to be movin' toward us. There came a rush of people through the city gates; the cloud came on with a rustling noise, like a roomful of women's fans working the air on a summer day, only louder. It was a flock of passenger pigeons, unfathomable numbers of the birds, and for the people, it was a carnival atmosphere. Men and boys hurled sticks and there was the boom of buckshot and a cheer as Big Bertha, a homemade blunderbuss built by an Albany blacksmith was rolled out.

Bertha was squat like a mortar, the maw of a stubby black barrel on a platform of wood, and even with her wide mouth gaping skyward, she stood just three-feet tall. Down her gullet was poured a bucket of musket balls, the men gave her a charge and lit her fuse. There was a resounding blast and cheers as multitudes of shot birds plunged out of the sky. The boys ran gleefully from one downed bird to the next and twisted their necks to finish 'em or simply crushed 'em beneath their heels. The girls, little images of their mommas with their lace caps, aprons and stockings, came along behind the boys, filling sacks.

Some of the men had muskets with especially long barrels, and a lively crowd, including Hans and me, gathered around them. The gun barrels required ramrods of unusual length, and loading the guns with powder but without shot and without removing the ramrods and with shouts and wagering around them, the men fired into the flock. The ramrods had sharpened tips and came down laden with skewered birds. The boys ran to retrieve the ramrods, to count and to shout out the numbers of impaled birds. One man managed seven with a single shot and took the prize money collected in a hat.

By the time the cloud had passed and the sun once more shone down, hundreds of the birds had got blasted out of the sky. The folks gathered up all they wanted and with so many birds left to rot in the bloody snow, Hans wondered if such wanton slaughter might someday lead to the birds' extinction. There were six or eight of us still there and we laughed to think we could ever dent the size of the flocks. We took the birds by the hundreds, they came in the millions. There could never be an end to them. That night and for some nights thereafter, we dined on Mother's pigeon pie which Hans declared delicious.

Chapter X – Sodbuster or Bearcat

Spring of the year 1756 and after two years of fighting, England declared war on France. The French reciprocated, the war was on, a war which, men said, would be different from all our earlier wars. Those had been fought over affairs in Europe which spread to America. This time, it was our affairs going in the other direction. Not just to Europe but everywhere, it seemed. This was a world war and would be to the finish.

Pops was still trying to sell the tavern to me, the outlandish price he had put on it not quite so steep now. I refused. I wasn't yet convinced I could become a farmer but farming was better than tavern-keeping.

With the ice broken on the Hudson, our new army went north. The redcoats, who had been fed by the colonists through the winter were out of garrison and on their way to Edward and to our new fort, erected, finally, at the head of Lake George and named William Henry, after two of King George's grandsons.

I worked hard to get ready for the spring planting. There was a piece of land I needed to finish clearing, the beginnings of which I had started in the winter by girdling the big trees. There was a lot to preparing a piece of ground. Cutting down the trees and chopping them up was hard, getting the stumps and roots out of the ground was damn near impossible. In between there was the plowing, the cows needed to be milked every morning and usually again come nightfall, and a hundred other chores. Monie was a city girl and though she worked hard and long, most of the work was too much for her to handle.

Besides clearing the stumps, there were rocks to be removed, some of them very large and lying undiscovered until the plow-blade banged against them. I had a mind to build Monie a stone house for safety and comfort and so I had begun to gather field stones. This greatly increased my workload. Each stone uncovered, big or small, and most were big, had to be moved to the side, to the piles I was making. If the stone was too heavy for lifting and carrying, I used my stone boat.

The stone boat was little more than a wooden sled, a toboggan, 'cept it was entirely flat, no gracefully curved front, and had neither runners nor wheels underneath. It required a man to get into harness and pull with his body, as if he were the mule. It was difficult but the only alternatives were either to lose time switching the mules from one harness to the other and back again or leave the stones until winter, when they could be moved with a sled. Gettin' into the harness was degrading for a mountain man, to hitch himself as if he were a beast of burden, and every time I got myself yoked, I feared the shame of anyone other than Monie seeing me thusly. It was just such a chore I was engaged in when Rogers showed up. He'd been canoeing north out of Albany where he had been recruiting and had decided to stop and see could he recruit me as well. Approaching and seeing I was in my harness, he snuck up and announced his presence with a shout, "They short a mules around here?"

He roared his laughter, I glared. "If I were an Indian," he said, "you'd be staring down at an arrow between your ribs instead of a fool harness." I started to get out of my straps, to go after him, and I got tangled and more angry, which made him laugh all the harder. "No, no, Sodbuster," he said. "Go on with what you be doing." I asked did he care to see did the sodbuster had any fight in him. He clapped me on the shoulder. "Hell no," he said. "I know you for a bearcat, not a sodbuster."

I invited him into the cabin, built up the fire, got out the rum bottle and poured each of us a healthy portion. Monie came in from the brook where she had been washing clothes. I introduced them and she spoke amiably enough but was bold in saying she hoped Rogers wasn't come to take her man away. He said it was hopeless and said he would settle for a little rum and maybe some supper. She laughed and for the entire time Rogers was with us, he said naught in her presence to disparage the life I now led, for which I suppose I was grateful.

Over a fine meal of beef and potatoes and afterward and with the three of us at the table drinking rum, we discoursed over the affairs of the colony. Especially did we lament the latest blow by the French, news of which had arrived not too long before.

A war party had taken and destroyed Fort Bull, our supply depot along the western Mohawk River. A hundred of our men captured and taken off to Canada, huge quantities of valuable supplies intended for our Oswego fort and desperately needed there, were lost. With Fort Bull gone up in smoke, there went with it any hope of victory this year in the western part of the province. Now it might be impossible even to hold the frontier out there.

Rogers told us about the fort the French were building at the mouth of Portage Crick and I imagined the hills and vales around Champlain ringing with the bite of axes felling trees for the sawmill. He said they were calling the fort Carillon, for the water going over the lower falls of Portage Crick which sounded to them like the ringing of bells.

"The fort," Rogers said, "is to be surrounded by a log stockade with bastions of earth on each side. The ramparts of the main walls consist of two parallel walls, ten feet apart, built of the trunks of trees and held together by transverse logs which are dovetailed at both ends, the space between filled with earth and gravel, well-packed." He told us the first of the redoubts, called Lotbiniere, was nearly completed. This was the western-most outwork and would control all passage in and out of the Portage Crick. Rogers said there would be four main bastions, a dry moat and a glacis. This glacis was a sloping ground rising from the moat to the base of the walls which, along with the bastions, would be dressed with thick stone. Rogers said the French were boasting how impregnable Carillon would be, once it was completed.

Me and Rogers grinned at this. Impregnable to the French, maybe, and the British, but not to us. We knew how to beat the place. Rattlesnake Mountain. The promontory where the French had situated their fort might be the proper location from which to control passage along the lake but the chokepoint was the top of Rattlesnake. The fort could not stand against anybody with sense enough to see the strategic value of the hill.

Rogers told us about our own fort, William Henry. Logs had been cut and placed in such a way to ensure the troops inside would be secure against cannons. So men said but neither Rogers nor me believed this, either. William Henry was maybe stout enough to dissuade Indians from attacking but it would not long stand against artillery.

"Only a fool," I said, "would get cooped up inside such a fort as you speak of. A fort where a man can simply wait to get blown up. If there are as many French regulars as you say up there at Ti, there's plenty of cannons, which I reckon them French can move through the woods well enough."

We talked, argued and drank deep into the night. Rogers put a dent in my rum supply. He told of the British generals on their way here to take control of the war and of our seven-thousand men, mostly colonials, garrisoned from Albany to the north. At William Henry, our men were engaged in building the sloops, whaleboats and bateaux which would take them north.

Rogers stayed the night and filled us in on the other news. We had heard many rumors of the activities of the French, about their various armies and parts of armies on the frontiers but Rogers had been out to the western edge of our colony and knew of the situation there. The French were aware of the English intentions and unlike us, they were by no means content to simply wait for the heavy blows to fall. They were taking all possible steps to counter the British. Their forts on the inland sea, the Great Lakes, Frontenac and Niagara, were getting strengthened.

Whilst Monie was over by the fire with her back to me, Rogers said loudly, "After your crops are planted and all else is in order, you maybe can come up and give us a hand." He winked at me when he said this, to let me know he was giving me the opportunity to state for Monie my resolve to stay home. I obliged, said he well knew how I felt about the British. "And I be not overly fond of our colonial officers. Some are competent and some, such as Colonel Williams, rest his soul, are damn good, but no part of the likes of Bill Johnson do I ever want in battle again. Or making any decisions for me. He's alright at the head of wild savages, to speak to them in council and to dance around their fires, but as a leader of white men, he's lacking. I'll never work under him again."

Gradually the talk shifted to General Shirley, whose march to the west last summer, the third of the big expeditions, came to no avail 'cept to slightly supply and strengthen Oswego. Shirley had slated another army for the west this year. "But now it has all changed," Rogers said. Shirley, who Rogers and me thought to be a pretty good commander, had been replaced by a British officer who knew naught of the colonies. Some fancy lord over from England. Rogers said Shirley was no great fighter, "But he is competent and his good sense is trusted by the colonial troops. They are not happy to have lost him." Rogers paused by the glow of the fire. He drew on his pipe whilst I poured us more rum. "Shirley," he said, "does good work in organizing expeditions and in keeping men active and fed once they are in motion. He has the respect of the men and now he is to be replaced. It makes no sense." I could only agree and said as how we could not have taken Louisbourg in the last war without Shirley's leadership.

Monie went off to bed, drawing the curtain around her; Rogers and me stayed up most of the night, quaffing rum and working out the problems of our world as we saw them. Every time one or the other of us threw another log on the fire, Rogers' big face lit up briefly, like a pumpkin in the fire glow. We talked in deep shadows, a rather mysterious and somewhat mystical experience with emotions deeply thought out, sentiments movingly expressed.

I finally went to bed and when I awoke next morning, Rogers was as I had left him, passed out in the rocking chair in front of the fire, beneath the blanket I'd thrown over his shoulders. After breakfast and outside on the doorstep and after Monie had said goodbye to Rogers, he asked me to walk with him a short way. I did, and whilst we went, he again tried to get me joined up. Truthfully, I was interested, but there was so much work, the farm certainly needed attention, and I was far from over my resentments. I had spent all the previous year up north and had to argue to get paid and I wanted no part of British officers who would have me risk my scalp and not pay me for my trouble. Rogers agreed but asked wasn't it all the more reason to go than not. To advise the green British. I was adamant and said, "You know as well as me, or better than me, how those snooty bastards feel about taking advice or even information from a bumpkin." I said I'd rather plow my fields and haul stones. My need was to protect my darling wife, not scout for some fat-assed general who would do naught but blunder through the woods and who would run away at the first sign of a Frenchman or an Indian.

"If you're to be nothing more than a plowboy whilst the rest of us is deciding the fate of the continent," he said, "then yes, by all means get to it." That stung. "By the time them French get done with the redcoats," I said, "the Indians will have a clear road south and I'll be fighting them right here where we be standing." I realized, even as I said this, how I might a been arguing for goin', not stayin'. Rogers seen it too. "When you be ready to come north," he said, "you'll know where to find me. I'll save you a seat by the fire." With that, he was gone.

Rogers had ridiculed me but I think it was because he was envious of the fine woman I had married and maybe even of the life I was makin' for myself, although he must have known on some level how it was the sort of life he could never aspire to or be content with, which might have been the reason for his spite. And what about me? Was I any more suited to be a plowboy than he was?

When I got back to the house, Monie was rattling pans and making more noise than usual for a woman cleaning up the breakfast dishes. She was pouting, and such a headache did I have, I could not deal with her and stayed most all day in bed, the curtain drawn around me. She was stiff toward me for a few days. After her little mad was over, she told me how hearing of Rogers' exploits up around the lakes and knowing how I felt about it and with how much rum me and Rogers had quaffed, she said when Rogers ask me to walk with him and I agreed, she feared she would never see me again. This was ridiculous, of course, but not in her mind. She and I had talked over the winter about the possibility of my going up there. She had never asked me not to go, she was a woman who believed in a man's duty, yet, and having been widowed once by a husband going off to war, she said she could not bear to lose another the same way. I was glad she talked to me about it and I told her I had heard Rogers' arguments before and could not be swayed by them. Which did not mean I didn't think often of Rogers and his men, the tribulations and dangers they endured.

****

The roads to the north were filled with long lines of redcoats heading for Edward, William Henry, and our smaller, scattered posts. Most of the troops went first either to Saratoga or Schenectady and whenever they came our way, Monie and me went out and stood along the Schenectady Road with our neighbors to watch 'em.

Once, what marched past was something I never seen before. Skirt-wearing soldiers blowing into what looked like inflated pig-bladders and which made the most god-awful squealing racket, as if the pigs was still in there. Monie said the skirts were kilts, the squealers were bagpipes, the men were Scottish Highlanders. She said they was sent here by the king on account of the bad blood at home between the Scots and the English, the former having been subjugated by the latter. Sent here so the British wouldn't have to fight 'em over there. The king considered the Scots a bloody nuisance and intended keeping them as far away from his throne as possible. According to Monie and to what I overheard from the Scots themselves, there was plenty of anti-regent bitterness in these men. A friend of mine, there with us, asked me what the Abenakis would make of going against men who wore skirts and powdered wigs. I said they might shake their heads in perplexity but their scalp halloo would ring undiminished through the woods.

Soon we heard how the camps to the north were once again turning into pestial holes. I could vividly recall the horrible smells permeating the camp at Lake George last year. More of our men would sicken and die. Bateaux-loads of the sick were already going south. The command post for the northern army was moved up to Half-Moon.

****

Thus did our summer of '56 go on, with the French active with their armies and raiding parties, and as inured as we were to the daily expectation of bad news, we were unready for the two heavy blows which now fell upon us in the west, the first blow dispensed by the French, the second by ourselves.

First, a French army came down the Saint Lawrence River and captured our Oswego fort. They took seventeen-hundred prisoners and the cannons, which was more than a hundred, and burned the fort and whatever else they couldn't carry back to Canada. Oswego was our sole presence on the Great Lakes, the loss of it meant we could no longer threaten the French supply lines to their more western forts.

Following the surrender, the French refused to allow our men what was called in Europe the Honors of War. This consisted of the defeated men marching out from their fort with flags and drums, a single cannon and shouldered guns, unloaded. The French said we had not shown gallantry sufficient to have earned the honors. This I did not doubt. The British officials so ineptly in charge of the war seemed more disturbed over the loss of the honors than the loss of all them men and cannons.

Whilst this was going on, a British relief column was getting rushed out there, and told the fort had fallen, the commander of the column, Lieutenant-Colonel Dan Webb, without even looking into what might be done about the situation nor sending out scouts to see was the French coming down the Mohawk Valley, which they were not, scurried back to Albany.

Who in the hell's side was Webb on, anyway? This so-called military genius. Who could believe a British army had been turned back without firing a shot. Was there ever a British leader who was both brave and smart? "How," I asked Monie, "could this English nation be so great?" She only shook her head. She loved very much the country of her birth and was embarrassed and troubled by England's inability to conduct a war. Monie said Webb maybe got misled by his scouts, she not meaning to implicate men such as myself but inadvertently putting the blame on us instead of putting it where it belonged.

Webb further shamed himself by burning our fortifications along his retreat, any and all of which might have been useful in forestalling an enemy advance. He also choked the water route with downed trees. Men said Webb was thinking on Braddock's road to the Monongahela which became an avenue of advance for the western Indians. Much later, when it was our men, not the French, who had to clean up Webb's mess, we heard there was plenty of grumbling.

I fully expected there would be trouble for us there in the Vlatche.

The Indians would be emboldened and would raid farther afield. Sure enough, within a few weeks, small raiding parties were sighted to the west of us. Not doing much damage but maybe scouting for bigger parties coming later. Militias were called up by all the northern settlements but the old questions arose again. Who was to pay and who to lead. These questions were debated more hotly than were ways to stop the enemy. With all the squabbling and the lack of money, nothing useful got done. In our own area, we maintained a vigilant watch with patrols out every day.

Scouts sent to Oswego returned with confirmation of the disaster, the corpses of a hundred of our soldiers rotting where they had fallen, everything burned. I never heard tell of any survivors. The loss of Oswego and the subsequent shameful retreat of our relief force created another problem, which too, was most serious. The territory of the more western Iroquois where, according to Indian legend, the Great Spirit, by pressing his hands down on the land, created beautiful blue lakes in long, thin lines, was opened to enemy incursion. Those Iroquois, already refusing to help us, were surely considering going entirely over to the French.

The work of Bill Johnson now came to carry the utmost importance. He was hard-pressed to even keep the Iroquois neutral, he and his Indian agents doing good work in preventing an open break. The situation was dire as more of the Iroquois embraced the French Papists' religion and went to the north. The Iroquois nations thus weakened, the prospect of their helping us was diminished. The neutrality between us and them was an uneasy hostility. They might go entirely over to the other side and if they did, nothing could survive the savagery and terror on this frontier. My contention to Rogers about not needing to go north to fight the enemy would be fulfilled.

I finally told Monie I was moving her to Albany for her own safety and we had a most vicious argument. Following the argument came a few days of her not speaking to me, then she huffily prepared a traveling bag and still without saying anything and without even allowing me to help her with the heavy bag, she got it up and into the wagon and she climbed up and sat there waiting for me, and with the damn mules not even hitched yet. I moved her into the tavern and with all the scouting I was doing around the neighborhood, I was exhausted trying to maintain the farm whilst finding time to get to Albany to see her.

By the middle of August, the mood in Albany was panic. Rumors flew on every wind as to the movement of the enemy. Indians were reported everywhere, and in truth, if they were in all the places they was said to be, we were doomed. There were surely plenty of 'em but the trouble caused by false reports was sometimes greater than the truth of the matter. Many more of the men moved their families away from the frontier. Those who stayed felt the danger closing in with the raids becoming more frequent. Small settlements and outlying cabins were gettin' hit and sometimes lost to the raiders.

I tried to find a man to come out and help with the farm, none would, and in one of my visits, Monie announced she was with child. This should have been a most happy occurrence to be shared between us and I suppose it was, but not without a cloud over it. Her condition had the effect of bolstering her desire to return to the farm. We argued some more but when smallpox struck Albany, I brought her home. I purchased four flintlock pistols and taught her how to use them. I kept them in the house, loaded and primed. I also purchased a flock of geese, the best watchdog known to man. The old gander was so protective of his harem, it was only with trepidation we dared cross the yard. He'd hiss and flap his wings and elongate his neck and snap at any intruders. He could run off a big dog and he once kept a coyote at bay long enough for me to get there and shoot it. And as I bent down to drag the coyote off for skinnin', the damn gander came after me! Any Indians thinking to sneak in on us would get a noisy reception.

The smallpox spread throughout the colony. Many in Albany were stricken. In the camps and forts to the north, soldiers sickened and died and were laid to rest far from home. For a month whilst the pox raged, we stayed away from town and discouraged all visitors. The pox would be too much for Monie in her pregnant condition. I would not take any chances with the life of the wonderful woman I loved so much. Despite our tribulations, she maintained a healthy glow. In my eyes, she was the most beautiful creature on God's bountiful earth. Her face did shine.

Our northern army, already debilitated by the camp sicknesses, was further weakened by the pox. If the French came now in force, as it seemed they might, we could not stop them. Luckily for us, they did not come, for whatever reason. Also lucky was Lord Loudoun instituting a system of inoculations for civilians as well as soldiers. This prevented many more deaths. The pox still spread, more people sickened but with the inoculations most of those affected were able to recover and go on to regain healthy lives.

With Monie once again refusing to move to Albany, I stayed close to home. If trouble came, I was damn sure going to be there to meet it. I spent less time with the militia, which gnawed at my conscience, and more time tending to the farm. I did no hunting and what little fishing I did was in my pond in the yard.

Beginning in the early spring and whenever I could, between my farm chores and my work with the local militia, I had begun working on my stone house. I got much needed advice from a neighbor who had built his own place, and with the threat of raiders abating somewhat, I was able to hire two men to come out to help with the work. One was an older man experienced in working with stone, the other, a younger fellow, was as strong as an ox. They worked in exchange for what little money I could pay and all the food they could eat, which was considerable. In truth, with all the work they did, they earned what they ate. Long days spent hauling stones and setting them into place, a strenuous and precise job to fit the stones just so. I worked sometimes with them, under the tutelage of the older man, and at the end of a day with them, my weariness was more pronounced than on the days when I did my regular farm work. I ached miserably, arms and legs, stomach and back. Monie rubbed the hurt and ache from my body. Her wonderful hands and her liniment, the boiled leaves of the wintergreen and whatever else she put in there, were a great comfort to me.

Chapter XI – Sergeant Tom's Purchased Bride

One day in late September, toward evening and with the last of my winter feed-supply for the stock about moved into the barn, I was in my field closest to the house, getting some hay loaded, when I spied a lone figure standing atop the hill, looking down at me. I jabbed my pitchfork into the hay and picked up my rifle, always close at hand. I jumped off the back of the wagon and from behind cover, I took aim. He had a rifle in his hand and a sack over his shoulder and with how solidly built he was, I thought it might be Rogers, back for another try at getting me joined up. But he wasn't so tall as Rogers, and with the way he stood and even without a uniform, his military posture was unmistakable, his gait, too, as he followed now the road as it came down off the rise. Long years of service stamped a man and it was my friend, British Sergeant Tom O'Brien. Waving my hat, I ran to greet him.

We shook hands and slapped shoulders warmly. He seemed in fine mettle. I laughed as he slugged my chest, hard. I slugged him back but could not get him to flinch, either. "Kenneth," he said. "How are ye lad? Good to see you. How goes the farm?" He was looking over my shoulder at the cabin and outbuildings, the half-erected stone house, the pond, the animals, and unlike Rogers, Tom seemed pleased with all he was seeing. "Heard you be a farmer now with a beautiful wife and with no regard for the woods life ye used to lead." He beamed 'round at my place some more and said he'd laughed when my father told him I was a farmer. Seeing it now, his eyes were lit up and he spoke partly in jest but with the utmost sincerity. "Is she pretty? She must be, if you are not up where the fightin' be." I, just as sincerely, said my greatest pleasure was watching my pregnant wife grow ever more beautiful by the day. I said my heart was filled to overflowing with love and tenderness for her.

He, then, gregarious as always, told me what was going on with him. He was no longer a soldier. "Now I'm a civilian as yourself and looking to become a farmer and settle 'round here and let you teach me the finer points of the work. Had enough of garrisons where naught but trouble exists for me. Enough of where the food is so poor me stomach is hurt so it'll never recover and the pay is bad, the work is hard. Oswego was the end for me, laddie." He shook his head with disbelief and sadness. Said he intended taking a wife and becoming an American farmer. "That way, I will at least know what the bloody hell it t'is I'm eating." His infectious grin was all over his big ruddy face. Tom spread good feelings to all, unless it be a private who had shirked his duty. Whenever his rank demanded it, Tom could be some tough.

"Well, come along," I said. "I'm about finished here. I'll unhitch my mules and we'll have supper and rum." He helped me with the mules, we went inside. I introduced him to Monie. He was gallant, respectful, almost reverential with how he took her hand and kissed it and I saw he was pleased with the woman I had taken. With the rum poured, Monie and Tom talked fondly of home, Dear England, although they were from different parts of the island nation and neither expected to ever go back. Tom told us his twenty-five-year hitch in the army was up and he had decided to get out. He had been with Webb on the fiasco to the west and I could only imagine his fuming when the expedition high-tailed back to Albany. The stink of it was too much in his nostrils as was the lingering regret he bore for not having gone with Braddock into the wilderness back in '55.

"Wi' so many of me friends dying along the Monongahela for their officers making 'em stand in the open and fight when cover was what they needed."

I replied as how he couldn't have done anything to save them and I saw the old temper flash briefly, then he sagged and said without much conviction how he might a done something for at least some of 'em. "And died in the doing," I said and I wondered how the British could win, with their folly knocking the spirit out of such an indomitable fellow as Tom.

For Tom, it had all decided his future. "Laddie," he said. "Our officers is unused to your way of fighting and refuse to learn or to change. The ways of the old country, they are of no use here. I don't ruddy mind to take my fair part in a fight, you know it, but I wanna have a chance a winning or at least surviving. Mark what I be saying. Webb is a coward and a fool and before this is done, plenty more good men will die for it."

"A coward and a fool," I said, "so they'll make him a general."

That was maybe striking too close to Tom's pride, and seeing a slight cringe in him, I turned the drift of the conversation by asking what were his immediate plans. He said he was now forty-years old, having started in the army as a drummer boy at fifteen. He had saved money in the army and was fairly well off and wished to invest in land. He was also intending to start a family. He had written to a cousin in the south of England and sent money to purchase a country girl for a bride. She was on her way and Tom wanted to arrange a home for when she arrived. My father had told him where I was and he had set out from Albany to find me.

I told him I was working hard to finish work on my stone house. It was to be a fortress with stout, thick walls and loopholes for firing and I told him once we were in, he and his wife could have use of our log cabin until they found something. They could use it to gather the things they'd need to set up housekeeping. I had discovered the hard way how expensive it was to acquire a piece of land and put oneself into service to a woman. Quite a change from the days of freewheeling and of necessities only, days when all a man needed was a bearskin, a fire and a bed of spruce boughs. In return for the use of the cabin, Tom could help with the farm work. I had been wanting to hire a man. There was a lot of work to being a farmer. A lot more than I was interested in doing, and in truth, I was not very good at it and felt as if the diligence necessary to my success was waning. Tom could cut and chop wood and tend to the chores on days I was scouting and his would be another gun around, always an important consideration in these times. There was sufficient fodder with what was crammed into the barn and silos to allow him to buy a cow and freshen her up for spring. We would have him a nice little situation by then; he could take his time finding the right place for him and his bride. She would feel better for having a woman from the home country close by and my pregnant wife would have someone to watch over her and to help her through her days of confinement.

That night, Tom and me struck a deal. He'd spend his time with us, learning to be a farmer whilst he awaited his bride. I told him he could sleep in the barn with the hired men or in the cabin, in the loft. If we could complete the stone house before his woman arrived, they could have the cabin. If not, Tom said she would have to wait in Albany until all was in order.

He got to work the next morning, hungover as he was from a long night of drinking, reminiscing and planning out the future. Monie could not believe how hard, nay, how ferociously he attacked whatever chores were to hand. "Stay out of his way," I told her. And when Tom took an interest in the construction of the stone house, my hired men were somewhat miffed with the way he just seemed to take over. Tom and the older man butted heads like two old bulls made to share a pasture and reluctant as I was to intervene, I thought I might have to, to keep the peace. It was the old sarge in Tom, gruff and demanding, but the hired men got over their disgruntlement and took a liking to him. They saw how hard he was willing to work and how much he knew about the building trades. How or where Tom had acquired his knowledge I couldn't say, just there didn't seem to be much about which he wasn't at least somewhat familiar. A truce was reached without my having to intervene and though there were still arguments, the three of them could be heard most nights in the barn, in their cups, singing bawdy songs that made Monie giggle.

****

We heard a most infuriating tale from a ranger who stopped by, and they stopped frequently for knowing Monie would put up a meal for 'em. It seemed one of our militiamen had begun to tell men's fortunes in the barracks. This was as much to pass the time, to amuse bored men, as it was for profit or to predict what might lie ahead, and our men were near to rioting when the British punished the man for this trivial offense by running him through the gauntlet. Sixty British with switches and clubs formed two rows and our man was made to run the narrow lane between the rows. The British laughed and joked whilst thwacking our man and when he came out the other end, he was bloodied and dazed.

It wasn't lost on me how the gauntlet was the traditional entry into Indian torture and the men most likely to get put into it were our rangers. My face flushed, I slammed my fist on the table, our cups jumped. "By thunder!" I said. "If I am ever witness to such as this, I'll knife the first British bastard who raises a switch to strike an American. This I swear."

Monie asked the ranger why the British would punish a man for such a trivial offense. He said punishments were getting handed out for all sorts of offenses and said it weren't so much for the offenses but was a mark of the British determination to remind us of our subordination to them in all things.

I asked the ranger if the British had put any rangers into the gauntlet. He said no, so far as he knew. "If I ever hear of a ranger put through," I said, "Loudoun's scalp will dangle from my belt afore our man reaches the farther end. This too I swear."

Then, and because Tom was across the table from me, I quieted down although I was yet steaming. I questioned from whence the British got the authority to punish us with such outrageousness. Heretofore there'd been maintained an official separation between their troops and ours.

The ranger said the separation had been breached by Loudoun who had decreed our officers, rangers included, were henceforth subordinate to British officers. Officially, any British with a rank of captain or above outranked any of ours. How it was playing out, their rank was in most every instance trumping ours, even were we getting subordinated by British of lesser grades than captain.

I looked angrily at Tom, he grimaced and admitted this was one of the reasons which had prompted him to get out. He had known it was coming and as a sergeant, he knew he'd be tasked with carrying out any and all foul orders and punishments conjured by his officers. Tom said it was an outrage, the ranger said our men were declaring they'd enlisted to fight only under their own officers and were vowing not to remain under these new circumstances. I exploded again by slamming my fist down on the table. "There'll be a mutiny, by God!" I said.

Imagine, with so many soldiers at posts separated by miles of savage-infested wilderness, the British were making an issue of who was to give the orders. Americans weren't the sort to tolerate British discipline. This the British should have known, or maybe they did know and it was their reason for doing it, just as our ranger guest had said. To remind us who was in charge. He said so many of our men was talking of going home, the British might find themselves in the wild without scouts, foragers, teamsters or bateaux-men.

"Do you mean to say," I said, and after thinking about Braddock and his officers who, even as they was getting slaughtered along the Monongahela, had damn near fired on their own colonials for them gettin' into cover behind rocks and trees, "any rat-faced lieutenant out from London could tell Rogers how to conduct his ranging?" The ranger said yes, at least by his understanding of how things now stood. Tom added as how this was not the way most calculated to get Rogers to do his best work. To this I replied as how I wished I could be there the first time a pimply-faced lieutenant countermanded Rogers in the woods.

What else the ranger told us, with lashes getting handed out for the most trivial offenses and with the British knowing the closeness within our ranks for our men coming often from the same families and towns, any and all strokes to be laid upon a man's back were to be administered by his bunkmates. I glared again across the supper table at Tom, a life-long lobsterback who, whilst not blind to the differences between his people and mine, nor to the things which made Americans in all ways more fitted for soldiering in the woods than his British, wisely declined to pursue an argument and instead, spoke with sympathy. He said he hoped the British interference didn't drive Robert Rogers from the service. I said it wouldn't. Rogers' devotion to our cause was spurred by all the Indian horrors he'd seen since he was a boy in New England and he would never leave the war whilst there were French and Indians to kill. Nor for as long as there were newspapers to recount his exploits.

It all brought back to me a conversation I'd had with Bill Johnson some time before. Bill hadn't got along so well with General Shirley. Shirley could be prickly and didn't really get along with anybody, but, Bill said, if there was anything good to be said about Shirley, it was his recognition of the differences between British and American troops. Shirley was English-born but had spent enough of his life in the colonies to have gained a better understanding of us than did those generals and governors who came over for a short time and departed without ever getting to know us. Shirley had always worked to maintain a tenuous separation between our two disparate sides, each fighting in its own way and for the same purpose. Bill said Shirley was in a tough place and with all his political enemies, he could not long avoid their intrigues. Bill said how all the men who had wished Shirley gone would soon enough be wishing him back. Bill turned out to be something of a soothsayer himself as Loudoun was now devoting his time and energy to putting the blame for Oswego on Shirley.

Whilst Shirley made ready to sail off to England to defend himself against charges and with Loudoun resolute in his determination to subordinate us, a mutiny was brewing. A New England officer in the British army by the name of John Winslow tried to mediate. Winslow laid out to Loudoun the reasons why the integration of the two allies, for we Americans were becoming more ally than adjunct, should be rescinded. Loudoun was unmoved by Winslow's arguments and when the matter was referred to king and council, they were as implacable as Loudoun, even going so far as to goad Winslow to declare mutiny or not. He did not, thank God, and through his patience, a compromise was forged. Not a satisfactory compromise as it only somewhat mitigated the standing orders without nullifying them but it did at least prevent a break between us and the British, which might a been the end of us all. Our men bitterly assailed Winslow when they might better have thanked him. Distasteful as it was, it was surely better to bury our feelings for the British at least for as long as the French threatened to swoop down from the north.

When the news came Shirley had been sent in disgrace to England, I agreed with one of my neighbors who said some of the charges might have had validity. Shirley was no saint, but the main charges, that it was Shirley, not Loudoun, who was to blame for Oswego, and the other even more outrageous charge, that Shirley's coddling of our colonial troops was a plot to build an army loyal to himself, was preposterous. Even men who disliked Shirley shook their heads at this and at the news the British had made a spectacle by draping Shirley in chains when they arrested him and put him aboard a ship bound for England.

****

I helped on the new house when I could and progress was rapid. We were about ready to move in when it came time for Tom to go to New York and meet the ship with his bride on board. Whilst he was gone, we finished preparing the cabin. We laid in what extra things we had and I put up a supply of wood. Then we waited, and finally, in late October, when Tom and his woman stepped off the sloop from New York, we were all there to greet her; Monie and me, Pops and Mother, Eric and Sarah. Her name was Jane, a pretty girl of medium years and build, long brown hair and with a bit of an Irish look to her features. We celebrated their wedding with a dinner at the tavern, then Tom brought her home.

She was greatly troubled and I couldn't help but pity her. She was from a middling-size city, not a girl of the country. New York and then Albany had seemed provincial enough to frighten her and now she was to be dropped into an isolated clearing in the middle of the vast American wilds. Tom told us how, as the sloop bringing them up from the city made its way along the river with its banks of immense spreading trees overlaid with meshes of vines and wild grape, a shadowy wilderness unbroken except for the occasional riparian hamlet or clearing of the patroons, she asked, nay, begged to get sent back to England.

Jane's first few days at the farm, she refused to come out of the cabin. Monie finally went in and talked to her, to allay her fears and to explain the workings of the farm. Jane listened, just she was unsure and scared. Poor child, she did seem well disposed toward Tom, he was devoted to her, but the grit necessary for life in the wilds, so different from the city, eluded and repulsed her. Still, she tried. Maybe she felt there was no getting out, but with Monie showing her all the things she, Monie, had learned for herself, not so long ago, and with her patient words and kindnesses, Jane settled as best she could into frontier life.

There was still plenty of work to be done before winter, which gave Jane little enough time to sulk. Tom and me worked long days and did some hunting, bringing home ducks and turkeys, deer, and a bear which I shot and which we dragged many a mile and which nearly, when we got it home, caused poor Jane to faint. The women dug the last of the potatoes and gathered the squash and the rest of the garden bounty. Tom and Jane went to Albany and came home with a new wagon filled with goods and pulled by a team of horses.

Monie's obvious love of our wild country never really caught on with Jane but Jane was a good sort and began to come around. Fortunately, there were no Indian scares and she could adjust without having to be all the time looking out for hostiles. We purposely avoided talk of them when she was present but it was impossible to keep her entirely removed from it, especially with small raiding parties hitting outlying cabins, killing, looting, carrying off the settlers. Where we were located, near the river and with Albany and Schenectady both nearby and with our Mohawks to the west and yet attached to us, thanks to Bill Johnson, we was fairly safe. Tom and me prowled the vicinity most every day for sign and found naught but the occasional skulkers. We spooked around the farm each night before retiring, but trouble, at least so far, had stayed away from our doors. The presence of my geese probably had an effect. Sneaking hostiles, seeing the honkers from a distance would veer off for knowing they could not get in on us unawares.

Inevitably, Jane began to hear more talk of the dread savages and she became obsessed with a surety they would one day come for her. Tom bought a pair of flintlock pistols and taught her how to use them, which she did, dutifully, but which only increased her fears. The idea of a civilized woman having to defend herself in this way was repugnant to her.

In late November, up the road came four-hundred British regulars who looked very cold without overcoats in the raw wind. They were to take over garrison duties at William Henry. Knowing her army was out there to protect her served to make Jane feel better. She didn't see how the Indians could be much trouble, with her countrymen watching the frontier. Neither Tom nor me told her the difference, better to let it go. If she felt safe with the redcoats up there, fine. I sure as hell didn't.

Riding along with the soldiers, gracing them as well as us with the sight of him was none other than Lord Loudoun. Sitting high atop a big horse and looking unfit for wherever he was headed. He who quartered troops on us wore a fancy uniform with gold lace on the shoulders of his coat and a powdered wig on his head. What else he wore was a scowl for our silence and for our looking down as he went past. He had come expecting we would cheer for him.

One day, Tom and me came home with puppies. Mine was the runt of the litter, a mongrel with an exuberance for everything. He was black with some white on his chest and reminded me of my faithful old dog of my youth, Blackie, with whom I had roamed the North Country. Me and Blackie had trapped beavers, hunted deer and the occasional moose, fought a war and mostly just lived the free life of the mountains. That old dog had been gone for many years and with how he loved running with the packs which sometimes got into the sheep around Albany, I couldn't much blame the herder who shot him.

I had trained Blackie to be a scout dog, to give warning in the Indian way, without barking. One bark in the woods at the wrong time could give away a position and spell disaster. The pups we would train not as woods-runners but as extra watchers around the farm. To stay in the yard and bark loud and long at the approach of danger, which was their natural inclination. We didn't have to teach the pups to give a wide berth to the old goose, he was clearly the boss around the yard and he let them know it, although they thought it great fun to bedevil him with nips at his behind.

****

The imperious Lord Loudoun announced the British regulars would spend another winter billeted by the private citizens of the colony. This created an uproar, the colonists well remembering having struggled last winter with all those extra useless mouths to feed. No one was eager to have the indolent soldiers with their gargantuan appetites foisted once more upon them. For us, well outside the gates of Albany, we were again not required to house our British masters, but oh! How those old Dutch burghers and dames in and around Albany did howl! The public arguments were long and loud, our colonial officials were very insulting to the British authorities, there was talk of open rebellion. I heard many a Dutchman say how it might be better to join the French and drive out the British, which talk was not serious but showed the extent to which feelings ran.

Through the winter of 1756 into '57, the rumors of Indian incursions were frequent, the savages were even reported at the gates of Albany. Small raids were impossible to stop, snowstorms often covered enemy sign and frustrated pursuit. From Scalp Point and Ti, the Indians were close enough to hit anywhere and be gone before our militia could get after 'em. We heard of deadly raids along the New England and Pennsylvania frontiers. Those poor folks suffered even more than us. Entire settlements burned, the citizens butchered and marched off to slavery in the north.

****

In early December, my son was born, Augustus Daniel, a fine healthy lad, lungs full of noise, and my proud wife and me began a new phase of our lives. The babe demanded a large amount of her time and seemed to me for a while to separate us, in a certain subtle sense to get between us. I suppose I was somewhat jealous of this diversion of her attention.

The times was hard, but we had sufficient food and the house was comfortable and warm. The wind blew, prodigious amounts of snow fell, the smallpox revisited our area. The inoculations Lord Loudoun had forced on the people served now to save many lives. As before, a large number of folks sickened but only a small portion died. About this time, on a day when the babe was doing his worst to keep us paying attention to him, making it impossible to think or sleep, there came a banging on the door; Rogers and his brother. They had just been cleared to raise the rangers' strength to seven full companies and they wanted me to take one of the commands. Richard Rogers, Stark, Spikeman, Kennedy and Parker were company leaders so far. These were men I had worked with, men good and true. Brave to a fault, inured to privation, able to manage any situation which might come up in the woods. It would be good to be in the company of such men. Still I held out, not wanting to be in a position whereby I could be ordered around by British officers. Their rank still took precedence over ours and from all I had heard, the British were exerting a powerful influence even on ranger operations, which sometimes put our men into situations of dire jeopardy. Did I accept a commission and get interfered with by an imbecile Britisher and did I tell him to shut his damn fool mouth or did I shut it for him, I would become a part of their unduly harsh military discipline. No, sir! I wasn't going to take orders from a pimply-faced lieutenant what didn't know nothing about the woods. I told Rogers I would only consider going as an independent scout, same as always, and not subject to the discipline which was getting many good men flogged. In truth, Rogers knew my feelings, he just couldn't resist asking me.

Rogers and his brother had been active all winter up around the lakes and they spoke of it with fervor and delight. Spooking the French forts, grabbing prisoners, though they admitted a lot of their success was due to French contempt of the English. This, they said, was changing with the French beginning to feel a heightened wariness for our rangers. With all of what Rogers and his men were doing, our losses had been severe and cumulative. Sickness and the extreme cold and hardship had opened gaps in the ranks which would be even harder to fill with the planned increase in the size of the force. According to Rogers, the French were moving large amounts of supplies down to Scalp Point from Canada, a sure indication our theater would be the scene of action this year. The illustrious French general, Louis Joseph de Montcalm-Grozon, Marquis de Montcalm de Saint Veran, the name and title rolling with smooth derisiveness off Rogers' tongue, for Rogers was fluent in the French language, was coming our way. Rogers, despite his mockery of name and title, said this Montcalm was a damn fine soldier, active and aggressive. It was he who had captured Oswego and if he was intending to come up the lakes and attack in force, we would be in for it when the weather broke.

Listening to all of what was gettin' said by Rogers and his brother, I felt I should go with them and I might have, except mid-winter was a time for Indian raids. There was no telling when a party might descend upon us on the Vlatche and so and despite Rogers' persistence, I stayed right where I was. I had a wife and a fine screaming baby boy, both of whom I didn't intend losing. Rogers tried enticing me with the news he was organizing a winter raid on the sawmill at Ti. He remarked, when Monie was out of earshot, how my little boy made plenty of noise and nasty messes and how the crying would drive me out of the house and up to the north. Given time, he was confident I'd be more willing to go.

Tom and Jane joined us and when I introduced Rogers and Tom and when Rogers learned Tom was no longer a redcoat, Rogers eagerly tried recruiting him. Blanch had told Rogers about Tom, a rare Britisher who could find his way around the woods. Blanch said if Tom were still alive and did Rogers ever run into him, he should get him joined up. Rogers tried, Tom shook his head, said his soldiering days were behind him.

Monie and Jane laid on a lavish supper, which the Rogers brothers were unused to of late and after dinner we had our rum and all of us at the table did what we did best and most often; we railed against the British. After a time, we got onto our colonial government. Ensconced in New York, a hundred miles from the war, our leaders showed no appreciation for the problems faced by our front-line soldiers and provided little in the way of pay and supplies.

Next morning we said our goodbyes. Monie and me, Tom and Jane all waving from shore as the brothers set out along the Mohawk River, toward Half-Moon and the north. Thus did I miss getting shot in a bad winter skirmish the rangers had up at Ti, in the Trout Brook Valley.

They engaged a large force of French and Indians, the fight lasting for several hours, and when it was over, nearly twenty rangers lay dead, their blood staining the freshly fallen blanket of snow. Amongst the dead were Kennedy and Spikeman. Half as many were wounded, others got hauled off as captives. Those what got out had naught but praise for Rogers. To a man they said only through his indomitable skills did any of ours escape.

One ranger, Thomas Martin, badly wounded and left for dead, came to and found himself alone on the field. Night was falling and with it the temperature plunged alarmingly. Martin, putting his gloved hands in the tracks left by our whipped and retreating rangers, crawled down to the Lake George shore. Getting there after dark and with the rangers gone and the Indians prowling, Martin made his way along the ice in the dark, still crawling, still placing his gloved hands in the footprints. By morning, this intrepid man had crawled many miles through icy winds and another snowfall which began late in the night. He was finally seen by a ranger patrol on the lookout for survivors. They first saw him as a dark spot on the ice and were cautious for fear of a trap. The inspiring saga of this man got written up in the newspapers and went some toward reviving our spirits. I met Thomas sometime later at a ranger camp. He was a tough bird and laughingly vowed to live to a ripe old age, he being but sixteen-years old at the time of his ordeal.

Another ranger named Thomas, Thomas Brown, got taken captive by the Indians and journeyed with them as far west as the Mississippi River. After many a harrowing adventure, Brown reached Albany and published a pamphlet vividly describing his captivity and escape and his fantastic adventures along the way. The pamphlet was a sensation and provided him with a tidy sum of well-earned cash.

Amongst the tales he related was an encounter with a pair of wooly mammoths, a momma and a babe. Mammoths, known by everyone from picture books, were elephants fitted with shaggy coats for survival in the north. As sketched by Brown in his pamphlet, the mammoths were taller than a moose and had feet and legs to trample a man and tusks to hurl said man to his death. Brown, half out of his mind with starvation and with just a crude spear, eluded momma long enough to slay the babe and eat a portion of it.

I once attended a public debate with Brown on one side and one of our learned men on the other. The latter said as how Brown could not have encountered the mammoths for the great beasts, even were they more than figments of the red men's legends, lived much farther west than Brown or any white man had ever gone. The learned man said it was something Brown put into his pamphlet so's to sell more copies. Brown, for his part, swore it was true and the crowd which had come to hear the debate, clearly with Brown, cheered mightily for him and cat-called the learned man.

What else came out of the battle was livid French condemnation of Rogers for having cut the throats of his prisoners when he retreated. Rogers defended this action by saying he regretted having done it but said he'd had no choice. He couldn't take the French along in his retreat and couldn't leave 'em for how much they knew about the weakness of his force. For this action, I did not fault Rogers. "Law of the woods, bucko," as old Hugh McChesney always used to say.

When news came to us of the battle and of Rogers being wounded, Tom and me made a trip up to Edward to see him. When we arrived, Rogers was nearly over his wounds but was very sick. He'd been hit twice, grazed on the forehead and shot through the hand, and in a weakened condition, he had contracted smallpox. This left him debilitated until spring, unable to perform his duties. Tom and me stayed but a short time. As soon as we heard there was smallpox, we departed and no more than a month after, we got word of a near catastrophe, which, had the French pulled it off, might have been the end of us.

It was an occurrence at William Henry, a tale spooky enough and made more so by our hearing of it on a winter's night whilst wind and wolves howled outside. The fort garrison was depleted, with most of the men having been granted winter furloughs. An alert sentry on the walls saw a pinpoint of light along the darkened west shore of the lake. Most sentries would have assumed it was men absent from the fort for one reason or another and would have ignored it. Instead, the alarm bells clanged and the entire garrison was roused from sleep. The men cursed the idiocy of it and called for whoever was out there to get the hell in so they could go back to bed. Even when the firelight which had alerted the sentry was extinguished, the fort commander would not allow the men to stand down and instead kept 'em all night on the walls. Come first light, our commander called out, saying he knowed the French were out there, although this he didn't know, for he was bluffing. As it was, and with our men cat-calling for the French and Indians to show themselves, fifty of 'em came out of the woods and onto the iced lake. They dared our garrison to come out and fight and some of our men, incensed by the taunts getting thrown at 'em, demanded they be allowed to go. Our officers wisely refused for knowing there were more French and Indians than what they were seeing. Thus thwarted and convinced we were not coming, the others of the French and Indians showed themselves. A thousand men. They set fire to our outbuildings and our boats too, which were pulled up on the shore, and after they had departed, our men found hundreds of crude woodland ladders in the woods.

We were somber, thinking on it. If not for the alertness of a single sentry and had not some few of the hidden war party got cold feet and built a fire, the enemy might have snuck up on the fort and got in with them ladders whilst our men were still to bed. Our entire garrison might have got massacred. The French officers surely gnashed their teeth for losing what might have been a great victory but they at least showed a willingness to take risks.

****

The smallpox raged most of the winter; fortunately, everyone around my house stayed healthy. Tom and me hunted and watched the forests for Indian sign. We cut down trees to clear more land for planting and spent evenings in the company of our wives, us men repairing harnesses and sharpening tools whilst the women mended and sewed. We acquired a young bull for use as a stud and soon all our cows were freshened.

When the ducks and geese began coming back to the north on their annual run to the summer feeding grounds, we took to the marshes and cornfields and filled our tables to overflowing with the tasty fowl. This was more to my liking than splitting and stacking firewood. With so much wood needed to get our two households through the winter, Tom and me spent most of our days at this most tedious of chores.

We had some time for sport, mostly shooting at the wild birds when they passed over. Tom never ceased to wonder how I could hit a pigeon or duck on the fly with bow and arrow. He tried but mostly he wasted arrows. I kept a constant supply, the arrows made specially for the hunt. Sometimes, when we went out, my wife joined us with the babe on an Indian-style backboard. Monie loved her days outdoors but it presented Jane with a stark choice. Stay home alone or tramp the terrifying woods.

The wintery feel of the cold was not yet out of the ground or the air, but it was warming and soon after and with the days getting longer, the ice went out of the Hudson and the shad run began. We took enough of the tasty fish to salt down barrels for the army, which paid lucratively, and to keep some for ourselves. I made more money peddling fish than I did with trapping around the Vlatche.

With so many bateaux, whaleboats and schooners needed for taking supplies to the north and with all the unloading and reloading at all the carries along the way, the British began improving the road from Albany to Edward. Heretofore crude in most places, the much-improved road facilitated the movement of supplies and provided opportunities for the local men. Tom got work hauling freight for the army. He'd ferry his wagon across the Mohawk River to the north shore and make his hauls from the lower portage at Half-Moon up to Stillwater and sometimes all the way to Edward. This kept him away from home days at a time, which greatly displeased his wife but the profits kept 'em in comfort.

He was home between hauls when his wife announced she was with child. It was late March and I'm not sure if these things are contagious or not, but shortly after, my wife said she too was once again pregnant.

Chapter XII – The Red Whirlwind

Spring of '57, it had been a year and more since I came down from Johnson's camp and married Monie. How my life had changed in the time. If only we could win this terrible war. Monie and me could move up to the Eagles' Lake, build ourselves a proper home and live in peace with our surroundings. Hope was all I had and I was feeling guilty, I suppose, for not having helped to win the war for some time. It was hard knowing someone was fighting my battles for me. I didn't like the idea too much. Tom and me talked about these things and decided there was naught for us except to get the fields ready for the spring planting. When the soil was dry enough, we put in our crops, wheat and corn, and with vegetables in the patches close to the house and mostly tended by the women. We shot plenty of partridge, they were thick in the fields, eating our new seed. Then the flocks of pigeons came, headed north. Stones hurled into the sky brought down more than we could eat of the winged delicacies. Not so easy to keep them out of the newly planted fields or to avoid their excretions, which fell like blizzards of snow.

In May, the first detachments of the British army came marching and floating their way up to the northern forts, on their way to take Ti and Scalp Point. We stood along the road as they went past with their drums beating, bagpipes blowing, flags a flyin'. Monie called them the Flower of Europe. I had a different name for them. So proud they looked to her, red coats shining in the bright sunlight, the gorgets and gold badges of the officers gleaming. So foolish looking to me. Did they never learn? Had they forgotten so soon the fate of Braddock and of so many of their illustrious generals? The vaunted redcoats going off to get themselves soundly whipped again. Monica and me had some bad moments whenever I spoke thusly. She was loyal to the British army, as were Tom and Jane, the British spit and polish were of considerable pride to my wife and friends. Whenever I denigrated the British, it upset Monie and Jane and an argument ensued. Thus, and in the interest of harmony, I learned to stay silent. Of course, I wished the army every success, they were a brave bunch, to wear those bright coats in the woods, and valiant to a fault. I could not help think how the wolves of doom to the north would be sharpening their knives in anticipation of the scalps to be had again this year. There would be plenty of dancing and bragging in the lodges. After the soldiers were gone past and with their attendant baggage trains hours passing, me and Tom would get back to work. There was so much to be done. Fields and stock to tend, tools to sharpen, axles and wheels to grease, storage areas to clean out. Each day, it seemed, more troops, redcoats and provincials, came up the river and along the road. So often did they go by, we stopped going out to see them.

Returning from one of the trips he made for the army, Tom brought alarming news which boded disaster for us. Loudoun had schemed up the idea to attack the French fortress of Louisbourg, eight-hundred miles away, at the mouth of the Saint Lawrence River. In adopting this idea, Loudoun was going to pull most of the regulars away from our northern borders. Loudoun, fool that he was, said we wouldn't suffer for this. In fact, he said, taking away our men would protect us as it would force Montcalm to take his troops to Louisbourg too, to defend it.

Tom and me spent much time in talking this over. He said it was often the way with generals. They saw things in a different light than we did. They saw it in terms of overall strategy, not on a particular locality or aspect and it was sometimes hard for us commoners to make sense of what they was doing until afterward. I said as I didn't care one whit for grand strategies, my only concern was for the trouble which was sure to be brewin' a-plenty right here at home.

None of us could forget how we had taken this Louisbourg once, in the previous war, and the British had given it back to the French at the war's end and now the troops we had fed all winter in expectation of their giving us protection during the campaigning season were to be put on ships for this far-off expedition. Many of our best militia units were to be sent too, and most of our rangers, including Rogers. Our frontiers would be unguarded except for some few regulars and the least of our colonials and with all the squabbling and arguing over money and command, even these were ragged and slow in coming together.

When our soldiers began marching south along our road, we went out to see 'em, same as we had when they'd gone north. Previously, we had cheered. Now and with them going downriver to Albany where they would board sloops for the run to New York, we were angry and sullen. Some of ours hissed and cussed, some threw stones and rotten apples, which disgusted me. One young man got up close and spit into a redcoat's face. The soldier marched on as if the gob dribbling down his cheek weren't there. I went for the spitter, to beat the hell out of him but Monie grabbed me. The youth was with five or six of his cronies and had the crowd with him too. As Monie pulled me away, I told the lad over my shoulder he was damn lucky Sergeant Tom O'Brien was off on one of his wagon hauls.

Our army was gone without having fired a shot. Once they got onto their ships and sailed, who knew whether or not they would return. As useless as the lobsterbacks were in the woods, they might at least have held the forts, their numbers might have discouraged the French from coming down. The departing redcoats took along such colonial troops as seemed the best of the lot, our frontier was left, if not unguarded, then certainly too denuded for any offensive action. Here was certain disaster in the making and sure enough and whilst Loudoun groused from the safety of New York about a lack of cooperation from the colony, we began to hear rumors of a great gathering of Indians around Montreal.

Our rangers, those few not gone off to Canada, confirmed the rumor, the Indian force, now moved down to Ti, was bigger than anything ever before in North America. A thousand Indians and with as many more on the way, some from as far away as the Great Lakes. How much truth there was to this or how much of it was being said because it was what men had predicted, we didn't know.

Mid-July and with so many of our men gone for Louisbourg, the first disaster struck. Three-hundred Jersey Blues on Lake George in whaleboats got attacked and suffered unimaginable casualties. The troop had been split into three parts, the van was taken stealthily by the Indians, who came in their canoes from behind the islands at a place along the lake we called the Sabbath Bay. Swift and silent, the Indians got in on our men with tomahawk, spear and bow and did their deadly work. With the van chopped up, the main body, under a Colonel Parker, entered blindly into the trap and was overwhelmed by a vastly superior force of the red devils. The Indian canoes were too agile for the more ponderous boats of the Blues. The horror of the savage yells and the loss of so many of their boon companions caused the others of the Blues, in their first fight, to panic. They thought only of escape and with so much confusion and fear, the Indians was all over them. Many of our men surrendered whilst others, just as foolish, jumped overboard and got speared like so many fish. The waters of the lake churned red with blood. Less than a third of the men got back to the fort, mostly from the rearguard. The only thing what got any survivors out was the Indians busily chopping up what men they had already. Of those taken, some was tied to trees, tortured and burnt alive. Rangers sent afterward found the mutilated remains. The captured Blues were taken back to Ti, guests of honor at a victory celebration. Or got disbursed deep into the hinterlands for the pleasure and enjoyment of the savages back home. Few of our men survived to tell the tale, but those who escaped and got back to William Henry said how the French made little effort to save 'em from torture or from their fate as slaves. Perhaps there was naught the French could do. Interfering with the Indians' centuries-old custom might have angered 'em sufficiently to cause 'em to go home. Worst about it was how it was just beginning. This summer of 1757 would be the most terrible summer of all.

****

The rangers who spooked the Indian assemblage at Ti reported more Indians arriving every day and said those from the far west were even more savage and wild than the more localized tribes. It would become ever more difficult for Montcalm to maintain control. The very capable marquis, beloved of the redskins, perhaps fearful of losing 'em in a fit of temper, was keeping 'em supplied with rum and with beeves for the roasting, which must have been in prodigious amounts. The ferocity of the wilderness fiends knew no bounds. They raided incessantly around the south end of the lakes and we were powerless to stop them. They raided up to the very gates of Edward where they killed and scalped a dozen or more men and dragged away fresh prisoners for the cook pot.

Feathered missiles from the woods found their marks on the ramparts of the forts, wagons along the roads were ambushed and burned, as were boats on the Hudson between Edward and Albany. Raids on the settlements and on lone cabins increased. With most of our rangers gone off to Louisbourg, those few still with us were scattered along our border and throughout western New England. The hornets from the Scalp Point nest buzzed over there, the raids frightful to hear about. Our rangers could do naught to check the raiding and by mid-summer our presence anywhere, even on the lakes, was scarce.

Then we got news which gave us cause for both hope and dread. First, the hope, the possibility Montcalm's army might be breaking up, or worse for him, devouring itself. The trouble was the enmity between his two factions of Indians, the more civilized eastern tribes, with years of close contact with the white man, and the wilder bucks out of the Ohio country and beyond. Each side disparaged the other; the easterners considered the westerners to be barbarians, the westerners taunted the easterners as no better than the the white man's dogs.

Montcalm brought them all together at the lower falls of the Portage Crick in a grand assemblage and soothed them with promises, roasted oxen and rum. Never in the history of North America had so many red men gathered in one place. One can only marvel at the nerve of the ranger who, disguised as a humble French habitant, walked amongst 'em and got back to tell about it. Montcalm, to keep his Indian factions from ripping into each other, separated them by sending the wilder ones up to the Tongue Mountains.

****

In August came the news we had greatly feared. The French army, more than eight thousand men, including all them Indians, was coming. Their advance was delayed as a consequence of Montcalm having sent his western Indians ahead to the Tongue Mountains. When he got there on his way up, the Indians were hunting the copious rattlesnakes. Hundreds of snakes skinned and eaten and only when the feast was over, the skins packed into bundles, did the Indians consent to advance. Montcalm invested William Henry and whilst our men put up a spirited fight, a call went out for help.

The commander at Edward gathered a relief force to march the fourteen miles to William Henry. I told Tom we should go. He was willing but was dubious about our whipping the French, which I suppose I was too, for the commander at Edward was Webb, the same who, nearing Oswego and getting word it had fallen, had fled so precipitately. Tom said Webb, now a general, didn't have the guts to relieve our beleaguered fortress. Still, we packed the women off to Albany. Jane was thrilled; Monie did not let on how she felt but with her not resisting and with the two of 'em settled into the Full Sail, Tom and me canoed to the north.

****

On the way up to Edward were hundreds of grim-faced men, alone and in groups of two and three and sometimes ten or more, on the road and in boats on the river. As we got in close to Edward, we heard the dull thud of the cannons up at the lake, a sign our men still held out. Webb wasn't ready to move, he saying he didn't yet have the men he needed but with plenty more arriving each day, swelling our ranks and eager for action, the grumbling started. We knew we couldn't afford any more delay. Our first few days at Edward, rangers from out of William

Henry arrived with messages pleading for help. After our third night, nobody got through. We had scouts out as far as they dared go, not far, and they could report little except much sign of hostiles prowling the woods. Tom and me went out one night with the rangers but with so much Indian sign, we turned back and in a few days, the cannons ceased thundering. Silence prevailed, and strain as one might, no sounds were heard from William Henry. Scouts began returning with survivors, all of whom told of French treachery.

The fort's defenders knew there was no hope of relief. This was made clear by Webb's response to a plea from Lieutenant-Colonel Munro, in command of William Henry. After saying there was nothing he could do, Webb, the son-of-a-bitch, wished Munro good luck. With the French artillery pounding him day and night, Munro made what he considered to be honorable terms of surrender. Montcalm guaranteed our people safety as prisoners and began marching them to Edward. The Indians, meantime and dissatisfied with their share of the plunder, had got into the English Milk, the whiskey and rum supply. On fire, they began to chop up the sick and wounded in the hospital. The French were remiss in protecting our men and the situation got rapidly out of hand. With our people trekking down the road toward Edward, unarmed except for some sidearms, the Indians got into 'em and butchery ensued. Here was treachery of a magnitude no man could fathom. Over two-thousand of our people, soldiers, women and children, cut up by the savages. This number of casualties, as first reported, proved to be an exaggeration, though the more accurate number of dead, wounded and taken was substantial. The survivors, as they came in to Edward, told tales of horror and cursed the feeble efforts of Montcalm and his officers to stop the massacre. We had patrols out searching for survivors, our cannons were fired every hour to help guide in any who might be trying to make it in. For days, they came, half crazed with fear and starvation.

Webb, meantime, had collected a sizeable army and our men felt we could go up with a fair chance of success. Webb refused, said he lacked the supplies necessary for a campaign. What he meant was, if he led us up there and blundered into trouble, it'd be another blight on his reputation.

Our men was near to mutiny and cursed Webb more vehemently than they did Montcalm, who was a true fighting general. Men demanded to be released, to go home to protect their own, since nothing was to be done here. Webb had deserters rounded up and flogged. Three or four were hanged. Webb's retreat from Oswego had opened our western frontier to the inroads of the French and now he was opening the northern route as well. Webb had never fired a shot against the enemy, so far as any of us knew, yet he expected men to abide by his decisions. Even with the floggings and hangings, or because of 'em, men departed. How could the British, who dared not venture outside their fort, stop them? By the end of another incredibly confused, fouled-up week, most all the colonials were gone. Luckily for those of us still there, the Indians were all mostly gone too, satisfied or not with their spoils and anxious to get back to their villages to dance out their scalps and boast of their prowess. The French dared not stay without their red allies and thus we were spared further disaster.

The survivors said the French had allowed the massacre to go on unchecked. Indeed, some said it was the French, Montcalm included, who started it. We could well imagine the fate of those who got taken. Running the gauntlet, from which not even women nor children were spared, often resulted in crippling or death and was the prelude to worse inflictions. Those who survived the gauntlet maybe wished they hadn't.

Two young British lieutenants told a tale, the truth of which I cannot verify. The lieutenants were assigned as bodyguards for Lieutenant-Colonel Munro when our people marched out of the fort. In the bedlam of the massacre, the lieutenants witnessed the tragic plight of Munro's two daughters, part of the civilian contingent in the fort. The girls had been claimed by a Huron warrior of some standing in his tribe, who had set out to the north with his captives. Further, the lieutenants said, two of our Mohicans, a father and son, the former a chief, the latter a princeling, and accompanied by a woodsman who, whilst not a ranger, had a near mythical reputation for woods savvy, had gone out to rescue the girls.

Here the stories told by the lieutenants diverged. One said he saw the Huron rip out Munro's heart and eat it, a practice of the Indians when their foe was worthy, which Munro, a stubborn Scotchman, surely was. The other lieutenant claimed to have seen Munro in the company of the scout and the Mohicans, in pursuit of the Huron and the girls.

Many of the men believed one version or the other, it was all repeated over and again, the men calling it a most tragic romance as the girls were said each to possess an alluring beauty and there was said to be a spark between the older girl and the scout and another between the younger girl and the Mohican prince.

As for the Mohicans and the scout, the Mohicans were once a proud and warlike tribe but no longer. They were a broken, scattered remnant, though among them were some very brave men, some even serving in the rangers' ranks, and I had heard over the years of these two Mohicans and their friend, the woodsman, he being a sort of phantom legend along our frontier. A white man raised in a Mohican lodge and who disdained white civilization, never, some said, having set foot in any of our towns. They say there were similarities between him and me. He was a Dutchman as was I, and he too had gained a certain notoriety with friend and foe for the work he did with his rifle. I had at times been mistaken for him, and in my wanderings, he and I had shared an occasional campfire and a meal. For a woodsman, he talked too much.

I cannot say how much of the lieutenants' story I believed; it seemed too fanciful. What I could say, Munro survived the massacre for I saw him sometime later in Albany, a man broken by the loss of his daughters and by what he perceived as Webb's betrayal and Montcalm's treachery. Men said Munro would not last long.

What else we heard, and it brought home to us what race of men we were fighting, some of the Indians, not satisfied with the scalps and loot, and with their blood a boilin', dug up the graves of our men who had died over the summer of the smallpox. One of those was my friend, Richard Rogers. I didn't know whether or not the insidious pox could remain potent in the scalps and in whatever other body parts, clothing and blankets, the fiends came away with, and having seen the horrors of the pox, I could never wish it on a people but it would well serve them did their ghoulish exhumations bring widespread death to their villages.

Tom and me helped to find and bring in survivors of what came to be called the Lake George Massacre. There were plenty of British and colonials, soldiers and civilians in the woods. Many were wounded and for some, the terror of being out there whilst Indians lurked was enough to drive 'em around the bend.

Three daring rangers, rash lads, went up to Ti to see the situation. They came back and reported the French and Indians were feasting on the food and rum taken from William Henry and said the screams of the prisoners went on day and night without surcease. When we heard this from one of Tom's old army friends who had been privy to the report, I thought back to my own nights up on the mountains overlooking Scalp Point and Ticonderoga and hearing the beat of the tom-toms below.

Tom and me stayed at Edward a few more days. Then and as we were under nobody's orders, we decided it was time to go. Nothing was being done to feed us, the fort was fast becoming a pestial hole. It was past time to go home and see to our neighborhood defense. The fall of William Henry could only heighten the possibility of trouble.

We canoed down the Hudson alone, which was a bad idea, and when, two hours downriver, we saw a thick pillar of smoke rising from the eastern shore ahead, Indians burning up a haymow or a cabin, we got in close to the western shore, pulled our paddles out of the water and had a quiet, hurried talk about what we should do. I was for abandoning the canoe and striking overland, away from the river. I was more familiar with the trails than any northern Indians would be and I was fairly sure I could get us safely home. Tom was for staying on the water. He wasn't the best of woodsmen but could get along better than most. We was still talking it over when came the dreaded war whoops and three canoes, each manned by three or four wild-looking Indians, shot onto the water from the other shore, two of the canoes at an angle to cut us off from the front, the other getting in behind us. We plunged our paddles into the water and got out ahead, thwarting their efforts to box us. Some of the Indians were shooting but they were not marksmen, their bullets hitting around us in the choppy waters of the wind-whipped waves. Then those which were firing put down their muskets and picked up their paddles.

We were going like hell, our elm-bark well-built for handling and more than a speed match for the bigger vessels. They were thirty yards behind us and weren't gaining, even were we putting some separation between us. Trouble was, they could outlast us and our only hope was the small riparian stockade which I knew was close ahead. The men there would have seen the smoke and might already be coming to investigate. If they was coming, it had to be soon, for not too long after the pursuit began, Tom began showing signs of fatigue. "Keep goddamn paddling," I said, and as I was behind him in the canoe, I was in readiness to whack him across the back of his shoulders did he falter. He dug in harder and we shot ahead, widening the gap, but when they began gaining, we didn't have to look back to know it. Their jubilant shouts told us. Bullets whistled around us, the Indians in the front of each canoe was firing whilst the others paddled. A musket ball hit our canoe and passed out at the waterline. We began to take on water, which made our canoe more ponderous and difficult to handle. With just one man firing, the others paddling, the Indians were pursuing us with their old tactic, one canoe coming fast to tire us whilst the others held slightly back, then the lead boat eased up and another came shooting across the water. In this way we were constantly pushed by fairly fresh men. Our situation was desperate. We could not last much longer. If help did not come, and if the soldiers in the stockade believed the smoke to be a ruse intended to bring ‘em out and they therefore decided to stay behind their walls, our hair would soon be lifted. If the soldiers weren’t coming, they’d at least be on the ramparts, and if we could get there and get in close, rifle fire from the walls might deter the Indians. Or our deaths might play out in plain view of the men.

I could sense the lead canoe nearly upon us and I risked a backward glance, into the triumphant countenance of a big ugly Indian. Angrily, rashly, I pulled my pistol from my belt and put a bullet between his eyes. The impact knocked him backward into the Indian behind him, their canoe veering, nearly capsizing, and with the other boats having lagged, this gained us some distance but it also brought angry whoops and a surge from the others.

Tom was near to winded, the game was about up when four whale-boats bristling with colonials came ‘round a bend with a few men in the front of each boat shooting, the rest pulling hard on their oars. The red men about-faced and fled. Just as the last canoe was turning, the Indian in the rear, who thus far had only been paddling, lifted his bow, fitted an arrow and fired. There was a terrible thud as the arrow was driven into the back of Tom’s neck and came out his throat, nearly decapitating him. Gushes of blood erupted from his neck and mouth, he slumped and pitched over the side and into the river. The canoe rolled, I kept it upright, wobbling, but poor Tom was gone. Three of the whaleboats went by us in pursuit of the savages, one boat stopped, the men fishing deep for the body with gaff hooks on the slim chance they might snag Tom by his clothing, though the waves and the current worked against their efforts. A round of shots came from upriver. The other boats had got up with the Indians, or were catching up, or had got ambushed. The men what was trying for Tom replaced their gaffs, got back on their oars and pushed on toward where their duty now lay.

I got off the water, my boat was sinking, and I had a notion to sprint up the shore to join in what was, by the receding sounds, a running fight. I’d vent my fury and frustration, but there might be more Indians about, they’d be going to the sounds too, and I had little chance of catching up on foot.

I started for home, bypassing the stockade and overwhelmed with grief for having lost my dear friend, and sick to think of poor Jane, who had come all the way from England to this strange, difficult land and who depended so greatly on Tom's massive strengths. I blamed myself for not having more forcefully insisted we abandon the canoe although I supposed the Indians had already spotted us and it was hard to say iffen we'd have fared any better fleeing on the land than on the water.

I arrived in Albany and when I entered the Full Sail through the back door, Monie was in the kitchen, working alongside Mother. Told them my sad tale. We three went together to where Jane was. By my sudden appearance without Tom and with the look of me, Jane knew before I spoke a word. She closed her eyes and as I began speaking, she shook her head, slowly at first then violently from side to side and with her hair flying, her hands over her ears, as if blocking the sound of me might make it not so. Finally, she looked up and I confirmed her man was gone. She blurted a sob and the tears came. She keened and shook like an Irish banshee, as if her very soul was lettin' go of her body. The wails from so deep inside were terrible to hear; wails for Tom, who I think she had come to love, and for herself, alone now in a strangely hostile world and with a baby coming.

Monie put the grieving woman to bed and prepared hot sassafras tea. Jane refused the tea, refused all offers of comfort. Monie stayed with her, I carried in food, Jane refused to eat or get out of bed. She became feverish. I fetched a doctor but there was little he could do. Something had broken inside of Jane. She miscarried, bled profusely and slipped into a trance-like state of shock, the fever more intensely upon her.

Jane's stillborn was a boy. I hammered together a tiny wooden box for him and with Monie, Pops and Mother walking behind me, I wheeled the box up to the Dutch cemetery where a grave awaited the tragic babe, Little Thomas O'Brien, the name we had carved on the lid of the box.

Jane lingered near death. The doctor came each day for a week and told us Jane was slipping away and without her wanting to live, there was naught he could do. We were resigned to preparing another box and a grave but after a few days, Jane surprised us by opening her eyes. I told her we had buried her babe, she gasped and sobbed, and I was sure we would lose her but she began slowly to get better and behind her grief, I sensed what was perhaps fueling her recovery.

She was seeing a way forward. Despite her affection for Tom and for how much she truly wanted the babe, she had never overcome her abject fear of the land and now there was naught to keep her from returning to

England, which place had grown in her mind into something more than probably what it ever was, or could be. I sensed in her an elation with her prospects. This I resented and she tried to hide from me.

A sad and melancholy affair it was, especially with my own beloved carrying a babe and with the dangers increasing every day around us. Monie cried pitifully for Tom and for Jane and the babe, for everything, it seemed, and I wondered whether Monie too had thoughts of returning to England. She and Jane had become like sisters and had talked so often of raising their babes together and now Jane could only talk of returning across the ocean, which would be a terrible loss to my own wife. I felt helpless, unable to comfort them.

Jane's resolve to never go back to the farm, not even to gather her belongings, had the perverse effect of convincing Monie she needed to go back at once. It was of course out of the question and when I told her I was going without her, we were near to the harvest and I had to get the crops in, we argued bitterly. She cursed and hurled plates and cups at me, this she had never done before. I lashed back, said her stubbornness would only serve to get her killed. Neither of us would budge and it was almost a relief when she stopped talking to me. Mother and Pops bore sad witness to my troubles.

I spoke to Bill Johnson, to see what he could do for Jane, some way for her to earn passage home, for now it was all she talked about. Bill secured her a position at a plantation well to the south of us, almost to New York Town, where she would go as soon as she was strong enough. There would be no Indian danger and she could earn her passage home, or perhaps, in the time it took her to raise the money, she'd reconsider and try life in America over again, just not so close to the frontier.

I went back to the farm and whenever I looked at the empty cabin where our friends had lived, I felt my own despair, and knowing Monie would probably get her way and come back to the farm before it was safe, I resolved to get someone into the cabin. Bring someone out here, as much for defense as to run the place. It would be a help to us in the work and in the matter of defense and in getting us over the loss of our friends. I discussed this with Monie. She agreed and there the matter rested. The harvest season was upon us and I forgot about everything except looking out for Indians and getting the crops in before winter.

Chapter XIII – An Atypical Redcoat

Our frontier did not go up in flames following our terrible defeat. There were plenty of Indian rumors and some raids but I reckoned the butchery at William Henry had sated, if just for a while, the Indian blood lust. Soon enough they would be paying us visits.

I was anxious to get someone into the cabin but I had first to get my crops in. Oats and wheat into the barn; corn, potatoes and squash, all the vegetables from the garden, into bins in the cellar.

I worked from sunup to sundown, day after day, and with the Indian threat much on my mind, I got frustrated with the never-ending amount of work. Frustrated enough so I left the farm one afternoon and walked to Albany and declared to Monie my intention of giving it all up; the farm, the woods-life, all of it. I would buy The Full Sail from Pops and become a tavern-keeper. Monie responded tartly. "Whatever it takes to keep me safely behind the walls of Albany."

She then became fervent in opposition to this latest intention, even admonishing me to not be a coward, for out of our tribulations, a new Monie had emerged. She spoke of revenge for the loss of Tom, who had meant so much to us, and of Jane and the baby. The vehemence with which Monie damned the French and Indians chilled me. She had never spoken this way before. I didn't really like the words or the sentiment. Revenge was never a good motive but her further point, we would not be safe until the French were beaten, was well taken and could not come to pass until all the brave men, namely myself included, went north and settled things. Only when we won the war would the raiding cease. She was tired of living in fear, of looking out and expecting to see Indians emerging from the woods with their bristly headdresses, painted visages and wild yells. Only victory could drive the Indians from our door and if I was serious about hiring a man, or men, to help us work the farm and defend it, I had better get to it. Winter was coming, she wanted to go home and she wouldn't abide a husband who shirked his duty.

She was right! For as long as there was war, the frontiers would not be safe and we could not realize our dream of moving up to the Eagles' Lake. Monie was a tough-minded woman and a realist, and in her heart, she knew I could never be satisfied with myself for as long as others fought my battles for me. "Get yourself up there," she said, her voice trembling with feeling, "and beat those damnable French so we can be free! You know I love you more than life itself and you know what it does to me, to have you up there." Her voice now dropped to a whisper. "But you must end this thing!" Who would ever understand the ways of a woman?

My father and mother knew we had been considering staying permanently in Albany. Mother was hoping I would accede to their wishes and take proprietorship of the tavern. She was thus disappointed when I told her our plans for going home but however she may have felt, she proved helpful when I asked did she know anyone who might be interested in going with us. She said she and Pops had just the right man. Joshua. I waited. Joshua what? Just Joshua. No surname? Mother shook her head. I asked was he Dutch. "Neither Dutch nor English," Mother said, "but a black man out of the South. A man who was once enslaved."

She and Pops were enthusiastic about Joshua and insisted I take him on, if he be willing. They said he had shown up in Albany some months before and was doing odd jobs around town, including work for Pops, a piece of which I had already remarked upon, a most beautiful mahogany top across the bar. I had admitted it was beautiful though I didn't understand why Pops would waste such a fine piece of wood and expert craftsmanship on something for men to spill beer and drool tobacco on, and besides, a clever artisan was not what I was seeking. Pops said Josh was a farmer and was only doing carpentry whilst waiting for a situation.

I agreed to meet with Josh and when he showed up, he came to the back door, not to the front, and entered with his tattered leather cap in his hands. I ushered him toward the common room, to a table where we might talk over supper. He demurred and made it clear he'd have trouble did he go into the front and presume to take a seat among the men.

So we had our supper and our talk in the kitchen and with Mother working around us. Josh, more a deep brown than black, was a tall, lean, slow-talking man, his words well-measured, thought out. He said he'd had a surname, but as it was his master's, he had discarded it and hadn't yet seen the need for another. His was a family of six; his wife Cybil, and the four children. Henry, the oldest, who was early twenties, another boy around fourteen, and twin girls, ages ten or eleven. Josh was unsure of his own age, around forty, he supposed, which made him three or four years older than me. Born into drudgery as a field hand on a plantation, he had developed and utilized his clever skills in woodworking and in so many other areas to purchase first his own freedom, then the freedom of his wife and two oldest children, each in turn. This was most unusual, and yet he told it in an unassuming way, as if it were perfectly natural. He said they all kept in their pockets manumission papers signed by a sheriff down in Tidewater, Virginia Colony. The girls, not born until after the family had bought its freedom, had papers attesting to their status as born of freed persons and so free themselves.

I said as how there might not be room enough in the cabin for such a sizeable brood. Josh said they were accustomed to being squeezed and with my permission, he and the boys could add an extra room before the snows flew.

I warned Josh about the savages; they would be as tough on a black man as a white. He said as how he was no stranger to the frontier, having been taken along by his master when said master had developed lands acquired farther west. Josh said I could maybe instruct them in the use of firearms. I asked how could a man spend time on the frontier without acquiring a familiarity with guns. He said his master hadn't allowed it.

I asked, "How the hell did you defend yourself against Indians?"

He merely shrugged, giving me to know there was much I did not understand about the life of an owned man. I had never been around too many slaves and had never given much thought to how they were made to conduct themselves. Mother always said holding a person as property was a terrible wrong. I suppose I had always agreed, and close up now to such a man, I felt the wrongness keenly.

The more we talked, the more I was convinced Mother and Pops were right about Josh. His wife and daughters could help Monie with her chores and do all the work when Monie slid into such a depression as I had seen lately, when she was incapable of doing anything. My big concern was how taking on an entire family would mean plenty of extra mouths to feed. Josh insisted they could all work the fields, even the twins, and they would produce far more food than they would consume. I said I could use them through the fall, to get in the last of the crops and get up our supply of firewood for the cold months and we'd see afterward. Josh said they were all of them God-fearing and would prefer not to do any work on Sundays. To this I assented, he and his brood packed their few belongings and we all went out to the farm.

****

Josh's wife was of a much darker hue than was he; she was short and husky. The oldest boy was not too tall and was dark and sturdy like his mother; the three younger children looked to grow tall and lean, like their father.

Josh and the boys worked in the fields, the girls took over the vegetable gardens and the kitchen, preparing and storing the food for winter. The twins doted on the babe, thus easing my wife's burden. Cybil and her girls, when it was necessary, did field work too, hard, physical work alongside the men, and when they were all in the fields, they sang joyously in praise of the Lord. I taught them how to shoot. They were terrible shots, worse than Indians, and I wasted a lot of powder and ball trying to get them to hit a mark. Whenever Monie asked how they were coming along with it, I said fine, never letting on and vowing to continue despite whatever frustration I may have felt.

Their eldest son, Henry, at twenty-three, had the habit of eating a fast supper and disappearing afterward. He'd be gone all night and returning just about the time the sun came up, he'd work the fields or cut firewood just as if he'd slept all night. Sometimes it seemed he could hardly keep his eyes open, yet he did his work, instinctually, or so it seemed. Josh and me kidded him about the woman who was putting such a strain on him. He would just grin and say nothing. Through the autumn he never let on who the girl was, making a mystery of sorts out of it. We knew she lived in Albany, friends of mine had seen him going in and out of the gates often enough.

Once the crops were in and with enough firewood cut and stacked and with Josh and his proving every bit as hard working as he had said they would be and them agreeing to stay through the winter, I decided to sojourn up to the north, to see what I might do. The campaigning was over for the year but we had plenty of men up there, newly returned from their failed expedition against Louisbourg. Our attempt on this mighty fortress which guarded the entrance into the Saint Lawrence River and thus into Canada, ended in failure when a hurricane scattered the British fleet which was to take part.

I joined Rogers' Rangers, again as an independent scout, assigned to Richard Rogers' old company, commanded now by John Stark, a good man in a fight, cool and intrepid.

Webb was still at Edward, his army on the improve. The colonial soldiers were more professional in their camp duties and in looking after themselves in the woods, at least in the vicinity of the forts and outposts. This freed up our rangers to go farther afield and in bigger numbers and we got into some nasty skirmishes. We took the enemy hard and more often than not, we came off with plenty of hair.

Some nights on Rattlesnake with the fog rolling in off the lakes and whilst listening to the dull steady roar of the water rushing over the cataracts and through the gorges of Portage Crick, we heard the beat of the tom-toms down at the mighty stone fortress of Ticonderoga. The drums sounded ominous in the blind night. Took a good set of nerves to sit up there. We would stay the night under the big oaks and look out over the valley, always careful to stay off the rock ledges, of which there were many, and the other open areas on the sides of the slopes. Those places were dangerous in the extreme and woe be to all of us if a single man showed himself up there. We were in and out often, in small parties. We watched our enemy closely and harassed their supply lines, often taking prisoners to be sent back south for interrogation.

One day, prowling the shores of Champlain and about ready to head back to Edward, one of our lookouts spied an Indian a way off in the distance, high up in an oak tree. Some of the men, having heard of my prowess with my gun and never having witnessed it, got me around to where we could better see the Indian. He had been watching the lake and was eyeing us now. He must a known we was gettin' around toward him because he began coming slowly down out of the tree. I raised my rifle, this didn't speed him along, he probably figuring I was too distant to plug him. I targeted on him, paused, targeted some more and squeezed the trigger.

Got him!

He tumbled down through the branches and got wedged in the crook of a big bough, his gun clattering to the ground. The men congratulated me, we left the Indian in the tree, arms and legs dangling.

****

With winter approaching, Loudoun announced his troops were once again to be fed by the colonists. Our resentment was loud and bitter. Feeding and quartering the troops which had been ordered away from our defense the previous summer, thus bringing on disaster. In the provincial governments and on the streets, wherever men met, all the talk was anti-British. There was, however, one Britisher who didn't feel our disdain, George Howe.

This Lord Howe, second in command of our northern army and as soon as he arrived, began accompanying the rangers on our scouts. This was not unusual. Plenty of eager young officers oftentimes came along but Howe, though young, was a general, and whilst those others were, with but few exceptions, a burden, Howe was a delight. Those others were contemptuous of us and sought to use us in the same manner as they used their own men, as manservants, by imposing on us, which did little for relations. They were thoroughly Old World; we were perhaps a mite too conscious of our rights as Englishmen.

Not so with Lord Howe. Here was a general who trekked along, eager and delighted to learn the ranger way. He was a welcome bother with all his questions. Rogers' Indian style of warfare was a revelation for a man steeped in the martial traditions of Europe. Rogers reveled in the attention he got for having along such a high-ranking officer.

What else Howe did, and he seemed to have a free hand in arranging things, was to change the way slackers and thieves were punished. Before, it had been with floggings, which only embittered a man, now it was with extra duty, which gave benefits to all. He had the tails cut from the coats of the soldiers and officers, even snipping the first few himself. He got rid of the big two-handed swords favored by the Scots and other useless equipment. The British officers were appalled at this departure from long-standing tradition; Howe cared little for what anyone thought, nor for tradition. He dismissed the officers' protestations and further outraged them in the matter of their personal baggage. Heretofore, much of the goods carried to the north were extras for the use and comfort of the officers. Mere necessaries, like powder and shot, food and medicine, piled up at the depots south of us because the officers' freight, the tables and chairs of the captains and majors, the fancy tea-settings, took precedence. Lord Howe severely cut into this practice. Using himself as an example, he went without his powdered wig and slept on the ground with only a bearskin for cover. The lobsterback officers carped at the indignity and it surely put smiles on the faces of the Americans, except for the bateaux-men and waggoneers who did not see the humor, now there was less money to be made in the hauling of useless freight. Lord Howe proceeded in a cheerful manner, more with exhortation than command, though it was surely commands, and so further endeared himself to all the ranks, even some of the British officers and even as he made their lives more difficult.

More importantly, Lord Howe cleaned up the camps. The sanitation rules were enforced, the troops were made to adhere to a new kind of discipline and slowly, a new confidence began to be felt throughout the army. Never before had there been such as this. Howe's style was infectious; few of the men could resist the new spirit. No longer did the camps stink like slops-ditches, as in Johnson's time. The camps and forts were still a long way from good, such change took time but the newfound pride driving the improvements was nothing our armies had experienced before.

One further thing Howe did, and it had the colonials and even the British howling with laughter. He began taking the dour skirt-men out of their kilts and putting them into pants. The indignant Scots became the butt of many bawdry jokes and verses, of doggerel and song.

****

I scouted around the lakes, usually with just a few rangers and still without any official connection to the army. The French were settled into their winter camps, most of their army was gone back north. Hard to tell just how many soldiers garrisoned Ti and Scalp Point. The Indians were mostly gone too, as were nearly all the Canadians so they'd not be undertaking any real offensive action. Except for raids of smaller proportion, there would be little trouble from them until spring.

The peasants who had been settled around were, in accordance with the usual winter practice, taken away, their huts and stone dwellings boarded up. Activity mostly involved moving supplies from one place to another, all their wagon trains were heavily armed and protected. I stayed around until the end of November, trekking back and forth between Edward and the lakes, and with not enough Indian activity to keep my attention, I went home for a longer stay.

Soon after I got home, we got news of a fresh disaster. A ways to the west of Schenectady was a settlement of German immigrants, the place known as German Flats. There was bad feeling between the Germans and their near neighbors, who were of English stock, mostly from New England. When Montcalm had come down to attack William Henry, he tried taking advantage of the enmity, his agents seeking to distract us by engaging the Germans against their neighbors. The Germans weren't interested and now the French were back for revenge. More than three-hundred raiders came out of the forests in the middle of a night and even though the settlers had been warned of the coming attack days earlier by the local Iroquois, and even with five blockhouses, five! the Germans were ill-prepared. Many did manage to reach the blockhouses but once inside and when the raiders demanded they surrender, the settlers came out. Fifty of 'em brutally murdered after they'd surrendered, many more taken away as prisoners, houses and barns torched, an untold amount of loot taken, the Germans being prosperous farmers.

The captives were taken on a heartbreaking trek to the north, which always took a heavy toll of the young and the very old. Lord Howe, who by chance was in Albany at the time, rushed up the river with a force of five-hundred regulars and colonials. They came along the road past my place and I joined 'em, promising Monie I would be back in a week.

Howe's European sensibilities were appalled at the scene of the massacre, this war on innocents, the scalped and butchered corpses terrible to see, houses and barns burned, flocks and herds slaughtered. "Not the sort of war you be used to fighting," I told Howe, "but it's how wars are fought here."

Howe was further appalled by the bloody trail we followed, the mutilated bodies of those who couldn't keep up. We pursued but we moved too slowly and with the head start the savages had on us, we understood we could not catch them, and frustrated, we returned home.

Soon after, in December, my second son was born. I said we would name him Thomas but Monie refused. One dear Thomas had been lost to the Indians, another had perished in the womb; Monie wouldn't put the name and the accompanying burden on our babe. I suggested Pieter, after my father. Monie reminded me our babe was American, not Dutch, and thus, Peter, a healthy babe with a lusty cry. Monie was infernally busy with the two infant boys and I suppose I was a little put out by the amount of attention they got, and how little time Monie had for me. It seemed me and my wife were drifting apart, she seemed so distant. Not that it was true, it was mostly her extreme busyness with the babies. We talked of this and I was gratified to hear her say she loved me more than ever before.

Still, and after the New Year, the pressure of being around the house got to be too much. There wasn't much for me to do. Josh and his family were relentless in attacking the chores, my wife had a good system down for the babes and got plenty of help from Josh's brood, especially the twins. Whenever I tried helping with anything, I seemed to get in the way of someone or other and whilst Josh and his family remained deferential, they knew a hell of a lot more about farming than I did, and there was constant friction between Monie and me, she carping often at my inability to do things right. Truth be told, farming wasn't the only thing I was not very good at and I began to feel left out on my own homestead.

Henry, Josh's oldest son, announced he was to be married, he finally letting on about his girl, a pretty negro lass, a servant girl in an Albany mansion. We put together a wedding breakfast for him and his bride at the Full Sail. They had hired themselves out to a wealthy Dutchman to the south, down along the Hudson where the patroons lived. I loaned ‘em the use of my wagon so they could move their possessions.

When the excitement of this goings-on died down, the boredom and sense of being out of sorts resumed within me. I set a few traps and took some fur, most of it small. My wife and me continued to quarrel over the minutest of matters, kitchen things not in their rightful places, wood not cut to the proper length, the new babe’s constant crying, things not worth getting angry about, yet we did, and it got worse instead of better. Finally, at the end of January came the breaking point. I could take no more. I needed to be away from those who had my eternal love. I could not abide having them so near and yet so distant. Feeling I had done all I could to ensure Monie’s safety, with Josh and his family there and with the stone house a fortress, I left for the frozen north, for the dangers and exhilarations, the cold and lonely vigils of the ranger life.

Chapter XIV – The Indomitable John Betts

Rogers, back from Louisbourg and with his rangers ensconced at the camp he'd established on the big island in the Hudson, adjacent to Edward, was glad to see me. We set out at once with a full company, sixty men, to see what damage we could do up around Ti. We skated a ways, then took to snowshoes and got up along the high series of hills and ridges that separated the two lakes until we was once again up on Rattlesnake Mountain. We were perched on the icy slopes of the sheer east side, high over the mouth of Portage Crick and Fort Ti. We grabbed a Frenchman, questioned him and sent him back to Edward under escort, and with not much activity around the forts, Rogers sent all but a few of the men home and suggested those of us still there go on up to my cabin. I had often told him about it, he had always wanted to see it and now seemed a good time. The men with us, four of 'em now, I had 'em swear never to speak about what they seen nor ever return to Paradise without my permission. I wasn't concerned about 'em. They were Hampshire men not likely to stay around after the war, did they get through it, and they were men I trusted.

We watched our backtrail and covered our tracks going up and when we arrived at the cabin, it was intact and undisturbed. I showed the men around, they were delighted by all the beaver sign and got as excited as small boys those few times they sighted one of the big rodents. Rogers pointed out what a superb base for smuggling this post would be. He knew the smugglers' trade was what had given me a start in the North Country and I was sure, though he denied it, it was how he got his start too, over in New England. Also how he spoke fluent French and understood French habits so well. We stayed three days, not time enough for me to trap, only time to think about it and wish for the day when Monie and me could move up here in safety. When it was time to go back down to the war, I wasn't alone in my reluctance to depart. The time spent had kindled in all of us, even in Rogers, thoughts of home and of peace, of expelling the French so we might live the woods' life without fear of savages questing for our hair.

Later in the winter, a month after our sojourn in Paradise, we were once again up at the lakes, this time with two-hundred men. We were on snowshoes in deep snow on the west side of Bald Mountain, in the Trout Brook Valley and we seen a detachment of French and Indians coming toward us. It looked as if they hadn't seen us and we split into two, some of us led by Rogers, the others by an ensign, Greg McDonald, our intention to trap the enemy between us, a nice little ambush. The foe got into McDonald before Rogers could get there. McDonald drove 'em back but he, wounded, was not able to stop his men from going off in wild pursuit of the enemy. Turned out McDonald and two other rangers were the only survivors of his contingent as the enemy referred to was the advance of a much larger party of three-hundred French and Indians. They wiped out McDonald's force and with those of us with Rogers now heavily outnumbered, we commenced retreating south down the valley. With rangers on each of our flanks and a strong rear, we didn't expect our main body would get overrun but we didn't move fast enough and the enemy came on and cut off our retreat. It became impossible for us to disengage in any sort of order. The enemy was up so close, we could see their faces and only thanks to Rogers, who always made sure our guns was clean, our powder dry, did we hold 'em off. We fought a fierce battle for some time, my barking rifle dispatched a few of 'em, and having sustained heavy losses, our only hope was we might survive 'til sundown; after dark we wasn't sure what would happen.

Rogers held a force in reserve, in readiness did the enemy try to turn our flanks. When they tried this inevitable turning, our reserve party went over and got itself shot up, which put us into a more precarious situation as we was now taking a firing from our left as well as our front. Many of our men got hit; Rogers got shot on the wrist, I got clipped on my left ear. Bullets whizzing, we was getting enveloped, it was time to depart. Rogers called retreat. Rangers' rules state that when retreat is sounded, it is retreat, not any kind of tactical withdrawal. It was every man for hisself. Get to hell out and get to the rendezvous, which was set each morning. The men too severely wounded to retreat of their own was left behind, something every ranger understood.

Just as the men started pulling out, the enemy made a rush into our position and the fighting became up close for those who could not get away. My rifle was slung over my shoulder, I used hatchet and knife, and with the flow of retreat to the south, I headed out due west, to try to avoid the main paths of action.

I had gone but a short distance when two Indians barred my way.

Both were armed with warclubs and knives, the clubs with nasty black spikes for driving down into a man's head. One Indian came straight for me, waddling on snowshoes in the deep snow whilst the other circled around behind me. I charged into the first one, he swung his big club, I avoided it and buried my hatchet in his forehead. I lost the hatchet when he fell and the other Indian, from behind, got his forearm locked across my throat. He whooped as he raised his knife in his other hand and he'd a plunged it over my shoulder and into my chest had not a ranger swung his musket with two hands on the barrel and stove in the Indian's face with the gunstock. I finished off the Indian as he kicked in the snow, his hands clutching his shattered face. I said something to the ranger about getting the hell out of there and I saw he'd got shot in the thigh and was weakened enough so he told me to get going and forget about him, as were our standing orders. I said as I wasn't a ranger and was only an attached, his rules didn't apply to me. What I meant was, he had saved my life, now, God willing, I would save his. I grabbed his arm and began pulling him and if he had resisted, I suppose I would have had to leave him. He, though, decided he wanted to get out too, and with me helping him along, we got off through the woods. Our only hope now was flight. Behind us we heard the exultant scalp halloos of the enemy who had carried the day. My ranger friend had bled profusely and had stopped the bleeding with a tourniquet which I now loosened. Better to bleed some than to let the rot get into it.

His name was John Betts.

We pushed west, deeper into the mountains until nightfall overtook us. We had not got far, the sound of gunshots could still be heard faintly down in the valley, our progress slowed for the severity of John's wound and because the higher we went, the deeper was the snow.

The temperature fell, the wind shifted back to the south, it began to snow and soon we were engulfed in a roaring gale of wind-blown proportion. This was not a bad thing, the snow would cover our trail, nor a good thing, for the night would be harsh.

I built a shelter of saplings and bark and got a fire going inside. By the firelight, I tried to do something for John's leg. The ball was still in there but didn't look to have hit anything vital, at least to my unpracticed eye, and the cold seemed to be cauterizing the wound.

We slept some and come morning, the storm had passed, the sky had lifted considerably and was a cloudless blue, the air intolerably cold. We pushed off, John using a branch for a crutch and our progress was slow.

I wanted no part of going back down into the valley so we headed south into the mountains around the lake. We moved along the precipitous ridges, difficult as they were snow covered and icy. John had a terrible time. I'd go ahead to break trail then return to help him. Step by torturous step he moved along. He constantly begged or cursed me to go on alone and save myself; each time I refused and we persevered with him stumbling and falling often. The sun had the effect of warming the body some though the glare on the snow made the way hard to see. All was white. I helped John along as best I could. I urged him with threats and pleadings to keep going, even did I shake and slap him when his urge to lay down and die got too strong, and when he demanded I leave him and save myself, I told him to shut the hell up. The forest was silent, though we knew the savages were hunting around for such as us. I was frustrated with our slow going and I knew we could make better time down on the frozen lake but we would have been too exposed out there to both the weather and the Indians. We had to stay in the mountains until we neared our rendezvous place.

The way was ice-strewn and difficult. Our snowshoes coming apart, we halted often to repair them. Betts had lost a lot of blood but he at least was no longer interested in arguing about keeping going. It was as if he felt he didn't need to argue, as he would soon be dead and I could go on without him. Yet each time I went ahead to break trail and came back expecting to see him dead, he was coming along. Step by step, mile by mile, he moved in this way, clinging to a thread of life, refusing to throw it up.

Darkness came just as we arrived at the top of a steep cliff. Below us a highland peninsula jutted south, seven miles or so up the lake. This was the Tongue Mountain Range which divided the lake into what was called the Narrows on our left, and to the right, the Northwest Bay. The range presented a more or less hogback appearance except the hog's spine was slightly east of dead center which made for less rugged going to the west.

Betts said the heights upon which we were perched were too steep to get down. I told him there was a way, to the west but we would have to wait until morning. Betts asked was we going to have a hut and a fire. I said no. Hunkered down inside and with a little warmth, we'd go to sleep, the fire would die and we'd not wake up. We'd have to suffer the night exposed on the windswept clifftop. The wind blew ferociously and as exposed as we were and with our clothes wet clear through and our bodies weak, it was a long night for staying awake and we both did sleep some. At first light, we were covered with ice. I shook John and was surprised to see his frost-encrusted eyes open. He asked for something to eat. We hadn't had much food when we started out, just some jerked meat and dried corn. Now just a handful of corn remained. We silently soaked the corn in our mouths to thaw it, and when it was eaten, we started out again.

Even moving off to the side of the mountain, we had a most difficult time getting down. There was much ice on the rocks, thick in places but there were enough footholds and crevasses and some small trees and exposed roots for the grabbing. Still, and with all John's slipping and falling, it was here he made his most insistent demand I go on alone. He began muttering about leaping to his death so I could go on without him. To counter this threat, which I feared he might make good on, and also for the steepness and the ice, I put a tether on him and tied the other end around my own waist. Thus linked together, I knew he would not leap off any of the innumerable cliffs for knowing he'd take me with him.

By long and slow detours, we made the bottom and from down there and looking back up at the steepness and what we had accomplished, I recollected the tale of the tragic lass which had played out here during the previous war. Captured whilst to bed and dressed only in a sleeping shift and taken north and escaping her Indian captors and attempting to get down off the cliffs, her shift got snagged on a thorn bush and she'd lost it. The Indians recaptured her and had thought it was a fine joke, the white undergarment of their now naked captive waving like a banner from high up on the hill over the lake. Her shift stayed there for some time and became a source of ribald amusement for any who passed by. I had seen it a few times myself.

Daunted we were with what was next, the Tongue Mountains. I was familiar with 'em, John was not, he asking how far must we go and how would it be for us. I told him it was seven miles to the southern tip of the peninsula and somewhere down there was our rendezvous. He asked would there still be men there. I didn't know and what was unspoken, if there weren't, we were goners.

Seven miles was a long ways for men who hadn't slept nor ate much for two days and with one of the men with a busted leg. The going was most treacherous for although not the loftiest of the eastern Adirondacks, the Tongue Mountains were damn near impassable in winter. There were a few slender trails along the western edge which made for easy enough traversing most of the year but which would be deadly now, in winter. With so much ice accumulated along the trails and with the way the trails rolled up and down and how they were squeezed between the rock formations, the trails, in some places, were death traps. Once down in 'em, we might not get out. We stayed as best we could partway up along the western slopes, these were less precipitous than what was to the other side, the ridges not as iced. The trees was mostly hardwoods which bareness exposed us to the weather and to any Indians what might have been hunting us.

All around was an empty landscape of white; the lake, the mountains rising along the far shore, all lay in a deep blanket of ice and snow. The air was deathly still. Nothing stirred 'cept the snow rising in gusts and sharp tossing in our faces. It seemed as if we was alone in the world, as if we could have fired our guns and there would be no ear, human nor otherwise, to hear the sound of it. But we knew better. Near to us, men were locked up in a terrible struggle for life and death.

With us looking for the easiest walking and going to it, we were wandering all over. This we knew by the glimpses we got through the bare trees of both the Northwest Bay to one side and the Narrows to the other. Neither John nor me had the fortitude to pursue a more resolute course and by mid-day, I knew we must go down to the lake if we were to survive. It would be a most desperate gamble but one we must take. The way through the mountains was too difficult, we were stumbling and wandering, unable to sustain a straight-forward direction. Another night in the woods and we would be dead. Our only chance was to go down to the lake and walk along the ice. With all the distance we had made, the rendezvous island must not be too far off and with luck, we might make it.

A short conversation ensued. Betts had been thinking the same as me. We got back over to the eastern side and slid down over the ledges on our arses, ten, twenty feet at a time, and whilst not yet all the way down to the lake, we came to a rock outcropping, a vantage from where we could see out over the icy surface. Any French or Indians would be dark specks against the whiteness and not seeing any such specks nor movement, we got down to the lake and stood along the edge, beneath the trees. The wind on the lake was ferocious with gusts lifting the snow and thrashing it about but at least the wind would be behind us and would be strong enough to push us along. Best thing now would have been to wait out the remaining few hours of daylight before going on but neither of us could endure it any longer. What we needed was an end to it, saved or dead, it didn't much matter.

We got onto the lake where a musket shot might at any moment take either one of us for we could be seen not only by anyone on the ice but by any up along the Tongue Mountains as well. And so close were we staying to where the trees overhung the lake, we might have got jumped by Indians whooping out of the bushes.

Darkness commenced, which increased our chances of making it in. The wind stayed at our backs, the stars were bright in the crisp air. Our breath froze throats and lungs. Snow to any depth was beyond John's strength so we avoided as best we could those places where the wind had piled the snow into drifts. We mostly traversed where the ice was blown bare. I kept us pointed in what I hoped was the right direction and once, wandering too far out on the lake, we came unexpectedly into a grove of trees. I thought we had got turned east instead of south and had crossed the lake to the other side. Turned out we had struck one of the islands in the Narrows and we righted ourselves. The wind got stronger, the air colder. Our progress had slowed almost to nothing. John Betts, Private John Betts, could not much more than stagger.

Having trudged for so many hours without food or sleep, I was as near to giving out as was John. My eyelids kept wanting to close, my body to shut down but I knew I must keep on. I still carried my rifle over my shoulder. With my powder soaked, the gun was useless and I would not have the strength to fire it, did the need arise. I started to reach for it a few times, to discard the weight of it, and each time, I thought on how long I'd had the rifle. How would I ever replace this great gift from my father? He'd presented it to me when I was yet a lad, when he could not convince me to abandon my resolve to become a woodsman, same as his own father, a farmer, had looked out for him when he was a boy and had disavowed the farm and declared for a life at sea. The gun stayed slung over my shoulder.

The wind intensified, the most frigid weather had arrived, and still thinking about Pops, it occurred to me if I had listened to him all these years and become a barkeeper, I'd be safe behind the walls of Albany. Maybe sitting before the hearth in the common room, biting down on a slab of roast beef between two pieces of Mother's thick buttered bread.

Thinking thusly, I hadn't realized Betts was no longer with me and when I turned and looked, I didn't see him nowhere. I went back along my own tracks as best I could in the faint starlight which glinted the snow and ice. Coming to where his tracks and mine parted, I followed his and found him hunkered down behind a snow drift. Hiding from me more than from Indians. He didn't say anything; his look wasn't defiant, just it was contemplative. "Get up, Betts," I said, "and get movin'. You ain't quittin' on me now." His will to survive taking hold, he sighed and came along, and when I put a tether on him, so to not lose him again, he neither resisted nor complained.

We trudged one pitifully short step at a time. I thought we must be close to the rendezvous. John asked what was the name of the island, I couldn't remember, I was damn near incapable of recalling much at all. I told him to persevere a little longer and we would get in.

Out of the gloom ahead came apparitions. Shadowy ghosts becoming shaggy men in bearskins. I couldn't tell were they ours or not and I reached for my knife. I maybe didn't have the strength to fight 'em but iffen they be Indians, they weren't going to take this Dutchman alive. "Rangers!" John said in a croaking whisper, all he was capable of, and as it was, he was right. It was rangers out searching for stragglers and spooking us in the dark. They said the rendezvous point was a quarter mile behind us. We had gone past it, so if they hadn't a found us, we would a died come daylight, frozen dead or tomahawked. The rangers carried rods and blankets and assembling two travois, they loaded us on. John asked for rum, they gave us splashes out of their canteens.

There were huts at the rendezvous and we were helped inside. Rude it was and smoky but it got us out of the wind and alongside a fire. Venison was cooking, the most delicious of smells, and there was beef broth besides. The men insisted we take the broth before the meat, rangers had to spoon it into our mouths. The other men, bless them, looked the other way as we were fed like babes. After taking the broth I felt revived and with my hands and fingers thawed some by the fire, I began helping myself to strips of the meat, tentative at first, then ravenously, though the chewing was both difficult and painful.

The flow of blood from John's wound had started again with the warmth inside the hut. They laid him on the floor and put a stick between his teeth for him to bite down on and they took hold of his arms and his good leg but with him far gone enough to think it was Indians what had ahold of him, he began struggling against the men. The surgeon, an old Scottie, conked John on the head with a chunk of firewood and with him passed out, the surgeon made his cuts with his scalpel and dug out the fragments of the bullet. He then cleaned and bandaged the wound.

Rogers came in and was glad to see me and John, although I don't think Rogers had heretofore been familiar with John. Rogers said a force of a few hundred British regulars was on their way from Edward with food and there'd be sleds for transporting the wounded. Rogers sat down and over rum and strips of venison, he said not too many of ours had got out, besides those what got out at once. He was anxious more might a survived and might get in.

Whilst we ate, Rogers resumed the argument he'd been having with one of his officers. When the retreat had been called, nearly every ranger who could, including Rogers, had, at great risk to themselves, brought out wounded men. This contradicted what we had been taught, which was every man for hisself when the situation demanded. To me, hearing the arguments, the lesson was clear. The way our men had stuck together under the worst of circumstances was admirable. To some few of the officers, it weren't so clear. One of our inviolate rules had got flouted and acts of selflessness, they said, had probably got more of us killed, a fact which could be neither proved nor disproved. I was of the opinion our men, including myself, had done right. Hard lessons were getting learned and Rogers ended the argument, perhaps unfairly, by nodding toward John and saying to the officers, "Ask Betts what he thinks."

During the latter stages of the night, the British came in, their arrival most welcomed for the food and rum they brought and for their fire-power, which secured our position against attack. In the morning, John and the other bad-off men were loaded into the ox-drawn sleds for the trip back to William Henry.

The rangers stayed on the island for a few more days; I stayed too. I worked long hours on my rifle and made myself useful around the camp. Patrols were in and out, day and night, searching for stragglers and alert for any Indians what was still around. The depth of the snow and the severity of the cold slowed the searching on both sides. A few more stragglers were found, a number of dead too. Some had froze to death afore the Indians got to them. We found the remnants of the fires for the Indians having warmed the heads so they could lift the hair. Few Indians were seen though they were present.

The bitter cold turned to an early thaw, weather to stop even the most intrepid of raiders, a world of mud and slush. We loaded the last of our wounded into sleighs and returned to the camp at the south end of the lake. I went on to Edward and to the hospital there. I had lost a piece of one ear and was suffering headaches for getting my head bashed in the fight and hit against the Tongue Mountain ledges.

After my short stay at the hospital, I went home. Monie was overjoyed to see me. I had sent her two letters from the hospital at Edward but she had received neither of ‘em. We quickly forgot our problems of the past and began to look ahead to the coming of spring, not too far off. She had realized, she said, how much she missed me when she heard of what became known as The Second Battle on Snowshoes and knew not my fate. She said she was sure I was safe, said she could feel it, but she had fretted terribly and her hopes were waning by the time I showed up at the door. It was such a joy to be with her again.

Chapter XV – Mrs. Nabbycrombie

I stayed home for the rest of the winter. I was slow getting back my full strength and could not shake the fever which had set in after my rescue. I was always tired and was of little use around the place.

Thank God for Josh and his brood! Each day they attacked the work and I asked and they agreed to stay on permanently. Even with most of my land still covered with forest, I knew what was cleared could provide sustenance for us all and in a few years, if we was still here, we might begin selling to folks in Albany and maybe even New York Town. I had made a wise bargain and I would prosper. No. We would all prosper together.

Toward spring, I shared my neighbors' incredulity and outrage when it was announced another expedition was to go to Louisbourg. Once again, a good many of our best soldiers, rangers included, were to take ship for Canada. Here was yet another mixed-up debacle of the British. Those of us with long memories thought once again and with bitterness back to King George's War, when we had taken Louisbourg from the French and our British Lords gave it back by treaty. We had said then how we would someday pay a price for this British folly and now and for a second time we were inviting disaster by denuding our borders of troops. Did Montcalm once again gather as large a force as he had the previous year, it might be the end of us. We were now so angrily cursing Loudoun, we hardly had time to curse the French.

Then, one day, mid-April, I was working in the yard and two rangers came down the hill. "Heading south?" I said with bitterness for thinking they were going to New York to take ship for Louisbourg. "North," one of them said. North? "To Scalp Point and Quebec." I looked sharply at each of them and with them trying not to grin, I suspected it was something good.

They gave me the tidings and it was so far beyond belief, when they finished, I tossed my hat in the air, slapped each of 'em on the shoulder, whooped, and rushed madly into the house, startling Monie, who was by the fire. "Fix these men a spread like they's never et before," I said.

The men had followed me inside and after one of 'em repeated to

Monie what they'd told me, she placed her hand on her breast. "Oh, dear God," she said. She hugged me, and with tears, she hugged each of the rangers, never mind they were dirty and smelly from the woods.

Mister William Pitt, of whom Tom had always spoken so highly, had become prime minister of England back in '56. It had taken him some time to get his sea legs, as Pops would have put it, but now Pitt was in firm control of the war and it was to be decided not on the high seas nor in Europe, where our wars were usually decided but instead right here in North America.

The rangers said when Loudoun's plans for another Louisbourg campaign reached England, Pitt summoned Loudoun home, which everyone assumed was the end of any talk of Louisbourg. Not so, and this is what caused me to toss my hat and Monie to shed her tears. The Louisbourg campaign had not been rescinded. It just wasn't going to be allowed to strip our northern frontier of men as it had done last year. Instead, and in addition to a campaign against Louisbourg, the biggest army ever seen in the colonies was to assemble in Albany, to march against Ticonderoga, Scalp Point and beyond. Three years before, when Braddock marched to the Monongahela with twenty-two-hundred men, it seemed an unfathomable number to take into the wilderness. Now we was going with fifteen thousand and incredibly, there was more. A third army was to go to the west, against the French fort, Frontenac, which was the doorway into the French interior, the Great Lakes and the Mississippi. Did Frontenac fall, all those interior posts would be cut off from succor from Montreal and Quebec. I could not help recalling what else Tom had said, how things would start to happen for the good if Mister Pitt got control of the war. Pitt, Tom said, was the only Britisher who understood North America to be the center of what was truly a world war, and may God rest Tom's soul, he was right.

After the men finished their meal, I got out the rum jug and even having already heard the news twice, I insisted they tell it again. Monie wondered how the hell Pitt intended to pay for it all. One of the rangers said this needn't concern us. Our job was to win the damn war and the bewigged heads could figure out how to pay for it later. Me and the other ranger agreed, Monie too, she laughing and saying she well knew her countrymen. They would find the money somewhere.

A week later, we were down at the river landing. I had our oldest boy in my arms, Monie had the infant in hers. A flotilla of ranger canoes was heading north and behind the rangers, bateaux with a regiment of fancy skirt-men. Happy we were to see them and in our delight, we laughed at how, even crammed belly to belly in their boats, the Scots were blowin' on their pigskins.

Soldiers and supplies became a daily spectacle, both on the river and along the roads, and once, when the Scotties came marching by, we got a close-up look at 'em. They were big, sour-looking men with ramrod-straight backs, stiff, impeccable bearing. "Invincible," one of my neighbors said. Looked to be, maybe, marching up the road, and I didn't doubt their prowess on European battlefields but woe to any of these who fell afoul of the red-skinned savages of Canada.

Even those of us who had witnessed it all before had never seen such numbers as this year and with so many of our soldiers situated between us and the French, Indian raids were as least likely to occur as ever I could remember, although I insisted we remain vigilant, both there at the farm and in the woods around us. By early June, our army of such proportions, all those thousands of men, was encamped at the south end of Lake George. British regulars, Highland skirt-men, colonial levies.

Optimism was high along the frontier; indeed, I imagined it was high throughout all the colonies. The only dark cloud was the man who was to lead us, General James Abercrombie. He was said to be a bungling clod, an incompetent, humorless, colorless man. "Not much good, just good and fancy." What else we heard about Abercrombie, the mere sight of an Indian in the woods or anywhere was enough to scare him out from beneath his wig. Recalling once again the high regard with which Tom O'Brien had held for British Prime Minister William Pitt, I said the rumors of Abercrombie's incompetence must not be true. Pitt, did he truly know how to conduct a war, would not put a blockhead at the head of such a large army, or any army.

How it was explained to us by one of our rangers, a Harvard graduate who was often immersed in the newspapers, Abercrombie was a political appointee much despised by Pitt but foisted on him for reasons which he must perforce accept. This got some of us hot; the ranger, calming us, said it would be alright on account of Pitt knew how to take the measure of a man. Abercrombie was so out sorts in the New World, he'd give Lord Howe broad latitude regarding the conduct of our forces so long as he, Abercrombie, reaped the laurels. Pitt knew Lord Howe too. Howe didn't give a tinker's damn for who got the credit, so long as we whipped the French. Still, we worried. With so much fighting over in Europe, why couldn't their Lordships find a place for Abercrombie over there? Or was sending him here a way to get him away from there?

After the spring planting and filled with the optimism that was going around, for none could deny the spirit of our army, our attitude of victory in the making, I returned eagerly to the war. Our rangers were spooking Ticonderoga and Scalp Point, engaging in forays, grabbing prisoners. The French had few Indians or woods-lopers and we had a fairly easy time raiding and prowling.

We rangers were constantly harassing the French. We intended no real damage, we just wanted to keep 'em on edge. Often did we fake what looked to be a serious nighttime raid, forcing them to arms, then and with them all awake and running about, we'd vanish back into the woods. We picked off an occasional sentry and grabbed anyone from a garrison who wandered into the woods.

On one of our forays, Rogers, just recently promoted to major, showed me the skeletal remains of oxen in a glen where, in mid-winter and having grabbed a French supply train from under the very nose of Ti, he and his men killed all the oxen, butchered a few and feasted on some choice parts. When the rangers had finished their repast, and in a note inserted into a pouch which he dangled from the horn of one of the slain beasts and to the delight of the folks who eagerly followed Rogers' escapades in the newspapers, our new major addressed Montcalm.

I am obliged to you, sir, the note said, *for the fresh meat you have provided me. I shall take good care of my prisoners. My compliments to the Marquis of Montcalm. Signed, Rogers.*

****

With the summer sun high up in a cloudless sky and the water a shimmering blue, I rejoiced to the fullest from the top of Bald Mountain as our grand army passed below. Never had I seen a more spectacular sight. With ranger canoes out front, the army came in three columns of boats, the colonials on either flank, the regulars in the center. Whaleboats and bateaux packed with men in every color uniform and in buckskins; flags a flyin', fifes tootin', drums poundin', the Scots' bagpipes a skirlin'. So many brilliant colors splashed over the blue waters, and behind the men, flatboats with cannons, horses, wooden barrels, boxes and overstuffed duffels, a truly magnificent sight. I confess here to gettin' a little choked up for seeing it come to pass, what I had waited so long to see. Surely such an army must prevail and we would no longer have to live in fear for our lives, for who could deny us? Who could prevent us from taking Carillon and Scalp Point and going all the way to Canada, to destroy the seats of French power?

With most of the army having gone past our position on the mountain and with the forward-most boats disembarking at the landing near the north end of the lake and whilst we were preparing to move down off Bald Mountain, a scout came in and said there was Frenchies in the Trout Brook Valley. We got down there and shot it out with them. We had more men than them and with our firing having a more favorable effect than theirs, they fled back toward Portage Crick. We pursued 'em through the valley, the scene of the previous winter's Battle on Snow-shoes. We passed by the bones and decay of our late friends. The enemy escaped us by a series of ambushes. The entire valley, no more than a good gunshot wide and thickly wooded, was a nasty place to get jumped and we declined to press too closely.

Then we heard scattered shots which quickly reached the scale of a full battle. We rushed to the sounds, leaping over dead logs and clawing through brambles and patches of thick juniper and briars. We advanced to whence the shooting was coming from, the place where Trout Brook flowed into Portage Crick. Rogers was there with two-hundred rangers and colonials. He was engaged with a force of something more than a hundred French, which probably included those we had been chasing. It was a nasty fight with both sides hidden in the brush and behind trees. We couldn't see more'n a few feet to the front or to the sides. The French retreated and the battle became a rout. We got into their rear just as they reached the fast waters of the crick and we shot most of those who tried to get across. We hurt them, but as it turned out, we was hurt far most grievously.

Lord Howe, he to whom the entire army looked for leadership, was dead. One of the first shots of the encounter had pierced his breast and as he lay bleeding to death, those gathered around him must surely have understood how the deaths of half a hundred of the enemy paled against the loss of this one man. All the confidence of our army, our men knew, would pass on with him.

By the time we got back to the landing, a general forward movement was underway and the cheer around us rang hollow in our ears. We knew a change in mood was coming, and as the shocking news spread through the ranks, there was disbelief, confusion. The forward movement was canceled and the main part of our army, which was mostly camped at the falls of Portage Crick, was ordered back to the landing. We sat at the shore of the lake, fifteen-thousand men doing nothing, then a part of our force was ordered forward. They crossed over the crick on the bridge which our men had rebuilt after the French had partially destroyed it.

I was with some rangers ordered up onto Rattlesnake to spy out French intentions. We moved cautiously up through Cold Springs, the back way onto the mountain. Gettin' to the top, I fully anticipated seeing the French in full retreat down the lake. What the hell else could they do against such numbers? Their camp at the lower falls was abandoned, the sawmill was intact. The narrow crick below the falls, where boats could navigate, was clogged with fleeing French and Canadians, rowing and paddling hard. Through the trees, thick with summer growth, could be seen more of the French, quick-stepping along the road to Carillon.

For years I had heard of the vaunted British artillery, now I had a perfect seat to see it in action, the top of Rattlesnake. I thought it was too bad about Lord Howe gettin' hisself shot. With all the good he had done, the victory should have been his, not Abercrombie's, but even as we mourned General Howe, we would prevail. How could the death of a single man make the difference between victory and defeat in such favorable circumstances? One of our rangers remarked as how we didn't need to bring up the cannons, all we had to do was cover the Scalp Point road, which would deny succor to the already ill-supplied Frenchies. Another man said how sitting on the road and starving the enemy was more Abercrombie's sluggish style than attacking, to which we agreed and laughed.

From where we were, we could see the French were under-manned. They had not been reinforced and weren't no more than a few thousand, mostly regulars. We had 'em five or six to one. Abercrombie had merely to point his cannons at the French. Montcalm was no fool; a look down into all them cannon barrels would surely send him back to Canada, and if it didn't, we'd pound his army to dust.

We got farther around the slopes of Rattlesnake to where we could see down onto the star-shaped fort. A mile in front of the fort, the French were frantically chopping down trees and erecting them into a ten-foot-high wall with an elevated shooting platform behind it. In front of this was a narrow flat ground bereft of cover, then an abatis of logs with tops and branches sharpened and all thrown together in a tangle, to deter any advance up to the redoubt. Our men sneered at this new fortification.

"Let's see how she stands up," one said, "to British cannons." Our artillery, laboriously transported up from Albany and ranging from the smallest bore all the way up to siege cannons, would make the French defense of their position a hazardous one.

"Did they understand the confusion amongst our leadership," another man said, "they'd have been less precipitate." I agreed and asked in turn why there was such flight from the sawmill to the fort but no such flight north down the lake. Did so few intend making a stand against so many? This possibility should have filled me with anticipation but gave me instead a bad feeling. A ranger sneered at the French efforts but his voice was filled more with gloom than with conviction.

"Today," he said unconvincingly, "is still to be our day."

I hoped to God he was right, hoped the French would be fools enough to stand against us, so dearly did I want to witness their annihilation. With naught but a shamble of knocked-down trees and a crude wooden wall blocking our path of glory, we could take Ticonderoga and advance to Scalp Point and beyond, possibly even taking Montreal this year. Oh, Great Day! How my hopes soared!

We returned to the camp and it was engulfed in confusion with orders and countermands and finally, late in the afternoon, our army, which had mostly sat all day at the landing place, marched back to the lower falls where it encamped. I thought it most ominous the cannons were left at the landing. I figured Abercrombie for a fool without much battle sense but the only alternative to cannonading the French was to choke their supply lines, which we were not doing, or to make frontal charges into and through their abatis and up to their wall. I told myself Abercrombie would bring up his cannons. Why the hell would he drag and float artillery all the way from Albany if he wasn't intending to use it?

Most of the men knew the cannons would not be brought up and I suppose I did too. Those few who insisted the cannons would be used asked why, if the cannons weren't going to be advanced, why, after the French had destroyed the bridge over the crick, why had we rebuilt it strong enough to support even our heaviest artillery? Most of the men just shook their heads and wrote melancholy letters home, dreading what they would be asked to do tomorrow. They went forward of our position for a look at the enemy lines. The French were furiously adding to their defenses, they'd be at it all night, increasing the hell we would be facing tomorrow. Our British and colonials were brave men, but none wanted a massed charge into a tangled pile of downed trees and with Frenchmen behind a wall on the other side.

Abercrombie took up headquarters in the sawmill and incredibly, he never ventured to reconnoiter the situation for himself. He was probably the only man in the entire army who hadn't gone for a look.

Just before sunset, the dread order came down, a frontal assault to convene on the morrow. I accompanied Rogers as he escorted an engineer from Abercrombie's staff up onto Rattlesnake to show him the ease with which the fort could be bombarded into submission from up there. The engineer, even looking down on the promontory, held fast to his commander's views. He bragged on the efficacy of British bayonets and said it would be stupid to haul cannons up the mountainside. He told Rogers not to concern hisself with strategy. Rogers cursed him for every kind of a fool. When Rogers gets this hot, beware! The argument grew more bitter, us rangers listening with disbelief as the engineer repeated the rumor which had been going around the ranks and which was now goading Abercrombie.

Johnson's Mohawks had reported large numbers of Indian reinforcements to be on their way and near to hand. I figured the Mohawks were French plants. Rogers thought so too but it appeared now as if the bait had been swallowed by the British commander, as hurry was added to his fears. His head was filled with hordes of painted Indians swarming up Champlain in war canoes. Rogers' argument with the engineer damn near ended violently when the engineer told Rogers to shut the hell up. Rogers retorted he'd scalp the officer and with Rogers reaching for the knife in his belt, the officer ran down the mountain. He reported Rogers for insubordination, which charge was forgotten in light of later events.

When we came down off the hill and with the orders having gone through the troops, the grumbling had become too loud for the officers to ignore. Our colonials talked about refusing to march. Said they would go home if the orders as they then stood, prevailed. A few men actually did head out for the south. Some were caught and court-martial was convened. Six men were accused, tried, convicted and sentenced to hang. Four Americans and two British. A gallows was erected, of all places, along the route our assault troops would march to the attack. At first light next day, the army mustered, the condemned men were led out and hanged. Gallows Hill would become an infamous byword when talking of our British military genius.

I wasn't witness to the hangings, Rogers having ordered me the night before to take a small patrol up to Five Mile Point, a peninsula midway between Ti and Scalp Point, the site of some old Indian burial grounds, to watch there for the expected approach of the enemy reinforcements.

July the Eighth, 1758, early morning, we were watching the lake and a flotilla of canoes came past, a hundred Canadians and Indians, heading south. We didn't even bother reporting this force as it was too small to matter. Looking back, we should have told Abercrombie every red man in North America and the ghosts of their departed brethren was coming for him. Maybe he would have called off the attack and hastened back to William Henry, coward that he was.

The first sounds of a battle started around mid-day, rifle fire, not what we most wanted to hear, the thunder of cannons. All afternoon we heard the distant firing, still no cannons, and we speculated on the ebb and flow of events. I sent a man down to Ti, to find out how the attack was going and late afternoon there came a single boat moving north at great speed, three paddlers, well out from shore. Frenchmen. I rested my rifle along the crown of a big rock, flat on top, and took aim. I fired and saw the fellow I aimed at, in the back of the canoe, topple over the side. His weight pulled the canoe over and the three were in the water before I could get off another shot. The shot man thrashed around some before sinking, the others swam for the eastern shore. My rangers were excited about the shot, which could only be accomplished with my famously accurate rifle. Reloading, I reflected on my poor judgment. No matter how good the shot, it gave away our position, a dangerous thing for a scout to do. I told the rangers it had been a rash action and said I hoped we would not be made to suffer for it. We gathered our gear and moved off to another hiding place, about a half mile or so closer to Ti.

Toward evening and with the air bereft of all sound, the silence sat eerily on us. These lulls had occurred at intervals all afternoon and into the evening, each lull bringing renewed hope the day had been carried but each silence was broken by loud firing commencing anew. I strained to see the remnants of the French army fleeing past us along the north-flowing lake but the waters remained void of passage.

In the morning was more of the ominous silence. We saw a great plume of smoke and some of our men cheered for the fort having got taken. We told them it was the sawmill, by the size and direction of the plume.

The expected resumption of the battle did not come, the affair did not sit right. All was quiet and I tried to puzzle it out. If we were victorious, at least some French should have been fleeing down the lake. We had kept watch all night, moonlight made the watching easy, yet none had we seen. Were the two armies still facing off with each other? The long summer day moved on into late afternoon; it was hot and with the horseflies and mosquitoes buzzing. We waited anxiously for the return of the man I had sent down to Ti but what came instead were ten Frenchmen herding twenty captive Scottish skirt-men. The Scotties were tied hand to hand. They were being led off to Scalp Point and were downcast, haunted looks in their eyes. The French were jubilant. They whooped and fired their guns into the air whilst laughingly prodding and cuffing their prisoners.

We spooked 'em for a short way and when they stopped to rest, the Frenchmen drinking their wine and eating British biscuits, we hit 'em. With our knives and tomahawks, we killed the French and cut loose the prisoners. We hurled the dead Frenchies into a ditch and covered up sign of our scuffle. We led the Scots a short distance off and getting 'em into dense brush, we demanded to know what had happened. It was as we had feared. The unthinkable had happened at Ticonderoga.

Our men had lined up all day and marched into the abatis and got shot to pieces. The skirt-men boasted of having fought bravely, of which I didn't doubt, and the colonials and redcoats too, plenty of good men killed in senseless attempts to get through the impenetrable tangle of trees and into the French and Indians behind their wall. Men hung up on branches made pathetic targets for an enemy shooting through loophole emplacements. Four times our brave men advanced into the death-trap and got themselves slaughtered. Our dead and dying lay in heaps, a tragic, needless loss of two-thousand brave men. The discipline which enabled our men to stay together in the face of such carnage was sorrowful to ponder. Finally, according to the Scots who was tellin' us, when the men were convinced of the futility of it and refused to charge again, Abercrombie took flight for the landing place, leaving his men to find their own way back to their boats.

I felt broken in spirit but my duty was to my men. We could not abandon our post, our presence might be vital. On the other hand, if our army was lost and French reinforcements was coming, we were situated between two enemy forces. I decided we better get to hell out of there.

Some of the Scots were wounded and would not be able to keep up. We had no choice but to leave them. We were sorry for it but we would not get ourselves out, did we take them. They seemed to understand or were maybe too beaten to care.

We gathered what gear we had and hastily departed.

We went west, in a single file along a small brook with which I was familiar. Where the brook turned north, we continued west, staying at a distance from the lake and road. Following another brook and coming to where a small waterfall splashed down over rocks and into a pool and with night coming on, we made camp. Had I been leading just rangers, I would have kept going but I feared losing the Scotties in the dark and with the brush probably too thick for way-finding. No fires did we light, there was little enough food for five rangers and fifteen famished Scots.

The Scots were Black Watch Highlanders from the Forty-second regiment. They spoke with anger and pride for their men's valor and said when the battle was over and with Abercrombie and his army fleeing, these Scots, the ones we had rescued, had stayed behind to try and bring out some of their wounded friends. That was how they got surrounded and captured. I cautioned the Scots against too much talk, for the danger to our position, but also for the bile I felt rising within me. I told them to discard their bright coats in the morning and said any who was slow or who wandered or made noise would be left behind. They bedded down and we kept guard over 'em through the night. Before first light we was underway south, and getting into the Valley of the Trout Brook from a ravine to the west, we passed single file between two of the Three Brothers Mountains. We were wary for being in the valley for its closeness to the French positions but we didn't figure the French, almost all of whom were regulars, would be out here.

We met up with some other rangers who told us they had seen the battleground, thick with red-coated corpses along with the greens and browns of our colonials. The rangers told of dying men tangled in the morass of sharpened branches and begging for help which the French would not give them. The rangers said our retreat turned into a shameful flight with the British officers out front, terrified of the scalping knives of the Indians. Shades of Braddock's defeat on the Ohio except Braddock got pursued by hundreds of Indians and there weren't nobody chasing Abercrombie. The rangers praised the efforts and steadiness of our colonial officers, men such as Bradstreet and Stark, who tried to put order into the retreat.

More than ten-thousand well-armed and otherwise stouthearted men fleeing from a few thousands and there was more shame for our army when it got back to the landing. The men fought for places in the boats and gave no thought to reloading supplies nor cannons. Left everything there for the French.

We waded up the stream to hide our tracks. I sent a man ahead to see were there any men still at the landing. He returned with the news not one Englishman was there, nor any French, neither. The French must a been still behind their wall, they not considering the possibility they had not only stopped an army five times their own size but had sent it fleeing in abject panic.

I decided to go down and see for myself, so I could report on it. I left my rangers with orders to keep heading south. I climbed Bald Mountain. I reached the summit, the outpost was deserted, as was the lake for as far as I could see, north or south. Our army had fled back the way it had come. Beaten. Retreated. Who could believe an expedition so conceived in victory could end in this way? My hopes fell to the ground, I thought never to rise again. I may have been inured to defeat, we had surely suffered our share, but those others paled before this one. This was madness for how certain we had been of victory, nay, not merely victory but decisive victory, an end to the war.

I went down to the landing place. Staggering amounts of supplies awaited the French, all of which would go over to them as soon as they grasped the enormity of their victory. I watched from hiding as the first of their scouts came up. They exulted for seeing we were gone and for the abandoned stores. In among the spoils were kegs of West Indies rum which was getting busted open, the spoils of war. The French fired shots into the air, laughed and slapped one another on the back.

I circled around warily to the north, on the lookout for trouble. I had to avoid another small camp of French woods-lopers situated along the shore where the muddy banks were steep. These Canadians, even without Indians present, were caressing two colonial soldiers they had taken. White men torturing other white men. Going on and coming to a swamp, I seen something on the ground ahead glinting the sunlight. I could not tell what it was, coins, maybe, but when I got to it, it was something to add to my disgust. Shoe buckles. Our British, fleeing through a swamp and with their shoes catching, was too scared to stop and put 'em back on. Shoes by the hundreds, a symbol of our shameful retreat.

What the hell were our men so terrified of, anyway? We had suffered grievous casualties in the stupid fatal headlong charges but even losing two-thousand men, we still greatly outnumbered the French. Why had we retreated? Were we all cowards? No, not all of us. Just one of us.

With more of the French coming out from their lines and up to the lake, I decided it would be too dangerous for me to go down to Carillon for a look. Instead, I headed back south through a narrow pass and back into the Valley of the Trout Brook, I cut around behind Bald Mountain and by midnight, I was back with my men. Most of 'em were asleep, some few of the Scotties was yet awake and they told me more of their story in their thick-tongued burred accents, their disgust for both the French and British obvious. They told of advancing through the abatis toward the wall under heavy fire, determined to get their hands around the throats of the French. Despite their great courage, they failed to even get close. They said our men fell by the score. The French, from behind their wooden wall, shot the hell out of ours whilst ours could scarce see the enemy to shoot at them.

The next morning, early, we started out. My rangers struggled with keeping the Scotties together and moving, not an easy task with the terrain which was mostly unfit for travel. We jumped a pack of wolves which was feasting on dead soldiers. One of our Scots raised his musket, taken from his French captors. I forbade him to shoot.

We arrived at the army camp at Sabbath Day Point, eight miles south of Bald Mountain. Rangers was posted there to receive any stragglers who might yet be coming. The rangers, as incensed as us for how badly Abercrombie had bungled the campaign, said few men had showed. The stomachs of these strong men churned at the thought of so many men lost and of glorious victory thrown away. We who had been through so much on this frontier and who felt we were finally coming to the end of our troubles, saw instead the dangers to our homes with the increased boldness the Indians would surely show now in raiding. A small band of Mohawks had witnessed the slaughter of our men from the heights of Rattlesnake, the very place I had anticipated watching the utter destruction of the French. The Mohawks would go home and retell the astonishing tale of our stupidity, the Iroquois' support for us would waver, our western frontier would be in even more peril. All for the incapacity of a commander who, astoundingly, had not actually seen the field of battle, indeed, had spent the entire fight inside the sawmill blockhouse for fear of Indians. The red men had played but a small role in the battle, yet it might be they had scored the biggest victory of this war so far.

The colonials had whaleboats and said there'd be plenty of empty seats on the return journey. They had only bad things to say about the British. Though they were of English stock, they considered themselves Americans, not Englishmen, same as I was American, not Dutch, as was my father. They said it was worse to have the English as friends than the French as enemies. Most of their scathing was for Abercrombie, they putting responsibility for the debacle, the needless slaughter of so many brave men squarely where it lay.

After dark, the Scotties were put on boats for the trip back up the lake. They were profuse in their thanks to those of us who had brought 'em in, the first time I ever seen any of 'em smile. Late in the night, rangers arrived from the south, their canoes ghosting silently to shore. Rogers was among 'em. They had met some others, southbound, so he knew I was back and was glad for it.

Rogers said there was trouble brewing down at the south end of the lake where our defeated army was encamped. Our colonial soldiers were in a terrible foul mood. Some of our men had refused, late in the afternoon of the battle and after what proved to be the final charge, to have another go at the wicked French emplacements. Abercrombie ordered some of the dissenters to be taken to Gallows Hill and hanged. The redcoats assigned to do the hanging had allowed some of our colonials to get away, either because they, the British, were repulsed by what they had been ordered to do or because they were eager to get to hell out of there. Probably the latter. British soldiers rarely disobeyed an order or considered whether it was just or not.

Ten men hanged by the biggest ass ever to set foot in the New World. No trial, no hearing, no nothin', just ropes. "To hell with him," I said. "Him and his bloody ilk. All their stupid rules and regulations t'ain't worth one damn colonial, same as Braddock, only he wasn't cowardly, just stupid. No more work shall I do for the addlepated sons-of-bitches." Me and my men were lucky to have gotten away with our hair, when what we should have been doing was celebrating a momentous victory.

Rogers asked about all the western Indians the Mohawks had said was coming and which I had been sent to watch for. I said we had seen no sign of them. He asked about the battlefield carnage. I told him what little I knew, none of which I had seen first-hand and had only been told. He got red in the face, filled with his own anger and shame and I thought he would explode. He didn't, and with the calculating I seen in his eyes, I sensed he had something other than our defeat on his mind.

Rogers asked if I thought the enemy was readying a move up the lake toward us. "Not until they finish off Nabby's rum," I said, and I laughed sourly to think of a handful of drunken Frenchies spooking Abercrombie all the way back to New York. Rogers knew the enemy wasn't coming but had felt a duty to ask and he wanted to know the situation around Bald Mountain. Had the French occupied it? I told him I had been to the summit; no one was there. He asked did I think they would re-occupy it. Probably, but why give a goddamn? The French were masters of the north end of the lake and we weren't going back up there anytime soon so what did it matter? Rogers asked more questions and he kept coming back to Baldie, which puzzled me. Surely there were more important things for him to be asking.

Rogers wrote out a brief report of all I had told him and dispatched it south, then he asked me to go along with him on a private scout to the north, just him and me. I thought this was even more audacious than usual for Rogers and I had a suspicion, by the look of him, it was for something other than a scout. He gave orders for the men to wait through the night, then another day and night for any of ours who might be forthcoming. He told them if we weren't back by the second morning, they were to go on without us. I got into his canoe and there were shovels, a pry bar and a stone boat, all concealed beneath a blanket. Something was afoot. Something to make me uneasy.

Chapter XVI – Rogers' Gold

We paddled hard all night, pushing rapidly toward the North Star. Rogers, in the stern, didn't hardly say anything and so neither did I. Toward morning, we approached Bald Mountain, which for me was too far, given the uncertainty of the situation. All was dark, no fires did we see at the top or along the sides of the mountain, which didn't mean the French weren't up there.

We went past the big rock-slab mountain, past a bay and a point and into another bay which, in the first light of dawn, was of a most wondrous beauty. If seen from the right hilltop, this bay was in the perfect shape of a heart, the water clear and clean smelling. Just into the bay and hugging the shoreline and with me feeling trepidacious for how much farther we might go, Rogers steered us to shore. We got in under some sheltering fir trees, the tips of the limbs nearly touching the water, which would afford us concealment even after the sun was up. Over a cold breakfast, I told him we ought not to go any farther. He said we had no need to, the bay was our destination. He then told me what we was doing and even already having figured we had come for something more than a scout, I was stunned by what he told me.

It concerned the army pay chest. Through some sort of army foul-up, the chest had accompanied our army to Ticonderoga. The night before the battle, Abercrombie, in full panic and learning of the foul-up, had ordered two lieutenants to take the chest back up the lake. The lieutenants, with four privates rowing and one steering, had set off in a whaleboat on the morning of the battle and never arrived at the south end. They, along with the chest, were presumed lost, which news was kept from the men. Meanwhile, a ranger reported to Rogers having seen from a distance a whaleboat moving fast with seven men aboard. This in itself was unremarkable and the ranger only told it because of what he saw next. The boat pulled into the Heart's Bay, the men unloaded a heavy chest and took it into the woods. "A few hours later," the scout said, "the privates emerged without their cargo or their officers." They rowed across the lake to the east shore where they disembarked and sent their boat drifting out onto the lake. They then trekked into the woods.

"Up over the mountains and heading for Boston or some such place," Rogers said. "To hide out until they deem it safe to retrieve their buried wealth." I admit to having been too stunned to say anything right away, such was the enormity of what Rogers was intending. "And what the ranger reported seeing," I finally said, "never got into your reports." He gave me his most wicked grin. "Abercrombie will have half his army up here looking," he said, "but not before we find 'er. May as well, eh?"

Having ascertained from the ranger as to where the soldiers had first gone ashore, Rogers was convinced the treasure was as good as his. He rationalized his intended theft by saying how, since the original thieves were probably murderers too, it was somehow noble to deny them their loot. "We can rebury it somewhere then come back later and reclaim it. What do you think?"

The way his eyes widened was something to see. The man was a wild one, game for about anything. "If I'd a had this figured out in time," I said, "I wouldn't have gone for it. I never would have come up here, but here I be." It was plain to me how wrong this was, but I suppose I was in such an angry state of mind toward the British, most anything done to punish them was alright with me. Except I didn't want them punished in a way to benefit myself personally. I also considered if I refused to go along, Rogers might brain me the first time my back was turned. He couldn't take a chance on my talking, now my reaction told him what I thought about his scheme. Money surely did things to men and with a fortune so near to this man's grasp, he was not someone to cross. I would have to go along, at least until I could get to hell away from him.

We took turns standing watch through what remained of the night, and with neither of us sleeping much, we discussed what action we might take in the morning. There really weren't too many directions we could go with a stolen treasure chest, not with a couple thousand French to the north and so many of our own to the south. The only thing was to bury the chest and come back for it later. Across the lake, somewhere on the eastern shore, might have been the best place but we would have to cross the lake at one of the widest points of the northern end. We might be spotted by either the British or French, or both, and with the chest probably as heavy as a small cannon, it'd be hard going and risky in a frail birchbark which might sink like a damn stone before we got across. South along the lake to the other side of Bald Mountain would have been a shorter distance but the depth of the water at the base of the cliff was two hundred feet. Did our canoe sink there, the treasure would be gone forever.

"Maybe that secret cave of yours," Rogers said.

The cave, low along the front of Baldie, ran slightly upward through the rockface. The entrance was sometimes underwater whilst the inside remained dry except for some dampness on the floor.

"Any Dutch or English who has ever smuggled or spooked the lakes knows about the cave," I said. "Same as the Iroquois and the rest of the devils. Put the chest in there and sure as hell some lucky Frenchies or red men will get off with it and you damn sure ain't goin' to dig a hole in solid rock for burying." I finished by saying as how the great Rogers, always so thorough in planning, hadn't done such a good job this time. "Greed got the best of you," I said. "Have to dig our own hole and stash it right here in the bay."

"With as many men as Abercrombie will have up here searching," he said. "Think they won't find it?"

"You're the great Robert Rogers," I said. "Some are even saying they ought to rename this here damn slab mountain after you, for all of what the newspapers are saying you did last winter to escape the Indians what was chasing you. Puttin' your snowshoes on backwards and goin' down the front of the cliff as if you was on skis. Surely a man as clever as you can dig a hole and cover it so's none but you can find it." He grinned and I suddenly got it, how he'd outfoxed me. I had chided him, saying as he hadn't thought it through, but he had, and had only led me on for knowing nothing of what he had proposed was workable. He had said those things so I'd suggest a plan and thus draw myself in deeper. My own feeling was, I was already in as deep as a man could go.

In the half-darkness of the morning, before full light and not wanting to get back onto the water to search for the place where the treasure boat might have come ashore, we walked the shoreline through the fog and quickly decided where the British had disembarked. From there, it did not take long to find the freshly turned earth, the chest buried just a short distance inland and a poor job done of it.

Rogers sent me back down to the canoe for the shovels, the pry bar and stone boat. I returned and we quickly dug up the chest. We brought it up out of the hole and I must admit to feeling a good deal of excitement as he pried it open. He pulled back the heavy lid and we gazed down at copper and gold coins, wads of paper money, silver and gold ingots, precious stones and the pay books for the army. On top, probably put in just before the chest was sent back from Ti was a fancy tea set, a serving for ten or so, each piece with Abercrombie's crest. Rogers lifted a few of the stones in a handkerchief for fear the rays of the sun through the gaps in the trees might glint the jewels and give away our presence. He offered me the stones. I hadn't ever thought I might become wealthy; prosperous, yes, but not so filthy rich as even these few baubles would make me. Truth was, I didn't want to take them for iffen I did, I was into it as deeply as Rogers. But if I didn't take 'em, I felt my death would be a surety before the day was out, such was the greed of this otherwise remarkable man. I stuffed the jewels into my pouch, telling myself I would manage somehow to not keep them.

He grabbed the handle on the front of the chest and waited for me to grab the back. I glared at him, then acquiesced. We grunted, lifted the chest onto the stone boat. Rogers tried to hand me the end of the harness.

"To hell with you," I said. "It's your treasure, minus my share, small as it will be, and only if I decide to take it," for I was still set against it. "Haul it yourself." He said he was ordering me to do it. "Rogers," I said, "what we're doing here is criminal, so I'm not obliged to follow your orders." He gave me a look as malevolent as I ever seen, for so great had his reputation grown, not even the most arrogant British officer dare speak to him in the way I was speaking now. "We're Rogers' Rangers, not Kuyler's," he said, yet, when I stood resolute in my intentions, he said nothing more and I suppose he couldn't argue with what I was saying, how, for as long as we were burying stolen treasure, rank meant nothing. I watched him get into the harness, my mirth nearly soundless, given our situation, but I damn near guffawed as he began pulling the heavy load. As I followed along, I taunted him, same as he had taunted me when he'd come to my farm and seen me harnessed and hauling stones. "Laugh all you will," he said whilst taking a break from the work and wiping his forehead with his handkerchief. He went a ways farther, stopped, and began disentangling himself from the harness, he maybe thinking I'd had my laugh and would now take a turn. "Stay in your traces," I said. "You've got farther to go, it's all mostly uphill and us short of mules. Pull!"

Now his glare was more menacing than I'd ever seen it and I suppose I could have taken a turn, or got behind the chest and pushed but the sight of him, like a yoked bull, his face red and sweaty with the exertion, the muscles and veins in his neck purred near to bursting with the leather thong of the harness tight across his forehead, was too funny. With the weight of it, he couldn't go downhill, the stone boat might have clipped his heels or run him over or it might have slid or tumbled down the slope and into the water and him going with it. He had instead to go side to side, uphill along the ridges. We found a likely place for the burying, it didn't much matter where we did it, just how well we did the job, and after he got out of the harness, he tried to hand me a shovel. I told him I'd cover our tracks, "Whilst you dig."

He told me to find the murdered lieutenants and clean up any blood I found. Blood on bushes or rocks would have the British digging all over the mountain. "Which they're bound to do anyway," I said. He got to work, I went off in search of the lieutenants and when I got back, he was still digging. I told him I had indeed found the bodies. He told me to carry them down to the boat. I did, and for the next three hours whilst he sweated over the hole, I worked on covering up our drag marks and footprints. He finished with the hole, we walked backwards down to the lake, swooshing branches over our disturbances. We wrapped the two stiffs, the shovels, pry bar and stone boat in the blanket and tied it all up with ropes. We attached a duffel full of rocks to the bundle.

After dark, we set out south and crossing in front of Bald Mountain, we dropped the bundle into two-hundred feet of water. We went on a little farther and in a secluded cove, we bathed and cleaned what dirt we could from our clothes. We got to Sabbath Day Point just as the others were preparing to pull out and we got in with them.

The men in the boats were drinking heavily, even the rowers, and all were morose, except for Rogers. He seemed gay, and now it was me glaring at him. Any investigation sure to come would look at the two of us for having gone north and for what reason, and when the British interrogated the rangers who'd been at Sabbath Day Point and who were in the boat with us now, as they surely would, the men might recollect how Rogers had acted more as if we'd won the battle than lost it.

****

We arrived back at the camp. The mood was dispirited for all of what had befallen us. The last remnants of old William Henry were finally getting cleared out, a bastion was getting erected. The feverish pace of the work got us even more agitated. How we seen it, Abercrombie, still haunted by the fear of all those Indians coming for his scalp was hurryin' to build something to cower behind. A ranger said Nabby, as scared as he was, ought to get on the next ship to London and leave the war to real men.

A crowd was gathered by the lakeside around one of those itinerant preachers so prevalent in our camps. He, a long-legged skinny fellow with whiskers, was up on a barrel eulogizing the late Mister Howe and as we passed by, he was saying how God had raised up a hero to end our travails and how could misfortune have befallen us at our moment of triumph? The preacher answered his own question by admonishing the men not to blame Abercrombie for our defeat. No. We ourselves was to blame. We were sinners and if we were to win the war, we must all repent of our worst sins, hubris, which I wasn't sure what it was, and insubordination, which I well understood. One of our men pulled the preacher down off his perch. The preacher vowed Perdition for the miscreant and with our miscreant holding onto the preacher's whiskers and with the preacher bent at the waist and windmilling his arms, our man walked him to the end of a pier, lifted him a way up into the air and tossed him into the lake.

When we got to our huts, the drinking got worse, our rage, too, as we began hearing the stories. One said Abercrombie, when he fled, had left our men hanging on Gallows Hill for the French who, when they got there, pulled down the corpses and scalped 'em, and before raising 'em back up, the French put placards around their necks. Cowards. I added to the indignation by telling of the French I had seen torturing our men and all those shoes with shiny buckles in the mud. Another man spoke of colonials pinned in the abatis and unable to go forward or backward and giving a hurrah for seeing a red surrender-flag rising up over the French wall. Our men ceased firing and were joyous for thinking the French had given up. The French played along, raising their arms whilst some of our men crawled out of the abatis and into the cleared area in front of the wall. "Quarter!" our men shouted. "We grant you quarter!" The gleeful French poured down a murderous volley.

We rangers got deeper into the rum. We cursed the British even more than we did the French. I vowed never to spook for the British again and I cussed their pompous fool of a general. We carried on past midnight with the drinking and with talk loud and rough enough so sentries came to quiet us. We, well-soused, insulted them.

"Get the hell back to England if you can find your way through the woods without us, you stupid sons-a-bitches."

"Get back into your petticoats, lobsterbacks, and leave men alone."

The sentries summoned the officer of the guard who came up with a detachment. We insulted them too and pretty soon a brawl got going. A few men got hurt, none seriously, and it ended with us stripping the sentries of their uniforms, tossing the uniforms into the lake and tying the British to trees in just their linens. We threatened them with tomahawk practice by torchlight but were content to leave 'em tied up, bedeviled by mosquitoes. More redcoats came and we whipped them too, except we ran out of cordage for tying 'em and had to let 'em go. It was a good thing there was not rope enough, else we might a bound up the whole damned British army and left it for the French.

Rogers wasn't present and when he come rushing back, he pointed out the British were not to blame, they had suffered same as us with advancing all day into murderous fusillades. He said their belligerence toward us now was on account of the anger and shame they was feeling. "So what you are saying," I said, "is those we want are the higher-ups." This was approved by the rangers.

Rogers shook his head and whilst he was trying to keep things from gettin' entirely out of hand, something snapped inside my drunken skull. Already fiery mad and with my hatchet in one hand, scalping knife in the other, I stormed out of camp intent on taking Abercrombie's hair. I didn't get far afore I got stopped by rangers sent by Rogers to fetch me back. Whilst I tried convincing 'em to join me, one of 'em, from behind, busted me on the head with a tree branch.

When I awoke sometime later, I was tied up alongside the redcoats and the ranger camp was in an uproar. Drunken, beaten-up men littered the grounds. Others were running and shouting, fists was flying, British regulars surrounded our camp with bayonets, all of which took place by firelight and in shadows, it being still a few hours to the dawn.

A British captain came along and demanded my name and the reason I was tied up. I rashly told him the truth, what my exact intentions had been and still were. To scalp his fat-bastard, cowardly general. Or, and if I could not have Abercrombie, I said, "Any high-ranking officer will suffice." I asked could he please untie me so I could get on with it. He ordered his men to take me to gaol.

I was put into the guardhouse with the rest of the culprits. Tying up the camp guard was a serious affront to British discipline and pride but we didn't think it would amount to much. Only as the morning wore on did we find out different. A court-martial was convened and a few at a time the men were led out and taken before the court, all but me, and each time someone came back, it was with grim tidings. The British, probably for feeling the shame of our defeat, same as we, were making it rough on our ranger outfit. Abercrombie was present at the inquiry.

He wasn't saying much but his presence was maybe goading the court into seeking harsh punishments, including hangings. The less-incensed of the judges suggested they could maybe hang just a few of us as an example and I figured I'd be amongst the few since it was I who had threatened to scalp the general.

Late morning, the gaol door swung open and the turnkey, a hard-looking sergeant with a lantern jaw and a nose which looked as if it had been busted a time or two, told the men they could go. "Not you, bub," he said as I tried slinking past him. He shoved me back inside and I seen there was another man with him. This was Jethro Stallworth, the ranger appointed to speak for me. I told Jethro my side of things, he didn't say much, just he kept shaking his head side to side and when we were done conferring, Stallworth went out, the gaoler slammed and barred the door, leaving me alone in there.

Well, about then I figured I was to die as a lesson to the rest of the men. What pained me the most was what it would mean to my dear Monie, the disgrace my hanging would bring her. And what would they tell her? That I died a valiant death? It's what they said sometimes about men who died less than heroically. It wouldn't matter, men would talk, word of my audacity would get out and Monie, so proud of her English heritage would be alone in a world as yet foreign to her and she wouldn't be able to go home to England, so great would be her shame.

One last thought reinforced my feeling of doom. Only one man had sufficient prestige to save me and that man, did he see me hanged, would double his buried fortune.

Mid-afternoon and with all hope having fled, the door opened. The usual protocol when a prisoner was to be taken out and hanged was for soldiers to come in behind the turnkey and get around the condemned man with bayonets. This time, it was just the turnkey. He was red-faced with anger. "Git!" he said, kicking at me whilst I was gettin' up from my bed of straw. Well, I did git, quick's I could, I not daring to believe my life had been spared.

Back at the huts, the rangers told me about the court-martial. They said the judges had decided to hang just one man and decided it might as well be the ranger whose belligerence had sparked the entire affair and who'd boasted he'd scalp the general. Stallworth apologized to the court for the drinking and in an attempt at levity, he said the incidents of the previous night showed as how we and the British still had some fight in us despite the whupping we'd taken from the French. This the judges met stone-faced.

Stallworth conceded threatening to scalp the general was not a good thing but with all the confusion and the shouting and with all of it taking place in the dark, wasn't it at least possible it was someone other than me? He turned to the rangers who'd been present and asked had any of 'em seen me heading out after the general. None had. The British captain, asked the same question by the court, said I had been clear about my intentions. Stallworth said it was just talk, a way of lettin' off steam, which was healthy for an army and wasn't it sometimes better to just ignore what got said? The captain, a young man reeking sincerity, after again re-affirming having heard it right, spoke eloquently on the infestation of rot which insubordination brought to the ranks.

Stallworth, a flamboyant lawyer in civilian life, countered with his own oration, which too was eloquent. He spoke glowingly and at length of my years of service but well-spoken or not, the judges weren't buying it and one of 'em finally stopped Stallworth by saying his pretty talk was a waste of the court's time.

Stallworth then played his trump card, what was called a point of order. He said, since I was an attached and not an official part of anybody's army, the British didn't have the authority to condemn me. This gave the judges pause. They huddled, whispering, and asked did I eat British rations and take British pay. My lawyer admitted I did and the judges said if they could feed me and pay me, they could hang me.

Rogers, hitherto standing by in silence, now brushed past Stallworth and ignoring the tribunal, he looked Nabby in the eye so hard and cold as to cause the general to shudder and turn his face aside. One of our rangers said it was as if no others was present, as if it were just Rogers and Abercrombie in an arena, the New World facing off against the Old. Another laughed to tell how whilst Rogers stoked the Mohawk rumor about all them Indians coming up the lake, Abercrombie's eyes got as wide as saucers.

Rogers said if the red men were coming, or when they came, Abercrombie would need rangers, which he would not have did he hang even one of ours for what was nothing more than feistiness. Because, Rogers said, if one single ranger hanged, every last one of us would be gone by sundown.

Abercrombie must have realized Rogers' threat to pull his men out of the war, as insensible as it was, might have been more than a bluff. Americans, in British eyes, could be a most exasperating people. We didn't always take the long view, often did we act out irrationally but we was always conscious of our rights as Englishmen, nay, as Americans, and had to be dealt with in a way different from Englishmen.

I think Abercrombie understood he was finished with the New World and was only thinking of getting back to civilization with his hair still intact beneath his wig. Or maybe the general, his spirit broken by the damage done to his reputation, just didn't give a damn anymore. Whatever it was, and with Rogers jabbering, threatening, Abercrombie threw up his arms and stalked back to his tent.

Rogers then turned to the judges and told 'em of a mission so fraught with danger he would not order any man to undertake it and so secret he could not even say what it was. He said I had volunteered and said I was going and did I come back, which was most unlikely, well then, they could hang me. This the judges latched onto. Better to lose a good man in an attempt to accomplish something than to gain naught by the forfeiture of said man's life.

The rangers finished telling the tale and everybody laughed. Except me. I realized how fortunate I was and I was grateful for the throbbing in my head from the clubbing and from all the rum I had drank. I felt the throbbing was somewhat of a punishment and would serve to remind me how dangerous it was to lose one's temper.

As for Rogers, I didn't doubt then, and I still don't today, that he was sincere in his defense of me, but I'd be a fool to think the stolen treasure didn't have anything to do with it. Rogers maybe feared what might be my last words up on the gallows. Maybe I'd call out the truth and laugh as the trapdoor sprung beneath me for us both knowing the next time it sprung would be for him. Or maybe Rogers did it for knowing he would need me to go back with him to fetch the treasure and now I could not refuse. The price I would pay for my life was a lesser share of the gold and did I decide I wanted no part of it, my gratitude would buy silence.

I thanked Rogers and asked about the mission for which I had volunteered. "You're to get yourself into feathers and paint," he said, "go up to Ti, talk your way into the fort and stick a knife into Montcalm's ribs." I stared at him and as I started to say he was crazier than I thought, he interrupted me. "Only get your arse up to Paradise afore Abercrombie changes his mind and don't come back 'til I give you the all-clear."

Chapter XVII – A Necessary Interlude

Staying west of the lakes, I followed a narrow creek to its source, a bubbling spring high up in a mountain ravine. I refreshed myself at the spring, crossed through the ravine and trekked down the other side, over steep ledges.

Getting closer in to my Paradise, I passed by familiar ponds, out of which I had taken many beavers and pretty-colored trout. The beavers, without me nor anyone to cull them, were increasing. Good blanket pelts they would be, come winter. I hoped I could get back to collect 'em.

I thought of my youthful days in Paradise, how naive I had been to think I could carve a life for myself up here, and yet I had succeeded, and I thought with regret how the war had diverted my life into a channel other than the one I would have taken. I remembered when my fight was with nature for survival in this rough country. Those times seemed now to be joyous. Hard times that made a man. How I longed for a return to peace and harmony, when a man worked to prosper and not simply to survive attacks by the cruelest, most inhumane race of men.

Monie would be eager to try it up here, once the danger was past, and even with all the British bungling, our time was coming. I imagined us raising the boys here at the Eagles' Lake. We would teach them to rely only on themselves and to grow up to be mountain men, not sodbusters or tavern-keepers.

I got up along the east end of the lake, the surface was tranquil with nary a ripple. I checked for sign, as usual, and found none. Saw a young moose browsing the shores, his presence another indication I was alone in Paradise.

I hurried along the cliffs and ledges and up into my canyon. I got onto the rim of the cliffs to look for sign of men. Again, none. I went back down into the canyon. My cabin was intact but was not without damage. The ravages of time had done their part. A stout limb had come down from way up and caved an entire side of the roof.

I opened the door and heard the scurry of little critters as they ducked into creases and dark corners. There was a strong smell of rot inside from the crushed roof having let in the rain. Back outside, I checked my cache, not digging it up, just assuring the area had not been disturbed. My first night back, with the air turning cool and after I got a fire going to drive out the dampness, I found a nearly full jug of rum on a shelf. Uncorked, it gave off the most delicious of aromas.

I settled in; a certain rough hominess was present. My first few days I spent putting affairs in order, even knowing my stay would be brief and I probably wouldn't be back until all the repairs I was now making would be erased. Still, it was work I enjoyed. I fixed the hole in the roof and stuffed moss into the cracks in the walls, between the logs.

Once this was done, I wandered the mountains, seeing all the familiar places again. The ponds so high up, some nearly to the top of the mountains, all full of fat trout, truly a paradise for a man good enough to make it so. I felt safe this far into the woods, away from the trails and forts. The French and Indians never seemed to come up here, and now and even with their victory at Ticonderoga, their hold on the lakes, with all their problems with resupply and reinforcements, was tenuous.

I shot the young moose for food and for the skin.

Walking the ledges and gazing down on my mountain lake, I wished there was a way to capture this picture. To bring it home so my wife could see for herself what I meant when I spoke of Paradise. I began thinking about where along the lake I would situate a cabin when the war was over, for I reckoned in a year or two the French would be driven out, the continent would be ours. To build on it, to farm it, was to own it. The French, for as often as they whipped us, were too dependent on their home country for things we provided for ourselves. All we needed was for the British to find some capable commanders. Not another Lord Howe, his type was rare, just someone to hold us steady to the end.

The north shore, though sunnier in the afternoons, was too sheer for all but the very rudest of cabins, the soil too thin for crops. There were just two possible sites. One was the patch of level, fertile ground along the east end of the lake, but with the swamps behind it, I feared the biters in summer would make it most untenable.

The other possibility was directly below my canyon, where the cut off the top of the mountain came down from the heights. Here was a most peaceful bay nearly entirely enclosed by the point of land which fish-hooked around it. The shore along the bay was flat and was broad enough for a barn and some few crops, whilst a house on the bay, with water on three sides and the cliffs behind it, would be defensible.

The summer sun, necessary for crops, would be pushed far enough north to splash its warming rays over my homestead and with a pebble beach nearby, I imagined Monie and me swimming and lazing about in summer. In the colder weather, we'd be somewhat exposed to the wind from the north and west but tight walls would fix this and in winter, the tall mountains would shield the house from any snow rolling in from the south.

My abode would be a proper house, not a cabin. Not so big nor fancy as what was along the lower reaches of the Hudson or along Yonkers Street but proper nonetheless. A stone house for warmth and comfort and protection against marauders. No telling when trouble of one sort or another might pass through here. Nobody ever seemed to come but this, too, could change. I must be prepared. There was plenty of fieldstone to build with. Constructing a house of these heavy stones would require a lot of work but I was ready, yea, eager, to start. So eager I began drawing lines in the dirt and on paper; where the house and outbuildings would stand, where the crops would grow. Just as well I did not have a shovel!

Off the lake end of the point, a few rods out, the water deepened and there was a small rock island where I would build a gazebo. My English wife had a fondness for gazebos, often mentioning one in a park close by to where she had grown up. I would build ours of cedar and recalling Josh's woodworking talents, I decided the gazebo would be an ornate work of art. Monie and me could swim to it in summer and canoe out when the leaves turned their colors and the water got cold.

Sitting on the shore in the cool evenings of what were mostly hot days, I saw us here in our garden spot with our two boys and with all the rest of the children we would have. I would offer Josh the farm on the Vlatche in return for his help in getting us started on the way to what I envisioned. The Vlatche farm was sufficiently prosperous to allow me to give a part of it to him and sell the rest to finance my new life.

The more I thought about Monie, the more I pined for her. News of our defeat would have her plenty worried and with her going down to the river or the road for word of me whenever soldiers went by, she'd know I had nearly got hanged and would think I was now on a mission from which I was unlikely to return. Such thoughts made my exile difficult, nay, unendurable, and I reckoned I could hide at home as well as I could here.

I went by way of the East Branch. I was avoiding not just the French but the British too, a precaution in case Abercrombie was having second thoughts about not having hanged me. The East Branch always held the possibility of encountering Mohawks. Go around a bend in the river and into a hunting party and I might wish I had been hanged. Still, I figured the western route would be safer and as it was, I made it home without incident.

I approached the house trepidaciously for what Monie might say about my drunken foolishness and the price we had nearly paid for it. There was a chance she didn't know about it. The only soldiers who ever stopped by the house were rangers, not militia, and sure as hell not British regulars, and Rogers would have been explicit with his men; they were not to speak of it. Loose talk might resurrect the hard feelings of the British and a reconsideration of my fate. Better it was for everybody to shut up about it.

Monie threw herself into my arms. We held onto each other with no words passing between us until she leaned her face back away from me and said it was lucky Abercrombie was a bigger fool than me, else I'd have hanged for certain. Then, and with how tightly she squeezed, she let me know how grateful she was for her fool having got home safely.

****

I was mightily pleased with how things were going with the farm. The crops in the fields, the stock, few but increasing, the gardens; corn, squash, potatoes, all the things we would need to see us securely through the winter, it all showed the results of dedicated labors. My hired man and his family were better farmers than I could ever be.

I had been thinking about moving Monie and my boys, along with Josh and his family back to Albany until we saw how things developed. An increase in the raiding seemed a surety thanks to Abercrombie, who, instead of securing our frontier, had opened it wide to depredations. I knew Monie would refuse to go. She had developed a bond with our tenants, especially Josh's wife, Cybil. It was as if Monie had regained the sister she had lost when Jane departed. All of them had a devotion to the farm, a zeal to work it, to improve it day by day. We were prospering, and Josh let me know as how there was naught but trouble for him and his family in town. Out here, and except for Barnes, men paid scant attention to another man's color, or at least let it pass, judging a man by who he was and of what he was capable.

Whenever rangers passed by and we had them in for supper, and as we got deeper into the rum, I'd get edgy, less they say something about the trouble I had caused. I would steer any and all conversation away from it because unlike when I'd first come home and Monie's overriding feeling was relief, now and when it came up between us, she'd get furious, or worse, derisive.

We heard plenty from the rangers about the lingering friction between our men and the British up at Lake George. Same as always, the British were contemptuous of their bumpkin cousins whilst we despised them for their stupidity and arrogance. Devoid of the sense of purpose inspired by the late General Howe, the camp was reverting back into a pestial hellhole, and with most of our supplies having been left for the French, rations were poor. "The French," I said, "must be grateful for all the barrels of meat and rum left by our fleeing army." The rangers said our colonials was getting sick and was dying. Many, disgusted with the ineptitude of the British, had begun to desert.

One ranger told us about the lost treasure chest, over which I feigned a dutiful shock. Abercrombie had sent a detachment of regulars to look for it. The ranger said they had dug just north of Bald Mountain, along the western shore of the lake and without success. I said, to test him, how if anybody could find the chest it was Rogers but I supposed he was too busy with recruitment and training. The ranger said no, Rogers had led the searchers, he determining the most likely places for digging. Of course. Places where a few hundred shovels would turn up nothing but dirt. What else the ranger said, and this got us laughing, after our men had dug all those holes and departed, the French got in there and did some digging of their own, not sure what they was going for but fairly certain it must be something for all the holes the British had left in the ground. My laughter was bitter for thinking the French might have got off with Rogers' gold.

The ranger said when our men found out about this latest official blunder, or, as some saw it, the swindle, and found out they wouldn't be getting paid, they nearly rioted. The British assured the men they would get their money, a vague promise which reassured nobody.

Rogers, with an audacity stunning even for him, was further endearing himself to our colonials with the fury with which he railed against British malfeasance. Rogers was loudly insisting the British had made it up about the lost chest so's not to have to pay us. I cagily questioned the ranger for more details, he said there was a rumor, probably started by the British, that Rogers might have had something to do with the disappearance of the chest. Me and the ranger scoffed at this, said it was just a way for the British to put the blame for their own ineptitude on us.

As stupified as I was by Rogers' boldness, I thought it prudent, with Monie there, to agree with the ranger when he said the British had somehow conspired to remove the chest so they wouldn't have to pay us. It made me feel guilty, my duplicity and the shame I put on Monie for her countrymen, but so deep was I into Rogers' scheme, I could do naught but go along. I griped for having been counting on my pay to buy things we needed for the farm and was troubled to hear we would not get our money, at least not for a while. I had buried my own stolen baubles in the woods there at the farm, still not sure if I would ever do anything with 'em and until such time as I decided and could figure out how to turn 'em into cash, I would leave 'em where they was. No matter the temptation or the need.

After the ranger departed, Monie seemed perplexed with Rogers possibly having been involved with the disappearance of the money. Monie knew Rogers was a scoundrel and what else she knew, or suspected, as tight as me and Rogers were, if he had something to do with it, I might of too. She didn't openly accuse me but she did say I had badgered the ranger for what more he might know about it.

I demanded, rather harshly and to draw out what she was thinking, what she meant. She said I had seemed to be barking around a tree for something I didn't dare go for directly. Something I was hoping wasn't there. "Something about the money?" I said, and she finally said as how it would be just like Rogers to have swiped the chest and if he did, she hoped he hanged. She later said she didn't believe Rogers would do anything so awful and stupid but if he did, and did I have a hand in it too, then God help both of us, she certainly wouldn't.

****

From another ranger, we heard how Rogers had got careless and it had cost him. Finishing a three-day patrol over near the Drowned Lands with a hundred men, a mix of rangers and redcoats, Rogers was camped for the night at the ruins of old Fort Anne. There hadn't been much sign, Indians didn't seem to be around, and the rangers got to boasting of their marksmanship and taunting the British officers for their own shooting which, our men always said, was poor. The British began giving it back, saying the rangers' shooting wasn't nearly as good as our reputation. In truth, the British accompanying us on our forays, the Light Bobs, as they were called, for they were light infantry which had cut their hair and discarded their wigs, could shoot pretty good. Trained by us and adopting our tactics, the Light Bobs were becoming capable enough in the woods.

Rogers, upholding the honor of his command, challenged the best of the Bobs to a shooting match. Targets were set up, distances marked off and Rogers showed what an American woodsman could do with a rifle. The Bobs were impressed, as were the four-hundred French and Indians who was within hearing distance and who had heretofore not been aware of Rogers' presence. The next morning, whilst our men was going through thick brush, they walked into an ambush. The fight was a hot one and with the French giving Rogers a hard sniping, our position was desperate. Another man might have panicked, made the wrong moves and got wiped out but Rogers' audacity and savvy held our men together and it was the French militia what broke off the engagement. Our losses, killed and wounded, were fifty men. The French lost more than us and the newspapers, whilst lauding Rogers, ignored his rashness, which had brung on the fight. Sometime later, we learned the commander on the other side was the noted French scout, Charles Michel de Langlade, he who had led them to victory in the first of the two battles on Snowshoes. This Langlade was known to us as the French Robert Rogers and the news Rogers and Langlade had met again and Rogers had bested him further enhanced Rogers' reputation.

****

Our disaster at Ticonderoga was overshadowed by news of important successes for our side, in this momentous year of 1758. First came word of our taking Louisbourg with a combined land and sea attack. Despite our earlier fulminations regarding this diversion of our men, the strategic value of Louisbourg was undeniable. Located at the mouth of the Saint Lawrence River, this mighty fortress was the gateway into Canada. Now and with Louisbourg firmly in our possession, any ocean-going French convoys attempting to land much-needed troops and supplies would be threatened by British warships out of Louisbourg. The Albany church bells must have pealed joyously and I could only imagine the celebrations which must have filled the Full Sail as well as the other taverns.

And, too, we were avenged for the loss of William Henry which loss could be at least partly attributed to our having sent our men to Louisbourg in '57. What else was erased was the shame for the British having given Louisbourg back to the French after we took it in the previous war. This time, and with Pitt's determination to win the world-wide war in North America, we knew there would be no giving it back.

Then came news of another great victory, the fall of the French fort,

Frontenac, which controlled Lake Ontario. Canada's lifeline was now severed in two places. The Canadian heartland, the settled areas around Montreal and Quebec, were cut off on one side from the mother country and on the other from the interior forts and trading posts. The two cities could be starved out or taken whilst the interior forts lay before us as ripe melons on a chopped vine. The flow of French trade goods to the western Indians would be seriously diminished which would prompt them to rethink their allegiance to the French. Most satisfyingly, the fall of Frontenac was the work of our colonials, not the British. American arms had once again scored an important victory. Three thousand of our men, led by the colonial, Bradstreet, whom I had seen in action many times, had taken the fort and garrison and all the French trade goods destined for their western posts, and even a couple of sloops of war.

Then came the best news. General Abercrombie had been bagged off to England, where he could hector his king with declarations of how none of the Ticonderoga debacle could be laid at his feet, never mind he was the commander. Probably say it was the fault of us colonials. Fine. Let him spend the rest of his life fighting us with voice and pen, seeing he never would fight the French with his cannons.

Another fancy general was on his way and was bringing five more regiments of regulars. This new man was Jeff Amherst, said to be solid. Rumors went around the camp. Amherst was intending another go at Ti. It would not happen this year. It would soon be too cold up there for the British. They could not fight in the summer, how in the hell were they to fight in the winter?

After a month or so of checking on things, and time spent with Monie and the boys and without much for me to do at home, I began to hear the call of duty. I had made plenty of noise about never aiding the British again but the overriding importance was to defeat the French. Anything other than the elimination of the danger was strictly secondary and with our successes, glimmers of hope in what had been an otherwise dark time, I was anxious to get back up there.

I broached again with Monie and Josh the prospect of their moving temporarily to Albany whilst I went north. I knew they would resist and I thought it not fair of me to expect Josh and his to stay at the farm whilst I packed Monie off to safety. I understood how they felt but I asked anyway and they refused.

What was a-building there at the farm was a community, with Monie, Josh, Cybil and the children all working together and glad I was for Josh and his family, not just for what they were doing for me but for what the farm meant to them. Albany had proven difficult as had most places they had tried, and if I insisted they remove themselves even for just a few months and for reasons of safety, I knew they must seek something more permanent elsewhere. I consoled myself with the knowledge our local militia had been upgraded due to the heavy raiding we had anticipated but which had not yet come. I was further assured by the knowledge my stone house was a fortress and by how Josh and his young son and even his wife and daughters had improved their marksmanship. They worked diligently with the muskets and pistols I had left with them and though they were not crack shots, they might yet take down an Indian running in their peculiar zig-zag loping fashion. I cautioned Monie to stay as much as possible within a short run of the house and I was grateful for Josh having dug a well close by to the front door. Heretofore, we had got our water either from the well by the cabin or out of the stream, now it could be drawn from right up close to the house.

After ascertaining from Rogers the way was clear for me, I returned to the north.

Chapter XVIII – Answering the Call

I was soon back at the ranger camp at Edward. I went to Rogers' headquarters. He wasn't there, the officer in charge was a man I knew. He welcomed me and we talked a few minutes. "Wait," he said as I was leaving, and he reached around and down and came back up with a crisp, neatly folded, forest-green ranger uniform. "This is for you."

The rangers had only begun to issue uniforms sometime earlier in this year of '58 and I had so far refused to wear one, my refusal couched on the fact I was attached and not a real ranger. I thought the uniforms were silly. A heavy coat, double-breasted and short-waisted with slash cuffs and pewter buttons, it seemed more fancy than practical and some of the jacket pockets weren't even real. Fake pockets, just where a man wanted to be reaching in a bush fight. The rest of the uniform, breeches and hose, a buckskin frock, leggings tied at the knees, weren't much different from what I mostly wore anyway. The headgear, though, was one of those green bonnets with a ridiculous frilly pommel on top.

"The major says you got to wear all of it," the supply officer said, "and iffen you don't, my orders is to run you out of the camp. He says you need to blend in, not just in the woods but in the camps too, so you don't stick out for the British to reconsider hanging you for the trouble you caused." Rogers and me had argued plenty over this, he was proud of the uniforms, having had a hand in designing them, and he considered himself most dashing in his. The officer grinned as I snatched the bundle and somewhere, Rogers was laughing.

My uniform, stiff for being so new, I was maybe stuck with, but I wasn't going to abide the hat. No, sir. I wasn't going to wear a damn bonnet like what the Scotties wore, else next they'd have me in a skirt. I went down to the piers. Our boatmen all mostly wore leather slouch caps same as Joe Blanchard had used to wear and I figured I could wear one in tribute to Old Joe. I saw a nice one with gold-colored embroidery and with the long sides curled up the way Joe had used to wear his. I asked the boatman did he want to trade hats. He looked at my bonnet and laughed, as did the men around him, and when I insisted and put a bottle of French claret into the deal, he got suspicious for thinking I was trying somehow to dupe him. We haggled some and with me trying to convince him I was on the level and him getting how intent I was on owning his hat, he kept raising the ante. When I walked away, the boatman and his friends were passing the bottle and laughing as he pranced around with the fancy green bonnet on his head and my shiny new ranger knife, hatchet and shot pouch on his belt.

****

I was soon with Rogers at the south end of Lake George. The camp was getting to be a fort again, with the new bastion completed, which was reason for optimism, as well as bitterness. Men who should have been on the way to Canada were instead at work preparing defenses, as if they were expecting King Louis hisself to bring the entire might of France up the lake. We were six-thousand men, the place was not fit for so many but not even the debilitating condition of the grounds, so near to the swamps, could daunt the British army from its task, so long as the task was something other than fighting Indians.

The raids were on the increase, the Hurons and Abenakis and all the rest stirred by Montcalm's victory. Snipers' arrows were a menace for the men, many of our supply trains got hit. The casualties we suffered were high, though the wagon trains got through. A big part of the army was on the roads, escorting the wagons and suffering for it. Any soldier who wandered off or straggled got hisself killed. The foe rarely showed themselves but were always watching. One of their tricks was to catch a man and make him holler within hearing distance of one of our patrols. Often this tactic was successful as no orders or warnings could stop the men, they simply snapped at the viciousness and acted rashly upon it. Or a man might be walking with his mates in a group of five or six and an arrow out of the trees would take him down, and if any of the men went charging into the woods after the villain, which they did, often, they would be lost too.

****

Fall came, the forests of the north were dazzling in their colors, the orange and red in the maples, the brown of the oaks, the yellow of the hickory, birch and beech, an array combined to make a trip through the woods or along the jewel of the lakes a most incredible journey. The colors also made the woods more dangerous for the woodland devils knew how to paint and conceal themselves so to blend in and to lurk in the play of sunlight and shadow. We lost scouts to ambuscades and traps. All these things were constant reminders of what awaited the unwary.

****

Early winter and on a cold night, we were five canoes, twenty men. We were moving north through the Lake George Narrows. The ice was just starting to form. In some places it was in thin sheets we had to break with our paddles, in other places it was chunks bobbing in open water. We were wary, as always, of what the ice might do to our frail birch-barks. One rip of a sharp edge against the skin could sink a canoe and in cold water, a man not immediately pulled out would lose the ability to save himself, so quickly would he lose the feeling in arms and legs.

On one of the islands as we passed, we heard what we thought was a voice calling to us and which, after careful observation, turned out to be a ranger named Williams, who had been a prisoner at Scalp Point. He had escaped and having located a hidden canoe, he was getting up the lake pretty good when the canoe gave out and he just barely got to the island. He had been marooned for a couple of days and was nearly done in with the cold and fatigue. We wrapped him in blankets and bearskins, got him up close to a fire and fed him. He gave us the news from Scalp Point. The French were breaking camp for the winter. The habitants were all mostly gone to the north, more regulars than usual was staying, compliments of Abercrombie and the large stores of food he had left for them. Williams said the news of the French losses of Louisbourg and Frontenac had cast a gloom over the enemy garrisons. They too saw the direction the war was goin'. Williams said the only concern the French didn't have was us coming down the lakes to hit 'em. Our British were not adept at hurting the enemy.

Rogers sent Williams south in the care of a few men. We pushed on. Rain and fog shrouded our passage. Winter was surely upon us, the rain colder and heavier now. Ice continued to form on the water and by the time we got along the precipitous slope of Bald Mountain, we could see little of the edifice, just glimpses through the fog, and we was having a hard time breaking ice.

We got into the Heart's Bay, I looked to the canoe in front of mine, to Rogers, who was in the back, his paddle out of the water, his neck and head twisted around so's to look at me. Then, grinning, he pushed away hard, vanishing into the fog.

We got up to Ti and with the French spy posts and lookouts drawn in for the winter, we ascended Lookout Rock, near the summit of Rattle-snake, and looked down upon the star-shaped fort below. The French were putting boats onto the lake. Despite the strong current from the crick, the ice was thick. Lake Champlain iced before Lake George. The latter was spring fed so the deep formations were slower to form there. Lake Champlain was much shallower and so more conducive to icing. Soon it would be sleds and horse-drawn sleighs replacing canoes and whaleboats on the lakes. The sloops getting underway had small boats filled with axmen going ahead, chopping a way through those places which had ice. On our second day in the area, the rain turned to sleet then snow. Rogers groused how, "If only the English would move, we could finish off Ti and Scalp Point this year, once and for all." He was right, we should come here in force and finish the job. All his grumbling was for naught, as the British would not hear of it. We trudged back south from Scalp Point through a snowstorm. Cold and miserable as it was, the snow served to cover our tracks. We regrouped at our boats and after the weather cleared, Rogers led us back to the Lake George camp.

****

I made some solitary patrols, up for a few days and back again, and after one of these patrols and entering Rogers' tent and before I could report and find out from him the news, he said my black man had arrived four days ago with word my father had taken terrible sick. I left within minutes on a borrowed horse, going south along the Great Carry road. I didn't make Edward until well after sunset. I spent a sleepless night at the ranger base camp and a half hour before first light, I put a canoe into the river. The current was strong from all the rain and snow and by ten o'clock at night, I was hurrying through the darkened streets of Albany. The tavern should still have been open and I was chilled to see it dark and shuttered. I went around to the back, there were lights and voices inside. I walked through the door. Monica, Eric and Sarah were in the galley with some few of Mother's Dutch friends. Dishes of food warmed by the fire. My wife and me looked at one another, she shook her head side to side. Pops was dead. We embraced without any words between us. I held her so tight, I didn't ever want to let go. Eric shook my hand and offered condolences. Sarah rose up on her toes, kissed me on the cheek and whispered something. Mother came out from the back room. "Oh, my son, my son." Mother sniffled, then, stoutly fighting to keep her voice steady, "It is good you are here." She broke down and sobbed, I tried comforting her in unpracticed, stumbling Dutch.

Eric told me what had occurred. For a few days, the men had been remarking how Pops had seemed more red in the face than usual and had been sweating heavily, and when they asked him was he ill, he, of course, gruffly dismissed their asking. Then, about a week ago, late in an afternoon, he went into the back room for a keg of beer and lifting the keg, he'd fallen. By the time anyone could get to him, which was no more than a moment, Pops was unconscious. He lingered a week, never regaining consciousness, the doctor saying there was naught they could do except keep Pops comfortable. The morning of the day I got there, with Monie and Mother at his side, Pops slipped quietly away.

Eric, with years at the apothecary, was more knowledgeable about these things than most of the doctors around and he said as how it was unlikely Pops had hit his head when he'd fallen, nor had the keg struck him a blow. What killed him came from inside, and further, Pops had an intimation he was about finished with this world and had gone to the apothecary and asked Eric vague questions about pills and potions but when Eric tried to learn more about the trouble, Pops stalked off angry. The old Dutchman would go out doing the only thing he knew.

When Josh came back down from the north with word I was out on patrol, they figured there was little chance I would get home before Pops passed. Even whilst Pops lingered, and with Mother's consent, Eric had begun making arrangements. A casket was readied, a stone was cut, the burial was set for the morning following my arrival. I was grateful for all Eric had done.

Monie and me walked into the bedroom, dark except for flickering candles and an oil lamp. A sheet had been placed over Pops' lifeless form. I paused at the foot of the bed, not wanting to take another step. Monie nudged me with her elbow, I moved closer. I sat in the chair up close to the bed, Monie lifted the sheet.

Pops looked peaceful, the lines of his face gone slack. I couldn't help but think he must soon open his eyes and grouse about all the sniveling and nobody minding the tavern. Even to one who had seen a lot of death it was hard for me to accept the loss of this vital man, to know he was never to rise again, his sardonic tongue stilled forever. I replaced the sheet, nodded to Monie and we returned to the others.

Mother was terribly haggard. The poor old girl had hardly moved from Pops' bedside. She hadn't taken anything much for food or drink and had only slept fitfully in her bedside vigil. If anyone thought she was cried out, she now showed she wasn't, probably it was my being there. Her lips quivered, she shook her head and called out piteously for her man. I held her in my arms, she sobbed into my chest. She shook with spasms, I thought how tiny she was.

"He was a damn good man," I managed, after Mother had somewhat recovered herself. "We shall miss him."

"I know, son," she said. "Even if you never would listen to him."

"My dear Mother. Believe me, I often did listen to him. And to you, too. I suppose it just never seemed so."

"Of course," she said, not believing it.

Gathering her strength and looking for something to distract herself, she moved away from me and went over to stir the fire. She was a strong woman but so much of her strength came from the powerful man she loved, her loss apparent in how frail she looked now, hunched down by the fire. She went back into what had been her and Pops' room, closed the door and continued her vigil, alone with him.

Mother's friends, women I had known my entire life, hugged and consoled me and departed. We had a drink, Monie and Sarah fixed us a good supper from what Mother's friends had left; beef roast, potatoes, cabbage, bread and butter. Mother came out and joined us at the table, and as we talked and ate, she chided me for cursing so much, something I did without realizing, it being natural in camp with the rangers. I contemplated how strange was my path, the life of a woods-romping scout in time of war, and how, when I was off to war, I was yet but days from home, my two lives thoroughly opposed yet entwined. Without the one, there could not be the other. It was hard to come down from the headiness, the constant alertness required in the wilds. Eyes searching and probing seemed out of place by a warming fire and with my wife at my side, as did a chiding from the old woman, offended with my language when only days ago I had stood in mortal danger of a fearsome enemy.

****

The funeral was held in the Dutch Church and was well-attended by the Albany folks and others from up and down the river. Pops was a legend of sorts among the frequenters of taprooms. He was known by many; army men, leaders of the colony, Indian chiefs and drunks; all were welcomed in the Full Sail, all enjoyed their time there. Pops' favorites were the sailors. Whether they plied the river, or, less frequently, the world, didn't matter. Pops would talk with them by the hour about ships' rigging or a sailor's life on the deep sea or the Hudson. He loved to gossip about the different characters among them. Those old sailors were worse than a women's church society. Pops always had a helping hand for the sailor who missed a ship or jumped because of a bucko mate or feisty bos'n. He never allowed the British recruitment gangs to steal drunken seadogs from his place.

There in the packed church, I recognized more than a few weather-beaten faces from my youth. Josh was there, standing in the back, cap in hand, there were rangers on furlough, and Baronet Sir William Johnson, bless his soul, took the time from his work to attend, accompanied by his beautiful Iroquois princess and some Mohawk sachems who had used to drink with Pops. After the service and the burial up on the hill, Johnson and me and his Mohawks spent the better part of the day in the otherwise empty tavern, drinking the old man's beer. We toasted Pops and talked about the state of affairs in the colony.

Johnson looked drawn. He was being driven about crazy in unending dealings between his Indians and our colonial government. Johnson was a most important man in the colony. The old rascal was ever vigilant in keeping his Mohawks quiet. He had spies and informers in every camp and spent endless hours haranguing his red brothers. His place as go-between in the constant wrangling between the two races of men was frustrating and difficult.

Bill's office was also very dangerous. The French had long offered a reward for his scalp. Never knew when some young buck in a smoky longhouse might bury a tomahawk in the back of Bill's head. This was a real threat. Johnson knew it but did not let the risk deter him. Worse in his mind was the constant interference of politicians who thought they know more about Indians than him. They often tripped him up, thwarted his efforts. "Sometimes not meaning to," he said, and frowning, "and more often for their own shady purposes."

Bill could always switch topics easily and with a benign smile he asked, "Do you intend taking over the tavern?" I told him no. He asked what would I do with so many kegs of beer, for Pops had just recently brewed a batch. I said I supposed I would take it home, unless Mother said no. "Hate to let it go," I said. Bill seemed puzzled and asked where I would keep so much beer with winter coming. "In the cellar, I reckon," I said. "Should keep from freezin'." Bill had always considered Pops to be the best brewer in town and with a sudden grin, Bill asked could I get them big kegs down into my cellar. When I admitted I could not, he said I might as well give it to him. I talked it over with Mother and whilst I filled some few small kegs for myself, Mother insisted Bill just take the rest. He refused.

"Dear Mother Kuyler," he said, sweet as sugar on a cake, his gracious smile had always charmed her. For twenty years Mother had reckoned the sun rose and set on William Johnson. "I would never stoop so low as to rob the widow of a friend. You shall have your fair price." Indeed, Baron Johnson did her more than right.

The day after the funeral, Mother, Monica and me sat in the dark taproom, Mother urging us to consider taking over the tavern so I might give up my dangerous bush-loping.

"You know I could never run this place right," I said.

"Is it too much to hope you might learn?" Mother said. "Think of the boys. Do you want them to grow up without a father, should something happen to you?"

Monica replied, "Do you wish for my sons to grow up as wild as their father around this taproom?" She said this whilst smiling so Mother would know she was intending levity. Mother misunderstood and gave Monie a cross look for thinking Monie was chiding her about my own upbringing. Putting the blame for what I had become squarely on Pops and Mother.

"I only want you to understand," Monie said, "that neither of us cares to live in town. I, too, wish he would stay home, to run the farm, but he has a greater purpose for which we should all be grateful, and we should all respect him for what he does." Monica placed her arm in mine in a wonderfully loving way and I felt a surge of emotion for her. It had seemed to me, when we had first met, how she had her sights as much on the Full Sail as on me, and now, with the tavern there for the taking and with Mother insisting and I refusing, Monie stood firmly, nay, defiantly, with me. I leaned over and kissed her on the cheek and her love-filled eyes told me she understood the reason for the kiss.

Mother saw clearly what had passed between Monie and me.

"He takes good care of us," Monie said to Mother.

"I suppose it is so," Mother said, half-smiling, surrendering. "Kenneth has not turned out so badly, just a bit undisciplined, and if anyone is to be blamed, it has to be me, doesn't it?" The tone of her voice and the smile on her beautiful old face spoke much for a mother's love of an only son, however errant she might think him.

"You did your best," Monica said, trying not to smirk; then, and with a smile toward me, "You just didn't have much to work with." This time Mother understood Monie's lightness and suppressed somewhat her own proud smile. "I'm sure you're right," she said.

Monie tried to convince Mother to come live on the farm with us by pointing out how much she would enjoy her grandsons. "We have plenty of room." Mother said she did not want to interfere. Monie told Mother she would be a joy, not a burden. I think Mother mostly wanted some time alone.

Despite the insistence of many of Pops' regular customers, I declined to open for business whilst I was selling the place. I feared staying open would entrap me and I might never get out. Instead, I sought to quickly arrange the sale. The sooner we got rid of the tavern, the better, not because it hadn't served us well but because it might become the source of more serious contention. With time to reflect and at Mother's urging, Monie might yet swing around to Mother's way of thinking.

Buyers came, eager for the chance. We soon had four or five solid offers lined up. Still Mother hesitated and we decided to go to auction, where we might get an even better price. The bidding was lively and would have upset Mother had she attended, which she did not. The tavern sold well and along with what money the folks had stashed over the years, Mother was assured of finishing out her life in comfort. Details were completed within a few days, the papers drawn up, stamped and official. The buyer was an Englishman new to the country. He was out from the city of Birmingham, a city dandy who expounded on what he called the Great American Wilderness.

Mother took lodgings, Eric and me moved her things. She told me she was considering a visit back to the old country. I convinced her a sea journey this time of year would be too difficult. With everything in order, I sent word to the farm for Josh to come with the wagon. We loaded Pops' tools and the beer kegs and some other stuff. We shipped Pops' clothes down to Henry. The clothes wouldn't fit the lanky Josh but might, with some stitching, fit Henry, shorter and thicker than his father. A few days later Josh was back to fetch us and we were on our way home, Josh driving, Monie and the babes in the wagon, me walking alongside, rifle in hand. It was a pleasantly warm late fall day and as saddened as I was by Pops' passing, yet I felt happy for our future.

****

The fall passed quickly and the Christmas season was soon upon us. Monie and me were looking forward to enjoying the happy season with the boys. I promised to stay home at least until the New Year. I didn't want to ever leave, yet I felt pulled by the call of duty.

Official dispatches came from the west. Another key French strongpoint had fallen to us. Colonel Forbes had taken Duquesne, the French fort at the forks of the Ohio, where Braddock was so soundly beaten back in '55. We cheered for knowing this would quiet the Indians out there. Forbes suffered heavy casualties in hard fighting but kept on to victory. A Swiss officer serving with the British, Major Bouquet, was given much credit for our success as were some of our Scotsmen from the Black Watch Highlander Regiments. The Scotties did some of the best fighting though not without losses. One of their advance detachments got wiped out and when our men marched into the fort, they seen the heads of the Scotties impaled along the tops of the walls.

****

I had a bad dream. My friend Tom O'Brien came to me with a stern warning. He stood stiffly at formal attention in his dress uniform and sash. He took my hand and said he was sorry, there was simply nothing he could do. Wished I understood better what he meant. I didn't say anything to Monica about it, afraid to scare her. More likely she'd have scoffed.

Chapter XIX – Scalp Hunters

Good news! We were to have a prisoner exchange with the French. I thought of Priscilla, wife of my late friend, Arnold Baldwin, and of Eric's father. Eric and me were not hopeful. So many years had passed since his father and Priscilla were taken away, and as it turned out, the exchange was for soldiers only, no civilians. Colonel Peter Schuyler was among those to be released. That influential Dutchman was a steadying influence on our colony. He took on a lot of responsibility.

Also included was one of our rangers, the celebrated Israel Putnam, taken prisoner when Rogers, deep in the woods, got into his shooting contest with our British friends, which drew in Langlade with his French and Indians. Ol' Putt, as we learned, had undergone the most harrowing ordeals in captivity. The gauntlet at every village, tomahawk-hurling games with him tied to a tree as the target and another time tied to a tree and getting burnt, he was saved by a late-afternoon thunderstorm. Putt was a solid man undaunted by all he had endured and as determined as before to continue the fight. The French were fools to give him back.

Many were against the exchange. They said it benefited the French more than it did us, which was true. Feeding prisoners and refilling the ranks were more difficult tasks for them. Still, the exchange was mostly welcomed.

Mid-December, the army muster rolls were verified, pay to be issued at Albany. Me, Monie and the boys went into town. On the appointed day, I carried along Augustus Daniel. Whilst I was standing in the pay line, the rascal wet all over me. The other men got a chuckle out of my misfortune and my little boy, seeing the men laughing, clapped his tiny hands and laughed along.

Long lines bogged down by frequent petty arguments; aggravating delays caused by the officials challenging the validity of our men's claims. I finally received a damn chit for twenty Spanish dollars. Not much! We saw Mother each day and spent most evenings with Eric and Sarah. We truly enjoyed the visit, impossible not to, in the company of such fine people. Mother, still grieving, came with us most nights to dinner. She was seen to smile more than once and she agreed to spend

Christmas with us.

Monica bought a green dress. One to set off her flashing eyes and delightful full figure to fine advantage. I found it impossible to keep my rough hands off her, with her charms so amply apparent. Such a woman! The first night she wore it we were an hour late for dinner. Eric grinned when we appeared with faces flush, Monie and me a little embarrassed. Quite obvious. Sarah winked and made suggestive remarks at which we all laughed, even Mother. In the laughter, our poor manners for such a late arrival were forgiven.

That night I had the same terrible nightmare again, except this time Tom seemed even more melancholy, the sadness in his eyes was most gripping. Again he apologized, saying there was nothing to be done for it. The ghost stayed but moments, accompanied by the tom-toms pulsing a steady rhythm which grew fainter as Tom's shadow dimmed. I awoke trembling and reached for Monie. Didn't she hear the drums? Her place felt empty and I groped around in the bed. Where was she gone off to? She was there and awoke growling, "What the hell are you wanting now?" I mumbled about a bad dream; she told me to go back to sleep. I didn't sleep the rest of the night for the dream having upset me so.

Monie presented me with an expensive new suit. I wore it to dinner the next night. Too-short sleeves restricted my shoulders and arms, the starched collar pinched my neck. A nuisance for a man accustomed to fringed buckskin hunting-shirts which hung loosely below the waist. I had a time just putting the damn thing on and I was nagged with how it restricted my movements. Couldn't figure why seeing me bound up so made my wife happy. Eric could not stifle a laugh and said to Monie, "I did not believe even you could tame our mountain man but look at him!" Monie smiled sweetly and damn near melted my heart by saying, "Isn't he handsome?" Sarah agreed as did Mother, who nodded before bending down and resuming playing with her grandsons. Having them around was a tonic for her.

The women shopped every day, seemed as if they bought something from every merchant in town. Monie and Mother, arms full of packages, laughed for spending so much of my money.

I was sad when the day came for us to leave. Monica was having such a time, who could deny her anything? Still, and with the way she was spending, it was time to go. I thought of the expensive gems Rogers had given me and of our fabulous wealth buried up along the shores of Lake George. I still wasn't sure I would take my share, or even keep the gems. I'd have to figure some way to cash it in without raising suspicion. One thing for sure, if I took it, I would never again have to worry about my wife's spending.

The women and babes were loaded onto the wagon for the trip home, the wagon half-full of boxes, and amid fond goodbyes with Eric and Sarah, we promised to repeat the good times after Christmas, when we would bring Mother back to Albany. Eric and Sarah promised they'd visit the farm come spring. Josh drove the wagon, Monica sat alongside him, Mother and the babes were in the back, the littler one in his carrier, wrapped from head to toe in a warm shroud blanket. Augustus sat in Mother's lap. I walked alongside, rifle in hand, comfortable again out of my city clothes and back into mountain-man attire. My loose-fitting clothes felt stiff with all the washing and ringing Monie had put on them. The women gabbled along the way. They sang clapping songs and fussed with the babes. Mother was already teaching Augustus to speak Dutch. Funny to hear the little guy struggle over the words. Mother said Augustus was a happy child and well should he be, with all the love and attention she gave him. Monie was excited for the chance to show off her home. This would be the first time Mother had visited us. It was heartwarming to listen, though I feigned disgust with the chatter.

The day was cold, clear and bright and with a strong east wind. The mules took their time. I did not mind going slow for Mother's sake. At first, we met farmers, itinerants, soldiers, sutlers' wagons and carts. A party of Irish immigrants bound for Saratoga. Passing greetings were cheery. People were encouraged. The future looked bright. Despite the troubles and sorrows, we looked forward to Christmas with a sense of well-being and a growing belief the coming year would see the end of the war in our favor.

According to the news in Albany, all was going well. The lads out to Oswego were eagerly awaiting spring, to continue the offensive started this year. They were doing good work, these young men. They were becoming a fighting force of considerable repute. By young Eric's letters, which his father had shown me, our lads had a growing confidence in their ability to defeat the French and Indians. The French were not yet driven from the Great Lakes or the Ohio Valley but I was pleased with our prospects for the upcoming campaigning season. Affairs augured well. Good leaders make the difference.

As we got closer to home, traffic on the road thinned. The mules became unruly, Josh had a time controlling them. Mother complained of the jolting. We pulled into the yard at noon, startled to find Josh's family at arms. The boy ran up and jabbered wild and fast about having run the stock in from the pasture and into the barn. Cybil hushed the boy and explained.

A patrol of militia had gone past less than an hour before with a warning. A party of Canadian Indians was in the neighborhood. A cabin on the Vlatche was burnt this morning. No one knew how big was the raiding party. Cybil said she asked Barnes from down the road did he want to come over to the safety of the stone house. So far, the fool had declined. Barnes and his woman didn't like black folks, yet, to me, skin color seemed a foolish enough reason for a man to risk his family. He had small children and his cabin, shabbily built, was hardly defensible.

We got into the house and made sure the shutters were bolted, loopholes securely plugged. I pulled the loads and re-charged all the guns, checked the primings, replaced all flints. When I began preparing myself for going out, Mother became frightened and begged me not to leave them and go where I might get killed. I told her the raiders, having made their strike, were probably already on their way home. If not, and this I didn't say, if the raiding party be still in the area, I would seek out their hiding hole and call in the militia before the Indians hit someone else. Told Mother I could not sit behind stone walls whilst danger prowled my neighborhood. I didn't believe raiders would try their luck against my fortress-like house unless they could catch us outside. I told everyone they absolutely must not go out for any reason.

"No matter what, stay in here and you are safe."

Mother persisted in saying she didn't think I should go and thus leave them defenseless at the worst moment. "Mother Kuyler," Monie said. "Kenneth knows what he is doing. He will take care of us."

"You will be in danger," Mother warned me with a city person's fear of the forest. I doubted there was any real danger. "I'll just make a short scout to make sure they're not skulking around here." I kissed my wife and promised to be back in time for supper. By the door, where no one else could hear and looking pleadingly, almost desperately into my eyes, Monie said, "I have a terrible feeling about this."

"Make sure Mother is comfortable," I said, "and cook up a big supper. I'll be powerful hungry when I get back." What I was most hungry for was my darling wife. That alluring body in the clinging green dress was hard to resist. Reaching again, I got my arm around her waist and pulled her close. "Tonight," I whispered. "Yes," she said in a voice become husky. She kissed me hard, obviously hungry herself. Her dancing eyes fair shouted, "Come on." I wanted her so bad, hard as hell to pull away. I put the dogs out, to sniff for trouble, and I paused in the doorway to plant one last kiss on Monie's sweet cheek. Her worried smile and love-filled green eyes were the last things I saw as she pushed me out the door. "Go!"

Filled with emotion, I circled the farm, looking for sign. Nothing. I worked away from the place in a widening circle. The only fresh tracks in the three inches of snow were the deer and other four-legged critters. By mid-afternoon I was two miles east of the house. That's when I found a lone track, Indian, by the look. Toes pointed in. Not an hour old. This raiding party hadn't gone anywhere.

The fresh prints led to a thick pine grove. I entered the pines warily, and from heavy cover, I viewed the hidden camp. Nobody there, only snowshoes and sleeping blankets bundled for a fast getaway. Looked to be about ten Indians; one, maybe two Frenchmen. I circled around the camp and following the tracks and seeing they was headed straight for my place, I took off at a trot.

Hadn't much more than turned my head toward home when a flock of crows rose up between me and the farm, squawking and causing a ruckus. Obviously spooked. Moments later came a barrage of shots. I stepped my stride up a notch, rash but necessary, and before I had gone another hundred yards there came more shots, then a burst of smoke rising up out of the trees straight ahead. Told myself it was the barn, not the house. Had to be. Seemed to take me forever to cover the last quarter mile, the smoke becoming a thickening column billowing high up into a clear sky. As I got closer, I heard Indian whoops and the crackling of burning wood.

Reaching the top of the ridge overlooking the farm and concealed in the trees, I looked down in horror. Three bodies sprawled in the door yard, I strained to make 'em out. Two looked to be Indians, the third was one of Josh's girls. I cursed Josh for his apparent failure. Why had he not kept his family inside?

Directly below me, smoke came from the opened doorway of Josh's cabin. A redskin watched the smoke. In one hand he held a torch, in the other, an old dress Monica had given to Cybil. Slightly to my left and also below me, my barn and the smaller outbuildings, coops, sheds, hay mows, all of it, torched. The stock bawled for being trapped inside the barn.

There was smoke around the stone house but it wasn't from inside and was instead off the piles of burnables, one pile beneath each of the two front windows, one on each side of the door. The Indians knew the house wouldn't catch but the windows, wooden shutters with greased paper, not glass, might let enough smoke seep through the cracks to force those inside to come out. An Indian was on the roof, chopping at the tiles with my ax.

The others of the raiders were prone behind the big chestnut tree and were sniping the house. The slight rise of ground by the tree gave 'em some cover and they dared not get in any closer for my insistence the yard immediate to the house be kept clear of anything big enough for raiders to get behind. Not able to get in close, they was shooting and making noise to panic those inside, flush 'em out. An occasional shot came from the house.

The Indians were mostly youngsters, maybe their first war party, and I only saw one Frenchman. With his back to the tree, he was waving his arms, haranguing the Indians. It looked as if he was trying to convince 'em to rush the house and they were for hanging back. Rushing a stone house wasn't anything Indians would go for, especially a house as stout as mine. I figured did I quick-shoot the Frenchie, it might convince the Indians it was time for them to go.

I'd shoot Frenchie then get the buck on the roof. Thus far the tiles had resisted his efforts but he couldn't be allowed to continue chopping. And I'd have to get both of 'em fast, else I'd see what I most feared. My loved ones coming out with their hands in the air. Putting themselves at the mercy of Frenchie would be a fatal mistake. No white man along on a raid could seek to deny the Indians what they felt was rightfully theirs.

I raised Nitpicker toward the Frenchie and rested the barrel across a stump. A middling distance shot, must make it a good one. I held my aim on him and fired. He crumpled to the ground, holding his belly and kicking his legs. I watched the Indians. They weren't looking around for who shot the Frenchie and were maybe figuring the shot had come from the house, through a loop-hole.

I reloaded my gun and raised it toward the buck on the roof but from where I was, partway down the ridge into the gully, and with the Indian slightly on the backside of the roof, I didn't have a clear shot. I'd have to get around and to the other side of the burning buildings and the only way to get there would be to go across the barren cornfield behind them. Crossing the cornfield, I would be out from the cover of the woods and with the cornstalks cut down to ankle-height stubble, I would be in plain sight did the shifting smoke uncover me and did any of the Indians look in my direction whilst I was making my dash. Not anything I wanted to do but from down there and after I got the Indian, I could circle through the woods around the house and get up the hill again and onto my road. Get out to the Schenectady Road and with all them Indians chasing me, I'd run as long and as hard as I could and hope the militia came along before the Indians got me. There would be plenty of patrols out and with the gunshots and the smoke, they'd be coming in fast.

Off I went, across the cornfield, in and out of the smoke and with my rifle over my shoulder, my pistol in front of me, cocked against the possibility of meeting an Indian. I got across the field without trouble and past the buildings and downwind from the fires and back into good cover, I seen the Indians were still not looking around for me.

The Indian on the roof had his back to me and was lurching forward and down with each stroke of the ax. I forced my lungs and arms to steady. I raised my rifle and when the Indian stood up straight, taking a breather and looking at the progress of his work, I adjusted my aim and squeezed the trigger. My rifle popped, hang-fire, a delay before the discharge for the flint striking poorly. I tried to hold on the Indian and hoped my gun would yet touch off. She did, but not before the wind, which was out of the southwest, gusted the smoke off the outbuildings and into my face. I wasn't sure I had held on him long enough. Got around behind a tree and reloaded, first changing the flint, fumbling to put in another, my trembling fingers making this precise work difficult.

Finished reloading, I peered around the side of the tree. The Indian was on the ground and with him not moving and with me having shot him from behind, I figured my ball had maybe broken his spine. Dead or not, he wasn't going to do any more chopping. I snuck through the woods and got down to the pond and behind one of my sheds, stacked wood beneath a tin roof and with poles at the corners, no walls.

The wind-whipped flames engulfing my barn roared up in a dreadful whoosh as the roof and walls collapsed inward, into a turmoil of flame and sparks and flying ash, embers of wood and of hay and straw on the wind. So much hard work lost in mischief.

A boy of no more than ten ran toward the house carrying an armful of hay, which he tossed onto the fire along one side of the front. He scampered back toward the tree and picked up more hay and I seen he was a white boy, the son of a man who was in the local militia with me.

I had taken the boy hunting a few times. He again ran toward the house with hay whilst ignoring the cinders and bits of burning straw drifting off the fires. I raised my rifle and targeted him. I asked God's forgiveness and before I could squeeze my trigger, there came the crack of a musket, the boy jolted, got lifted into the air and throwed backward. The shot which struck him had come from inside the house. He lay without moving.

A bullet from behind me whacked the woodpile inches from my face, kicking a splinter into my eyes. I plucked at the blinding chip which was blurring my sight. A second ball smacked into the wood, so two Indians, at least, were back there. The Indians up at the chestnut tree were yelling and shooting at me now too. I was cornered, my only way to get back up to the road was to go across the front of those Indians which had first shot at me but before I did, I had to get a better notion of where they were. I waited, crouched, whilst they reloaded. A ball zinged the woodpile just over my head. Too close for me to wait for the other of 'em to shoot, I took off running, away from the pile of stumps in the field from whence the shot had come, thirty yards from me.

I stayed inside the narrow, twenty-foot-wide strip of woods which separated my clearing from the closest of my fields. Partway down the wooded corridor an Indian sprang out from behind a tree and leaped onto my back as I was going past him. He got his forearm across my throat. I staggered some with his weight but before he could put his knife into me, I got my arms up behind myself and dropped to my knees the way Blanch had taught me and I tossed the Indian over my shoulder. He hit the ground, I put my knife deep into his belly.

I rushed on, my rifle back on my shoulder, pistol cocked. I was out of their trap for the moment. Bullets fussing through the brush presented not much of a threat to me; Indians were notoriously poor shooters. I got to the end of the swath and into the woods along the bottom of the hill.

I ascended the hill and getting onto my road, I ran toward Barnes' cabin, the only other place on the road. Give him a chance to pepper any Indians what came after me. The one behind me whooped and came straight on down the road. I approached the cabin and as I went past, Barnes fired. At me! The damn fool was too scared to know what the hell he was doing. I cussed him and without stopping running, I leaped into the brush across the road from his place. I knew he had more than one musket in there and he'd have his wife loading and sure enough, a second shot came close behind the first, this one intended for the Indian. The shot raised puffs of dust at the Indian's feet and just before he bolted the road, he raised his arm toward the cabin and gave his halloo. He turned toward me and I seen what the hallooin' was about, what was in his hand and getting shook now at me. Hair. Fresh taken and dripping blood and brain soilings. I froze at the sight of those long black tresses.

My Monie's tresses.

Oh, no. Oh, no!

The Indian was leaping about in an exaggerated way, hallooing and shaking my woman's hair. I raised my rifle, took careful aim, fired and missed, an impossible shot with so much between us to knock down or deflect my rifle ball. He issued a savagely filthy taunt and once more shook the hair of my beloved at me. A sudden surge of choleric rage exploded inside my simple brain. I gave my own whoop, a throttled cry, and was in hot pursuit.

Through the woods we went, he mostly staying in my sight which must have been intentional with how he howled and rattled the deep carpet of leaves as he ran. Then he'd get silent and I, not seeing him, would slow up and creep toward where I last seen him. As I closed in, he'd bolt whooping from cover and I'd whoop too and get after him again. My unloaded rifle was over my shoulder, my long-barreled dragoon pistol in my hand but with all the trees and brush and with him bounding, I was unable to get a clear shot.

With his long legs and his youth, he could have got clean away and since he didn't, I figured he was leading me into an ambush. Taking me to a rendezvous with his party and if he was, so be it, I would go straight in and once I got him, the others could have me. My crazed mental state had driven all sanity from my mind and what else worked on me was him laughing as he ran, a high-pitched cackle meant to goad me. With how hard I was blowing, it was naught but a game for him and if he couldn't add my scalp to Monie's, he would content himself with getting away.

In deep woods and without much underbrush, for it was an area with trees tall and thick enough along their tops to keep out the sun and rain, he stopped to catch a breath and looked about, so this was where they intended their ambush. I kept on, straight for him and made up the distance whilst he stood there and only as I got close and raised my pistol did he streak away. He went now at a lung-wrenching speed, either to get far enough ahead to set another trap or, and confident there was no way this old man could stay with him, he would simply outrun me.

He got onto the Schenectady Road. This enabled him to go faster but it helped me too for it increased the chance we'd encounter the militia and it gave me a better target for my dragoon pistol but still not a sure shot, which again was maybe how he intended it. For me to take my one shot and miss, which I most surely would, with all the turns in the road, and once my pistol was emptied and with me not able to catch up with him, further pursuit would be pointless.

The road ran close along the Mohawk River and I hoped the buck's worriment with my staying after him might induce him to try and swim across. He was young and if he was desperate enough to shake me, he might try it and iffen he did, I could plug him, even with a pistol, but as it was, he stayed on the road. I gained slightly, which might have been intentional, he still trying to goad me into taking the one shot to decide our contest.

I pressed on as best my heart and legs would allow, mile after mile, not closing the gap just maintaining it. Refusing to quit so I might erode his confidence in his ability to get away.

Each bend in the road we came to, I looked for the militia or teamsters to be coming the other way but the road remained empty of all save him and me. Going around one wide curve, he got off the road and back into the woods and I would have gone past and lost him except for the one glimpse I got of him slinking from behind one bush to another. I came on warily and when I was almost onto him, he bolted and ran. I again had my pistol raised but still didn't have a good enough shot.

Huffing, bathed in sweat despite the cold, I kept on. If his will to live be stronger than my determination to kill him, he would escape. No! I could not allow it. My Monie's hair would not decorate his wigwam, he would not regale his kinsmen with the mirthful tale of the old man who chased him in vain. I would endure until he gave out.

Then, by luck or design, he got onto an old Mohawk hunting trace. The roughness of the little-used trail did not faze him. Extremely powerful from his lifetime of forest living, he bound as a panther over fallen logs and splashed through cricks and down into and up out of deep ravines. With his steady stride, he knew he could outrun me; youth was too much in his favor. His legs and lungs against mine, yet he would not get away with having murdered and scalped my Monie, she never again to speak in the lilting accent which fit her so well.

Her beautiful green eyes, closed forever, would be avenged. I would stay close enough until, convinced he could not shake me, he must turn and face me. Dog him until the instinct took over from the mind. My strength of will against his youthfulness. The only chance, for did he not quit soon, it would be I who dropped out. The thought of taking my shot I pushed from my mind. I could not hold my gun steady and with us now back into thick woods, I would surely miss. I must run him down!

****

My legs nearly done in, each breath searing my lungs with fire, I seen a faltering in his stride, his body refusing his mind. His knees buckled and after running a short way farther, and vexed for my refusal to drop out, he stopped, turned, raised his pistol. I stopped no more than thirty feet from him and called out.

"Va tres voux!" I said. "I am going to kill you!"

I ran in screaming, my pistol held straight in front of me, gripped in two hands. He fired first, his ball ripping across the top of my shoulder, cutting my shirt, tearing skin, whacking bone, enough to knock a man down but not this man, not this time. I pulled my trigger, my pistol scant inches from his face. There came a roar out of the barrel, his mouth and jaw exploded, we collided. We both went down. I got up first and with him trying to rise, I gave him the butt-end of my pistol, skull-crunching whacks to the top of his head until the gunstock shattered and he fell onto his back.

I checked him, he lived. I removed the knife and tomahawk from his belt and flung them aside. I stripped him of shirt and leggings and using rawhide cords from my satchel and driving four sticks into the ground, I looped the cords around his wrists and ankles, tied the other ends to the sticks and pulled 'em tight. With him spread in naught but his loin-cloth, I began gathering up twigs and bark and when he awakened, I had a small fire going.

I straddled him, leaned down, and in his dark eyes looking up at me from inside painted black circles, I saw what might have been regret for his having stayed to taunt me, thus losing the chance to escape. The eyes hardened and what was in them now was a summoning of the fortitude he would need for the only thing left for him, a warrior's death, as all the young bucks was taught from infancy to seek.

"You know what be next for you, don't you, you little rat bastard," I said. He began trying to sing his death song which, with so much of his lower face blown away, was denied him.

I ripped his totem from around his neck, a small leather bag on a string. I sliced it open, looked inside. It held some few colored pebbles and what might have been the gossamer skin shed by a snake and which I figured to be his umbilical cord. I crumpled it in my fist and opened my hand so the crumbs might blow away on the wind.

I built up my fire, unheedful the smoke might draw in others of them, and with the fire getting hot, I thrust my knife and hatchet blades into the glowing coals. I would have him beg for mercy before he died, to burden him with a shame he must carry into his afterworld.

The knife blade glowing hot, I showed it to him. His resolve not to cry out I saw in the shake of his head, side to side, and with my eyes looking into his, I touched the blade against his forearm. I pressed down hard. There was the sizzle and odor of burnt hairs and flesh, no sound nor movement did he make.

Deep into the night, I re-heated and applied the blades of both knife and hatchet, the one getting hot whilst I used the other against every part of his bare skin. Arms and legs, cheeks and stomach. His eyes, mostly closed, did follow me sometimes but the only other thing telling me he yet lived were the involuntary spasms of muscles and tendons beneath his copper skin and the reflex jerking of an arm or leg from the touch of a heated blade.

Much else was I determined to inflict upon him, same as his people did to ours. Cut off his ears and nose, his fingers and toes, incise his stomach to extract and distend his innards. Anything which might induce him to beg for mercy. All these things might I have done for I had descended to his level of barbarity but when I put the red-hot knife up close to one of his eyes and the flesh around the eye blackened and his eyeball bubbled and popped, my guts roiled. Vomit gushed from my mouth, splattering him and seeping down into his wide-exposed throat. With my arms clasped around my sides, I foamed at the mouth as a dog gone mad. My body shook, I collapsed and lay alongside of him.

Chapter XX – Grim Reckoning

When I awoke, it was late morning, by the sun. I was mortal drained and shaking, sick at heart, wretched of body. I could think only of the abyss of emptiness I was fallen into. A black hole so deep in my mind no bridge could span the depths. I cursed the others of the Indians for not having come along and brained me whilst I slept.

I got over the top of the Indian. The dirty snake yet lived. Not entirely bled out, he was taking shallow breaths and exhaling through his nose. His eyes were empty pustules. He was repeating a single word over and again. I kicked him so he'd know I was there. The kick silenced him momentarily, then he resumed speaking his word, as if my presence no longer mattered. The word was Momma, said in the French tongue for he was a Caughnawaga, a Praying Indian, a Mohawk who had embraced French Popery and gone to live in Canada. I told him he was well beyond anything his momma could do for him and I said as how both our lodges would be filled this winter with wailing.

I got behind him and kneeling and using one hand, I gripped tight his topknot, the sprout of hair in the center of his otherwise shaved head. I used my grip on his hair, twisted in my fist, to raise his upper body off the ground. Using the tip of my knife, I began cutting into the top of his head. I didn't gouge deep lest I pierce his brain and with a circle of blood cut entirely around his shank and with the skin loosened, I pulled hard thus robbing him of his hair and plenty of skin too. He emitted a god-awful shriek which was neither human nor beast and followed it with a copious weeping.

It was the first time in my life I had ever scalped a man.

I rubbed his hair in his face and jammed as much of it as would fit into the wreckage of his distended mouth, for his jaw hung now by tendons and cracked bone. I whacked his nose with the butt end of his tomahawk so his final breaths, which might last a few hours, would be more ragged and difficult.

Before I had begun working him over, I had cut the thong which held my Monie's scalp to his belt and stuffed the scalp into my bag. Then, sometime whilst I slept, I had awakened screaming and hurled the bag into the darkness. Now I searched around and retrieved it.

I began walking. My going was slow. Sore legs achingly stiff with every step, I stumbled over roots and sticks, even did I lose my way on familiar ground, so wrought was I with despair. I got turned around and floundered plenty before I got myself straightened out. I stopped often and knelt weeping with my face in my hands. Late afternoon I came onto the Schenectady Road.

Darkness was fallen 'ere I arrived home. The smoke and stink of cabin and barns, the near-suffocating stench of charred wood drew me in. Wind-stirred tongues of flame shuddered and flared in the ruins. All else was dark save a thin beam of lantern light showing through a busted shutter hacked by the raiders. Overwhelming rushes of grief struck at what remained of my spirit. My legs buckled as I rapped on the door and heard Josh's voice, "Who be dere?" I said who I was. "Dat u'uns?" he said and I heard the bolt move. The door opened, I slipped inside; Josh closed it up behind me. "Been watchin' fo u'uns," he said, and with his wife standing alongside him, I stared at them. There was a chance Monie had survived the scalping. It happened sometimes. Horribly disfigured yet alive but I didn't have to ask, or maybe I did ask, and if I didn't, the look on my face was enough. Their own looks told me Monie was gone.

"De militia say de Injuns not comin' back," Josh said. "Us'uns bin watchin' de day, prayin to Jesus u'ns'd come back safe. Hallalooa! He done gib us de anser. De way u'ns lit n' outa here, I tinked u'ns mighta got kilt." I told them I had ran down Monie's killer. "Dat right?" Josh didn't sound surprised. "Hallalooa, Jesus!"

"If you had only done what I told you," I said, more pleading than angry. "If you had only all stayed inside." I will always remember the look he gave me. I think he half expected me to kill him and the look said he didn't care if I did and he only waited for whatever I would do.

"Yo' boys and yo' ma be safe," he said.

We shook hands firmly, melding our grief.

"Your girl is gone, too," I said.

"Both a muh gals and muh boy," he said and I looked at him. I only remembered seeing one girl dead in the yard.

"One gal scalped'n murdered, de udder fetched off to de north wit de boy."

I could only stare at him. So much lost. I looked at Cybil, her chin was trembling. I put my arms around her, held on tight, a silent sharing of grief. I lowered my face onto her shoulder and began an unmanly keening. She hushed me sternly. "Yo' boys be sleepin'." Those round black eyes shone bright with tears. Mother came out of the back bedroom. We embraced, she looked up at me. "Oh, my Kenneth, thank the Lord you are safe." She looked gray. I said if I had heeded her and not gone out, Monie might yet be alive. "Bosh! How could you know what would happen? They might have succeeded in burning us out had you been in here instead of out there. They were near to doing it when you arrived back and chased them off. It will do no good to blame yourself. And don't be blaming Josh for Monica going out there. With the child carrying on so, what would you have done?"

The child? They explained what had happened, each of them relating a piece of the story, one picking up when another faltered.

Just after I went on my scout, a little white girl of no more than three or four years had wandered into the yard, calling for her momma. Monie had insisted they bring her into the house. Josh was equally insistent nobody was going out to fetch the girl and he planted hisself in front of the door. The child began wailing. Monica pointed a pistol at Josh and said she'd shoot him if he didn't get out of the way. Said she'd go out, grab the girl and come right back in. Josh unbolted the door, Monie went out, Josh's boy too, both armed, and with Josh covering them from the doorway.

One of the twins, watching from inside, must a seen a flash of color or movement over by the outbuildings because, and leaning her head out the door, she shouted a warning. An Indian, having got up alongside the door, grabbed the girl by her hair and pulled her out of the house. The yard filled with Indians, all whooping and jumping around.

Monie and Josh each shot an Indian and the second twin, seeing her sister getting dragged away, ran out and grabbed the sister by the arm. With the girl holding one arm and the Indian holding the other, they was both pulling until another Indian tomahawked the girl who was pulling. Whilst this had been going on, Monie and Josh's boy ran for the door. Monie they grabbed; the boy, running ahead, about got there, would have got there but with Indians close behind with raised tomahawks and with the way in wide open for 'em, Josh slammed and barred the door.

"Did they kill Monie here in the front?" I said before anybody could tell me what happened next. "Did you see it?"

"No, suh," Josh said and whilst shaking his head vehemently. He said the Indians killed Monie out of sight of everybody in the house. With

Josh, Cybil, Monie, and even Mother shooting at 'em from inside and to get out of the line of fire, the Indians had dragged Monie around the side of the corn crib, which was the closest outbuilding to the house. Mother said Monica called piteously for me to save her, to save all of them. Mother and I broke down in tears, Josh picked up the story. He said Monica's anguish had become screams of pain. I said the pain was probably intentionally inflicted to bring the others of them out of the house. Josh said he would a gone had not the screaming ceased. I looked away, far away, for the longest time. Much of the rest of what happened they only pieced together after the militia arrived and looked around. With the militia getting told how the Indians was all grabbing at Monie as they went around the side of the corn crib, they speculated what had gone on back there had started as the Indians trying to draw out those inside the house and had devolved into an argument over which Indian owned Monica. An older Indian, seeing younger bucks arguing over a captive might kill the captive for fear the bucks would turn their tomahawks on one another.

Mother said Monie had put up a fight as she was getting dragged 'round behind the corn crib. She said this to make me proud but I could only shake my head. I had always told Monie, were she to be taken by the Indians, not to resist, no matter what awful things they did to her. Resistance only brought worse trouble. "Just go along, no matter what," I had always told her. "Keep up, carry your burden, stay silent. Survive the trek north and there was a chance you'd get ransomed someday and come home."

"It's something Indians can't abide," I said. "Captives putting up a fight. As savage as they be and as scairt as they make us, them Indians is scairt too, scairt if they don't get away quick-like, the militia'll be onto them. Resistance gets 'em boilin' and as soon as they seen they could not drag Monie to Canada without her struggling all the way, they killed her." Hard for me to bear the thought of the anguish Monie must have felt for getting separated from her babes and for me not being there to make things right.

I asked Josh about his other girl and his boy. "Was they killed too?" Josh shook his head. The militia hadn't found their bodies and Josh and Cybil held onto the hope they were yet alive.

"And the little white girl?" I said.

Dead and scalped, she was the sister of the boy who had been putting straw under the windows of the house. Three dead children in the back room with my wife. Josh and Cybil had prepared the bodies. Cybil said they were washed, their heads wrapped in tight shrouds. What she meant was, the gruesomeness of the tomahawk blows and the scalpings had been covered so I might look upon my beloved. Cybil said the neighborhood men were working up coffins and would be back in the morning. The militia had tossed the dead Indians and Frenchman into the river.

There was no way to tell Josh how grateful I was for his shutting the door on his boy. Had he not made this awful sacrifice, all those inside would have got carried away to the north. Except for my babes. Not old enough to survive the trek, they would have got their brains bashed out against the stone walls. Josh had acted courageously, we both knew it, and what else we knew, he would live the rest of his life with the torment of having slammed the door on his boy, thus dooming him, along with the girl, to unspeakable tortures followed either by death or a lifetime of slavery. Indians were always eager to exchange captives for trade goods but black folks didn't generally fetch much in return and were seldom worth the bargaining. The best Josh's children could hope for was adoption, a buck's life for the boy, for the girl, the drudgery of a squaw.

"Why de lay dat on po' black folk?" Josh said. I replied, "Savages, Josh, from another world. So savage none of us can comprehend." And what Monie had done, to try to help the little girl, much as I had insisted they not go out, I couldn't really blame her. Unlike me, she hadn't spent a lifetime dealing with Indians and didn't have my fatalism, although the fatalism could in no way assuage my loss.

Monie's dog, over by the fire and heavily swathed in bandages and panting with each breath, began whimpering for wanting to be noticed. "They get the other dog?" I said. And the gander, too, I was told. "He going to make it?" I said, still looking at the dog. Cybil said she figured the dog would survive if infection didn't set in. The arrow put into the dog hadn't hit anything vital; Josh and Cybil had extracted the projectile and cleaned the wound.

Mother had been looking me over closely in the dim light and she told me to go down into the cellar so Cybil could clean me up. I went; cloths and a pail of water were set out. I took off my soiled shirt. The buck's musket ball, whilst not penetrating, had dug a gouge across the top of my shoulder and raised a tight bruise under the skin. This I had scarce noticed before now. Cybil came down and tended to me. Her probing and scrubbing was painful but she knew what she was doing and when she finished, she coated the wound with a foul-smelling, pasty yellow concoction.

Back upstairs, I gazed at my boys, asleep in their wooden cribs. Their peaceful repose and soft breathing made it impossible for me to not conjure images of what would have been their fate, had the Indians got in. My body shook, I couldn't make it stop. Josh gave me a glass of brandy. I drank it down in a gulp. That which I didn't spill all over myself.

"I should have stayed," I said in a low voice and more to myself than to anyone else.

"What youse talkin' bout?" Cybil's voice challenged me out of the near darkness on the other side of the room. I went to the table by the fire and fumbled in trying for another drink. Cybil took the rum bottle out of my hands and poured. "Don youse fret none. Ain' nuttin' nobody cudd'a did. Po' miz Monica be dead fo she knowed it. What youse wuz goin' do?" Cybil shook her head. "Youse be 'ungry? Got's dee' stew a keepin' in de kettle." I wasn't hungry and doubted I could keep anything down.

Later, Mother said how during the raid, the Frenchman had taunted them in English by calling out he knew the Rogers' Ranger with the long rifle was inside the house. Frenchie boasted they were going to kill Kuyler and all his family and take his scalp and gun. "They knew my name?" I said. "Yes'm," Josh said. Of course. With most of the houses around made of logs, they wouldn't attack a stone house unless there be someone inside who they much wanted. Warfare for them was about prestige; my scalp and gun and the bragging on it would have been valuable coups.

"Somebody must a told 'em," I said, thinking out loud: "The Indians was closing in on somebody around here and to save themselves, they told the raiders who I was and where my house was." Josh's glance told me he'd been thinking the same thing and we both had a notion who the scoundrel might be.

Barnes, with his insatiable hatred for Josh and his family on account of they were black, and his dislike of me for the reason I had always made my disdain of him obvious. Maybe he'd grabbed at the chance to save hisself and his family, eliminate Josh and all of his, and maybe take possession of the stone house.

The militia company having arrived shortly after I went off in pursuit of Monie's killer was, I supposed, what accounted for why no others of the savages had come along after me. Too bad they hadn't come, either to help their friend or to take revenge on me for killing him and as I lay out there defenseless. I'd have taken a few of 'em with me afore I died.

Mother set a plate of stew before me. My stomach churned. I ate but little, meantime downing another cup of brandy, still shaking awful.

Josh told how Barnes had bragged to the militia how he had saved me when the Indians chased me down the road and into the woods. Barnes said he'd fought off the attackers whilst I ran from 'em and said over and again how he saved my life. Josh said Barnes had been over twice to see had I come back. "He bin eyeballin' dis heah place all de day long," Josh said. I said as how Barnes had damn near shot me. I said to hell with it.

They talked about how intensely hot and smoky it got inside the house. Mother tearfully said how mad she got for thinking what might happen to the babes. Mad enough so it was she who shot the boy who was feeding straw onto the fires under the windows. "Dat mamma a your'n," Josh said, "she sure nuff haf de spunk." So Mother, too, had something which would haunt her for the rest of her life.

I went into the back room. Cybil followed me in and lit the candles which was placed around Monie. Cybil went out and closed the door behind her. The four bodies, Monie, Josh's girl, the white boy and the little white girl, were beneath their shrouds. I went to Monie's form, knelt, and after a time, I lifted the sheet. I stared down, she looked peaceful, her beautiful face tightly-wrapped. I caressed her cheeks, kissed her. My emotions broke, I blurted a denial, buried my face in her chest and wept.

How awful must it have been for those on the other side of the closed door, to hear my gasping sobbing denials, yet I could not stop myself. When I came back out, the babes were awake, my weeping had awoken and upset them, and they were wailing now too, for their mother and her milk. I looked helplessly at Cybil, she was already getting things ready. Augustus, the older of the two, was partially weaned. His usual fare was pap, bread crumbs soaked in water or milk. I had often seen Monie and the girls feeding him from his pap boat. Peter, the younger, had so far subsisted entirely on Monie's breast milk and now and with Mother spooning the pap into Augie's mouth, Cybil showed me how to work the suckling-bottle brought over by Barnes' wife, along with a pail of goat's milk. These would see us through until the militia returned, they promising to bring along a nanny goat for our use and for as long as was necessary.

I managed to get enough milk into Peter to quiet him and with him and his brother fed and back to sleep, we all soon after retired, Mother to the bedroom, Josh and Cybil up into the loft, me under a blanket by the fire. I lay there whilst everyone got settled and when they were quiet, I went into the back room and sat a silent vigil alongside my woman. I spent the night planting kisses and dropping tears on her face. Toward morning, I returned to the front room. I built up the fire and poured some brandy. The house was quiet except for some low sobs from the loft, poor Cybil reliving her losses. I stayed there in front of the fire. I slept some but was soon up, and when Mother came out from the bedroom and began fussing around the fire, getting breakfast going, I went into the bedroom, closed the door, got onto the bed and with my face pressed hard against a pillow, I let go with enough silent tears to float a damn river schooner.

I fell asleep and not too long after, I heard a wagon and didn't bother getting up to see who was there. I heard talk, heard the wagon depart and Josh come back in. He called to me from the other side of the door. The coffins had arrived. I came out. I told Josh my wife's resting place would be up in our little clearing on the ridge overlooking the homestead. Monie and me had used to sit up there in the evenings, on our stone bench. There, her bones warmed by the late afternoon sun, her spirit could look over her house and watch the boys. I told Josh his girl should be buried there too. He nodded his appreciation.

I picked up my gun, walked down to the river and when I returned, two hours later, the boxes, two large and two small, were on sawhorses in the yard. Josh told me the bodies had been put into the boxes but he hadn't banged down Monie's lid yet. I told him I had finished saying my goodbyes and I went inside, got back onto the bed and fell asleep to Josh's hammering.

The sound of voices and the bleating of a nanny goat woke me. I got up, stumbled to the door and looked out. Josh was with a crowd of fifteen or so neighbors come to help with the burying. The men had picks and shovels and rifles; the women had baskets of food. I pulled myself together the best I could and went out. Must have looked a sight though all were cheered for seein' me. They, yesterday, must a doubted they'd ever see me again.

The women went inside with the food, the men lifted the boxes of the little boy and girl and put them into the back of a wagon. They would be taken home, to their burned-out cabin, to be buried alongside their momma and poppa. The men went up the hill and commenced digging, a melancholy and difficult labor with the ground frozen. They all talked of helping with other things. A new barn and cabin come spring. These were good people, well-intentioned.

Barnes came down the road with his family. He bragged as how he'd done so much good shooting. "Saved your life, Kuyler, your babes too. Too bad about your wife." His unruly young 'uns caused a continual ruckus. He and his fat, dirty wife didn't see fit to scold them. I shut him up, his children too, with some hard looks. He read my thoughts in the looks. It was him. Sure. Raiders always went for the easiest pickings. They would have gone for his place, a cabin with old logs dry enough to burn and with enough chinks in the walls so musket balls could be put through. Desperate, Barnes must a shouted from inside about the ranger in the stone house. The Frenchman had understood what Barnes was saying and had convinced the Indians to have a try for me, which probably explained the reluctance I seen in the Indians for rushing my place for fear a sharpshooter was inside.

The militia had tracked the Indians and said some of them had been in pursuit of me whilst I chased the one who had slain Monie and taken her scalp. I had simply outrun them, they probably not having pursued far for not having the Frenchman pushing them and knowing the militia was around. Probably they figured their buck would get away and meet up with 'em later. The militia said Josh's boy and girl appeared to have been taken away, not killed, this gave us at least some hope they might be saved. What else was talked about was the escaping raiders having headed off toward Iroquoia. The men pondered the meaning of this. The raiders were Huron, so why had they gone toward the homeland of their ancient foe? Had fear driven them to do something desperate or had the overwhelming French victory at Ticonderoga so emboldened them they no longer feared the Mohawks? Or was the Mohawks' attachment to us so loosened they was giving sanctuary to our enemies?

I told them the buck I had killed was a Caughnawaga Iroquois. There yet remained a bond of kinship between the Iroquois factions, and if one or some of the raiders was Mohawks, the entire party, even the Hurons among them, might have gained refuge with our Iroquois. Which meant Bill Johnson might be able to do something for Josh's children, iffen they be still alive.

The men asked did I want them to search for the body of the Indian I had slain. I shook my head, no. Let his stinking corpse serve as fodder for the beasts of the forest, let his disgraced spirit wander, forever denied whatever afterlife his primitive religion promised him. Whilst the men were digging, I went inside, shaved and put on the suit Monie had given me. To look more presentable than I felt. The weather turned cold and it started to spit snow. Eric and Sarah arrived before the digging was done. The militia had sent a messenger on horseback to Albany the day before and my friends had come out as part of an armed posse.

That afternoon, there on the windy, snow-blown hillside, Sarah read from Monie's Bible and when she closed the book, I began eulogizing my wife. My words sounded inadequate, my voice quavered and broke. My inability to think straight or hold myself together made me stumble time and again over heartsick words. So many things I wanted to say, likely should have said and mostly didn't. Eric, watching me flounder, stepped forward and asked quietly did I want him to do the speaking, for which I was grateful.

Whilst he talked, the snow blew hard, a squall of raw, sharp flakes slanting sideways into our faces. Sarah stood beside me, beautiful Sarah with her arm around my waist, her head leaned into me. Mother rocked baby Peter in her arms to keep him quiet; Cybil held Augustus' hand. Eric finished, the squall stopped, the sun came out and as Josh began speaking, Barnes walked away. I would have gone after him, furious at his disrespect but one of the men, a neighbor who well knew my feelings toward Barnes, gripped my arm, his look saying not now but later. Surely later.

In a voice so strong and rich, so full of emotion, Josh spoke. His strength and the simplicity so moving, his words full of feeling as he confronted his own awful truth. One child dead, two more taken from him, and did he contemplate how he had struggled for most of his life to put aside money enough to buy his and his family's way out of bondage only to have his children taken into a different, perhaps worse servitude? An impossible blow for any man. Cybil stood beside him and was stiffly erect in the wind and in the presence of so many white folks, she not restraining the silent flood of tears down those high-boned, coal-black cheeks, the tears mixing with the snow melting on her face.

We said last prayers over the graves and it was done. We went inside and ate and as everyone was departing, hunched against the cold, Eric and Sarah wanted to stay. I told them to go in company with others for safety. With everyone gone, there was a dreadful quiet; the wind blew through the trees around our clearing.

Around midnight, there came a loud rapping at the door. "Who be dere?" Josh said at the loophole. "It be Henry." I looked too, saw it was indeed Josh's older boy. I picked up my pistol, cocked it and motioned to Josh. He unbolted the door, opened it, Henry slipped inside, Josh closed and bolted the door. Henry hugged his ma and pa and looked me straight in the eye as he shook my hand and told me how terribly sorry he was. Eric had sent a messenger to Henry down to Kinderhook, below Albany, and Henry had run all the way, a distance of more than twenty miles.

Chapter XXI – The Lone Wolf

Cybil and Mother were taking care of the babes. I knew little enough about it but was learning. How Monie would have laughed at my clumsy efforts! The wound across my shoulder stung fiercely but was healing. Whenever Cybil applied her witch's brew of a concoction, she made sure I had nips of what she called Oh-Be-Joyful, which was to say, rum. The ruins of my log cabin and outbuildings, whilst still smoldering, had cooled enough to investigate. We found little worth salvaging. All the buildings and farm implements were destroyed as were the tools and whatever else I had got from Pops. We would have to start over. Tough enough in itself; without Monie, I feared it would not be possible.

The next morning, rifle in hand, I walked over to Barnes' place, and when I returned home a few hours later, Josh asked had I killed Barnes. I said I hadn't intended killing him, just maybe beat his brains out, what few he had, but I only hit him once, and with him on the ground and too scairt to get up, I said, and blunt was my threat, "I suspect you had something to do with it and I won't kill a man on a suspicion, but if the truth ever comes out and it's as I suspect, you'll die for it." I told Josh I could not prove anything and surely it would be no great loss to the neighborhood but we needed as many men along the frontier as we could get, if we were to beat the French. And beat them we would. No matter what misfortunes they brought down on us or we brought on ourselves, we would always be here. And with what it would mean for Barnes' wife and brats, it wouldn't be right.

****

Me and Josh talked over how we were situated for the winter.

"Reckon de be 'nuff taters, corn, an' groun' nut put by in de cella to las de winta," he said. "Us uns gets by. An plenny a pickled venison 'cause u uns such a good shot wid dat bad gun but us uns needs a cow for de babies. De needs ta hab more milk dan de she-goat gives. Mister Abner Stebbins, he gots extra milk cows an' they be fresh. He owe u uns, fo he ain' neba 'turn de fabor fo de bull bangin' his herd two times. Tink u uns gits one if'n u uns akse."

Josh and me went together to see Stebbins, who agreed to loan me a cow for as long as I needed it. Josh offered to do some things in return. Stubbins shook his head; he'd ask no payment.

****

Christmas Day the house smelled of good things cooking. Mother and Cybil baked two young male geese, the last of my flock. The Indians had killed the others, along with the chickens and all else. Just as well, with the feed stored for winter having burnt up, we'd of had to slaughter the animals. We had a bit of pork and bread brought over by a neighbor, along with vegetables from the cellar. We finished with coffee and pie. Not much was said whilst we ate although plenty enough was eaten. Truth is, nobody said much all day.

My boys loved the Christmas toys Josh made for 'em. For little Peter, a wooden flute, brightly painted and melodic, at least when someone other than him blew into it, and for Augie, a whirligig. This was a ten-inch-tall stick-man perched at the end of a wooden paddle, a sailor in a red sock-cap, striped shirt, flared trousers and wooden shoes. Augustus was not able to master setting the spring, necessary for the boatman to do his clog dance so we took turns doing it. All day, Mother and Cybil clapped along and sang ditties as the boatman danced, his hands on his hips, his oversized wooden shoes clomping loudly on his platform.

A moment to temper our sorrow, until Augustus, abruptly and most crossly demanded his mother come out from wherever she was hiding and do the winding. None of us knew what to say, which confirmed for Augustus his suspicion something was terribly amiss. He threw down the boatman and with Peter blowing into his flute, Augustus grabbed it out of his hands and began smashing it against the wall. Peter wailed, I snapped for visualizing what I couldn't get out of my head, the savages swinging my boys by their ankles, their little heads battered against the stone wall. I got Augie by the shoulders and shook him so, Josh had to pull me away. I looked in horror at my terrified, confused little boy, at the fear inside him. I tried to pull him back to me, he screamed and fled into Mother's arms.

Christmas night I stayed up, drinking rum, chasing it with beer. Josh joined me before the fire. I told him I was going away and asked would he stay on through the winter to look after things. He spoke, his voice low. "Us uns'd sho nuff lak' stay on de winna'. Don' wanna leab jus' now. Dat ol' wind blow mighty col' out deah."

He poured himself another drink, I took a long pull on the rum. I intended to get good and drunk. His voice raspy and slurred from the rum, which he was not accustomed to taking, he said, "Us uns gots no place to go, fo su'e. Ain' holdin nuttin to go wit. In any quantity." Even harder to understand than usual but he did ask would I rebuild, come spring. Rebuild or sell the place, I didn't care to think much about it just then.

****

Gripped by an unhealthy lassitude, I was constantly gazing upon my boys. Mother, Josh and Cybil knew why I gazed, sadness and pity, yes, but also because both boys favored their mother. Every time I looked at either of them, I saw Monie's eyes and face. Mother finally got after me about it. I knew she was right but what was I supposed to do? I had never been a religious man but was feeling now even more vehemently hostile toward God. The others all looked to God for succor in their travail so I kept my blasphemes hidden from them.

I had never considered the possibility I could lose Monica and have to go forward without her either at my side or waiting at home for me. We had discussed death often, always with the notion it would be mine, not hers. Life does take strange twists and turns, seldom does it deal the hand the way we would expect, for how much do events we can't control affect our lives. If God was trying to teach me some profound lesson, its significance was lost on me. My feelings were punctuated by violent rages, although, and still haunted by the sickening way I had gone after Augie on Christmas Day, my rages I never directed at any other than myself.

I spend long days aimlessly traipsing the woods around the farm, bringing back an occasional deer. Thinking on Monie and brooding on Abercrombie and Howe. Abercrombie, the son-of-a-bitch, if he had only done what any competent general should have done back in July, both Ticonderoga and Scalp Point would have been ours and there'd not have been a hostile Indian within a hundred miles of my place. Lord Howe I cursed for getting hisself killed in a meaningless fray. He should have stayed alive to lead us to Scalp Point and beyond. But no. Hearing the sounds of battle in the Trout Brook Valley as we approached Carillon, the goddamn fool had run to it. Elan, the British called it, a word they borrowed from the French.

****

Stebbins lent me a team and wagon and I took Mother and the boys to Albany. Mother promised to return when the weather turned warmer or any time she was needed. Sad to think of her passing a long winter alone in her own grief, housebound until spring without Pops and with so much to ruminate on.

I told Eric and Sarah I was going north and would not be back until spring. I asked could they keep the boys through the winter. They said they could and with how Eric looked at me, I think he knew I had in my mind the possibility I might not be back. Sarah must have seen it too because she said if I didn't ever return, they would raise the boys. Eric added as how it would not be a problem for them, who had raised so many of their own. I told them if I didn't come back, the farm was under their guardianship, to sell to provide for the boys or keep with Josh and his family as tenants, was Josh willing.

We hashed out some few details and it was time for me to go. I lifted up my boys and held them close, one in each arm and so tight I feared my thick, bear-like arms and my emotions might crush them. Reckoned it might be the last time I ever held them. The thought struck me hard.

I went to see Bill Johnson. He was off to the western end of the colony on Indian business. I wrote out a letter to him and left it with his secretary with instructions to get it into Bill's hands as soon as possible. The letter was asking could Bill see about bringing Josh's children back.

Back at the farm, I told Josh I was going away. "Whe' u uns goin', boss?" he said. "What u uns fixin' ta do?" I gave him a letter too. "This," I said, "states if I don't ever come back, you have use of the farm until such time as you and Eric can work something out. If he decides to sell, you're the first buyer, if you want, and iffen you don't, one-third of the money is yours. Meantime, I be heading north. Varmint hunting."

"Varmints?" He knew what I meant but asked anyway, "You goes fo furs dis late in de year?"

"No, Josh. Not fur. Hair."

He maybe wanted to argue but knew it was useless.

****

I was up before first light. I lit a candle and stirred the ashes in the hearth into flame. I slipped shivering into my clothes. It was a cold, damp morning. I heard Josh moving around in the loft and I knew I could not face him. He was a good man and was no doubt appalled at what I was intending, although he wouldn't say anything. I picked up my rifle, pistols and powder horn, knapsack and possibles, and walked stiffly out of the house, tears welling in my eyes for all of what I had lost and for what I was leaving behind. Sick with emotion, I walked fast, stopping only at Monica's grave.

The day was mighty raw, a strong north wind was in my face. It made for hard walking. Slept the night in a barn, and walking all the next day, I got in to Saratoga. Another day brought me to Edward, where I stopped at the sutler's store only long enough to pick up a few things and again slept in the hay of a stable, avoiding the ranger encampment. Early the next morning I had breakfast with the stable hands and went to the northwest, along the ridgetops, headed for my cabin in the mountains. Anger over my senseless loss was sometimes a numbness, at other times it was a red-hot poker of smoldering white heat stabbing at my guts. The quest for revenge seared my insides, I cared not for the consequences. Only scalps might ease my pain.

Took four days to get to my cabin for the snow deepening the farther north I got. Along the way were lean-tos and the ashes of fires. Arriving at my Eagles' Lake cabin near sundown, I got a fire going and slept, and at dawn, I set to upon my first wretched task.

Along the shore of the lake, below the edifice of my sanctuary, at the tip of the point which jutted into the lake and where I had intended building Monie a house, I cleared the snow and commenced digging a hole. I worked at it most of the morning, chopping angrily at the frozen dirt, the sweat rolling off me. When the hole was three feet down, I held the satchel containing my woman's scalp against my cheek. I placed it inside a small wooden box and put it into the hole. I covered it up and rolled a big rock over it, so to always know its exact location.

That night, in my cabin, I got drunk on the rum I had brought north with me and with what was already there. The rum had been a burden to carry but getting drunk the first night was something I thought would be necessary. I slept some, and in the morning, I began preparing my worn-out cabin for the work ahead. Executing French and Indians would require a stout base, such tasks as putting by enough wood and food, patching roof and walls.

It took me a week to get it all as I wanted, and the entire time I was haunted by thoughts of my last time at Paradise Valley, when Rogers had banished me and I had laid out in my mind what me and Monie would build together, the joyous life we would have here.

****

A storm was brewing as I hit the trail for Scalp Point. The outlet brook was high. A new beaver dam just below the outlet had iced over and was backing up plenty of water which made for a slippery traverse.

It occurred to me how for many years there had been no beavers here on the eastern slopes, wiped out same as in so much of the country in the frenzy for wealth. When I had first arrived so many years ago, the timing of my arrival had been perfect, the population had just begun to revive sufficiently for me to take advantage of it but not so much revived it might seep out to where others might discover it. Now, and with the beavers expanding outward, the Indians, either Mohawks or Canadians, would perforce find them and drive them once more into extinction. The discovery might come before the winter was over. With the first beaver sighting, the cry would go out, the rush would be on, the red nations fighting to decide who would profit from it. My Paradise would become the scene of yet another beaver war, disastrous not only for the beavers and me but for the Indians as well. In times past, their most destructive wars had been fought over furs.

I was well prepared. The leather pouch covering my priming was fairly in place, the priming intact and dry. Same for the priming of the dragoon pistol I carried in a leather holster. Guns were not my weapons of choice for how they would echo around the valley. I would kill with the bow and arrows slung on my shoulder and with the knife and hatchet in my belt. I carried near a quiver-full of arrows. At the cabin I had a stash of steel arrowpoints, feathers and glue. My intention to kill silently meant I had not totally abandoned thoughts of coming out of this alive. Or was it a determination to kill as often as I could afore I was killed? Truthfully, I was not concerned with how it might end. Only revenge mattered.

****

From the crest of the ridgeline along the western slopes, I watched the smokes of the breakfast fires rising up over the Champlain Valley. Then and with the day turning brilliant in the sunshine, I approached within a few miles of the Scalp Point fort and hid along the road. Soon, a train of sleighs pulled by oxen came along. Too many men for me, I stayed in my concealment and they passed by without disturbance. A bit later and after I had moved around some, there came what I had been watching for, a lone man. Out from the windmill redoubt, he carried a wooden bucket with fishing gear; hand-lines, sinkers, bait. He walked northwest at an angle across the promontory and got onto the bay which was just north of the point. The bay was where so many of them fished. It was often crowded but today it wasn't, maybe because of the cold. He walked the ice along the shore whilst I spooked him from behind trees and brush. He got into a cove, chopped a hole in the ice and let down a line. The cove was secluded enough so did I kill him silently, nobody would know until I was done and gone, but with him pulling up fish and tossing 'em onto the ice where they flopped around, I decided to give him a few hours to catch me some supper.

I stayed in hidden vigil, the day turned colder. New ice was forming underneath what was already there, the ice cracking, roaring, shooting great splits across the frozen surface, lifting chunks of ice and spouts of water high into the air, all thrown up by the pressure underneath. Like volleys of cannons, the roars echoed around the rim of the valley. The cold was becoming too much for me, it was time to leap out and make a try for the man's scalp but before I did, I heard voices, three more men coming to join the first. They walked close by my hiding place and onto the ice. They began chopping holes with axes and chisels. Soon they was set up, catching fish, drinking, laughing. I cussed myself for having waited and was it for wanting his fish or was it my reluctance to kill a man?

Now and with my hiding place too close to them, I dared not slink away. They might see I was not one of them. I huddled through the remaining daylight hours and felt the cold for not having a fire. At dusk, with them still fishing, I snuck back into the mountains and sheltered in a cave.

A small fire in a hole scratched in the stone floor gave off scant heat against the bitter night. I hung a blanket over the entrance to keep out some of the wind and cold and keep some little heat in and to ensure no light showed. Just before I had come down from Paradise, I had shot a bear and skinned and carved it. Now and with a fire, I thawed some bear steaks and cooked 'em. Dawn the next morning I breakfasted on more of the steaks and resumed my quest. This time at a different place along the road. All day and most of the next, I sat in fruitless vigil. It seemed I could not even bushwhack unwary Frenchmen.

Finally, on the third day and along the road south of the fort, I heard a horse's whinny and there came a lone sled pulled by a tired old gelding. The driver walked alongside, switch in hand. The sled was empty, likely come from Ti for provisions.

I put an arrow into the man's back. He toppled to the ground. The horse stopped and stood patiently alongside the downed man. I listened for the sounds of others then I darted into the road. The man was dead, face down in bloody snow. I scalped him and took his weapons, a loaded musket and a knife, also his bearskin and possibles sack. More wagons were coming, I got back into the trees and seeing how many they were, ten wagons and thirty men, and with my tracks plainly visible in the snow around the dead man, I fled up along a rocky creek bed, trying to stay more on the ice than the snow, my tracks would be less readable to Frenchmen though not to Indians. I came to a massive cedar tree, newly fallen and spanning the crick. The snow around the tree disturbed in the falling, I climbed up onto the trunk, walked the length of it and leaped into the boughs. From there I got into some juniper bushes and walked more dead logs. I waded upstream in a small crick, or more likely a fork of the same crick and high-tailed deeper into the forest.

I returned to my cave-lair, my refuge from the cold and danger. My feet were wet and cold. I kindled my fire, removed my moccasins and socks and put them on sticks up close to the fire. I rubbed my feet and put on dry wool socks and high moccasins. I was plenty nerved up for having killed a man from ambush and scalped him and nearly paying for it with my life. My only other scalp, the Indian who had slain my Monie, I had taken in a rage. This one I took as proof of what I had done.

"Christ," I realized. "I am no better than they."

I spent the night picking the graybacks out of my victim's bearskin and with the wind howling outside and limbs crashing down, I sat up all night in watchful repose, listening for any what might be coming for me. None came, I got through the night in good order.

Thoroughly shook by my actions but determined to strike again, I waited for another covering storm. I ate bear steaks, along with some corn taken from the dead man's pouch. Inspection of the area around the caves revealed the presence of a pack of wolves also using the caves as shelter. Before many hours, I was in possession of two skins and some tasty dog meat.

During the warmest part of the day, I slept. Late afternoon, I gathered cedar boughs for the making of another pair of snowshoes. The dark came early. It took me another day to work the shoes into shape. I gave 'em a test by stalking a turkey what made the mistake of gobbling close by. The shoes worked; I ate well.

The next snow was not long in coming and was heavy. Before it stopped, I went for scalps. So much snow made it hard to move around. Took me extra time and tired me considerable. Down along the road, I got into good position behind a fallen log and waited. Snow mantled my shoulders and head. My pistol, bow, and two arrows were set on a rock in front of me.

I thought how Monica would take to knowing the manner in which her man skulked in dastardly ambush. I remembered her speaking of revenge, nay, clamoring for it following the death of our friend Tom. Then, I had told her revenge was not a proper motive to live by. Now, it was all I had. Sat there for as long as I could tolerate the cold. The bow-string was still in the inside pocket of my bearskin. The string didn't work well when wet, I would not bring it out until I needed it.

Finally, and with the snow nearly stopped, two sleighs hauling barrels approached, heading south to Ti. Each carried two men, a teamster and a guard, all with muskets across their knees. Four men, maybe too many for me to attempt with as close as I was to the fort but if it was scalps I was come for, there they be. I strung the bow and set an arrow. I waited and as the second wagon went past my hiding spot, I stood up and shot the driver a mortal blow. Buried the arrow nearly to the feathers in his side. The other man jumped off the wagon and looked wildly about. My arrow slammed into his back and showed neatly between his ribs. He, too, toppled into the snow. With ax and knife, I waited for the other two to come for me. Instead, and having jumped down out of their wagon, they ran in precipitous haste up the road shouting "Iroquois!" as if the very hounds of hell was at their heels. The dumb oxen bawled for gettin' left behind.

The barrels held wine. Useless to me, I chopped holes in those I could reach and I meanly cut the throats of the oxen. I took the men's scalps and muskets along with their pouches of parched corn and cooked meat. I carried it all into the trees, into the gloom of late afternoon.

That night, I again stayed awake alongside my small fire in my cave, alert did the French come for me. They didn't, and I thought it was for the ruse I had used to deter them. My arrows and snowshoes were made in the Mohawk fashion. Nothing spooked the French and Indians as did a Mohawk. So great was the fear, the presence or just the thought of a single Iroquois would make the French and Indians most reluctant to pursue me. Before I was done, they'd know the truth, either discovered for themselves or revealed to them.

****

A few more days spooking with no opportunities, I gathered up my loot and walked back up to the cabin. The bear carcass I had left hanging from a high limb of a tree behind the cabin was undisturbed. No wolves nor other critters had got to it although there was sign they had tried. I put a pot of water on the fire, chopped off a roast from the carcass and threw it into the boiling pot. Soon, the inside of my cabin warmed, the meat thawed. I cut some steaks and put ‘em on a spit, the sizzling meat filling the cabin with its tantalizing aroma.

A few days later I was back, spooking the road from the Ticonderoga fort to the sawmill at the falls. With no one coming or going and with darkness about fallen, my face wrapped against the cold in wolfskins, just my eyes showing, I came out of the trees and walked boldly along the road. In my hand, beneath the loose cloak I wore over my bearskin was a hatchet. Did I encounter anyone, I’d walk as if I belonged and as bundled as I was and did I greet them in my crude French, they wouldn’t take me for an enemy until it was too late. In this way I arrived at the sawmill and the bridge, the water flowing over the falls visible beneath an encasement of ice. A bayonet-wielding sentry was posted at the bridge. I approached and mumbled a response to his challenge. I pointed to the blockhouse and indicated I had business there. He nodded. “Oui, Oui,” He, thinking I was naught but a habitant, a dumb provincial, asked no more questions. I considered killing him. My hatchet against his pig-sticker but I did not, for knowing the time it would take me to bring out my hatchet might be fatal to me.

I crossed the bridge, not looking back, and around the bend and out of sight of the sentry, I headed for Rattlesnake Mountain. I got up along the side of the mountain and disappeared over the top of the ledges into the trees, headed for a cave my old mentor Hugh McChesney had shown me years ago. Hugh had sometimes used the cave as a hideout and to stash things. It would be near impossible to find by someone who didn’t know it was there. A slight path led up the side of the ledges to the cave. Scrub birches around the trail and the entrance obscured it. I had often used the cave in the years I had been spooking and now it would be my refuge. It wasn’t on any of the maps and even did the French and Indians know about it, they wouldn’t think I might be in there. Both my strikes so far had been up at Scalp Point.

Inside, the cave was damp and with no bears or wolfpacks holed up. It went twenty feet into the side of the mountain and had a low ceiling. I hung a bearskin a short way in from the entrance and with fresh meat cooking on the fire I wondered about myself. How many more scalps would it take to erase the pain of losing Monica? These three had done naught but make me as savage as the Indians I so detested. They at least were Stone Age people. I had become as them, yet was I unwilling to give it over.

During the night, a snowstorm raged, wind shrieked through the trees, enough snow fell to cover all sign. In the light of morning, the land lay fresh and clean under the white. I ventured out, but not far. No squirrels nor mice nor any of the other animals had begun moving from burrow or sheltered refuge, an indication the storm was not entirely past. I returned to the cave. The storm resumed on the mid-part of the afternoon and for three more days it kept me shut up inside my hideout. I went out only for firewood and I was heedful of direction and distance so not to lose my way back. My world was silent, the only sound the soft thud of snow falling from the trees.

The cave was cold, damp, drafty, smoky. But better than outside. When the storm abated, the wind shifted north of west, the sky cleared, the clouds blew away. I came out from the cave and trudged back to my cabin. The new snow was above my knees. Without snowshoes it would have been impossible to do anything but flounder for the fresh snow not yet crusted over.

Once back at the cabin and in the few days I took to rest and thaw out, I tried to smother my conscience, which was telling me I had ought not to go back for more scalps. This struggle against whatever decency remained within me was won, or perhaps lost, and I went down.

I spooked the road which led from the lower falls of the portage to the Ticonderoga fort. I sat shivering whilst waiting for a mark. None came and when I could no longer abide the cold, I returned to my cave to spend the night. Next day I was back again at the road, though not at the same place. Again, nobody, just did I see the faint traces of sled runners getting filled in by the falling snow.

Discouraged, I walked along the upper crick and crossed over the ice-encrusted natural stone bridge, and on the west side, I got to where the crick turned east. Here was a hill the French used as a burial ground. The hill overlooked the steepest part of the gorge, where the crick water, not fully iced for how wildly it roiled around the sharp bend, had formed a deep permanent whirlpool. The road to Scalp Point ran below here and I watched for the chance to perpetrate a dark deed on some unsuspecting French or Indian.

The day was wicked cold, I moved twice, when I couldn't sit any longer. The second time it was to where I could look down on the sawmill on its north side. Burned by Abercrombie when he fled from Ti, the mill had been rebuilt and was in full noisy operation.

I finally gave it up and returned to my cave. I was back the next morning along the road and there came a lone sleigh, one man aboard, headed up the hill. I watched awhile to make sure nobody was coming behind him. Then I took off in pursuit. The sleigh continued climbing up out of the gorge, the driver unaware of my presence, of the fact his end was near. I closed up behind him as fast as my snowshoes could carry me and put an arrow high up on his back. I took his scalp and anything else worth taking, which weren't much.

Circling back around toward my cave, I had gone about a mile and up on a ridge from where I could reconnoiter my back trail, I seen I was gettin' followed. Ten men. The two out front I figured for Indians, the others, by the flashes of white and blue uniforms beneath brown bearskins and with how clumsily they went in their snowshoes were French regulars.

If the eight be true sons of Europe, woods-loping would be entirely foreign to them and did I draw them deeper into the mountains and kill the Indians, the soldiers would be helpless against me. Even though they were eight and I but one, I might pick 'em off one at a time and over a considerable distance.

****

I led them west and south for two miles, staying well ahead, even increasing the distance between us. I got into the Trout Brook Valley and half a mile in, I turned south and climbed up out of the long ravine between two of the Brothers Mountains.

Up in the high country and in a place where the Indians couldn't see me, I went fast and got out onto a ledge overlooking my back trail. I checked my priming and waited and up the ravine came the Indians, well ahead now of the regulars, as I had anticipated and coming quickly, anxious to finish me. Not considering I might be doing anything other than fleeing, and thinking I was a Mohawk, they didn't expect I was a marksman what could take them from long range. Their mistake. I got one at a distance and reloading quickly, I got the other, he misjudging from whence the first shot had come and hunkering down where I could get him.

I scalped the Indians. One of 'em had a nice new bearskin, the other's was ratty. I took the good one. I took their food pouches too, and their muskets and knives and whatever else, and all of what I took, except for the food and hair, I stashed for retrieving later.

I got into hiding and waited for them others. I figured the echoing gunshots would slow 'em down, the loss of their guides, once they seen the bodies, might send 'em home. If it did, I would kill as many of 'em as I could whilst they made their way back down to the lake.

They came to the dead Indians and after talking over what to do next, they surprised me by keeping on. Must a been a dutiful officer leading less-determined privates.

I got back out ahead, far enough so I looped around and put 'em onto their own backtrail. From hiding, I watched 'em studying their tracks. Was they pondering who else might be up there with them? I stayed out of their sight and on we went, west and south through steep, icy country. The wind blew, the tall hardwoods bent, swayed and dropped limbs the size of small trees, something else to maybe send 'em back down into the valley. Yet did they come on.

I picked off two of 'em and when they switched direction to skirt a difficult piece of terrain and it seemed they might get themselves off my track, I stepped boldly out onto a ledge and gived 'em a halloo to point 'em back in the proper direction.

There was just five of them now and where was number six? Might have turned back and gone home or was he an Indian or an accomplished woodsman dressed as a regular and working around to set his own trap? I figured to watch for him whilst I dispatched these others.

I tried to determine which of 'em was the officer. They would thank me for killing him, iffen they didn't do him first but did I kill him, it'd be the end of our game. Besides, there wasn't much to identify officers 'cept for the gorgets they wore 'round their necks and no gorget did I see for the distance. Any officer wanting to keep his hair would remove his insignia and with them rotating who was out front, the officer knew I was eyeballing for him.

****

On they came, floundering in the deep snow, each seeking his own path. They had heretofore been walking with plenty of space between 'em; now and maybe for feeling fatigued, the two damn fools in the rear had got careless and was walking side by side. Close enough so I might bag 'em both with a single shot, something I hadn't ever done before, so far as I knew. I got out ahead a ways and came down off the cliffs so when they came along, we was on the same level and I weren't no more than forty feet from them. The two was still side by side. I had an extra charge in my gun and lining up the man closest to me and with the other man also in my line of fire, I squeezed the trigger and high-tailed into the rocks behind me. I got up a short way to where I could see them and they could not see me. The two lay in the snow. One, the first to have received my bullet, was dead. The other was down, wounded, although perhaps not mortally, the force of the musket ball having been checked for its passing through the first man. The others had gone to cover in some rocks on the side of the pass opposite to where I was ensconced.

The shot man revived and began crawling on his elbows toward where the others was hidden. They, from their sheltered place, urged him onward. With him close enough to the cover so the others were reaching out to him, I shot him in the head, they recoiling from the splatter of blood and brains. Now and with them yet pinned, a long, deep silence ensued. With a cliff towering behind them, their only escape was to come out from the rocks and go back down the pass, which would give me easy shooting. They stayed hidden for not knowing was I still there or not and knowing iffen I were, I would shoot the first one who bolted from cover. The waiting got to be too much for one, he came out and fled down the pass. I let him go on a ways, to give him the hope I was maybe gone, then did I come out to where the others could see me. I raised my rifle. They shouted a warning, the fleeing man looked behind himself and up at me. Holding my aim on him, I laughed loudly, which echoed around the rocks and cliff-sides. One of the hidden men took a desperate shot at me, his ball kicking up snow nowhere close. I let the fleeing man get a ways down the pass, and far enough to where he might a been thinking he was beyond the range of my gun, I shot him in the back.

I hunkered down in plain sight and waited for what the others would do but after awhile and as it was getting late in the day and with seven dead, two cornered and one unaccounted, I figured my game was played out. Besides, I wanted for one of ‘em, at least, to bring word to Scalp Point. Let ‘em know it be an American what done the killing, not a Mohawk for no Indian could shoot so well.

I backed off the ledge and into the trees and moved west, then north. I laughed for thinking how long the two men might stay hidden for the fear I was lurking. The man unaccounted-for worried me enough so I switched often from one side hill to another. He was probably naught but a regular and was more likely to get lost and die in the woods than to come for me. Still, I would be wary.

The awful night came on, stars shining bright, no wind. Just terrible cold. Ice crystals in the air seared my nose and throat. My teeth chattered so, I reckoned they’d be heard for miles. Colder than a Huron heart as old Hugh McChesney would a said. I built a shelter in the lee of an overhanging ledge. I wrapped myself in bearskins, coonskins covered my face. Not daring to sleep for fear my blood would freeze, I abandoned the shelter and trekked through the dark.

Around midnight, clouds came in from the south and thickened as the night wore on and toward dawn, it began snowing. The first hour the snow came straight down in small, grainy flakes, then I was caught in a raging snowstorm. With the storm making it hard to see or tell direction, getting lost was a more dangerous possibility than getting trailed and bushwhacked by a Frenchie and as it was, I had to reverse myself a few times afore I got straightened out. I had been watching for Outlet Creek and figuring to have overshot it, I thought about turning back but kept on for the vague notion I was alright where I was.

The snow stopped and with a new foot of it upon the ground, I seen I was in familiar country. I came to a gorge between side hills and was now just a few miles from my cabin. The walls of the gorge lay close together and sheer to a height of a hundred feet on either side, they made a man feel small to walk through 'em. The cut opened and ran between the summits of two hills.

I was quickly over the mountain and down the other side. I got into a swamp and followed the easier going along the ice. With the winter sun halfway across the southern sky, a smudge behind thinning gray clouds, I arrived at the cabin, hungry, thirsty, bone-tired.

Chapter XXII – The Lone Wolf Continued

I spent a few days re-provisioning my cabin. So many fresh scalps drying on a stick-rack in the yard, all treated with oil to preserve 'em and to cut down on the smell. Whilst I had been hunting the French, I had cached all of what I took of theirs, muskets, pistols, uniform coats, pants, shirts and socks. Now I went back dragging my toboggan and collected it all. I found the two men I had corralled behind the rocks. The new-fallen snow undisturbed over 'em told me they hadn't dared to come out, frozen more by fear of me than of the cold. I had to kick around in the snow to find 'em and I had to thaw their heads by a fire afore I could lift their hair. I looked for sign of the one who had got away or had been tailing me, as unlikely as it was, and I never did see anything more of him.

****

I set traps close by to the cabin, fished through the thick ice of the Eagles' Lake, and soon I was back down in the valley. I got a Frenchie my first day. I took away his scalp, musket, powder horn, sack and bear-skin. The horn was a beautiful work of art. It was made from the tusk of an animal not native to the Adirondacks. Someone had spent consider-able time in the delicate work of hollowing and etching the horn, an epic with sailors in a longboat and in a titanic struggle against rough seas and an angry whale. So life-like, I damn near smelled the salt air. Gazing down at the face of the driver, had I killed a budding artist or a scalawag who had acquired the horn in a night of gambling or with some skull-duggery of his own?

A few days after and drawn to the sound of a shot, I advanced warily into a cedar-covered swale and heard someone talking. I decided where it was coming from and approaching, I came upon a man talking to him-self. Here in the swale, with the snow less deep, the deer had herded up, a dozen or so, and the Frenchie had got right up and shot one. This far into winter, the deer were thin, their meat was without nourishment but the French were so hungry they killed even these sour deer. Frenchie was gutting his kill, his back to me, and so quietly did I get up on him and so joyously loud was he talking to himself, a sure sign of debility, he remained unaware of me. The herd, on his other side, watched my approach, same as they had probably watched him, and if he had paid attention now to the deer, to the look coming into their eyes, the stiffness into their front legs, he too might have been alerted to my sneaking up behind him. I tapped him on the shoulder, he turned, I, grinning, shot him. He dropped, the herd not scattering with the muffled sound, just a shudder went through them, their front legs buckling with the eruption of noise in the silence; dull witnesses to murder.

Whilst taking the man's scalp, I contemplated how I, too, had begun talking to myself, even arguing sometimes, although never loudly and never when I was stalking. I had not used to do this, in all the years I had spent alone in the woods so I reckoned, same as the Frenchie who had just paid with his life for his jabbering, I too was gone more than a little daft. I took the man's gear, and good bearskin but left the deer meat. Even fresh-killed it is high.

****

All winter at the cabin I had worked on a pair of skis, trying to devise a way to keep 'em tight to my feet. After several false starts on the ice of my secluded lake, I got so I trusted 'em. Cumbersome to carry, useless in deep woods, they would only work in open country, such as the iced-over surface of a big lake. With the skis strapped across my back, I went down into the valley.

Late afternoon, my first day back and through a deepening gloom, I seen a lone man walking in the distance on the wide-open lake, and with no one else around, I strapped on my skis and approached swiftly. He, hearing the swish of my skis on the thin coat of snow on the ice, looked over his shoulder, sensed trouble and began running, his long braids flapping behind him. Cruising along, I laughed demonically as if I were one of the Indian windigos he'd grown up fearing, for he was an Indian. With my laugh echoing, his exertions only served to exhaust him whilst my skis gave me the deadly advantage. I closed in, he cast one last terrified look over his shoulder and I put an arrow high up on the back of his leg, in a place to stop him yet not prove immediately fatal. He fell and bleeding out, he reached behind hisself with one hand and clutched the deeply-driven arrow. I got over him and removed his knife from his belt. He looked up at me. I grinned and gestured with the knife. His own look back was him asking I kill him afore I took his hair. I, still grinning, shook my head, no, and whilst I twisted his hair in my fist and pulled it tight, he cursed me as spawn of the devil and as I took his scalp, he emitted a most awful scream.

Dear God!

Now and with skis, the scalps came oftener; Lake Champlain became a deer runway for me. A place to hunt men and to speed away from any and all pursuit. I became ever more bold and with the boldness, nay, the rashness, was I asking the French to finish me? To put an end to what I could not? Or had I become so contemptuous of them, I did not think they could ever kill me?

One night, my boldness took me up and over the walls of the wooden stockade across the strait from the Scalp Point fort, same as the Indians sometimes did when the snow got piled up against our own fort walls. I killed a sentry, took his scalp and leaped back over the wall and into a snowbank. I slid and ran down the hill to the shore. I put on my skis and escaping swiftly along the lake, I got down to Ti with time enough afore first light to go over the wall and get me another scalp.

****

More days of fruitful hunting on skis and now I was hurrying, more anxious than ever to get up to my cabin. So many scalps, I carried them in a bag and what else I carried rattling over my shoulder, three canteens. That morning, a three-man patrol of regulars had come along the road and after I had slain and scalped them and checked their bags for food, I took a swig from one of their canteens. Killing is thirsty work. I tasted brandy. Tried the other two canteens. More brandy.

The canteens were bulky and had made for hard carrying up and into my mountain lair but I was grateful for having lugged 'em. Until, and in my half-drunken state, I began having visions of my beloved Monie in the only way I could see her now, in her box, her head wrapped tight in a white shroud, like a stern Catholic nun. Her face, the only part of her visible, was shrunken in death. Then came thoughts of my boys. I knew did I not ever get home, Eric and Sarah would give them care and upbringing but what sort of man abandoned his youngsters when they most needed him? How twisted must a man be to abandon his children for the bloody path I had taken?

A couple hours of this acute melancholia, the canteens were drained and I felt a desperate need for more. I found a jug on a shelf and raised it to my mouth and getting nothing out of it, I hurled it against the wall. Then, cursing and sobbing, I furiously swept all of what was on the shelves and table off and to the floor where I kicked and hurled it against the walls. Finally, exhausted amidst the shattered ruins of my cabin, I fell onto the bed. My sobs raised up great gulps of air and with tears flowing, so despondent was I for Monie and for myself and the boys, I thought I must either go mad or go home now, today. It would not be possible to get there with so much snow and ice but the thought of trying seemed better than keeping to my murderous course. Yet there was naught for me except to get over the feelings and get on with the killing. I was trapped here for the winter and trapped as well by my own evil-ness, for so far was I gone 'round the bend.

In the morning, clear of the effects of the brandy, I remembered why the bastards down in the valley were getting a measure of what they had given me. Reckon I be not done yet! The French inside their stone forts must know how any time they left the safety of their bastions, the Lone Wolf would be after them. May the thought make the winter so much tougher on their minds!

****

A young girl and her beau came along the road south of Scalp Point. Wrapped in furs and in each other's arms, he with a rifle; her, secure in her man's embrace and emitting the trilling laugh of the mademoiselle. I determined to kill them both but as it was daylight and we were close to the Scalp Point castle, I would have to do them quickly, him first, and her before she could scream. I got back into the woods and coming out farther along the road, I hid behind a tree. They were too taken with each other to be aware of the danger and passed just a few feet from where I was hidden. I stepped out, brained the man with my hatchet and threw the girl to the ground.

I thrust back her hood, put my blade against her throat and with one fist wrapping her hair, my face close to hers, I hesitated, struck by her beauty. She had the classical features of the French-Canadian lass, the sultry lips, the creased almond eyes and brown-toned skin, and she was young, Christ, she was young. Her eyes looked into mine, nay, looked directly into my soul. Her lips moving in what might have been a Papist prayer, she seemed more resigned than afraid, her unquivering, jutting chin defiant toward a death she neither deserved nor feared. I realized cutting her throat might doom me to seeing her eyes each time I closed my own in sleep. Two pair of eyes staring back at me, this girl's browns, Monie's greens, the spirits of the two murdered women kindred in an abhorrence of me. Deciding the filthy acts of war could have no place for the killing of the fairer sex, I sealed her mouth with a strip of rawhide and tied her legs at the ankles so she might not give warning until I was well away.

Later, trudging home, I imagined her life. A peasant girl sold into marriage by her father or brothers or was she an adventurous lass run off with her soldier beau? A peasant girl's beauty faded quickly, she became bitter and crone-like from a lifetime of incessant toil but whilst they flowered, the French girls were as fetching as any girls in the world, or so I had heard from the salts and smugglers in Pops' tavern. I thought I should have taken her back to the cabin for use as a slave. She might have submitted, it was maybe all she knew, or would she have planted a knife in my ribs, first chance she got? Then I thought of Josh's heartbreak for his own daughter carried off into slavery and I was glad I had neither killed nor taken the girl. So my heart had not yet turned entirely to stone, or more properly, ice.

****

An Indian came up from Scalp Point to hunt me for the prestige he would garner did he return with my head on a stick. Or perhaps he was sent as their best tracker, maybe brought in from far away to have a go at me. He was good, I was better, and after a few days of him stalking me, me stalking him, I got him with a hatchet blow from behind a tree. I left him dead in the snow, scalped and bloodied, meat for the wolves.

****

Days I fished the Eagles' Lake. Sitting on an upturned bucket and dangling my lines down through holes chopped in the ice, a welcomed interlude but soon enough I was back at the deadly business of trophy-hunting. Days of lonely vigil, the wariness of staying alive, of waiting in freezing bushwhack for the next poor fool to come along.

I knocked on the head a Frenchman who was hunting and later the same day, I came upon a habitant fishing in a secluded cove along the Verd Mont side of Champlain. He was a giant of a man, so big I contemplated passing him by. This I rejected and with my face wrapped in fur against the cold, I walked right up to him, as if I were a friend, and got him with my dragoon pistol, the sound of the shot somewhat muffled for the barrel pressed into his bearskin. I gathered up his fish and gear, and when I stooped down to take his scalp, his arm shot up suddenly, his big hand got around my throat. We tussled in the snow, he got on top and was choking the life out of me, then I felt his grip easing, so I had shot him well enough. Even with their last breath, these bastards were treacherous. He rolled off me, I plunged my knife into his stomach, finishing him, but not until after I had scalped him.

****

My beard was longer and more scraggily than ever before. Usually, I was bearded in winter, clean shaven in summer, but in winters past I had the habit of at least somewhat trimming my beard with my knife and my little shard of a mirror, and before descending into civilization or immediately upon arriving there, I would shave entirely and cut my hair. Now I gave no thought to it, not even disgust did I feel at how unruly my appearance must be. Streaks of gray showed in my beard and in my long, shaggy, wild-looking hair, most often in a frozen ponytail, greasy, filthy, yet it would be one fine trophy for the man good enough to take it. My clothes were worn out and ragged. I patched them against the cold and the wind but cared not how they looked. Monica had always fussed over my appearance and how sorely disgusted she'd have been to see me as I was now. Or smell me. Likely she'd have dumped me into the nearest icy lake or pond.

****

The days lengthened, the wind was sometimes out of the south; rain mixed with the snow. The forests were drab and stark. This change in the weather aroused the French. They were out more and with a watchfulness in their lines and along the roads. They were patrolling in more numbers, ten, twelve men, enough so I could do naught with them. They still weren't venturing too far out from their forts but with more Indians coming from the north, they would soon launch a foray to search me out and kill me. I laughed to think for how so many years Scalp Point was so called for the scalps brought there and now it was the Scalp Point raiders who were losing their hair. I didn't laugh to think of a hundred men in a widely cast net coming up into my Paradise, discovering my beavers and wiping 'em out.

Then came mud season, the most awful time of year, the interlude between winter and spring when hunting of any kind, man nor beast, was near impossible. The French pulled back closer to their forts and when they were about, it was most always in numbers intended to keep me from trying them. For days, I was not able to make a score. I couldn't hunt nor did I dare venture onto the softening ice to fish. I was growing weak for subsisting on bark soup and ground nuts. I feared I might starve to death, my bones all the French would find in the spring when they would surely come for me.

What few kills I did make, and I was making then now as much for food as for scalps, I was frantic to get into my victims' packs for what I might find there. Often my only sustenance was strips of leather to chew on and too often was I stranded without shelter against the piercing, near overwhelming cold.

Yet and despite the mud and cold and the lack of anything much to eat, I prowled, and when a situation arose, I went for it. Swift and silent, taking advantage of cover and speed, I avoided the long chance and adapted my ways to the wily fox.

Over the winter, I had seen occasional sign of my rangers. I had even raided one of their unguarded caches for food, or had they known I was prowling and did they leave the food for me? I thought about getting in with them but they, same as the game animals and the French, had become scarce. This was for the mud and for the French having pulled in and tightened the cordon around themselves and for the rangers staying south to get ready for our own spring campaign. With no sign of rangers, I would not wait for them to reappear. They might come too late for me and besides and as a stubborn Dutchman who had survived the winter without the aid of anyone, I would finish the same way. Alone, or perish in the doing.

Back at Scalp Point and feeling frustrated for not having made any kills, I again went over the walls of Depeuw and took a sentry. Moments later and having crossed the lake to the windmill redoubt, I came upon another sentry, this one having chosen the wrong time to venture out to relieve himself. Him too I left lifeless and hairless, the snow around him red with blood. "Sans cheveux," might my Frenchmen have said, were their lips not sealed forever. As I was fleeing on my skis, the alarm bells commenced ringing, so the entire garrison was called out. They would stand to arms through the bitter cold night, unsure whether or not I might attempt something more. Doubt they cared much for it. I spent the night in a shelter I used sometimes, under the rock ledges on the east side of the lake behind East Creek.

****

Scalps hung on a pole outside my door, my cabin overflowed with loot; weapons and accouterments on the walls and piled in the corners; guns, powder horns, shot pouches, knives and tomahawks, fancy shirts, robes and blankets. An aristocrat's sword. It would all fetch a good price, especially my burgeoning collection of French muskets and pistols which I kept loaded and primed. Did Frenchie discover my hideout before I got away, he'd get a most hot greeting.

All of what I had taken, did I sell in Albany, I could use to get started on rebuilding and restocking the farm. Thoughts of the farm were an indication I was considering a life beyond my winter of killing. So much death, yet, taken all together it could not near avenge all I had lost. I was coming 'round to the acknowledgement of how taking the hair of every last French and Indian at Scalp Point and Ti was not going to bring my Monie back. It was time to go. Time to stop this thing and face a most wretched future, to become human again. To put aside all thoughts of revenge and return to the living. This revulsion, which I was feeling more often, was dangerous for a man who would prowl enemy country. Distraction by abstract thoughts could get me killed.

More often now I pined for my boys. To hold them in my arms and hear them laugh. And how was Josh getting along with the farm? With his promise to build a new barn over the winter, did the weather allow? So much needed to be replaced. A new beginning, a return, as hard as it might be, to the place where my Monie had been taken from me. That was the awfulness I would have to confront if I were to live again. With the onset of improving weather, it was time to end the killing. Time to go home.

****

I built a bark shelter down at the first of the Paradox Lakes, well-hidden in thick pine. Then I got started on a canoe. As early in the spring as I would be departing, I understood this had to be the stoutest canoe I had ever built. Stout enough to withstand the massive amounts of snow-melt sure to be pouring down out of the mountains and filling the rivers. It would have to be the biggest, too, if it would carry all my accumulated booty.

The canoe took a week to construct, what with framing with just the right cedar, the pine pitch to be boiled, the cutting, rolling and unrolling of the sheets of the white birch, and when I finished, the boat was a good one. Fifteen-feet long, light enough so I could carry it, strong enough to withstand the bashing it would receive. I carved four paddles of swamp cherry, the strongest of woods. My paddles I made slightly wider at the bottom than usual. They would be as much for steering as for propulsion. I built two sets of outriggers. One shorter set for use on the East Branch, a longer set for the Hudson. These would give me stability, yet and with the danger they might hang me up on snags, they could be cut away with just a few slashes with the polesaw I had rigged, a French cutlass at the end of a stick. I also built a rudder, something I hadn't ever used before. With work on my boat completed, I spent two days lugging my loot down to the Paradox and stashing it in my shelter.

I grew more nervous each day with waiting for my way to open up. The air warming, the muddy ground drying, I was filled with anxiety, certain the Indians would come whooping up out of the valley before I could get away. The early spring nights were yet cold and even with a lessening of the mud, the hunting was poor, the woods devoid of game. I'd have taken a cedar-fed deer about then, if I could a found one.

Finally, I awoke of a morning to the ice broken away from the shores of the Eagles' Lake. Not sufficient for me to depart but a good sign, and with enough open water along the edges of the lake, I was able to take some fish. A few more days, anxious beyond telling, noisy action with the east wind shrieking during the nights, heralding the imminent break-up of the ice. Soon I could travel but not before one final task which I had been savoring and which I nearly abandoned in my anxiousness to be away but with how fitting a close it would be to my winter spent man-killing, I remained firm in my determination to go through with it.

Warm in my cabin and with my scalps in a pile on the table, so many different colors, red, black, brown, gray and white, so many different textures. I took snips of hair from each and twined them into a slender three-foot braid. I trekked down into the valley and nailed the braid to a tree. My message, written out beforehand and stuffed into a pouch, I now attached to the braid.

Frenchies, my note read, *some dirty skunks among you have no doubt boasted of having attacked the Vlatche house of the English ranger, Kuyler. These may think they succeeded in killing him and of a certainty they have lifted the hair of his woman. It is for this deed and for these boasters I have perpetrated my winter of foul deeds. So many of your scalps have I collected, vengeance is mine saith the Lord, for I am no Iroquois. I am but a single man, Kuyler, the Lone Wolf.*

****

Back at my cabin, I slept but little and awoke before dawn. The water shone a dark blue in the moonlight. I packed my canoe and was away, moving fast along the first of the Paradox Lakes, a cold wind at my back. I made good time until I arrived at the channel which flowed into Second Lake. An hour's paddling was usually sufficient to get me through the channel but now the narrow way was clogged with chunks of ice which had got driven there and wedged in by the wind. I unloaded my loot and hauled it down to Second Lake. It took three trips to get it all moved and with darkness come again and knowing I would not sleep or might oversleep and get awoken by Indians, I kept going, across Second Lake and down the short stretch of the upper East Branch and into Big Lake. I moved fast before the wind and steered south by Orion, the Celestial Hunter. A terrible cold night. The wind blew wild; whitecapped waves roiled the lake. I hugged the shore.

With my shorter outriggers attached, I got onto the East Branch. The current was strong, swollen by the snowmelt. Surely my fastest trip ever on this ordinarily placid river. Often had I grumbled at its lazy meanders and cursed at those places where sometimes in the summer and fall there was not enough water and I had to drag my canoe at the end of a rope. Now the roiling sped me along at a good speed. I had sometimes to go ashore to avoid the fastest water as well as the worst snags and for short intervals of rest, and I was all the while trepidacious for what lay ahead, the joining of the East Branch with the Hudson. From the confluence, it was thirty miles to Edward. I feared those miles would be impossible to traverse this time of year, with the snowmelt, yet I was hopeful, or plain foolish in thinking I might somehow manage it.

Nearly down to the confluence, I came to where the river opened into what I called French Pond for the time in the earlier war when me and my dog Blackie had snuck past some French and Indians camped here. We had nearly died in the sneaking, and spreading the alarm downriver, we set the stage for the onset of a major campaign by the British, which, like so many of their efforts, ended in disaster.

****

The roar of the East Branch meeting the Hudson was loud ere I got close, and with the current strengthening, I disembarked along the east shore a mile or so north of the junction. I stashed the canoe and staying back in the brush and trees along the bank, I walked down for a look. I got below the merging of the rivers. This put me at the bottom of the falls which marked the confluence. Still back in the trees, I stepped out and was stunned by what lay before me. The Hudson as I had never seen it before, the sight filling me with trepidation.

Oh, Lord!

Here at the bottom of the falls the river broadened into a lake and what a lake! Roiling, rumbling water, dense fog, a tempest at sea such as Pops had sometimes spoken of in awe. A frothing spew rolling up over the banks, crashing and receding as it broke from the confinement of the riverbed and flooded in amongst the flat, tree-lined shore, same as up at French Pond. The roar of the falls was as if the Indian Thunder

Gods was awakening beneath the waves.

So much water rushing over the falls and bringing down out of the mountains the limbs of trees, even entire trees, and ice flows, massive white leviathans. These blocks of ice, as big as cabins, when they arrived at the lip of the falls, plunged. Striking at the bottom, thumping, they sent torrents of water into the air, the blocks submerging, and coming back up to the surface and resuming their bobbing journey down the swollen river. The massive chunks of frozen water, same as the trees and limbs, would be deadly for a man out there in a canoe and I knew it would be thus all the way to Edward, with so much of the melting snow yet to be moved down to the sea at New York.

Not even my lifetime of skills could see me through. A single misjudgment would be fatal, there would be no escaping the dire penalty for error or bad luck. I might do everything right and still die for it. I could not attempt it, nor could I survive waiting out the weeks it would take for the river to calm itself.

Might be the only thing would be to build a travois and go overland. Drag my boat and loot down to Edward. Or stash everything and hoof it the rest of the way. Refreshed and after the waters had somewhat abated, I could hire men to come up and help retrieve everything. This seemed the most reasonable course though it was not a surety. As weak as I was, I might die a madman in the forests long afore I got to Edward.

I returned to my boat and with so much indecision yet present in my mind and as late as it was in the day, I would sleep on it until tomorrow. Impatience can kill. I spent the night shivering with just a bark shelter against the rain which fell steadily. I kept a small fire in a hole. A dismal time with the rain getting in and the wind howling through the trees. In the morning, I trekked back down alongside the river. Seen by first light, it was a more daunting tempest for the waters having risen considerably overnight. I walked back upriver and at the top of the falls, I got a whiff of something familiar.

Bacon!

I swung my rifle down and to the front and still crouched in the trees, my eyesight swept the river and the far shore. I saw no sign of anything and figured to have imagined the whiff until I got another, and still in the trees and perfectly still and through a break in the fog, I seen a most glorious sight.

On the other side of the river, there at the top of the falls and with the shoreline in front of it partially denuded of trees and brush, was a fort.

British, had to be. A stockade within cannon range for blasting anything coming along the carry trail or through the woods on the side I was on.

I couldn't tell from where I was and with the distance and the mist off the falls, whether or not there were men on the walls and no flag did I see waving over the parapets. It could be the fort had been closed up for the winter and not yet re-occupied. Might be the smell of bacon was from ruffians. Or Indians. Or something conjured from inside of me.

Still, and remembering the talk which had gone around last summer, I thought myself a fool for not having anticipated finding a fort where previously there had been none. The talk was Abercrombie's replacement, General Amherst, was a builder of forts and roads, so busy at it he sometimes forgot he was supposed to be fightin' a war. If he was a man with any sense, which he was said to be, this junction of the East Branch with the Hudson would be an obvious strategic place for him to build.

I was one wild ride away from getting in to a warm fire and a breakfast of bacon and probably coffee too. Thoughts of trekking through the forest paled before this sudden new possibility. But how the hell was I to get over? It might as well have been on the other side of the moon.

Stayin' back in the trees and with the waters plunging at my feet for how close I was to the top of the falls, I pondered how I might get to the other side. With my familiarity with the confluence and spurred by the smell of the bacon, an idea began taking shape in my head. Foolish and crazy, yet it might work.

I walked downriver a mile to where I knew there was a big island. A quarter mile long, oval shaped and heavily wooded, the island was half as wide at its widest, in the center, as it was long, and tapered to points at either end. The rocky upstream end of the island withstood a constant bashing from the water breaking violently against it.

At times of high water such as now, I knew most of the flow would be through the main channel along the island's south side, enough so I might navigate the northern channel, if I could get into it. This northern channel, though I couldn't see it from where I was and for the tall trees on the island, I knew to be the narrower of the channels. The narrowing would necessarily increase the speed of the water, it would be moving as fast or faster than what was there in front of me, but toward the bottom of the island, the river made a steep descent through a sweeping curve which might drive me up and onto the shore.

I could put my boat in somewhere between the falls and the island

and make my way across the breadth of the river and could I get to where the current split around the island, I might get into this lesser channel. I would have to choose my debarkation point carefully. Far enough out from the falls so not to get wrecked at once yet not so close to the island to not give myself time enough to get over.

So much could go wrong. I might choose the best place for getting on and still not make it. I might get knocked out of my boat by one of the big waves off the falls or get clobbered by a massive block of ice or rammed by one of those trees which were riding the current. Or, and did I fail to get over, I must perforce traverse the faster-moving southern channel, and even did I succeed in riding it to the bottom of the island, unlikely as it was, down there and with the currents reuniting, the tempest would be at its most ferocious.

Some other things I knew for having often come this way, some in my favor, some not. Firstly, the water above the island where I must cross, as fast as it was and with all the flotsam, was without shoals. As forbidding as any water but just water. Still, and with so much debris, there would be no maneuvering around it. I must trust to luck.

Another danger was the debris which had got piled up along the shore and with arms reaching into the river. There was plenty enough of it in the south channel and probably on the north side too. My hope was, this early in the spring and with the speed of the current over there, most of what was getting washed down might have kept going and got flushed out the bottom.

One other possibility made me laugh. Did I fail to get far enough out and did I strike the island with enough force to wreck my canoe or did I tumble out and did the canoe go down the river without me and did I get onto the island, I'd have neither the strength nor the means of getting off. There'd be naught the British could do for me and I could starve or freeze to death agonizingly close and in full view of 'em. Hell, we could maybe converse whilst I awaited my death.

Daunting as it all looked, I was of a mind to try it but not without first making sure there was men in the fort. Men who wouldn't kill me did I take the trouble to cross over to their side. I got back up across from the fort. I raised my rifle and fired, knowing at once no one there could have heard it over the rumbling of the falls. I took off my shirt and waved it on a stick whilst walking up and down the skinny of the shore. If there were British, I hoped they had sense enough to have sentries posted on the walls, though with them, one never knew. Nobody coming out, I took a pair of French linens from my loot and cut them into strips. I climbed up into a pine tree which, though not too tall, stood by its lonesome and leaned precariously out over the lip of the falls. The top of the tree was scorched black and bare of limbs for having got hit by lightning. The water boiling and plunging directly below me for the closeness of the falls, I tied the strips to the top of the tree and climbed back down. The strips snapped in the stiff wind off the falls. I hid in the bushes and watched. It took some time but the fort gates swung open and as much as I loathed the sight of those red coats of the British, seeing 'em now, ten or so soldiers rushing out, was a most awesome sight. They were unsure who or what the hell was up there in the tree and how it might have got there and with them deploying behind the downed trees and icepacks littering the shore, they were no more than forty yards from me. I stepped out with my arms in the air and hoping to God none of 'em took a shot at me. Their sergeant and me shouted some, neither of us able to make out what the other was saying for the rumbling of the falls. I tried telling him with gestures what I was intending and not sure he understood, I bade him and his men to watch, which they did, most intently as I pulled my canoe out of the woods and carried it down along the riverbank.

In the few hours it took for me to get everything moved, the British went back and forth with me. The place I chose for getting onto the river was an inlet behind a point a hundred yards down from the falls. Inside the little bay, I could get on without immediately plunging into the worst of it. I attached my longer outriggers and my rudder, which for now I lashed tight against the back of the canoe. I reloaded my loot and gear and secured it and with all in readiness, I gazed into the thick mist over the raging river. I tried to convince myself it was possible, my judgement no doubt clouded by the thought of being done with it in minutes instead of days or weeks. My thoughts turned near reverential for the feeling Monie was looking down on me. Watching, urging me to make it to the other side for the sake of our boys. She could no longer do anything for them, I yet could. I checked my gear and outriggers one last time and lashed my paddle to my wrist. Then, and for my wife and boys, I raised my paddle to the British, gave a whoop and shoved off.

Getting out of the bay and into the main flow was more difficult than I had supposed. With the pushback of the current against the less-riled waters of the bay, I got rebuffed each time I tried and with how violently my boat rattled and shook in the attempts, it was as if the River Gods was raising their hands against my foolishness. Pieces of cedar, the extra framing I had put on my canoe, splintered off and I could feel the rocks and submerged snags, even the gravel, clawing the bottom of my boat which fortunately, and though weighed down, was not too deep in the water.

I tried pushing with one of the long poles I carried, even did I stand up to get more of my strength into the poling, and fortunate I was to not be standing when a mighty wave came off the falls with a height and force sufficient to sweep over and across the bay and take me with it. Spun about and shrouded as I was in the mist off the towering wave, the British must a figured they'd seen the last of me. Yet did I come out, buoyed by my outriggers and perched precariously atop the wave, or another following wave, which I rode downstream at a most horrific height and speed. It was wild and harrowing for surely no man had ever taken such a ride nor been so at the mercy of a river, the speed exhilarating if it did not kill me. With so much of the length of my boat suspended off the wave, first the front, then the back, I was certain my boat must break in half yet she remained intact for being stoutly built.

Riding one wave then another, sliding down into troughs and rising up again on the crests, I shot downriver same as the limbs and ice cakes, the limbs like spears, the cakes as big as blockhouses. Much of the detritus moved as fast as me, some went past on either side; others did I pass by and leave behind. Some banged the sides of my boat; one ice mass coming up from behind was the shadow of death with its great height looming up over me. It chugged along a ways, even did it bump me a few times and I wasn't sure it wasn't going to crush me though it did veer aside.

Farther down from the falls, the waves were less ferocious though even here and as caught as I was in the swift current, I only stayed afloat for the steadying of my outriggers. My rudder I thus far had dared not use for the certainty I would lose it did I unhinge it against the current; my paddle, when I tried steering with it, kept getting thrust forcefully back at me until finally, and even tied to my wrist, it flew up into the air behind me and was lost. I quickly grabbed another from where they lay at my feet.

****

I had taken some glancing blows from the waves and detritus but had so far avoided the one solid blow which might have doomed me. Now, though, and with the trees of the island looming taller for closing in, it was time to loosen my rudder. Said rudder was skinny boards held together with nails and pine pitch. With how crudely it was built and with the ferocity of the water, I was fearful, nay, certain the rudder would snap as soon as I released it, which would doom me, yet there was no other way if I were to cross the river. I unhooked the rudder, it swung out, I held tightly to the crank and felt the pressure of the current. The rudder creaked and I seen a big crack spread the length of it, yet did it hold and I began edging my way across the river.

My instinct was to get over as quick as I could yet this notion I must resist as a single moment broadside to the river would surely be the end of me. Slowly, gradually, and whilst navigating as best I could the flotilla of trees and burgs, I nudged myself out far enough so I felt an easing of the pressure of the water, an indication I was passing from the southside current into the lesser current of the north.

The soldiers were shouting and waving and if their intention was to dissuade me from getting into this other channel, they were too late but as I got around the island, I seen what was riling 'em.

The northside channel was clogged. So much debris had come down, not all of it had flushed out and where it was piled up along the shore, it extended arms into the river. The water crashing against it, boilin' and workin' around it, sent up violent spouts, rooster tails twenty-feet high. Enough to wreck any boat which ran up against 'em.

The river narrowed as I got down into it. My outriggers began banging and catching. Rocked side to side, I had near to hand my sword and chopped at any and all of what caught me up. Even would I hack off my outriggers were it necessary though I knew not how I might get on without 'em. As it was, I was able to free my outriggers each time they got caught and only would I cut them did they get irredeemably bound up.

I came to the biggest of the debris piles, a blockage of trees, limbs and ice floes which extended nearly to the island. I had but a skinny gap to thread and as I got close in, I seen what must have been what the British had been warning me about. A massive log with one end locked into the snag and the length of it laying across the gap. Moved by the action of the onrushing current, the log was in perpetual motion, rising ponderously to a height taller than a man and crashing back down again. A most powerful fulcrum, the anvil of an angry Poseidon which might pound me as a carpenter's hammer on a nail.

The British were seemingly right over the top of me as I dropped down into the gap and with the log rising when I got there, I might a got through alright except for what else was there. A whirlpool beneath the log and formed, same as the movement of the log, by the upriver snags having broken the current into lesser flows which all came back together here for the river descending more steeply. Captured by the vortex, I got spun madly about, round and round in a tight circle. I hit against the debris on one side, the shore of the island on the other; water poured down on me from off the piles of debris, all whilst the log creaked and strained overhead for its apex.

The log came down and again it was the River Gods looking out for me, for had the log come a moment sooner, I'd have been beneath it. As it was, my boat took a glancing blow to the stern which not only failed to finish me but which served, with how it struck, to give me a propulsion sufficient to drive me out of the eddy and I was again hurtling down the river, now in its fastest, steepest descent. I bounced and skimmed the surface and without hinderance for there was less debris down here than above for so much of it having caught on the big snag and most of the rest having washed away.

My rudder snapped and the last of my paddles, when I tried to use it for steering, got ripped from my hands and there was naught for me now but to grip the sides of the boat as I traversed the curve and the downslide and it was as if I was going down an icy hill on a toboggan except what man had ever gone downhill so fast as this? Clutching the sides of my boat, I screeched defiance, my face into the wind, my long hair flowing wild behind me. The British were feeling it too, whooping and waving their hats as if they was at the horseraces and I was the nag they had their shillings on.

My boat was skipping and bouncing and throwing its own roostertail as the current swept me around the last part of the turn and pointedly thrust me in toward the British. Some of them had a rope which they had looped around themselves to form a human chain which extended into the freezing cold river. Bless them, they would try to snatch me did I not get all the way in. The bravest of them, those farthest out of their chain, was prepared either to grab for me or toss the end of their rope. There wasn't much they could do but they was at least willing to try and did they fail, I figured to raise my hand in thanks and farewell as I rode to my death.

My canoe grounded with such force, I hurtled forward through the air and over the heads of the men. I crashed and rolled and got to my feet. I would grab my canoe afore it went down the river but I seen the soldiers was already dragging it up onto shore, the water bashing 'em.

Others of them gaped silent for having seen me take on the river at its wildest and having survived. Surely I must have seemed an apparition, surely they knew not what to make of me. In truth, drenched and obscured beneath so much filth and grime, hair and beard, I could have been most anything. French, even, or a spook, or the legendary Old Man of the Mountains returned to life, a relic, perhaps, of an earlier war.

"I say, Yank," their sergeant said after a silence, and what he meant was, it was the craziest bloody thing he'd seen in all the time he'd been watching the river. Too damn right, I thought, for it being one hell of a way to break up the boredom they must have felt for watching a place where probably nothing much ever happened.

Regaining my voice and with arms and legs yet shaky, I was profuse in my gratitude for their willingness to risk their own lives for mine, had it been necessary. Mostly I was grateful just for them having been there. How I had got across the river I figured to be a miracle from God, or, I suspect, from the Indian spirits who dwelt beneath the waters, although I wasn't sure why those spirits would have looked favorably upon me, a white man what was defying them. For pluck and skill, or foolishness. Indian Gods were known to have an affinity for those who were not right in the head.

I began to laugh, which further confounded the British. Some few of them laughed along although they maybe knew not the reason for it. As it were, I was laughing because when I had come in and with their bayonets in a thrusting position and with me hurtling over the top of 'em, I might have got a pig-sticker jabbed up my arse, a funny enough story for these British to tell, the crazy American who survived a suicide ride on the river only to die skewered on a British bayonet.

"What day of the year is it, please?" I said.

"Twenty-seven April, 1759," the sergeant said.

I asked did they have anything to eat. One private had some biscuits in his pocket. He dipped them in the water and gave them to me. The sergeant said he'd have my canoe and bundles brought in and he said they had just been sitting down to breakfast and would I be pleased to join them. Coffee, and a side of bacon.

Chapter XXIII – Homecoming

The fort commander, an affable young lieutenant of regulars, had been watching, arms folded. Told him I have been scouting for Rogers in the north. He said as how he'd want to talk to me about the situation up there but first, breakfast with the men, and "Would ye consider a bath before ye eat?" I said I would. I'd noticed he'd raised a handkerchief to his nose when he got a sniff of me.

Two soldiers, one on either side, held my arms and helped me up the hill to the stockade, a modest square of upright logs, not probably very defensible but something a man could run to, did Indians get after him. Inside the fort was a barracks, one side for the men, one for the officers, a storehouse and not much else.

I was taken to the soldiers' quarters. Some privates fetched a wooden tub and set it by the fire. I got in and soaked, the men joshing each time they came in and dumped their pails of heated water, saying how badly I stank.

Whilst I was having my bath and a shave, the lieutenant had a look at my loot. He came in and asked how a scout could come away with so much. I said it was common for us to take whatever we could. I figured he was new to the frontier and wouldn't know any better and I would spare him the grisly details, the dark side of things. Besides, and maybe it had to do with the bath, I was feeling ashamed of all I had done. I scrubbed as if rubbing away my skin would erase what I had become. The lieutenant said as how he'd have been vigorous too, was he as filthy as me, but, he said, as there wasn't much skin on my bones, I ought maybe to leave what little there was. I didn't let on it was more than dirt I was trying to remove. I got into fresh clothes, a lobsterback uniform which was loose-fitting but warm and dry, and much as I would have preferred a set of buckskins, I reckoned I could be a redcoat for a day or two.

I sat down to breakfast with the men. They put a bowl of porridge and a mug of coffee, both steaming, in front of me, then came the bacon, a fat, glorious, sizzling slab. I savored the smell whilst a soldier did the carving and the first trencher got put in front of me. There was chatter whilst we ate, they had plenty of questions and were entirely in awe of my having spent the winter to the north, which territory was unknown and scary in their minds. Mostly, though, their awe was for my having conquered the river. One of those who had seen it was telling some who hadn't how I had rode fearlessly into the flume and exactly gauged the rising and falling of the pendulum log, not only to avoid it but to use it to thrust myself out of the whirlpool. Another spoke of my screeching defiance as I rode the current. I shrugged, as if the dangers I had faced this day were not so different from my usual fare, wolfpacks, big cats and Indians.

They kept giving me more bacon, I kept eating and kept trying to steer the conversation back on them, if only to keep it away from me. I got plenty interested when they began telling about the road getting built from somewhere west of their fort and down to Edward. Said road was crude but was passable by wagon and there was a wagon train heading down in the morning and as a scout with information, there'd be a place in it for me. They seemed to think this would disappoint me, as if continuing downriver in my canoe was what I would have preferred. I didn't tell 'em different. Let 'em think this old river rat was rarin' for more.

They asked had I seen much Indian sign, they saying they patrolled every day and only rarely saw anything. I didn't figure them to recognize sign even was they standing on it, but I again didn't say so. They had been willing to make a play for my life at the risk of some of their own. Inept they might be in the woods but their quick thinking and probably a deft handling of their ropes, had it become necessary, were undeniable. It took brave men to do what they had been prepared to do for me.

After breakfast, back with the lieutenant in his office and over rum, he questioned me about the situation at Scalp Point and Ti and all points north. I answered as best I could, he writing it all down to forward to his superiors. He seemed awed with all I told him and with me, too. In his mind, same as in the minds of his men, I was a living version of the fantastic notion of Americans which some of the British brought with them from over the ocean. Dirty and uncouth, a bit crazy but never daunted. The lieutenant admitted he'd been told to be on the lookout for me and he confirmed my place with the wagon train in the morning.

I presented him with a French officer's sword and a bearskin. We toasted the king and afterward, I joined the men in their barracks where I spent the rest of the day regaling them over rum, those what came in and out as their various duties allowed.

Had a good night's sleep in a bunk and in the morning after breakfast and with my loot and canoe getting loaded into a wagon by the men, the lieutenant asked what was in one particular bag. It was my scalp bag and with a French braid snaking out the top. I tried to brush aside his inquiry, and when he asked again, it was in his strictest officer's voice although still polite. "What be in the bag, sir?" I felt deeply ashamed and tried again to brush aside his inquiry. I had begun to like him; he was a refined fellow with less of an obnoxious bearing than most of his countrymen and I didn't care to be showing him the terrible proof of my misdeeds. He persisted, and with him not to be deterred, I grabbed the pouch out of the wagon and opened the drawstrings to give him a look.

"Blimey," he said. "T'is human hair." I looked him steadily in the eyes. I think the young man's opinion of me dropped considerable and yet and as offended, nay, repulsed as he was, he could not stop himself from staring into the bag. I stuffed the strands back down inside, drew the drawstrings tight and tossed the sack into the wagon. He shook hands gingerly, as if my taint might rub off on him. I thanked him for the bath, the food and the ride, for everything, and despite my gratitude toward him and his men, I couldn't help a parting shot. "Woods warfare," I said. "You loathe it and you despise me for fighting in my own fashion but it's something we cannot win without." He didn't argue, he just turned in the stiff manner of his breed and walked away.

There were four wagons and a guard detail, a few guards in the backs of some of the empty wagons. I rode in the front with the teamster. He was convivial and had rum enough for both of us. Each time a wagon got stuck, which was often for the crudeness of the road, we all worked to get it going again. Arriving at Edward, I invited the teamster to take something from my loot. He chose a fancy powder horn, not the horn with the whaling epic, which I did not show him. After reporting in and telling again about the enemy doings up north, I went over to the ranger camp.

I went to the main hut, opened the door and stood looking in. There were about fifteen rangers, all glaring at my uniform. They didn't any of 'em care for the British, especially British without courtesy enough to knock but a change came over 'em with the realization what they was seein' weren't a lobsterback. An apparition out of the night, maybe, or out of the past. One man approached me, cocking his head side to side, as if trying to see me from different angles, to see what the hell I was.

He got his face up close to mine. He then turned to the others. "T'is Kuyler," he said. "Cain't be," another man said. "Hell if'n it ain't," the first ranger said, and he put one hand on my shoulder and with the other hand, he gripped mine, and still with his face up close, he said they all thought I was dead. Now all the men, getting who I was, got around me. They pumped my hand, slapped me on the shoulders and about knocked me off my feet. They'd had an idea of how I'd spent the winter and to a man they had not figured to ever see me again and now here I was, back amongst the living.

Someone put a tankard of rum in my hand.

"Tis ye been doin' all that raiding up and under, ain't it?" someone said. "Sure and damnation iffen it don' all fit now. Since the buggers hit your farm, we ain't heard nary a word from ye. Your black man says he ain't seen ye in four months. Says he don't know nothin', and the French we been bringing back all tell of a phantom Mohawk been raising hell up there all winter. Shit." He spat on the floor. "T'weren't no Mohawk a'tall, nor a phantom, neither. It were ye."

"It has to do with revenge for the death of your beautiful wife, don't it," another ranger said. "Can't say's I blame you."

In short order, my loot was brought into the hut and we were settled and drinking. They provided me with a ranger uniform and happy I was to be out of my lobsterback garb, as entertaining as it had been for the rangers. The uniform had one of those silly bonnets and having lost my slouch hat, probably whilst riding the river, I wore the bonnet.

I told them what I had done; with rangers I didn't have to hold anything back, and someone asked, "Satisfy yourself?" I went over to my loot, lifted the scalp sack and tossed it to him. "See for your own damn self." He dumped the grisly contents out onto the floor. "Yep, you got plenty. Wanna sell some?"

I felt more shame and wondered what right did I have to feel revulsion and only nodded, no, I did not care to be selling hair. He grinned. "Just askin'," he said and he and another man counted out the scalps. "Thirty-three," he said with awe and to the others who got around for a look.

The men related to me some of what they had been hearing all winter from prisoners brought back and the occasional French deserter, about the fear I had put into the French garrisons, the Indians more than the French. The Indians were convinced I must have been from the world of the dead. This supernatural fear of me had chased many of them back to Canada, they having no inclination to fight spirits, and those who had stayed the winter had most often refused to go looking for me, which maybe explained how I had managed to survive. The French had gained a pretty good idea of my whereabouts and had prepared an expedition for the spring, to invade Paradise and put an end to me. We laughed to envision the French and Indians trudging the snowy, muddy mountains whilst I was at Edward, alongside a fire in dry clothes and with venison, rum, and a bubbling cauldron of pork and beans. We all laughed too for thinking the French and Indians had maybe arrived at my hideout just after I departed, maybe even the same day. I didn't laugh, though, to think it might be the end of Paradise for me.

We celebrated my survival long into the night, they telling the news, most of it good. The British navy dominated the waters around the Gulf of the Saint Lawrence. Fort Duquesne on the forks of the Ohio was getting rebuilt and was garrisoned by British regulars and colonials. The fort was now known as Fort Pitt, in honor of the Lord Minister capably in charge of this war whilst the village already rising up around it, men were calling Pitts' Burg. General Wolfe was said to be near ready to ascend the Saint Lawrence and assault Quebec. He was only waiting for the ice to clear. Wolfe, the rangers said, was a fighting general and if he was successful in going for Quebec, a most formidable fortress, it would be the end of the French empire in Canada.

"And our own Amherst t'isn't much for fightin' but t'is a'buildin' everywhere," a ranger said. "He's the ol' boss beaver, makin' sure all is workin' hard." The ranger's eyes creased as he continued, "Amherst and Wolfe. The British have finally turned the conduct of the war over to the sort of professionals we have been wanting."

The rangers said we was about to commence operations in the Champlain Valley. Troops would soon be moving north; the fate of both Scalp Point and Ticonderoga were sealed. In the meantime, a ranger said, and whilst we waited for the spring campaign to get started, "Amherst has men building roads and fortifying the routes such as you never before seen the likes of." He paused for a pull on a rum jug. "Even old Fort Anne is gettin' rebuilt."

"After all these fifty and more years," I said.

"Stockades built between Edward and the lakes and along the rivers and roads," one of the men said. "Places for ducking into in times of trouble and from which to get on the trail of raiders iffen they hit. Old Jeff," this was a reference to Amherst, "he got angry when he first come here and seen his supply convoys gettin' jumped. One convoy nearly wiped out here at the Carry, right under the nose of the garrison. Amherst won't abide it."

"It's how he works," another man said. "From the ground up. Putting in the foundation so the wind don' blow down the house."

"I'll drink to all of 'em, each in his turn," I said, and we did. Over and again, and we raised toasts and huzzas for my depredations, so much more effective than I could have thought possible.

I stayed a few days to recuperate, and on the third day, I got a ride south with a wagon. I gave the teamster a nice French musket and rode with him as far as Half-Moon. I said it was foolish of him to travel without other wagons or an escort. He said going alone instead of waiting for convoys meant more trips and more money. He didn't think there was any danger. I must admit to shaking my head but he exemplified the confidence running through our people, an eagerness, now we were so close to the end, to get there. Or to believe we were already there, and truthfully, it was foolish of me too, just the two of us on what was still a wilderness road, although it was not so dangerous as in the recent past, and I was as anxious to get home as he was to make money.

Bouncing along in the wagon, I had time to reflect on all of what the rangers had said and what the teamster was saying. Finally, the English were using their fleets and armies to good purpose. Who could deny it? And as anxious as I was to get home, I was anxious as well to get back north, to be there when we blew the walls off of Ti, and after Ti, on to the devil's den, Scalp Point, and all points north. Put an end to pestial camps, savage raids, suicidal attacks by brave men sacrificed by stupid officers. I would not miss out on the final blows to be dealt in this tragic war. First, though, what I most needed, besides time with my boys, was a chance to recuperate in both my body and mind.

I rode in the wagon to the confluence of the Mohawk River with the Hudson. There the teamster kept south and we parted. I canoed the short distance up the Mohawk to the Vlatche.

Soon I was standing on the rise overlooking my home. The memories of my awfullest day came back to me. How much I longed for the impossible, for my Monie to come running out of the house and throw herself joyously into my arms. How bitter I felt for not having her to share with me in the certainty the war would soon be over, the French would be gone. I had a hard time to keep my footing as I walked down off the rim of the hill and to the house, and I probably only made it for having so long been preparing myself for this moment and for what was stirring within me. A small fire in the ashes, a fire too long dead, the feeling a strong one, a revulsion at the wrongness of my perpetrated deeds.

In the dooryard, two little boys, my Augustus and a brown boy about the same age, were playing in the dirt with a collection of tin soldiers, redcoats, Indians, and a ranger wearing a double-breasted coat and a pommel hat, same as what I was wearing.

Henry's wife, Isabelle, came out of the house, and behind her and to my utter astonishment came one of Josh's girls, with my little Peter in her arms. Isabelle saw my astonishment and smiled. "Mista Bill Johnson," she said. "He promise to fetch Kate back from thuh Injuns an he done keeped his promise." Kate put Peter in my arms; a moment later, Cybil came out. She and I embraced.

Josh and Henry, in the fields and having spotted me, came running up, rifles at the ready. We shook hands warmly, they all gaped silently at me. I had got another bath, a shave and a haircut before departing Edward but with my ranger greens draped loosely on my nearly skeletal frame, they couldn't any of 'em stop their gaping nor could they believe I was alive and home. Henry had brung his family back to the farm not too long after I had departed for the north.

"And your boy," I said to Josh. "Didn't find him, eh?" Josh said they had indeed found him. Johnson's Indian agents had located the boy, Timmy, and Timmy had sent back word, wishing them well but saying he was gettin' adopted into a northern tribe and declined, at least for now, to come home. This I understood perhaps better than Josh. The Indian life, hunting, fishing, warring, often held more appeal for a young fellow than the drudgery of the plow. Or maybe Josh understood better than me. Once made a member of a tribe, Timmy's skin color wouldn't matter.

I felt overcome by it all and leaning down toward Augustus, who had been looking up the whole time at me, "Son," I said, not sure how he would react. He was maybe old enough to feel resentment at having been abandoned, first by his mother then by me but he lurched forward with a little cry and wrapped himself around my leg. I lifted him and with one of my boys in each arm, I looked into the face of first one and then the other. They were healthy and doing fine. They were living with Eric and Sarah but with plenty of time spent at the farm, which seemed to suit them. All whilst I gazed at my boys, my thoughts were on Monie. I could feel her presence here on this land which she had grown to love.

I was certain she was smiling down at her three boys. Josh and his family were respectfully silent until Henry's little boy, with his hand visoring the sun, asked, "Be's you Kuyler?" I said I was. "Bejeezus!" he said and he slapped his palm against his forehead. We all laughed, even the boy's mother, and even as she admonished him for his profanity. Josh said the boys were always playing with the toy soldiers and in their games, the tin ranger was me, and only Augustus could be Kuyler.

I set my older boy on his feet and handed the younger back to Kate, and with the black dog following gimply behind, I walked up onto the knoll where my beloved was buried.

Josh had erected headstones for Monie and his girl. I sat on the stone bench. Grief and the sense of loss overwhelmed me. It locked me in a grip so tight, I had a fleeting notion of going back up to Scalp Point to collect more hair. Then I smiled, shook my head and spoke to Monie. "It's not what you would want, is it?" She was gone and scalps weren't going to bring her back. Whilst she lived, no man had better. Always my succor in time of need, as fine a lady as ever there was. The perfect life-mate, delightful in the good times, solid in times of trouble. Always steadfast. She had precipitated her own death but only with the truest of motives and courage and without fully grasping the barbarity of the natives, for hers was a more civilized society.

Death was always close to hand on this frontier. I had seen much of it but never had it come as close as it did here and it was too much for me to accept. The loss of my friend Tom last year, and of Pops, and the cruelest blows till now, the deaths of my first wife, Mary, and my first-born son, and the death nearly fifteen years ago of another woman I had loved, Lydia Moncton, the wife of another man. She too had got scalped and murdered by Indians. I had never got over these losses yet I had carried on, but now it all felt so bloody empty, I didn't know how I could continue.

Snow had begun falling, even without clouds enough to block the sun, which shone brightly. The snow put a mantle on my shoulders and on the dog's back, as unmoving as we were, until finally the dog shook off the snow, looked at me and whimpered. It was time to go back down.

Whilst Cybil and the girls prepared a homecoming feast, Josh, Henry and me went down to the river and fetched the gear from where I had stashed it. I gave each of them a new musket, French issue, and a bear-skin. We took a walk around the place. It all looked in fine shape, they were about ready for the spring planting, and as all the stock was gone, there had been little enough for 'em to do all winter and with the weather cooperating, they'd got started on a new barn. With help from the neighbors who came by whenever their own burdens allowed, work on the barn was well along. It would be two-stories and well-fixed for housing livestock and with the spacious hayloft and so many stalls, Josh was seeing prosperity for whoever would live here, be it him, me, us together, or someone else.

Supper was venison from a deer Henry had shot, he having become a most capable hunter; vegetables, potatoes, fresh-made bread with butter, cornmeal pudding with maple syrup, some of Pops' beer, and my favorite dish since childhood, Dutch apple pie, which Mother had taught Cybil how to make.

Late into the night, in front of the fire, with rum, and with Josh puffing on his long-handled clay pipe, we talked. He said he and Cybil had been talking to Eric about leaving. The farm held awful memories for them, the smoke and terror of the attack, their one girl tomahawked before their eyes, the other taken, the boy's screams as Josh slammed the door against him. Josh said even with his daughter returned to him and with his boy living the Indian life somewhere to the north, he and Cybil still struggled with it and felt it would be best for them to start over somewhere else. Anywhere to not be constantly reminded of their sorrows. The only reason these good people had stayed as long as they had was because of their loyalty to me. A fact I much appreciated. Josh said what they had planned, with no word from me, was to get the barn finished, do the spring planting and go back down closer to New York Town. One thing holding them back, I think, was knowing if I didn't return and they departed, Barnes would move in.

I told Josh I would be very sorry to see him go but if it was what he wanted, I understood, and I said I would help him in whatever way I could. I said I would buy him mules and a wagon and give him money besides. For myself, I told him my thoughts were to go back north to finish the war. My longer plans I had not yet formulated though his leaving meant I would have to sell the farm for the truth was, I could no longer be a farmer. It was not what I could do well, nor what I cared to do, with Monie gone.

A couple days later, paddling toward Albany and alone on the river, I lifted my scalp sack which, tied tight at the top, contained, along with the scalps, some few heavy rocks picked up along the shore, and what else was in there, the gems given to me by Rogers up at the Heart's Bay.

I dropped the sack over the side and watched it sink. With the sack gone, the bile went out of me and I felt as if I were coming back from the dead and rejoining the living. It didn't get me past the terrible blackness but it got me started. Like a logjam on the river, when the release of a single log could break the entire thing apart.

First stop in Albany, after securing my loot with an auctioneer, was to find Mother. Not sure where she was abiding, I went to the apothecary. Eric and Sarah were overjoyed to see me. They, knowing how I had intended spending the winter, had doubted they would ever see me again. They gave me assurances Mother was fine. She was living in a large house partway up the hill with two other elderly women.

I found the place and gazed at it from the street. It was a large brick house, almost a mansion. It had a picket fence and a slate walkway from the street to the porch, both the walk and the porch lined with cultivated flowerbeds, dormant now but no doubt Mother's beloved tulips, which reminded her so much of her home country, would soon be bursting out of the dirt. There was a shapely maple in the front and with spruce trees and some smaller cherry trees along the sides. Toward the back was a stable, chickens and likely a cow.

I smiled at the rocking chairs on the porch. Mother had always said how one day she and Pops would get out of the tavern business and spend their days idling. I never could see Pops being content rocking on a porch.

I banged the knocker. Mother answered and seeing me, she fainted. I caught her before she hit the floor and carried her through the foyer and into the parlor. There was a divan, I set her on it. Her housemates rushed into the room. One was around my mother's age; the other was considerably older and was shriveled; mother and daughter, as it was.

The littler one, wielding a broom, began beating me. "Varlet!" she said. "Scoundrel! Put her down!" I, whilst shielding myself from the blows, insisted I was neither varlet nor scoundrel. "I'm her son!" The woman stopped hitting me, the other spoke. "Truly," she said, "are you Kenneth?" I said I was. "The wild man of the north?" the older one said, and when I screwed my face up into what I hoped was a most spine-chilling scowl, she got behind her daughter and peered around at me. I winked and grinned. "Well!" the old one said. "Hush," the daughter said. She got smelling salts and we revived Mother, who, whilst gazing at me, shook her head and said my name over and over in what was a whisper. She sat up and clutching my shirt, she pulled me toward her and held me there, my head in her lap, awkward for me but which I endured. She finally released me, I sat next to her on the couch and held her whilst she wept gently into a handkerchief. The other women went discreetly into the kitchen. After a time, Mother sniffled, composed herself, and the women came back with tea, bread and butter. Mother asked about me, I told her I had been scouting, was all. I don't suppose she believed me. She told me, now the winter was over and with the French threat receding, she'd be spending time out to the farm with Josh and my boys.

The next morning, I reported in to army headquarters. They didn't seem interested in what information I gave 'em and acted as if the damn war was already over. I told them it would have been, a long time ago if not for the very arrogance they were showing me now.

I spent a week in town, evenings with Eric and Sarah, sleeping at their house, my days spent with Mother and with the four of us dining together most nights, sometimes at Eric's, sometimes at Mother's. I told them I would be going north to join Rogers, and Josh would be leaving. The last time I had seen Eric and Sarah, we'd reached an understanding. Did I not ever come back from my winter in the north, they would raise my boys as their own. Now, and with me back amongst the living but going off again to finish the war, they would keep my sons until I got back.

Later, Sarah got me aside and urged me to find another woman as soon as the war was over. "For the boys' sake, don't waste any time." I had a notion to tell her about the scalps and what dropping them into the river had done for me but the telling would necessarily involve how I came to have them and so I said nothing. Sarah was not of the woods and could not be expected to understand. I said as how all my thoughts for now were to be in on the finish and I couldn't really see clear to what might come after. She told me I was a damned fool and hadn't I done enough? "You have fought our battles for so long. You have faced the dangers so we could be safe, we would be ungrateful to not help in your time of need. But why not do something for yourself? Find a woman. Of course, none could replace Monica in your heart but it would be the practical thing to do." That was Sarah. Gorgeous, charming, often flirtatious but never impractical.

I stopped in at the Full Sail a few times, now called something else, and felt strangely uncomfortable in the place where I had been born and where my childhood and so much of my adult life had been spent. Ran into a few men I knew. My loot, guns, knives, bearskins, canteens, sold well, I was most happy with the returns. With the war winding down, French paraphernalia was in big demand and with not much quality fur having come in for a few years, my furs, though few in number, brought a good price.

On the way back to the farm, my mind was filled with thoughts so overpowering about the goodness of such people as Eric and Sarah, Josh and Cybil, goodness to balance against the evils in the world, and what about me? Was I evil for having gone over to the dark side? I supposed I was, but I was bringing myself back.

I told Josh if he was anxious to get started somewhere else, he should leave at once and I would find someone to do the spring planting and maintain the farm whilst Eric arranged with an Albany lawyer to get it sold.

"Mista Ken," Josh said, "we's bin thinkin' and talkin' whilst youse was to Albany. Thissa here place ben the bes' home we ever gots. We haz given so much of our lives to thissa here farm, so much of ourselves is buried here under dis very grount dat we don' wants to go. We wants to stay where we is home. And thassa fact, pure and simple." So something had taken hold of them too. They said farming was what they knew and here they farmed as they saw fit and they'd be mighty pleased to stay.

Cybil spoke, then. "Mista Ken, you is our fambly, you and your two beautiful babes. We is real close up to 'em and we 'members how good your missus was to us'ns. It jes cain't be right, leabin you here now, jus when you needs us de mos'."

I told them as soon as the war was finished, which I expected would be this year or next, I would come home, settle my affairs and go north, to build. I said if Josh would go with me to get my start, we could work up a deal to transfer the Vlatche farm to him. He was willing and I was gratified at the strength of his emotions, the firmness in his desire to stand by me.

We then turned to the more immediate matters concerning the farm. Here I pretty much acceded to Josh's words, he knew farming and stock from working them all his life. From the money I got for the winter's returns and with some of the money I kept stashed with Eric, we soon set out to buy a wagon and a team of mules, cows, pigs and chickens. Josh said as soon as they finished putting up the new barn they'd get started on a cabin. I told him to stay in the stone house. The threat from the north was waning but there was no certainty what was to come and we had reason to be wary of disaster, especially with everything seemingly in our favor. Besides, stone houses were warmer in winter, cooler in summer than were log and board cabins. I said I could hire a few men to finish the barn and raise a cabin and outbuildings so Josh and Henry could do the planting and acclimate the livestock. Josh asked weren't workers expensive, with all of what the army was contracting to build; forts, roads, bateaux, and if it was all the same to me, he said him and Henry could take care of things well enough without help. I smiled for knowing how my farm would soon be humming with activity and noise.

On the morning of my departure for the north, I felt a reluctance to go, with all the good things going on, but unlike the last time, I felt certain I would be back. I saw ahead, saw there could be a future for me. I said my goodbyes and up on the hill, where the road entered the woods, I turned and looked back. They were all standing in front of the house, watching me. Cybil had Peter in her arms, Augustus and Henry's boy were saluting me. I came to attention, shoulders straight, head high, and returned a smart salute back to 'em. Then I was into the woods, pointed resolutely north.

****

So concludes Scalp Point, Book Two of the Skywaters Series. Thank you for reading. In Book Three, it's victory, and peace at last, but the successful conclusion of the French wars, the expulsion of the French from the continent and the subjugation of the (Eastern) Indians brings changes which will shake the world. With the colonials and the British no longer held together by an external threat, loyalties are discarded, hurts recalled, and the magnificent Champlain Valley is once again the scene of intense conflict.

Made in the USA
Middletown, DE
16 April 2023

28942056R00177